# MORE BOOKS BY
# IVAN F. INGRAHAM

*The Patrol*

*Athena*

*22: A Journey to the Edge of Darkness*

*Dream Job.*

# MORE BOOKS FROM THE SAGER GROUP

*The Swamp: Deceit and Corruption in the CIA*
*An Elizabeth Petrov Thriller (Book 1)*
by Jeff Grant

*Chains of Nobility: Brotherhood of the Mamluks (Book 1-3)*
by Brad Graft

*The Deadliest Man Alive: Count Dante, The Mob and the War for*
*American Martial Arts*
by Benji Feldheim

*Death Came Swiftly: Novel About the Tay Bridge Disaster of 1879*
by Bill Abrams

*Vetville: True Stories of the U.S. Marines at War and at Home and at War*
by Mike Sager

*Three Days in Gettysburg*
by Brian Mockenhaupt

*Secrets of Ash: A Novel of War, Brotherhood, and Going Home Again*
by Josh Green

*The Living and the Dead: War, Friendship and the Battles That Never End*
by Brian Mockenhaupt

*Hunting Marlon Brando: A True Story*
by Mike Sager

*The Sing Sing Follies (A Maximum-Security Comedy): And Other True Stories*
by John H. Richardson

*Going Home to Die No More: A True Kentucky Story about a Train*
*Robbery and a Hanging after the Civil War*
by Russ Witcher

See our entire library at TheSagerGroup.net.

# ONCE WE PLEDGED FOREVER

## A NOVEL OF COMBAT, MARINES AND THE WAR WITHIN

Ivan F. Ingraham

Cataloging-in-Publication data for this book
is available from the Library of Congress.
ISBN-13:
eBook: 978-1-958861-64-6
Paperback: 978-1-958861-65-3
Hardcover: 978-1-958861-66-0

Published by The Sager Group LLC
(TheSagerGroup.net)


*The views expressed in this publication are those of the author and do not necessarily reflect the official policy or position of the Department of Defense or the United States government. The public release clearance of this publication by the Department of Defense does not imply Department of Defense endorsement or factual accuracy of the material.

# ONCE WE PLEDGED FOREVER

## A NOVEL OF COMBAT, MARINES AND THE WAR WITHIN

Ivan F. Ingraham

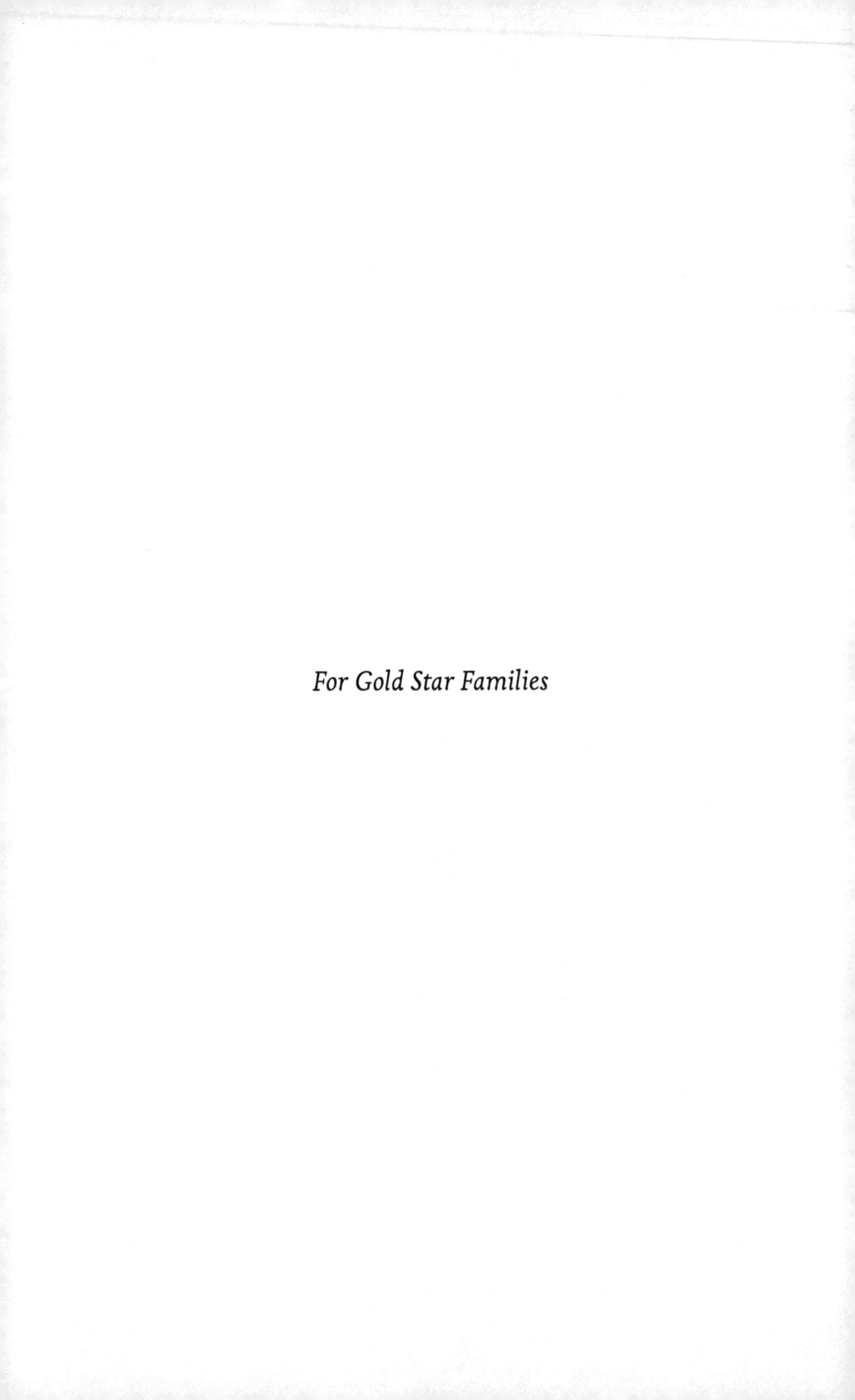

*For Gold Star Families*

# CONTENTS

# AUTHOR'S NOTE

I served twenty-four years as an officer in the United States Marine Corps, most of them in Special Operations. Although a work of fiction, this book is influenced by true events. These all happened in some capacity over the course of my career and helped create a story I feel is worth telling.

It's one of distance, shame, fear, anger, longing, paranoia, and vigilance; a lack of closure, doubt, betrayal, the loneliness of leadership, and overall difficulty. It's about pure vulnerability. It's based upon the most talented, funny, cruel, base, and interesting people I've ever known, interspersed with humor that sometimes was hard to identify and at others seemed starkly out of place.

Where the real names of people are utilized, it is with the permission and approval of the individual or their families. I used real names in some cases as an homage to who these people are. Some of them gave the last full measure with their lives. It's the least I can do. All other characters are figments of my imagination, and any resemblance to people living or dead is coincidental.

Military service is unique. Tight bonds form between disparate groups of people who come to rely upon each other in dire situations. Sometimes these relationships are lifelong, but most often they dissipate with the passage of time. My experience was no different. We once pledged forever to the other, now we never talk.

# PART I

When they go to war, the first stage service members undergo is one of ignorance. They think they're invincible and view being wounded or killed in combat as something that will happen to other people. A young person joins the military convinced of their luck and that they'll always be alive to enjoy the warmth of a lover's smile in the rain, to feel adored, and to never take things for granted since they're in the prime of their lives. Of this, the acclaimed author Paul Fussell wrote: "It *can't* happen to me. I am too clever / agile / well-trained / good-looking / beloved / tightly laced, etc." *Wartime* (Oxford University Press, 1989), 282.

All young people have these feelings before they first experience combat. If they felt otherwise, no one would even attempt it. It's also why the old veterans ignore or subjugate war's horror and instead focus on glory by telling stories that ignite the feelings of duty in the breasts of young people who hope to be tested and deemed accepted by the warrior caste. And the foolish youth believe them.

# 1



A red-tailed hawk circled in the crisp October sky, calling in a high-pitched screech. The changing leaves, usually vibrant in the autumn sun, were muted under leaden clouds that threatened rain. Steve Keller, fifty-nine, and long-retired after a twenty-four-year career in the United States Marine Corps, emerged from a tree line into a wide field and walked slowly up the hill toward his cabin. His gaiter-covered waterproof boots swished through the wet, knee-high bluegrass. Under his left arm was an open, 12-gauge Browning Superposed shotgun, old and trusted. In his right hand, he carried a seasoned walking stick, which he leaned on as he ascended. A game pouch with four grouse from the day's hunt rested on his left hip. Steve's black Labrador retriever, Kelso, kept pace at his side, ready to retrieve, moving neither ahead nor away from him, black snout sniffing the air as they ambled easily together. Steve glanced up at the hawk above them. It flew across the field to land behind them in the tree line they'd just exited.

These days not much hurried him, and Steve reflected that today had been a pretty good one, even though his hips hurt on damp days like this, a constant reminder of his service so long ago. Temperatures would drop enough in the coming weeks that he'd forgo going out to hunt too much more this year.

A cold, damp wind shook the trees making them sound like a freight train while churning loose leaves into the air. Steve stopped to adjust the game bag and pull the hood of his waxed green hunting coat up over his head, already covered with a red watch cap. He was further glad for the oatmeal-colored wool sweater he wore. Light enough to breathe and heavy enough to retain warmth. He liked everything purpose-made.

With the light fading, it was getting chilly, and the growing mist reduced visibility. He turned and checked behind him. *Old habits die hard,* he thought. He swept his eyes across the field and along the trees, scanning deeper into the woods to gain a full appreciation of the terrain as he paused in the grass to finish buttoning up his coat.

There, in the opposite tree line across the field he'd just crossed, stood a figure dressed in Marine Dress Blues looking at him. Steve froze. Was he seeing things? Maybe he was tired and imagining the ghost. But he knew better. Another gust of wind-driven mist, and the figure disappeared.

Kelso, unprepared for the stop, settled ten yards ahead of him, waiting. Sensing Steve's unease, he began to whine. Steve looked a little longer at where he'd last seen the figure, then closed the distance to his companion and onward up the hill to the next tree line. He placed his hand on Kelso's shoulder, and the whining ceased.

Steve's foot slipped a little inside his left boot. He frowned at his own neglect. He should have attended to it before they stepped off to return home. Steve stopped in the trees to sit on a familiar stump and tighten his laces to ensure no blisters formed on the remaining short trek. Toughing it out was for fools, and the best way to treat a blister was not to get one. Another lesson from MARSOC Selection. What was he in such a big hurry to get to, anyway? Home to clean and cook the grouse? And then what? Another night alone by the fire?

He drew in a deep breath of damp air and looked down at Kelso, "Come on, boy. Let's get inside. We're both too old for this kind of weather." In Kelso's defense, the dog hadn't suggested they go hunting. Steve chuckled at that thought and turned the walking stick in his hand. Smooth and worn, it was a gift from his wife, Elena, and he smiled as he leaned on it to stand and continue the walk through the woods joined along a small path. Trees sheltered him as Kelso trotted forward, knowing they were nearly home.

Steve and Elena had built the cabin in a glade after purchasing the land while he'd still been on active duty. Completed just after he'd retired ten years earlier, the solid structure could house five people comfortably. Now, only he and Kelso occupied it.

The dog shook off the water from his fur, then dutifully waited for his owner, sitting in his self-appointed spot to the left of the door. Steve reached down and petted his head. Kelso responded with a nudge. "Ready to go inside and get warm?" Kelso would never answer him with words, but a tilt of his head and a small, throaty bark spoke volumes. Steve smiled.

He worked the latch on the heavy oak door, which he'd assembled with care and by hand, like all the facets of the cabin. A labor of love that appealed to his sense of exactness and that had ostensibly helped him develop patience. Elena had thought the hand work would have helped him with post-traumatic stress. He entered the mudroom of the quiet home and leaned his shotgun and the walking stick against the inside of the door, then removed the hunting jacket, gaiters, and wet boots. *Guns, gear, self.*

Kelso brushed past him into the interior of the house to drink from his bowl, then to Steve's study to lay on the dog bed in front of the fireplace.

The rich scent of oak and hickory permeated the house. *I'll need to split more wood for winter to be on the safe side.* Staying ahead of requirements was best, but even he got behind on boring chores at times, mostly because he didn't want to do them.

With his jacket hung and boots laid out to dry, Steve slipped into comfortable navy-blue suede Puma soccer shoes and shut the door to the mudroom. He picked the shotgun back up and confirmed it was unloaded then carried the gun and game bag through an adjacent hall to the garage work-shop, a repository for discarded debris of a long life lived. He turned on a light and placed the bag next to the small refrigerator. Leaning on the door, Steve set the shotgun on his workbench. He stooped to retrieve a cold Harpoon IPA beer and popped the cap with a wall-mounted opener. The cap bounced off the trash can beneath it and clattered on the floor.

"Damn it." He bent down to retrieve it and dropped it into the can. Sipping his beer, Steve tasted the hops of the IPA coat his tongue. He swirled the first sip, enjoying the tart, robust flavor. *I'll thank Michael for these.* His son occasionally came to see him and had gifted Steve the case during his last visit.

At the workbench, he disassembled and fully cleaned and oiled the shotgun. He checked the action and safety, then wiped his hands with a rag on the bench. Turning off the light, he walked back into the mudroom and loaded the gun with two cartridges meant for larger game than he'd taken in the afternoon.

If he were to ever need to use it on a larger animal, it would be the worst kind of animal on the earth: humans. In his past life, he'd hunted them and been himself hunted.

Steve sighed and shut the door to the garage. He walked through the hall adjacent to the mudroom and up a flight of four stairs into a comfortable kitchen area. The cabin was one story except for the mudroom and garage. He and Elena had wanted a flat floorplan in case one of their hips gave out. At least, that had been the idea, that they would grow old together. But cancer doesn't discriminate, and it took her three years earlier. He'd loved her when she was sick; he loved her still. He'd promised her he always would in that hospital room in Knoxville that smelled of antiseptic, the air thick with forlorn hope and unanswered prayers. Though she died holding his hand, surrounded by the kids—after a lifetime of breaking promises to various people and himself, he'd at least made good on that one.

He placed the beer on the kitchen island and turned on the soft lighting. Steve looked toward his study, where Kelso dozed, trying to absorb the warmth of the near-extinguished logs from a fire built earlier in the day. "You deserve better than that," Steve mumbled. He entered the study to rub Kelso's head, then strolled to the mantle to stoke the embers with a poker. Only a small amount of heat danced in the hearth, so he piled on kindling and brought the fire up, added two oak logs, and the room was finally enveloped in comfortable heat. Kelso shifted slightly, only raising his dark eyes to Steve in a motion of gratitude.

Steve returned to the kitchen and retrieved a glass from a cabinet for his beer. *The Raider Patch*, a fraternal newsletter for the Marine Raider Association and former members of Marine Special Operations Command (MARSOC), of which he was a lifetime member, lay on the counter. On the cover was an older photo of a Marine Raider, as badged members of the organization were called, dressed in combat equipment while serving in Afghanistan, with a Silver Star medal inset on the picture. The headline read, "Master Gunnery Sergeant Marko Pech to Receive Upgraded Valor Award at this year's 25th Anniversary Reunion."

He sighed. "Marko. Damn."

Steve strode into his bedroom. He sat on the edge of the bed and removed his shoes and clothing to shower. In the bathroom, he reached for the faucet to get the water as hot as he could stand. The stream cascaded over his head and shoulders, and Steve braced himself, breathing deeply, trying to cleanse his mind and maintain discipline against the near-scalding deluge.

*Remember, this is what you asked for, and you did what you said you would when they asked you what you were going to do after you left the Marine Corps.* He wanted to live a peaceful life, but his past reached out to him time and time again in ways he still didn't understand, such as seeing the ghost of his dead friend Major Roland Joyce earlier in the day.

Steve grew used to the hot water and kneaded an old knot in his shoulder from carrying the weight of war and shame. Not all scars were external, and the internal ones also manifested in odd ways, bringing pain at times. After so many years, it was a wonder that the pain, mental and physical, hadn't overtaken him. He carried within him lasting wounds that would never heal and constantly reminded him that he still had a lot of things to endure.

His Marine Recon and MARSOC instructors had said, "You are constantly earning." Selection to get into Special Operations had been continuous, and he'd needed to earn his place each day. Earned. That's how he felt about how he lived his later life. That he'd earned it.

*That isn't the same as getting what you deserve.* The difference between earning something and having another outcome meted out couldn't be more acute.

Scrubbing his body, Steve traced the scars from wounds; long-faded souvenirs he'd never lose with the past so close behind. He examined the constant crook of his left arm, which hadn't been the same since the parachuting accident.

He studied his faded tattoos. The artists who'd done them were long gone, but the images created and what they signified still mattered to him. Elena hadn't cared for tattoos on anyone, let alone him, but he'd gotten them regardless as a form of self-expression. She'd sobbed when he returned with them, not wanting to argue over how and why he'd wanted them. She hadn't sought to understand—she'd just wanted her husband to be who she knew, not whom he was becoming because of his experiences. Steve still carried guilt. Not for the tattoos themselves, but for how he obtained them, the malfeasance of it all, of ignoring her. She'd deserved better than him.

The water colored the top layer of his skin red. After rinsing off the last of the soap and shampoo, he turned off the faucet. Steve looked at the tile work in the shower stall. A professional contractor, Michael, had done a great job. Like Steve, Michael took great pride in his work. Inheritance was not always monetary.

He grabbed a towel and wrapped it around himself. Back in the bedroom, he changed into a pair of soft blue jeans and a black cotton T-shirt and once again slipped on the Pumas. Steve finished his beer, then returned to the kitchen to prepare dinner, realizing he should have cleaned the freshly killed game before showering. Now he'd get his hands dirty with offal and blood.

Sometimes, doing so was by choice. Other times, it had been forced upon him while his own men bled out, shattered and broken. How could he ever explain such a sight to someone who'd never experienced it?

Steve shook his head. He checked on Kelso, still asleep in front of the fire, and stepped back out to the workshop.

He grabbed another beer from the refrigerator and poured it into the glass, slow and measured. *Take your time and do it right.* If only he'd heeded that advice over his life. Steve opened the game bag and stared at four grouse nestled together in their final, colorful resting forms, peaceful, like they might come awake and continue flying. Sighing, he retrieved the grouse and cleaned and dressed them. Well-versed in the steps, within twenty minutes, he was finished. Steve cleaned up the mess, putting all the unusable parts in a plastic bag and knotting it at the top.

After rinsing the blood from the interior of the game bag in the deep sink in the garage, he set it upside down to dry and took the grouse inside to place in a marinade he would copy from an old *Garden & Gun* food issue. Referencing it from the library of cookbooks and other tomes, he quickly assembled the marinade and decided on fresh asparagus and potatoes to round the meal.

His gaze caught on the shelf as he set the cookbook back in place. They'd been Elena's. Used with love and care when she'd cooked for them. His heart ached.

Letting the grouse settle into the marinade, Steve moved to the study and eased into his chair in front of the fire. Intended to be his retreat, a sanctuary of sorts; he'd designed the study off ones he'd seen in London, private clubs in New York City, and vintage firearms dealers' rooms who took care of their customers—ones who appreciated fine culture and considered the guns more tools than weapons. He was firmly acquainted with the difference but also knew one could be another.

The walls featured built-in bookshelves full of long rows of ready knowledge. He'd read all of them, some with notes in the margins, dog-eared for future reference. While the world had become more and more automated, Steve appreciated the longevity of a printed book. No Nook or Kindle for him, though he ironically recognized their utility. He wasn't a total Luddite, but having a real book meant enjoying the ritual of reading, the smell of the pages aging along with him. He never wanted to get—to be—old, but the years carried on irrespective of his thoughts of the aging process.

As Keith Richards of the Rolling Stones had been quoted, "No one wants to get old, but who wants to die young?"

And in the vein of Mr. Richards, Steve's own 1967 Gretsch Country Gentleman rested upright in its guitar stand. He hadn't played it in a few weeks and promised himself to do so soon.

A well-appointed gun case was a centerpiece that housed and displayed his collection. He admired the metal contained therein. Utilitarian and something for each task and requirement, they represented his history. It would be hard to explain the significance of those items to the uninitiated, so he generally didn't say anything about the things inside the case. Though there were also a few firearms in various locations in the house only he knew about.

Hanging on the wall to the right of the case was his collection of edged weapons, physical records of the past to hold in his hands. Fifteen swords; thirteen dating to the US Civil War; the remaining two being a United States Marine NCO sword from the Spanish American War and his own officer's sword, the Mameluke, designed after the Berber swords found in Libya by Marine Captain Presley O' Bannon during an 1805 raid on Tripoli, it symbolized a timeless link between Marine officers, more ornamental than functional. Steve thought of the six Marines who'd carried out that raid, perhaps the first Marine Special Operation in the Corps' storied history. He was proud he'd continued that legacy in his own career.

Steve stood and added more wood to the fire, then scanned a wall of mementos and photos of another life. Sipping his beer, he scrutinized the pictures. Young, physically hard men in their prime. Strong, well-trained, fit, and motivated; if one was going to war, those were the people with whom to do it. Some gave their lives to allow him the opportunity to spend his own wondering why the roles hadn't been reversed. As if the dead had answers, and the photos could speak.

Did he even live through all of it? A group readying for a parachute insertion. Another after an operation where all returned safely, only to run out of luck on the next one. One taken in Djibouti of him and two others in 2009. He studied his own young face in the photo. He was no longer young. In fact, old was what came to mind as he considered himself in the present. More gray hair than the original brown. Gray stubble on his chiseled jaw. High cheekbones and sharp features but soft edges. Kind blue eyes with lines along the sockets he wanted to believe were due to hard laughing, but they came with the strain of his career. Steve considered the younger version of himself. How naïve he'd been, he and the others in the picture and the other pictures beside that one. Faces, with surety of purpose that masked their individual issues. He hadn't talked to any of them in years.

His eyes settled on a photo taken of his family years earlier on the day of departure for a deployment. In it, Elena stands behind Steve whose arms wrap around their three children, Michael being the middle child between his sisters, Sammie and Marta. The image captured their forced smiles ahead of Steve's leaving to the unknown with the rest of his unit. Elena and Steve's relationship while he'd served had been strained because of the affection he'd placed in his men. It was returned to him, but it was his alone, and when the dead had to be buried and people sought solace, they'd come to their old house. From there, those men and he retreated to his study and celebrated the memory of another friend through the misery of loss and a bottle of whiskey. She'd called it a closed, tribal society in her house. She'd both envied and hated it. Not due to his duties but that he'd chosen them over her and the kids.

But clarity was shortsighted. Elena was gone, Steve was still alive, and in the end, the investment he'd made in their relationship hadn't paid off enough to create the conditions in which she would have fully accepted them. He'd ruminated over his poor decisions and expenditures to his men in the interest of loyalty, sometimes with money and others with integrity. A few of those men had been his best friends, and others had betrayed him.

Betrayal begins with trust. Caesar found that out from Brutus.

Outside, the stormy weather continued, wind-driven rain rustling and pelting the trees. Facing the fire, Steve set down his empty beer glass. He went to the liquor cabinet and chose a smooth bourbon. Two fingers should do it, trading the empty glass for a tumbler etched with the insignia of a long-distant unit that had seemed important to him when he'd bought it. He raised his glass to the photos on the wall.

"Cheers."

Then he prepared dinner.

Kelso came from the study to await the scraps Steve inevitably fed him. The grouse and vegetables came together well. He washed the dishes as he went, a trick his father showed him, and one Elena had insisted on, to minimize the mess. There'd been dinner parties they'd hosted over the years where he'd been constantly cleaning, his job while the guests conversed. He finished washing the plate and utensils and set them to the side of the double sink since they didn't warrant the use of the dishwasher. Steve considered having dessert, then decided against it, smiling at the thought that he had all his own teeth, though a few were crowned long ago, casualties to an incessant sweet tooth.

He washed and dried his beer glass and looked out the window over the sink, straining to see into the meadow through the dusk. The only visible items outside were the runs of rain sliding lazily down the pane, the light from the kitchen reflecting in their cleansing streaks. He turned off the light and coaxed Kelso down the hall to the study.

Settling back in the chair, he watched the dancing fire. Kelso lay down, content on his bed. The whiskey glass placed on his reading stand, Steve folded his hands on his lap and exhaled, releasing the physical strain of the day's hunt. There was a time when a physical training session of hiking hills with rifles and packs had been the perfect thing to do with his team and they'd end the day with three drinks in the team room. Selection had been commonality between them from the start, arduous tasks shared by men who understood the stakes.

Steve looked across the room to a photo of him and Roland Joyce, his friend and mentor, the ghostly figure who'd been standing across the misty field earlier that afternoon. He felt he hadn't lived up to Roland's expectations of him, but that too had been a long time ago.

As Steve dozed, his final thought as he drifted off was of Roland occupying the chair opposite him.

"Hello, old friend," Roland said. "It's been a long time."

# 2

---



Captain Steve Keller had been carrying a rucksack and M16A2 rifle for ten hours. He was nearly finished with the arduous three-week MARSOC Assessment and Selection Course, or at least the most vaunted and dreaded part of it—essentially a long walk. A light breeze under cloudy skies ushered in spring and a few trees budded, though patches of snow covered the fallen leaves on the forest floor. When any precipitation came at lower elevations, it was in the form of rain, but higher up in the mountains, it was snow. Big, fluffy flakes, wet and heavy.

Steve was happy he'd reached that leg of Selection. He felt good; his feet didn't hurt too badly, yet, and he was in a rhythm of sorts. But the physical effort was superseded to the mental requirements of the course and being selected to join MARSOC would put him in an entirely different class of operator.

Adjusting the pack on his back, heavier now than the fifty-five pounds it started at due to the weight of the melted snow that soaked the material and straps, Steve kept moving forward. Wet and chilly from falling in a swollen creek early in the march, he felt sweat streaming steadily from his pores. His naturally warm body heated him, and he would stay warm as long as he kept moving. Occasionally he'd see another candidate, but they were few and far between, although he walked with small groups of people if he caught up to them or they to him. Generally, though, he was alone.

At thirty-one, Steve already demonstrated he was among the best, having served as a platoon commander in 2nd Force Reconnaissance Company, one of the most elite units in the US Marine Corps. Just being invited to the course set a person aside from others, and although Steve arrived in great condition, the pace and duration of the sessions impressed him. The first grueling day alone dropped ten candidates, most of them MMA wannabes and body builders embraced by SEAL Gorilla stereotypes. A physical fitness test; more running, jumping, the obstacle course twice, loads of calisthenics, a ruck run with a monstrous, heavy pack for an unknown distance over broken terrain called the "washboard," a horrible session in the pool for "water confidence" testing, and another five-mile run at full pace to the end. When he looked at the remaining candidates, there wasn't any real average. Some were tall, others short, and most didn't seem the typical Special Operations Forces (SOF)-archetype.

Sixty people started the selection course. Steve and the rest of the candidates were identified only as a number. The training cadre, stone-faced and grim, weren't interested in much else since most wouldn't complete it. They didn't encourage nor discourage, didn't seem to run on anything Steve knew of and were always fresh and ready to deliver another sermon in silent agony. Those men were the fittest professionals Steve had ever seen.

Dark mornings began with physical training. Each day there was a pace setter called a rabbit, and all were told to keep up with him. A difficult task. Steve kept up with the lead pack, but at the back, in case he needed to find another gear. Most days were hard, but he would give it everything he had, plus a little more.

Selection was an interesting environment. People who'd never met each other developed strong friendships in a short period, and even those who might not get selected derived positives from the experience, though no one wanted to get dropped.

One evening during the first week, Steve sat down to dinner with two other candidates. "Mind if I join you, gents?"

"Sure, dude. I'm Alex Chan," one of them, an Asian, said. Steve thought he was Vietnamese but then reconsidered. Chinese maybe. Alex wasn't very tall, just under six feet, and Steve guessed he weighed 185 pounds of fighting muscle.

"I'm Guido," the second one, a tough-looking man, introduced himself. He had a wrestler's build and an easy demeanor.

"Guido?"

"Well, my real name's Anthony Larosa, but everyone calls me Guido. I'm from Long Island, New York. What's your story?" He clearly didn't see his nickname as a slur.

"Steve Keller. I'm a captain at Second Force—"

"No shit? I wouldn't have guessed!" Guido wore large glasses and sported a shaved head that was growing out; he looked like a Mon chichi toy.

"I'll take that as a compliment."

"I meant it that way!"

"How about you guys?" Steve asked, looking between them both.

Alex answered first. "Dude, I'm from Third Reconnaissance Battalion in Okinawa, Japan. I'm a sergeant."

"He's also from New Jersey, but don't hold that against him!" Guido looked at Alex, who brushed it off with a wave of his hand. "I'm staff sergeant at First Force Recon Company in California."

"Good to meet you guys."

From that point forward, Steve, Alex, and Guido shared meals together, getting to know each other during the commonality of suffering through the course.

After every morning PT session, they returned to the barracks to shower and go to breakfast. The food was excellent, all the meals served were, and everyone stuffed their faces with everything they could. Steve estimated they were burning close to five-thousand calories a day, and even with hearty meals, Steve had been at a deficit since he'd arrived at the course with trousers that were slightly snug. The looseness of the fabric earned through training was a good feeling in some ways and concerning in others. He feared muscle deterioration, but anything might derail a candidate. A nagging pain, a blister that didn't heal, a twisted ankle, yet he wasn't programmed to quit.

From breakfast, they received their instructions for the day, written on a dry-erase board, and prepared to go out on another tough land-navigation excursion. The candidates would stand and wait for their names to be called and be given a color and number. Then they mounted canvas-covered trucks that were sealed with zippered doors so they couldn't look out and were driven along circuitous routes into the countryside to be dropped at their starting point. All day, up and down the hills, each day named something ominous like Heavy Carry, Pipeline, and Bloody Thursday. Sometimes, Steve would walk for hours with only a sketch map drawn by someone else.

Each night, Steve would make it back to the barracks on time while the search-and-rescue helicopters fired up to go find the hapless and lost in inhospitable terrain. It was comical, sort of.

After readying his gear for the next day, Steve lay in bed and assessed his performance, mentally preparing himself for the next evolution, though he didn't know what was in store. *Today was horrible. Worse than yesterday. And tomorrow's going to suck even more,* he recounted before drifting to sleep.

At the conclusion of training each day, there were fewer and fewer candidates. The most disturbing thing was that it was as if they'd disappeared. At breakfast every morning, there were only the exact number of seats available in the chow hall or lecture classroom as there were candidates remaining.

Earlier in the course, Steve witnessed a candidate at a land-navigation rendezvous checkpoint fruitlessly arguing that he was in the correct spot. The unemotional cadre repeated the mantra, "This is not your RV," to the candidate's consternation. Steve moved away from him as fast as possible. He never saw that candidate again.

Another time, Steve awoke in the middle of the night as another Marine was in the final stages of packing his equipment. "Where you going?" Steve asked.

"I'm done. My legs won't do it." The Marine handed Steve the remains of his nutritional supplements and looked shyly down at the floor. "Good luck." He shouldered his bags and departed, one of the few Marines dismissed that Steve had ever seen physically leave.

It was eerie, and no one mentioned a person who got dropped.

Then came the final test. Steve was one of the last members of the class to start. Another check of his watch revealed he'd been moving for nearly twelve hours. At a conservative pace of three miles per hour, he estimated he was close to thirty-six miles into the movement, but with a realistic rate of two and a half an hour, he'd probably traveled closer to thirty miles. Still respectable, though, considering the terrain and weather.

Some places were covered with snow, but a trail cut by those who'd traveled ahead of him allowed Steve to follow it, trusting it would lead him in the appropriate direction. He arrived at his next checkpoint and saw two cadre members. They'd been camping in the middle of the woods for at least a day with the best of all camping supplies and stoves, which impressed him since those were unit-provided. There were four other candidates in the area.

"Color and number," Gunnery Sergeant Marko Pech demanded. Steve dutifully reported it. Though Marko didn't show any recognition, they knew each other from having served in Marine Force Reconnaissance together, though not in the same platoon. Marko was a plank owner, or founding member of MARSOC, and one of the first to pass selection in 2006. He also set the course land navigation speed record; Marko was an Operator's Operator.

Marko continued with his part of the script. "Show me on the map where you came from, bro." Steve did, and his point of origin confirmed he was in the right location. "Your next point is on this sheet." Marko handed him a small piece of laminated paper. "Come back and show me where you're going once you plot your next checkpoint."

Steve mapped his next stop and returned for confirmation, handing Marko the coordinates. When he demonstrated he knew where he was going, he stepped off into the gloomy forest. "Hey, Keller!" Marko called. Steve turned. "Have a good 'un!" He winked at Steve, and Steve laughed. Even if the cadre knew a candidate, familiarity was to be removed. He waved and continued on his way.

The brief stop had chilled Steve as he hobbled stiffly down the trail. His feet burned, and every muscle and tendon in his ankles and the soles of his feet were electrified, but he pressed on despite the pain. Parts of the trail washed out, covered with flowing, icy water. His feet numbed as he sloshed through the cold liquid. It was heavenly.

One advantage of the course was the confidence gained through application and sound reasoning behind the choices made. Or at least, that's how he felt.

He linked up with a few more candidates, and they walked together until some members became confused on the trail they should take. Steve pulled out his compass and got a bearing, deciding on his own how he would continue. He stepped off away from them, sure of his decision.

Steve came over a rise in the trail to find Alex sitting on one side, a Meal, Ready-to-Eat (MRE) spread out on the ground. He was seated on his pack as if at Thanksgiving dinner. Steve smiled. "You good, Alex?"

"Dude, I had to eat *something!*" He possessed a stiff work ethic, and nothing seemed to get him down. Alex just did his job. His reputation with his fellow candidates was of a selfless, humble but confident person.

"Have a good one, Alex!" Steve nodded but kept walking, his own hunger ignored. Stopping to eat would waste valuable time. Eating on the march throughout the day was a more advantageous method. Then again, Alex was ahead of him, so maybe he could afford it? *Besides, if I sit down, I won't get up again.* The dull ache crept up his lower body from his feet to his back and legs. At least his shoulders didn't bother him, having gotten used to the heavy pack long ago.

Another check of his watch. Fourteen hours on the move. He found, after his next checkpoint, that he'd have to ascend a mountain. On the map, there was a road that looked a long way around and a trail that appeared more direct. Unsure of how to depart, he chose the trail. It was nearly vertical and extremely difficult the entire way up, but others had taken it, too. He checked his map, and if he'd calculated correctly, he'd intersect another trail that would lead to his next checkpoint. From there, he would be nearly finished.

He expected, anyway.

The terrain was brutal. He fell a few times, nearly breaking his arm in the process. There was no easy route, however, and Steve continued up the steep escarpment, ever closer to the top of the mountain. A few more elevation changes, and he reached the summit. Relieved to be on level ground, and true to his reckoning, he stood on the trail he'd sought and walked smartly into the RV through the drifting snow. Fifteen hours had elapsed. He felt confident, but the day's fatigue was insurmountable, and it seemed he might collapse. That would entail passing out, however, since there was no way he would quit.

The same check-in, check-out procedures and script were followed, and he was on his way.

People who'd made it that far had a better than average chance of being selected to join MARSOC and go on to continuation training. Though it wasn't really in his control, Steve hoped he'd be picked at the Commander's Board. It was a rightfully worrisome event. People before him had passed the final physical test only to go to the board and be BNS, or Board Non-Selected, for no other apparent reason than they "weren't the right man." Steve knew many people had left that room in dejected frustration and bitter disappointment, and he didn't want to be one of them.

He encountered another few candidates, including Guido, who strolled along munching on a granola bar. They walked together but didn't say much, and Steve wondered if anything ever excited the relaxed Italian New Yorker. Even-tempered and calm, Guido was a great addition to any unit.

Breaking out of the woods into a powerline cut, they saw a truck covered in thick, icy fog ahead of them. Through waning daylight, Steve spotted two small figures with rucksacks marching away from the vehicle, uphill into the gloom, one much farther ahead of the other. The lead figure disappeared in the mist.

They stopped at the truck. Both he and Guido went through the same reporting routine with the cadre and were told to stand off to the side. Fifteen minutes later, Alex arrived and was directed to do the same.

Steve winked at Alex, whose face bore his trademark smile. Alex flashed him the "hang loose" shaka sign with his hand and mouthed, *Duuudde!* Steve laughed for a second before suppressing his smile and looking away from Alex to maintain his bearing. Guido drew in his lips and rolled his eyes.

They waited in silence.

The snow increased. *I couldn't create this in my dreams. The weather must work for them, this really sucks.* Steve's feet seized up. He looked for a puddle to stand in and found one that was iced over. It was a godsend, and his feet numbed again.

At last, he was called forward to the truck and told to proceed. That was the final checkpoint.

Steve stepped off, deciding he would finish strongly, his rifle at the alert position, a wool watch cap pulled down on his head, standing tall and squared away, despite feeling destroyed. Away from the truck, Steve said out loud, "Of course the last approach to the finish is uphill, and the weather is worsening!"

He ascended the hill regardless.

The dark figures that had been ahead of him were no longer there, and he didn't look back to see if Guido or anyone else was behind him. It didn't matter anyway, and he kept moving.

Through the fog, the outline of another truck was silhouetted against a large fire. The very thought of it warmed him. He quickened his pace, or thought he had, filled with a euphoria that he might actually finish his final trial to joining MARSOC. The truck grew clearer, and a hooded figure stood in front of it. Steve straightened his back and stood taller, ready for anything, even if they were to spring a surprise additional challenge on him last minute. There wasn't any choice.

He arrived at the truck, and the gravelly voice of Master Sergeant Brian Geraghty, the Selection staff non-commissioned officer-in-charge, met him from under the hood of his jacket. "Color and number."

Geraghty had briefly been Steve's platoon sergeant at 2$^{nd}$ Force but left shortly after Steve arrived. Steve provided his information, and after stepping forward when prompted, Geraghty extended a hand to him. "Sir, congratulations. You've made it. And you've done a hell of a job, sir. Fergus will take care of you." Geraghty squeezed Steve's shoulder.

Gunnery Sergeant Jarlath "Fergus" Sullivan, another cadre member from his Recon days, arrived and took his pack and rifle, smiling at him. Steve felt weightless. It was harder to walk without the heavy weight of the equipment. Fergus was an accomplished sniper with a few confirmed kills in Iraq, and, like Marko, a MARSOC plank owner.

Steve checked his watch. Sixteen and a half hours. "Holy shit," he muttered, grinning, still unsure. He walked to the rear of the truck like a newborn fawn on unstable legs with Fergus trailing beside him, his equipment in hand.

"I'll meet you at the fire, mate," Fergus commented in his Irish brogue.

Steve enjoyed the moment as he reached the rear of the truck and was intercepted by another hooded figure. "Captain Keller, I'm Major Roland Joyce, the Selection and Training OIC."

"Yes, sir. I know."

Roland was also a MARSOC plank owner, and like Guido came from 1st Force Recon Company in California. He was already a larger-than-life hero in the Marine Corps due to his combat experience as both a Force Recon Platoon Commander and as an Infantry Company Commander in Iraq in 2003 and 2005. "Congratulations on finishing the physical part of selection." He didn't offer his hand.

"Thanks, sir," Steve replied, unsure of where the conversation was going.

Roland's dark eyes looked into Steve's eyes from under his cap. "You're not in MARSOC yet. You still have to pass the board interview."

Steve nodded. "Yes, sir."

"And you may find it harder than the physical portion," he delivered in a grim tone. "Captain Keller, Officer Selection begins now." Roland stepped back and melted into the darkness.

Steve's exhilaration at completing the test lasted ten feet, the length of the truck. Still, he'd finished. He'd take whatever came next in its parts.

He was brought to the fire and stood staring at it along with a few other candidates. Then Guido, followed by Alex, arrived. Fergus met them with mulled wine and sandwiches. It tasted so good. When there were enough of them to return to the barracks they'd started from a week earlier, they loaded into a van with their equipment.

Steve was wet, cold, and exhausted, but with the van's heater on full blast, he passed out. Guido shook him awake when they pulled up to the barracks. His legs hurt so badly, he had to walk upstairs backward since he couldn't put any pressure on his quadriceps.

Soaked and sore, he stumbled to an individual room away from the rest of the candidates. Food was waiting for him, although it was cold, along with an electrolyte drink. The room was sparsely appointed. The single light bulb from a small desk lamp illuminated a computer and complete stock of office supplies neatly arranged on the desk. Aside from a bed and a wardrobe, the room's furnishings were otherwise plain.

Steve took a hot shower, standing in the water until it ran lukewarm. Fatigue overtook him the moment he stepped out, and he lay down on the bed. He was hungry but couldn't eat anything. He was out of energy.

The pain in his feet that had eased on the ride over returned with a vengeance. They hurt so badly, he couldn't keep them still, and sleep became impossible. He massaged them to no avail. Yet, somehow, Steve nodded off eventually, only to be awoken by a loud knock at the door.

"Who is it?" he yelled, annoyed. It was late, and Steve wasn't impressed.

The knock repeated, louder, and intense.

"Goddamn," Steve growled. He strained against his aching abdominal muscles to sit up, his legs wooden, and when he put his feet on the floor, sharp needles shot through them. He stood and slowly regained his equilibrium as he headed to the door. Marko, smiling pleasantly, stood on the other side. "Here you go," he said, handing Steve a manila folder. "Have a good one." Marko turned and walked away before Steve had a chance to process, let alone respond.

He shut the door and leaned his forearm against it to take pressure off his legs and feet. Steve hobbled over to the desk. After dropping into the seat with a wince, he looked inside of the folder.

The assignment was clear. A due date and time were established for twelve hours away. It meant staying up to do it while attempting to ignore the pain in his legs.

Steve sighed and got to work.

# 3



*Appalachian Mountains, Western Virginia, March 2007*

Steve surmised officer selection would be another challenging experience, but he underestimated; due to his exhaustion it was a mentally taxing ordeal. Coming after the excruciating physical portion, any officer who undertook it achieved a modicum of respect. Another week of tests followed. Gone was the sense of supreme triumph of finding his way in the woods, but Steve enjoyed the independence and ability to work on his own, sought-after traits in the Special Operations community. Then came the board interview presided over by Major Joyce.

Balding, with close-cropped hair and deep-set, dark brown eyes, he had an intimidating intensity. Of five board members, Roland was the senior officer, and the board members comprised MARSOC officers and noncommissioned officers. They asked tough questions.

"What would you do in this situation?"

"Can you work alone?"

"How about with a small team?"

"What if your men have more experience than you on a subject, how do you handle that?"

"Have you ever lied to get what you want?"

"You've got plenty of training and schools under your belt. Why should we take you here if you already know everything?"

"Don't tell us what we want to hear. Tell us how *you'd* do it."

On it went. There were more correct answers, but they were ascertaining how Steve thought and the conclusions he would reach. What went into his thinking versus the "right" answer. It was unlike anything he'd been a part of, and midway through, he was summarily dismissed.

He was sure he hadn't passed.

Steve remained outside of the selection building and enjoyed a sunny day in late March. On his way out, he'd looked at the photos of MARSOC men, units, people, locations, the paddles on the wall, the tradition; even for a recently formed unit. A unit that was proud of its short lineage, of its culture, and guarded it fiercely. One had to be invited to be there; to be selected—the very definition of elite—and Steve was captivated.

He was taken out of his observations by a terse "Report to the Selection OIC" from Master Sergeant Geraghty.

Steve's interview had already lasted two hours. Roland, nonplussed at what they'd discovered about him, started in on Steve. "Here are some highlights from your evaluations: 'An inveterate rule-breaker who believes the rules do not apply.' 'Not well-suited for working in strict, systems-based organizations.' 'Capable of working long-term as an individual or in a team, but thoroughly independent.'"

Roland paused for a moment to presumably let those observations sink in. The room was quiet.

"I see you went to VMI. Lacrosse player. History major. Why did you join the Marine Corps?"

"I wanted to be the best, sir." Steve hoped he sounded confident.

"We aren't looking for the best man here. We're looking for the right one."

"Yes, sir." But did he fit the criteria?

"You're an infantry officer. You went to Second Force in . . . ?" Roland paged through Steve's record.

"Two-thousand, sir. I served there until early 2003."

"But you didn't deploy?"

"No, sir. I completed all the special schools like jump and dive, but then I got assigned to permanent staff at OCS and missed the big push into Iraq." Steve sounded sheepish. Training candidates at Marine Officer's Candidate School in Quantico, Virginia, was hardly glamorous.

"Wait! *Really?!*" Roland sat up in his chair; not deploying was a rarity.

"After my tour with Second Force, and with all that's happening in Iraq and Afghanistan, I moved to Camp Lejeune, but I refused Infantry Company command to attend selection." Steve paused and corrected his quick words to a more paced and comfortable measure.

"MARSOC gave me an opportunity to get back in the Force Recon community. Honestly, it's home for me."

"Hmm. Doing that is probably career suicide, Captain Keller." Roland shook his head slowly. "It's clear you'll take risks, but you're probably at the end of the road, you know?"

Steve nodded.

Roland put his hands out. "And now, you want to come to MARSOC. So, why *are* you *here?*" He pointed at the table for emphasis.

Steve looked at the floor, considered his response. "Nine eleven. I lost an uncle in the North Tower."

Roland raised an eyebrow. "You're here for revenge?"

Steve shook his head. "I admit his memory drives me, but I don't have bloodlust, if that's what you mean. I'm here to lead men in combat, sir."

"How much combat time do you have, Captain Keller?"

Steve looked at the carpet in front of him. "None, sir. I've never fired my rifle in battle."

Roland half closed his left eye and tilted his chin upward. "I see. Combat can be ambiguous. I'm going to ask you a hypothetical question: Let's say your best friend was in trouble with the cops, and you knew you could get his charges dropped if you lied for him on the witness stand. Would you do it?"

Steve pursed his lips. "No, sir."

"Really?! Your *best friend*?!" Roland sounded shocked.

"Sir, given the circumstances, I'd be as loyal to him as possible but not at the expense of my integrity."

Roland looked sternly at Steve and pushed back from the table. "You're going to be faced with very complex situations, and I believe you're equipped to make the right calls. Further, we think you're perfectly suited for Special Operations work. I'm going to bring you on for continuation training. Welcome to MARSOC, Captain Keller." He stood; his hand outstretched.

The words rang hollow in Steve's head. He couldn't believe it. "Thanks, sir!" Smiling, he stood and shook Roland's hand as the other board members also congratulated him.

Steve was handed a letter proclaiming his selection to take to his unit and generate the military orders to assign him and his family to MARSOC's headquarters in North Carolina and what would become his home for the next fifteen years. Holding that piece of paper made Steve feel amazing. He was escorted out of the room, barely understanding what happened but flooded with relief that it was over.

Steve was taken to a barracks where Alex and Guido, also having passed, waited for other successful candidates.

"Man, am I glad that's over with!" Steve walked to a small table and pulled out a chair to sit with them.

"Me too, dude!" Alex said.

"So, now what?" Steve asked.

"Dinner, hopefully!" Guido grinned, and shortly afterward, Marko came and got them for their evening meal.

At dinner, Steve compared his selection experiences with them. "How'd it work out for you?" he asked Alex while piling spaghetti and meatballs onto his plate.

Alex shook his head slowly. "It was hard as hell!"

"No shit!" Guido blurted. "What a ballbuster! Did you guys take the road up the mountain?!"

"No, like a dumbass, I took the trail!" Steve laughed.

"Me too!" Alex's voice was that of someone admitting a bonehead mistake.

"Well, I did, and several people had a rough go of it after they made a wrong turn. They didn't complete the event in time! Can you imagine reaching the end, only to be told you'd failed to meet the standard?!"

"I'd be crestfallen!"

"Thank God it didn't come to that!" Alex took a bite of spaghetti.

They finished dinner and went to bed. It was the final night before they left to return to their respective units the following day. They had little idea what was going to come next in the training continuum.

At the end of the punishment, Steve, Alex, Guido, and seventeen others out of the sixty who'd started were selected.

The next morning, they boarded a bus to the airport where Steve delightedly called Elena to tell her the news, then drank a celebratory beer with Guido and Alex. By the time their plane was in the air, Steve was asleep.

# 4

———

Steve returned home to his family. After what he'd completed at Selection, there was just three weeks before continuation training began. His body would barely have enough recovery time, and he wanted to be ready, but that meant expending yet more individual time and family capital preparing.

Spring was in bloom, and he and Elena sat in their backyard enjoying an afternoon drink; Steve sipped on a beer and she on a vodka tonic. They'd met at a cocktail party eight years earlier, hosted by one of Steve's friends. She was the sister of one of the guests and had been in town for the weekend. Elena had taken his breath away with her little black dress and strappy heels.

They'd been married six years, and Elena, thirty-four, remained athletic and fit, with raven hair and intelligent brown eyes, coupled with an upbeat, sparkling personality.

Their three children played on the jungle gym while she and Steve discussed the news. "Congratulations, baby! How was it?"

"Tough. And thanks, babe!" They clinked glasses.

"I'll bet. What now?" She was curious but concern also lined her tone.

"I go through six months of operator training. I'll be gone a lot." He looked at his shoes.

Elena sipped her cocktail and sighed. She drew her legs up beside her. "Nothing new there."

Steve leaned toward her. "Yeah, but this is different. The people, everything is different than other units I've been in. I'm *so* ready for this!" He grabbed her hand, squeezing it with excitement.

"*We've* been in, you mean." She returned the gesture, then let go and indicated toward the kids. "Just be sure you make time for them, OK?"

"Of course," Steve replied. "It's like someone told me, 'The Corps will not always be there for you, make sure your family is at the end.' You guys are important to me!"

"And what about deployments?" Elena asked with a hint of hesitation.

"To be determined. We don't have a schedule since I still have to get through the training." Steve again reached for her hand.

Elena clasped his in return. "Being honest, I'm nervous for what being in this new unit will entail. But I know MARSOC is what you wanted, so I'm happy for you." Though he didn't doubt her authenticity, her tone seemed guarded.

"Let's take it one step at a time." Steve understood her apprehensions and tried to put her mind at ease. "It'll be an amazing experience, babe. Wait until you meet some of these guys!"

# 5



MARSOC Operator Training was an arduous six months long and encompassed a variety of skills, including military free-fall, and helicopter assault; survival, evasion, resistance, and escape, also known as SERE; evasive driving, unarmed combat courses, and a host of combat marksmanship. Each day began with a difficult physical training session and the process also involved a lot of shooting with the M4 5.56 mm carbine and M1911A1 .45 caliber pistol.

Steve, Alex, and Guido were part of a forty-man operator course, and the instructor cadre included Fergus and Marko, with Brian Geraghty and Roland respectively being the staff non-commissioned officer and officer-in-charge.

Dressed in body armor and helmets, the candidates conducted close-quarter-battle small-arms marksmanship training on a crisp, cold day. It consisted of quick reaction shooting from behind barricades, firing while moving and closing with the enemy and engaging multiple targets in rapid succession. Under the watchful eyes of Roland, Fergus, Marko, Brian, and other instructors, the staccato noise of forty M4 carbines being fired filled the air.

Guido talked smack to Alex between firing rounds. "You suck, Alex!"

"Really?! That's *just* like you. Just good enough. I mean, you say you're from New York, but you're from Long Island—that's not New York!" Alex fired two more rounds from his carbine.

Guido laughed. "Yeah?! You may as well be from Philly with as far south in Jersey as you are! No wonder you shoot well, you Chinese gangbanger!" He loved giving Alex a hard time, but he maintained an immense respect for his friend. The feeling was mutual.

"Fuck you, Guido. Quit shooting on my target!" The banter was meant to keep the stakes high and push the other to perform at their best. In this course, it took hard work to be considered mediocre.

Marko stood behind them and overheard the exchange. "Shut up you two." He stepped in between them, faced down range, and smoothly presented his own M4. He fired two rounds into the head of each of their targets, demonstrating he was adept at all facets of shooting weapons. "When you can shoot as good as me, you can talk shit!"

"Aye, aye, Gunny!" Guido said, looking at Alex. Marko stepped away, and they resumed shooting.

Further along the firing line, Roland took a position next to Steve. Standing six foot two and powerfully built, Roland was physically impressive. "Am I making you nervous, Captain?" he asked.

"Nope." Steve remained focused on his sights.

"Then why're your groups so big?" Roland dug. Steve's target centered on a large hole ripped in in the middle of the paper. "You rusty or something?"

"Whatever!" Steve said, squeezing off a controlled pair. The rounds impacted on top of each other.

"That's better!" Roland complimented.

"Cease fire! Cease fire!" Brian's yell echoed along the line and all the Marines stopped firing and put their weapons on safe. "Take a break, gents!" The Marines went to sit on benches and get off their feet. Shooting in full body armor and helmets, the gear was heavy.

Roland and Steve stood to one side. It was chilly, so Steve removed his shooting gloves, replacing them with fleece-lined ones to keep his hands warm. Roland smiled.

"What're you smiling at, sir?" Steve asked.

"You up for a little competition?"

"What do you got in mind?" Steve raised an eyebrow.

"Walk-back drill. Pistols only." Roland's eyes gleamed.

"Done."

Roland turned to Brian. "Brian! I've challenged Captain Keller to a walk-back drill!"

"Roger! Center line, gentlemen!"

Steve was already changing back to his shooting gloves as a murmur passed through the Marines. Some placed bets on the victor. Roland was an accomplished marksman.

Fergus and Marko glanced at each other. Steve overheard Fergus whisper, "My money's on the captain!"

"Shiiittt . . . you've seen the major shoot! Twenty bucks?"

"You got it." They shook hands.

Steve and Roland moved to the two-yard line and checked their pistols while the rest of the Marines gathered to watch. A walk-back drill entailed shooters taking turns at a small steel plate. At close range, this was easy, but with each subsequent hit, they moved back another five yards. Both continued to shoot the plate until they were seventy yards back—far for a pistol shot.

Steve asked, "Wanna pack it in?"

"Hell no! I'm not letting you beat me!" Roland fired—and missed. A collective buzz rippled through the Marines.

"Oh, shit, sir." Steve gave him a thin smile. "I hate when that happens."

Roland stood stunned and silent.

Brian chided, "You still gotta hit it to win!"

The witnesses, who'd been talking a lot of smack to both of them, fell quiet.

Steve sighted over his pistol and raised the barrel slightly. He fired and hit the plate. The Marines went crazy. Marko dropped his head, and Fergus raised his fists in victory.

Steve lowered his pistol and turned to Roland. "Guess I win."

"You sure did!" Despite the results, Roland appeared elated for his success. He grasped Steve's shoulder and squeezed, then clapped down a few times in celebration.

With the break over, the Marines returned to training.

# 6



Halfway through the course, Roland brought Steve into his office to counsel him on his performance to date. Steve entered, and Roland, seated in a chair across a coffee table with a carafe and two cups on it, motioned toward a couch in front of him. "Please, sit down. Have a cup of coffee." Roland poured one for Steve and topped off his own. "You've done well so far. In fact, you're the only officer remaining."

Steve held his cup and smirked. "I've noticed, sir."

Roland sipped his coffee. "This isn't for everyone. Most people don't have what it takes. You, however, are an exception."

"Thank you, sir."

"I'm serious. I see this as a valuable opportunity to develop you as a leader, if you want it . . . " Roland set his cup down and leaned forward.

"Yes, sir. Of course."

"Good. It's also my understanding you have a lot of history with people here, to include some of the cadre."

"I do, sir. The ones I know were people I serve with in Force Recon during my assignment like Fergus and Marko. Brian was briefly my platoon sergeant. I really only know two of the students since we bonded during Selection and they're in my team: Alex Chan, who joined us from Third Recon in Okinawa; and Tony Larosa, who's from First Force. I've never served with either of them, though."

"Yeah, I know Guido. And that's good commonality. Switching gears, you're from—"

"Montana, sir." The words slipped out before he could think. Steve pressed his lips shut.

"No, no. Please, go on," Roland encouraged, unbothered by the interruption.

"My brothers are co-owners with my father on our cattle ranch," Steve clarified.

"I guess the family business wasn't for you?"

"No, sir. But not because it isn't good work. I wanted an adventure, and I guess I'm still looking for it." Steve shrugged.

"But as I recall, your uncle died on 9/11?"

"Yes, sir. He was my mother's brother," Steve explained. "He was a broker living in New York at the time. I didn't know him very well."

Roland nodded. "Are you married?"

"Yes, sir. My wife's name is Elena. You, sir?" Though the conversation was objectively out of place compared to the rigid daily communications throughout training, the fraternal nature of their discussion offered Steve a sense of comfort.

Roland's eyes lit up. "I am, but I'm a geo bachelor. My wife's name is Pam. She still lives in California with our daughter, Kayla." He gestured to the framed photograph of his family on the corner of his desk. "Do you have kids?"

"Yes, sir. Three. Samantha—we call her Sammie—is six, almost seven, Michael is five, and Marta is three."

Roland smiled warmly. "Wow. That's great. Keeps you grounded on deployment. Gives you something to hold in your heart to come home to."

"I agree, sir." Steve smiled too.

"There's actually not much left in the course. We're about to start platoon assault training, then it's just the free-fall module, followed by resistance training. After that, you'll take a platoon."

"That's not long when you put it like that, sir." Steve took another sip of coffee.

"I want you to focus on leading these men. After selection, some of them may be members of your unit, and you'll lead them in combat. You need to be ready to make hard decisions. And live with their results." The softer, more personable quality had faded from Roland's tone in favor of something more serious again.

"Yes, sir. I think I'm most comfortable leading small groups. This is an extreme appeal of being in MARSOC."

Roland stood and shook his hand. "Excellent. Stay focused. You've got a bright future."

Steve swelled with pride when he stood. Roland was the Marine officer he wanted to emulate. "Aye, sir."

# 7



Dawn came bright and clear, the air already warm from a desert wind gusting across the airfield. The remaining members of the operator course were on a three-week deployment for training conducting the military free fall parachute module. *Arizona's nice this time of year,* Steve observed while studying the desert's unique charm through the large bay doors of an aircraft hangar, twice the size of a basketball gymnasium.

The class packed parachutes the night prior; the gear assembled for the jump to make an easy transition when they arrived in predawn darkness. Sunrise brought ideal conditions for perfecting skydiving with beautiful blue skies and unlimited visibility. Of course, they weren't merely skydiving. They were practicing a military insertion technique, and the addition of gear and equipment reduced much of the maneuverability. Plus, being an earthbound missile before the parachute opened was enough to worry about, never mind other people in the air. It wasn't something to be taken lightly.

"You ready, Steve?" Roland called as he approached from the back of the hangar, almost yelling over the low drone of aircraft engines in the marshalling area next to the hangar mixed with Schtum's "Skydiver" blaring from ceiling-mounted speakers.

"You know it!" Steve replied with confidence, looking up from his equipment. Roland's unmatched presence and charisma commanded respect upon entering a room, and he extended his hand to shake Steve's. The moment he accepted the offer, Roland pulled him into an embrace, then stepped back.

Steve buckled his equipment while the natural banter of other Marines filled the hangar. People ribbed one another, talked smack to break the tension. Jumping was hardly natural, and certainly not routine, something Steve found exhilarating.

Putting on his own parachute, Roland said, "I love doing this with you!" and smiled in a way that made Steve pleasantly embarrassed at Roland's admiration. Roland moved to another part of the hangar to interact with other students.

It was a mystery to Steve why Roland decided to mentor him—befriended him, even. In his own estimation, he possessed few, if any, of the qualities he admired in Roland. One thing they shared was a love of sweets. Steve marveled at how Roland would drink a milkshake, claiming it was part of his preworkout carbohydrate loading plan, and snack on Twizzlers candy, only to ostensibly not work out half as hard as Steve did after enjoying the same things. Roland also loved pizza. Yet none of his guilty food pleasures ever seemed to slow him down.

Roland was genuine and kind but also confident with the right amount of endearing cockiness. He made everyone feel special and important. It was his gift. Steve always felt good around him. Conducting military free fall parachute training was dangerous enough, but Roland's ease and confidence made it fun, even before they'd jumped.

Guido approached Steve, carrying his own parachute. "You excited, sir?"

"You bet! You?"

He chuckled. "Honestly, sir, I don't like jumping out of airplanes." Guido observed Roland on the other side of the hangar. "But I like hanging out with people who do. Makes it easier for me!" Guido raised his chin. "Do you know Major Joyce?"

Steve looked at Roland, too. "Not really. I mean, mostly what people say, that he's a bit of a legend."

Guido shifted the large parachute to his back and slung it over one shoulder. "The legend's true. I served with him at First Force. The guy's a machine in combat. He was also an incredible infantry leader, apparently. His Marines loved him."

"Wow."

Guido nodded. "Yeah. He was an All-American wrestler at the US Naval Academy. And he's got two Bronze Stars with a 'V' and a Purple Heart. Just a badass."

"I think the most admirable thing is that you wouldn't know it." Roland's humility was impressive and made Steve respect him even more.

"Anyway, thought I'd ask, sir, being that he's taken a shine to you." Guido smiled, then left to prepare his equipment for the jump.

Steve snickered, his gaze shifting from his retreating buddy to Roland, moving easily among the students and cadre.

Steve, Roland, and the rest of the Marines in their stick would be the third lift that day. To complete the requisite number of jumps for certification, a total of four jumps would be conducted to make up for a previous weather day where the winds were too high to safely train. War in Iraq and Afghanistan was ongoing. They didn't know what would be required of them, but they had to be ready.

One of the students was named Staff Sergeant Dave Porter. He was a bodybuilder and thickly built with thin black hair and a round face. He talked like a jock while drinking protein shakes, farting loudly with accompanying immature commentary, and extolling his most recent lift in the gym. He was annoying, at best, but Porter and Steve had been jumping in the same stick for a few days, and he at least respected Porter for having completed the tough training to date.

The rest of the Marines in the ten-man stick were other future MARSOC operators. With Brian as one of the two jumpmasters, and Fergus and Marko flying helmet-mounted cameras to film their jump, that totaled fourteen on the plane.

The lead jumpmaster's name was Hillman. Retired military and now a civilian contractor, he'd served on the Leap Frogs, the US Navy's elite showcasing parachute team, equivalent to the Army's Golden Knights. His jumps, numbering in the tens of thousands, backed a cocky arrogance. He certainly didn't look the part of a former Special Operations commando. He was dumpy with a bald spot and curly hair that jutted out from the side of his head if he wasn't wearing an ever-present ball cap. He had spastic mannerisms exacerbated by his intake of coffee and energy drinks, as if he needed any more stimulants. His diet consisted mainly of junk food. Still, he was the most experienced jumper of all of them, and his expertise was unquestioned.

All the jumpmasters were well-trained to rescue a jumper who was out of control, if that happened, and to pull their parachute if the person got into an unrecoverable spin.

As a cautionary tale, all the Marines jumping knew of a fellow recon man named Miller, who'd been killed in a training mishap in 2001. He'd lost altitude awareness, forgot to pull his parachute, and his reserve parachute opening device had failed. His body hit the ground traveling at terminal velocity—120 miles per hour—exploding on impact and creating a three-foot crater in the rocky desert. By the time Miller was located, there wasn't enough of him to put into a trash bag; the coyotes had already been feasting on the remains.

Steve and Miller were in Force Recon together and students at the Army's basic Free Fall course when the event occurred. Steve had been packing his parachute inside the hangar when the dreaded line "There is an unconfirmed jump fatality" came over the radio. It sent chills through all who'd heard it, even though it was only a formality. The body hadn't yet been located and only a coroner could officially pronounce someone dead, even if they were in pieces, or pieces of pieces. No one wanted that, but a heartless wag stated, "It's good job security for the coroner!"

Even in the most serious circumstances, someone was morbidly humorous.

Jumps were unmistakably dangerous training. Everyone took precautions and practiced their emergency procedures.

They would leap from a Marine KC130, four-engine, turbo-prop aircraft. It was noisy, and the lowered rear ramp was slick with hydraulic fluid.

Steve and his stick boarded the plane, got seated, and prepared for the jump.

The KC130 powered up and took off, quickly climbing to the designated jump altitude of 12,500 feet. The interior was warm and smelled of old oil and exhaust fumes, though the scent disappeared when the clamshell door opened, and a rush of chilly air flooded the enclosed space. The ramp revealed a cobalt sky over distant snowcapped mountains, the brown desert juxtaposed beneath their peaks.

The jumpers stood, calming their nerves, focusing, a rivulet of sweat coursing down a cheek, cold due to the temperature, but hardly noticed. Hillman took one last gauge of the wind and eyed the release point. One minute. Steve was third in the stick behind Roland, and they'd all exit together. A final check of equipment, looking to their own and that of the person in front of them. Porter, standing behind Steve, checked his parachute. Steve did the same for Roland.

Thirty seconds.

Everyone moved to the edge of the ramp.

The point of no return.

Hillman, with a maniacal smile, knelt in front of Roland. "Stand by!" he yelled and gave the thumbs-up signal that each jumper passed back.

Steve inhaled slow and deep. An adrenal dump pushed his heart and mind to an overdrive. Upon leaving the aircraft, inputs came at a jumper so fast, if a person failed to stay in control of what was happening, they'd die wondering what went wrong.

"Go!" Hillman yelled and led the team into the void.

Steve stepped off the ramp. The brief drop was followed by instant acceleration. Icy air collected the jumpers, straining to hold them in the sky, but gravity couldn't be repelled. They were free-falling.

"Get in a place in the sky that's yours and stay in it," Hillman had admonished during the prejump brief that morning. Steve heeded that advice and checked the altimeter on his left wrist; he'd already burned through 2,000 feet. Hurtling through the beautiful clear desert sky, he had just forty seconds until he needed to pull his parachute.

Steve scanned for other jumpers and checked his altimeter again. Nearly time to break away from the air formation and find his opening point. To gain separation, he turned his body and shot across the sky in a high-lift tracking maneuver.

"Never sacrifice altitude for stability," Hillman had said. "If you're tumbling through the sky and seeing blue and brown, pull on brown. Get a parachute out and in the air so you don't end up a stain on the earth!"

Steve systematically performed the pull sequence at the proper altitude, and his parachute deployed. *Next to sex, this is the greatest feeling in the world.*

The blossoming canopy snapped him violently into the sky and slowed his descent to a crawl, though he was still moving through the air aloft on the winds, controlling his movements like a bird. Taking stock of the other jumpers, he counted thirteen other gray canopies. Everyone else's parachutes had opened, too. No one would end up like Miller.

They would "stack up," playing follow-the-leader with one canopy behind the other, lowest to highest, and ride to the drop zone, Hillman leading them into the designated landing area. "Jump, land, and fight together," he'd taught.

Steve remained number three, following Roland, with Porter above. Being beneath Porter, the lower jumper always had the right of way.

They approached the landing point. Hillman and Roland were already on the ground, their gray parachutes behind them in limp heaps.

Roland shouted up at Steve, smiling, "Bring it on in, brother!" A slight wind came at a quartering angle. Inside of five hundred feet, it was easy to get fixated and only incremental changes were possible. Being so close to the ground and unable to make drastic maneuvers, Steve applied a small adjustment to his parachute.

A shadow came over his canopy—someone above him. The soles and laces of a pair of jump boots; Porter's boots. He was too close and hadn't made the same adjustment Steve had. Porter drove into the rear of his parachute.

Steve's parachute collapsed and he oscillated wildly to his right. His speed accelerated downward. The ground rushed to meet him. *This is going to hurt!* Though he attempted a parachute landing fall, his analysis was wrong. The situation was worse, and he was out of options.

After an accident, to paraphrase Winston Churchill, the terrible "ifs" accumulate. The postmortem is conducted on how things transpired. People blame others, details are misremembered, and everyone has an opinion, particularly those who witnessed it. First impressions and initial reports are often incorrect, but all add up to a narrative of poor sequencing that seem preventable after the fact. The one thing left out is fate, for it is fate that leads people to the place they're supposed to be, regardless of outcome.

Witnesses said Steve tried to get up after he hit the ground. After falling one-hundred feet through the air, he was travelling twenty miles an hour when he impacted on the left side of his body, destroying his arm, fracturing three ribs and his pelvis in three places, dislocating his hip, crushing his goggles against his face, and lacerating his head resulting in a lifelong scar.

Steve was knocked unconscious and came to in excruciating pain. The sun shone crimson through blood pooling in his eye sockets. He wasn't sure why his hip and left arm seemed twisted, simultaneously numb and burning, and he lolled from the intense pain as Roland rolled him onto his back.

"Don't move. Medics are on the way!"

The medics cut off all of Steve's clothing to make sure he could be safely moved and administered a morphine shot to blunt the agony. As they sliced off his boots, cold wind blew across his toes. His spine might be fractured, but Steve decided instead that *this* was the greatest feeling in the world. An odd sense of clarity settled in place of the pain, and he examined the entire chain of events.

If the order of the stick had been different, would things have happened as they did? It was contemplatable but hardly changed anything.

After an indeterminate amount of time, a Marine Huey helicopter landed to evacuate him. The flight Corpsman leaned in. "How's your pain on a scale of one to ten?" he yelled over the noise of the turbine engine.

Steve, weary, replied, "Fifty."

"I'm gonna bump up the morphine dose. I want you to count back from ten, calling out each number as the pain subsides. Only change the number if the pain is going down, OK?" The Corpsman administered more morphine through the IV they'd intravenously attached to him.

Steve counted, loudly, painfully. "Ten! Ten! Ten . . . Seven . . . Four . . ."

In his drug-induced state, he counted each rotor blade individually while they clicked through the air.

Roland had forced his way on to the helicopter to ride with Steve. His face came periodically into view as he held Steve's hand. "Hang in there, brother. I've got you!"

The flight to the hospital dissolved into a blur. Steve passed out, and all was relief.

# 8



"How're you feeling?" Roland pulled up a chair next to Steve's bed. It was the day after the accident.

Steve, groggy from painkillers, smiled. "I'm not on fire, so it could always be worse."

Roland laughed. "You mean your condition's improving! Ha!" He studied Steve's face, taking in his racoon eyes with bruising around the sockets and the stitches in his head. It was almost dehumanizing, being in the hospital in Phoenix, unable to even use the toilet without significant help.

Steve chuckled but held his ribs. "Don't make me laugh, dude, it hurts!"

Roland waited for him to relax again. "I want to reassure you that we're going to retain you so you can complete your training. No matter what it takes."

"Really, sir?"

Roland nodded. "Hell yeah. You're tough! What you went through would've killed a lesser man! You survived a midair parachute collision! Under canopy? Falling nearly one-hundred feet?! You're lucky to be alive!"

Steve looked at the IV attached to his hand. "So, I guess my condition *is* improving then."

Roland smiled. "Keep that sense of humor. You've got a long road to recovery ahead of you, and you're gonna need it. But I'll keep tabs on you, and when you're healthy, we'll get you back into training. Deal?"

Steve nodded. "Sound's good, sir."

Roland clasped Steve's hand and stood to leave. "Hang in there, man."

# 9

From his hospital room, Steve called Elena. "Baby, it's me."

"Oh, thank God!" she said, distress flooding into her voice.

"Baby! You all right?"

She spoke in between sobs. "Major Joyce called and said something about you being in an accident, that you were hurt but were going to be OK." She took a deep, shaky breath. "But I didn't hear much afterward! God, I've been so worried." Her voice trailed off, simultaneously relieved and scared.

"Oh, baby. I get it. And don't worry. Really. I'll be home soon!"

"You don't understand, Steve! I thought the worst when he called. I was terrified, and the kids." She cried harder. "I couldn't stand. I slid to the floor, and the kids came and lay with me. They were confused and worried, but I told them you were OK."

Steve tried to soothe her over the phone, but a long-distance call offered little comfort. "Thank you for doing that. Like I said, I'll be home soon. I'll tell you all about it then, yeah? I love you."

They stayed on the phone while Elena collected herself and only hung up after she said, "I love you too, Steve."

A few days later, Steve flew home via commercial aircraft. Landing late at night, and after a day of travel in his condition, he probably looked as awful as he felt. He limped off the plane on a crutch, his arm in a sling. His children, sitting in the back of their Jeep Cherokee, didn't know what to make of him if the way they stared was any indication. Elena gently hugged him and helped him into their car.

"Daddy, what happened to you?" Michael asked.

"I told you, Michael. Daddy's been in an accident." Elena wiped away her tears. Was she still worried about if the extent of his injuries would have lifelong effects?

"What kind of accident?" Samantha asked. She spoke for the younger two, too young to really understand, despite the tears lining their lashes.

"I got hurt jumping out of airplanes, Sammie, but I'm OK." Steve looked back over his shoulder. His answer seemed to stem their curiosity, but even they detected their mother's tension.

They arrived home, and Elena helped Steve out of the car. Their life would be different for a while, with her caring for an invalid as he learned to walk and regain the use of his broken body. It was a hard pill to swallow for them both, but they were committed to one another and his career.

Once they settled inside and the children were distracted, Steve told Elena of the events surrounding the accident. "Roland told me I'm going to be able to rejoin training once I recover. It's gonna be fine, baby."

"For whom?" She laughed nervously, though she seemed to be trying to remain calm. Most people would give up on returning to such an environment, but she understood her husband was different, which is exactly why he'd been selected to serve in MARSOC. Steve's drive and work ethic would only fuel his recovery so he could complete operator training.

"For us," he said.

It was late. He offered a few more consoling words of reassurance to the kids, and Elena prepared them for bed, but they ended up sleeping as a family with all three of the children in their bedroom.

# 10



Steve began his long road to recovery. His primary care doctor had served in US Army Special Forces and looked like Tom Skerritt with an easy yet firm demeanor.

"I've seen people in way worse shape than you make a full recovery to full duty status, to include jumping."

Steve laughed. "Worse? Is that possible?!"

The doctor nodded. "You'll achieve your goals, but understand with the injuries you sustained, your body may not come back the same way. In short, you may never be one-hundred-percent. You can get close, though. The process will be frustrating, but you'll also find ways to cope with it. You've got to want it."

Steve supposed he was right; just being at home was nearly impossible for him without Elena's near-constant assistance. He had to learn to do everything over, tying his shoes with one hand while his left arm healed and how to walk with a new hip, never mind taking a shit since he could barely sit down.

He was paired with a physical therapist named Kyle Tierney. The first day they met, Kyle asked some questions about him and his background and the accident.

"And you?" Steve returned, curious. "How'd you get into this line of work?"

"I'm from Maryland originally, but I loved North Carolina, so I settled here after a brief stint as a Marine Corps officer."

"Really?"

"Yeah. I wasn't destined to be a long-term career Marine due to my temperament and not adjusting to the life the Corps offered. I'm too independent and being the executive officer of an infantry company became the killing blow."

"How'd that happen?"

Kyle's intensity bordered on high-strung. "I was supposed to get an infantry platoon, but our XO got fired. I'm a capable organizer and good at my job, so I got moved up by my company commander. I worked for an ungrateful ass who saw himself as a vastly intelligent scholar of war, but we generally assessed him to be an idiot. Plus, no one joins the Corps to be an XO!"

"It seems a gross injustice that the other lieutenants got platoons while you toiled in administrative purgatory," Steve reflected. He studied Kyle's small USMC tattoo on his forearm. Kyle at least liked being in the Corps enough to emblazon a permanent memento on his skin.

"It's fine. Leaving the Corps, I found I had a knack for this stuff." He looked around the rehabilitation room. "I'm in the right place. Now, let's get to work!" Kyle's encouragement was infectious, and for good reason. The physical therapy recovery regimen Steve underwent bordered on excruciating.

The hip was difficult, but not impossible, though compounded with his pelvic fractures, he really was in a delicate condition. He was admonished by his doctor for walking without his cane when he came for a session since, without an X-ray, the doctor didn't know how his pelvis was healing. Though despite his own assurances that he felt fine, Steve knew the doctor was correct.

When he was able, Kyle took Steve on long, slow runs across the sandy terrain around Camp Lejeune in the hot sun. These not only built the body but also allowed him a fair amount of personal venting and catharsis. His injured left arm protected in a brace, Steve ran awkwardly, but Kyle loved hard physical training and pushing people past their perceived limits.

"The harder and stronger you are, the more you can take! You can do this!" Kyle said, running slightly ahead to ensure Steve would keep up.

Steve kept running, subjugating the pain of his legs to a corner of his mind.

Kyle was a superman, an Adonis. He trained Steve, taking him under his wing, and rebuilt him. He taught Steve how to lift weights with his reduced capacity, how to understand the mechanics of the human musculature to push his body to accept—maybe even enjoy—the pain of hard training and its tie to mental endurance. So much so, during his recovery, Steve tattooed Endurance on his arm under the Recon Jack one his Marines had bestowed on him.

The wrist was the worst. That, and the entire arm since his ligament ladder in the forearm had essentially exploded on impact. Essex-Lopresti, it was called. After another round of surgeries to his left arm, he restarted another long, slow path to recovery. He finished each therapy session sweating and in pain, but he was determined to get better, to return close to whole. Physically was easier than mentally, but spiritually, he struggled the most.

He didn't share that last part with anyone, not even Elena.

One day, Steve was panting after a difficult session where his wrist was turned with a machine to improve its lateral movement. "God, I just want to be healed." He massaged his wrist.

Kyle patted him on the back. "I want that for you, too. Hell, I want to see you succeed!"

"You know. You're one of the rare people put into another person's life to help them along. Some ignore such a guide, and others embrace them. I'm lucky as hell to have you on my side." Steve shook his hand.

Kyle pulled him into an embrace, confirming his mutual support. "I'm proud to help, but this is all you. All the effort. The sweat. The pain. It's all building toward your goal to achieve full duty status."

*Camp Lejeune, North Carolina, June 10, 2008*

Steve's future service in the Marine Corps remained uncertain. He'd been relegated as one of the myriad staff officers at MARSOC and seated at a desk in a stuffy headquarters. He had yet to complete operator training, which meant he couldn't deploy and lead Marines. It was worse than being in the hospital. At least there, his recovery gave him a goal, even if the desk job allowed him to attend his physical therapy.

Each day he entered the office, his soul ebbed in the daily doldrums of staff work. He wore a formal uniform, complete with tie and tie bar. The gabardine wool clothing chafed, both physically and spiritually.

Steve sat at the desk, typing on his computer against a mundane task when Roland burst through the door with his unmistakable energy. By contrast, he was dressed in camouflage utilities, the polar opposite of Steve's attire. "Hey, Keller!" he shouted.

Steve looked up from his computer. "Hey, sir! What're you doing here?"

Roland smiled. "Lookin' for you, dude! I've got a job offer for you!"

Steve winced. "I might be getting separated from the Corps. I'm awaiting the results of the medical board. If they deem me unfit for duty, I'm outta here."

"Bullshit. Besides, I'm true to my word. You have work to do!"

"I'm doing it!" Steve chuckled, gesturing to the computer.

"Nah! Real work! I just turned over my Selection OIC duties, and I'm taking command of a Marine Special Operations Company. I want you to be a part of it."

"An MSOC? Dude, congrats!" Steve stuck out his crooked left arm, a permanent result of the accident. "But I think I'm gonna have to hang it up. They keep telling me I might be too broken."

"No way. I saw the results of your last medical board evaluation. You're good to go! I'm getting you out of this desk job!" Roland nodded, emphasizing his commitment to his promise. "You gotta get outta this shit!" He swept his hand across the office. Some of the other occupants looked at him but he seemed oblivious to their gazes. "By the time you finish your training, you'll be ready to lead troops again! And the timing will be perfect for you to do it with me as one of my platoon commanders!"

"The med board. Seriously?" Steve beamed.

"Yep. Don't worry, I've got you." Roland squeezed his shoulder and walked out of the office.

Steve felt hopeful, and for the first time in a while, happy.

***

A year after the accident, Steve finished his last treatment and completed a Marine physical fitness test consisting of a three-mile run, sit-ups, and pull-ups. He ran slow but met or exceeded the minimums for each event, which meant he passed. Though not at full strength, it was still a momentous achievement.

"I'm glad I made it!"

Kyle looked at his results. "Hmm, I going to recommend to the doctor that you be retained on active duty."

"I guess we're finished, then?" Steve was a little emotional, an odd ball resting in his chest.

"Yeah. This is it. But it's supposed to be this way," Kyle reassured him.

"Thanks. For everything."

"You've earned it." Kyle offered a proud smile and shook his hand.

Steve walked out of the hospital and never saw Kyle Tierney or the doctor again.

# 12



In October, Steve rejoined the next available operator course and completed his training. True to Roland's word, Steve was assigned to his MSOC. MSOC Papa, 2nd Marine Special Operations Battalion, totaled 120 personnel. The HQ had thirty enablers of administrative support, and intelligence personnel. Two platoons constituted the unit's maneuver elements. One consisted of forty-five infantrymen, commanded by a lieutenant named Mark Hackett; and Steve's, also of forty-five men, comprised of those who'd passed from Force Recon units to become a Direct-Action, Special Reconnaissance (DASR) platoon.

The DASR was uniquely structured with a five-man HQ element with Brian Geraghty as the Platoon Sergeant, and four ten-man squads of two five-man assault teams each. The squad leaders were Marko, Alex, Guido, and Fergus. The platoon had Special Operations medics and snipers integral to its ranks. As a precision raid force, it was a small but formidable combat formation.

Through two months of training, Steve worked closely with Roland and Brian to develop the DASR to the highest standards of performance. He loved the autonomy of his role, and Roland was a steady, guiding hand, the first he'd really had in his career. Roland also taught Steve and Hackett how to integrate their platoons to operate well together. Hackett's Marines primarily drove the DASR in combat vehicles to and from objectives and provided a security cordon for them during raids. The MSOC became an effective team.

On a chilly evening, Roland, Steve, and Elena went out to dinner at a trendy bar near their home. They sat in a booth, chatting while Roland looked admiringly across the table at them.

"God, Steve. You didn't tell me how beautiful your wife is!" Roland smiled warmly at Elena. She blushed.

"Yes, I did!"

"It's nice to meet you under better circumstances than when you called me last year," Elena chided Roland good-naturedly.

"Yeah, sorry about that." Roland bit a corner of his lower lip. "But look at him now!" He squeezed Steve's arm and smiled. "Man, I'm glad we're serving together. You good? How do you like the MSOC?"

"I love it! And I've got you to thank for it. God, I would've died in that office." Steve took a sip from his beer. "But truthfully, I'm full of self-doubt, man. I don't know if I've got what it takes. The platoon is full of experienced combat vets. Compared to them, I'm not, and I'm expected to lead them? Taking command of the DASR was like checking into the 101st Airborne after they got back from Normandy. What do I have to offer?"

Roland dismissed that with a wave of his hand. "You're doing a great job as a platoon commander. You offer leadership and strength of character. You deserve to be here, no doubt in my mind!" He looked intently at Steve. "Brother, you were born to do this job."

"But maybe it was luck. And I sure as hell still hurt physically now that I'm back on full duty. Then there's the mental energy of being a leader in combat. I feel so . . ." he shrugged, "inadequate."

"Well, what would you do if you left? Not be a Special Operations Marine anymore? That's what defines you!"

"Steve, let me ask you something," Elena interrupted. "What's the hardest thing you've ever done? And don't say it was recovering from the accident."

Steve considered the question. "I'm . . . I'm not sure."

"C'mon! It doesn't have to be tough-guy stuff. It can be anything."

Steve pondered again before saying, "Telling you that I loved you. When I did that, there was no going back, and if you didn't return it, I had to accept the outcome. That was one of the hardest things to express. It was a gamble."

Elena smiled and leaned over to kiss his cheek. "Aww, babe, I love it!"

Roland reached out, grabbing Steve's forearm in a tight grip. "That's what I am talking about! Don't ever doubt yourself. Say it with me, 'I was born to do this job. I can do anything!'" He glared at Steve with an unknown intensity. Staring deep into his eyes, Roland's gaze bored into his soul.

Steve looked directly back. "I was born to do this job. I can do anything."

"Yes, you can. And never forget it."

Steve nodded, took a sip from his beer, and smiled at Roland who smiled back.

Elena put her arms out to both of them. "Cheers, boys!" She raised her glass of wine.

They toasted, Roland's hand still on Steve's arm.

# 13



*Camp Lejeune, North Carolina, April 19, 2009*

Steve had been in command of the DASR for six months. As his platoon sergeant, Master Sergeant Brian Geraghty was responsible for the daily operations of the platoon, as well as the discipline and well-being of its members. Steve was indeed overall in charge, but this division of labor kept things even. In good organizations, the officers and senior enlisted had a solid working relationship fostered through frequent communication.

Steve and Brian sat in Steve's office enjoying a beer after a day of training. Steve touched the long neck of his bottle to Brian's. "Cheers, man."

At six foot three inches and powerfully built, Brian was a giant. Strong and athletic, Brian had short-cropped brown hair, gray eyes, and a scar on his right cheek from a shrapnel wound from his tour in Iraq that gave him rugged definition.

"Cheers! It's been a solid week." Brian leaned back in a chair. "It's good to be working together. I didn't think we'd get that opportunity again."

Steve sipped his beer. "I know! I was pissed when I left Second Force, and the timing didn't work for us to go out together. I deployed in the infantry, but I got OCS as a second prize." He drew his lips into a tight line.

"Some consolation prize!" Brian took a pull from his bottle, then stood up. He went to the open door of their office and glanced quickly into the hallway outside before gently shutting it. "There's something I want to discuss with you."

Steve nodded. "After doing that, you have my attention. What's up?"

Brian sat back in his seat, leaning forward, the late afternoon sun reflecting in his pale gray eyes. "What do you think of Marko?"

"We get along well enough. Friendly. I briefly knew him from my previous tour, but we weren't in the same platoon. I know he's good at jumping, handling explosives, or any other dangerous task. He's got a hell of a reputation within the unit." Steve pinched his eyebrows together in a squint, unsure of where the conversation was going.

"I'll be blunt. I don't think he's team leader material."

"Why not? He's got the rank and experience; he's the best shooter in the company." Steve sipped his beer.

"That's true, but that doesn't always equate to having the right leadership qualities. Some people are solid operators but not good leaders."

"Marko's pretty popular, Brian."

He gestured with his bottle. "Yeah, people like him—he's charismatic. But that's not what I'm talking about."

Steve leaned back. "Lay it on me."

Brian slightly cleared his throat. "After you went to OCS in o-two, Marko joined our platoon. Always talking shit, he felt he had a lot to prove. So, we trained up and went to Iraq in o-three, but he didn't exactly perform the way we expected with all his talk."

"How do you mean?" Steve asked.

"Marko would be on assaults but hang in the back. He was a great shooter—still is—but would maintain he was holding rear security or backing people up on clearances. I don't remember a time he was first in the door. He always found a way to let the action happen, then come on the scene. That shit wouldn't have flown in the Det." Brian gestured with his beer bottle. Steve was afraid he might spill it.

"Tell me about the Det, really quick."

"Marine Special Operations Detachment-One stood up in 2003. The unit was handpicked. Everyone in it had spent their entire career with recon units and had a lot of combat experience. I myself was a two-time combat veteran; one with First Force in Afghanistan in 2001 and one to Iraq with Second Force during the invasion in 2003. When I deployed back to Iraq with the Det in 2004 I felt lucky to even be an assistant team leader in an organization stacked with talent, many of whom formed the core of MARSOC when it stood up after the Det disbanded in 2006."

Steve nodded, and Brian continued. "So, anyway, we stood up MARSOC. We found Marko has a checkered past, mostly petty criminal stuff, so how Marko got into the Marine Corps—let alone MARSOC—is a mystery. But I'll give him this: Even though he's pretty free-spirited, he's tough and intelligent, and he passed the first class of operator training. But I'm getting off topic. I know Marko. This'll be his first combat deployment in a leadership position. He's nervous and not a good candidate for team leader."

"Why is he one of our TLs, then?" Steve was curious.

"Well, he's a Gunny, for one. His rank puts him as a match for the billet assignment. And two, he has all the schools and training. He appears to be a natural pick to be a team leader of a Special Operations Assault Team, on paper anyway."

"Then I still don't understand what the problem is."

Brian sipped his beer. "Reputation is everything here, and while Marko is solid in training, in combat he didn't perform under pressure. He's been passed from one unit to another because of this perception. He's crafted a facade that allows him to squeak by."

"You're saying we should relieve him ahead of deployment due to a lack of confidence?"

"Exactly."

Steve thought about it for a long moment. Marko hadn't technically done anything wrong. He just didn't act the way others thought he should. "Marko may not be the best leader, but to this point, he hasn't proved he can't do the job either, right?"

"True," Brian reluctantly agreed.

Steve raised his hand slightly. "Marko will be given a chance to lead a team. If he comes up short, we can reevaluate. It isn't fair that he hasn't at least been given a chance to fail. We'll take him on with a clean slate in the hopes he becomes the leader people expect."

Brian twisted his face. "Hope isn't a good thing to rely upon here. We need guys we can trust."

"I know what you're saying. But it's on us as leaders to develop him. Otherwise, we'll continue to pass the buck." Steve finished his beer and reached into the refrigerator behind his desk for a fresh one.

"That's fair. I only wanted to get it out there, OK?" Brian indicated he was going to pass on a second bottle. "I'm afraid I have to get home, sir."

"You got it, and no worries! Though I have to laugh at the thought of you being a family man!"

"Why? Because my wife's petite and I dote over my two little girls? I have to!" Brian smiled.

Steve looked at Brian's tattooed arms. The art depicted violence and disturbing images peering through decaying flesh. A detailed belt of machine gun ammunition enveloped his left bicep. "Exactly." Steve laughed.

# 14



Pre-deployment training progressed. The Direct-Action Platoon conducted live-fire urban combat training at an area consisting of a small town with purpose-built buildings designed for close-quarters battle. An explosive charge detonated against a wooden door, blowing it off its hinges and into a room of one of the buildings, followed by another one. Smoke and dust filled the air and MARSOC Marines, dressed in full combat equipment, conducted assaults through the destroyed doorways. Gunfire and shouted commands, punctuated by the crack of flash-bang diversionary devices, echoed from within the building.

Brian Geraghty directed the chaos. "That's it! Push the fight!"

Alex yelled, "You got it, Top!" then moved down a hallway toward Guido, who was holding security on a closed door further up.

"I need support!" Guido shouted.

Alex strode toward him, "I'm with you!"

Hearing the call, Marko said, "Me too!"

They closed on Guido, who moved to open the door. He nodded to Alex and pushed it open. Alex and Marko moved forward and into the room, followed by Guido. There were paper targets set up on moving carriages, and they each engaged them with precision gunfire.

Marko finished his sweep of the room. "Clear?"

"Clear!" Alex responded.

Guido completed his scan, too. "All clear!"

Brian looked through the door at them. "Cease firing!" The command echoed through the building and the training evolution came to a pause. Roland and Steve entered the building after the gunfire stopped.

Since their meeting, Steve kept Brian's observations of Marko in the forefront of his mind. He was always judging Marko, perhaps unfairly. Steve watched him walk among his team, making corrections, and providing advice on how to shoot faster and more accurately. Marko removed his helmet, revealing thick black hair. He looked at Steve with brown eyes that sat behind an angular nose and nodded. His tan, tattooed skin showed years of hard living. Steve nodded in return. He had to respect Marko's capabilities, even if he had a sagging reputation. Marko still deserved his support until proven otherwise.

"Your boys are looking good, Steve." Roland brought Steve out of his private evaluation.

"Thanks, sir."

"How're you holding up? Any issues?"

Steve shrugged. "I'm good. A little sore at times, but I've been that way since finishing selection. Bound to happen, I guess."

"Good deal. Let's step outside." Roland pulled Steve to the side as the rest of the unit emerged from the building. Other Marines with new doors and targets moved in to set up another training scenario. Roland motioned to Steve's Marines. "What they did in there doesn't happen without good discipline."

"They're on autopilot. Brian makes it easy." Steve gestured toward Geraghty.

"I'll bet you're glad he's your platoon sergeant again."

"Oh, I am, sir. It's also great having Fergus, Marko, Alex, and Guido as team leaders."

"That's a dream team. It also means they'll have things in hand when you join me on our pre-deployment survey to Afghanistan." Roland looked at Steve, gauging his reaction.

"What? You're bringing me on the PDSS? Why not Nate? He's your XO." Captain Nathan Caldwell, the MSOC Executive Officer, would have been Steve's first choice, if it were up to him.

"You're the next senior man. And I need you to see what I see just in case we run split operations or something."

"OK, you got it. When do we leave?" Steve smiled.

"Two weeks. Nate'll run the company while we're gone, and if anything happens to me, you'll get your first MSOC command," Roland said in a wry tone.

Steve narrowed his eyes. "Let's hope it doesn't come to that, sir."

Roland laughed. "Relax, we'll only be gone ten days."

# 15



That night, Steve arrived home, excited. "Babe! Roland asked me to go on the PDSS with him! We leave in two weeks!"

"Great," Elena replied unimpressed. She returned to washing dirty dishes as she prepared dinner. The kids sat at their kitchen table, drawing on butcher paper with crayons. Michael held up a child's interpretation of a Marine. "Daddy! I drew you!"

"Nice, buddy!" Steve smiled and hugged his son, showing interest in his artwork. "What are you two drawing, my ladies?" Steve admired his girls' art too as Marta continued scribbling. Whatever it was, it probably made sense to her, and she seemed proud of it as she held up her work. "Very nice!"

Sammie had stopped drawing. "Daddy, where are you going?"

Elena stopped washing to stir the soup she'd been heating and turned toward them.

"I have to go to a place called Afghanistan," Steve explained.

"Where's that?" Michael asked.

Steve sat in a chair so all three of his children could see him. He held hands with Marta and Sammie. "Grab Michael's hands, girls." They did, and Steve glanced at them each in turn, squeezing his daughters' fingers. "As part of my job, I have to go away sometimes. Afghanistan is far from here, all the way on the other side of the world. And there are people there who don't have as many opportunities as you do. We're trying to help their country to allow their little boys and girls a better life. Does that make sense?"

The kids nodded, but Sammie's eyes teared up. "But I don't want you to go," she sniffed.

Elena set the soup to simmer and moved to sit beside Sammie, brushing back her hair. "Daddy won't be gone long," she said with an eye on Steve, indicating his cue.

"That's right. Mommy's right. I'll only be gone for two weeks. That's fourteen sleeps, OK?"

"That's a lot of sleeps!" Michael said, perhaps trying to envision how much time that would entail based on the furrowing of his blonde brows.

"I know. But it'll be good for you guys to keep track of it together." Steve stood up. "Let's have a family hug!" All the children and Elena moved in together with Steve to share in a warm embrace.

After dinner, baths for the kids, and putting them to bed, Elena and Steve sat in their living room having a cocktail.

"Two weeks, eh?" she stated.

"Yeah. It'll be good for us, getting a lay of the land." Steve nodded.

Elena put down her drink and moved to sit on his lap. "I need you to come home safely, Steve."

"You know I will, baby. What's with the worry?" He placed his own drink on a side table and wrapped his arms around her.

"That's what Alan Chisolm's wife thought." She put her head on his shoulder. Alan had been a friend of theirs who'd been killed on a PDSS to Iraq. He'd served in the infantry with Steve and had been in Steve's recon training class as a lieutenant. His death was a sobering reminder of the dangers of any mission, regardless of duration.

"I know. But he wasn't supposed to be where he was when it happened. We'll be careful. OK?" Steve kissed the top of her head.

"Promise?" Elena said, sighing into him.

"Promise." Steve looked at their reflection in the dark full-length sliding glass door that led to their backyard, enveloped in the blanket of night. He thought of Alan's family in the aftermath of his death. Did Alan have a similar conversation with his own wife before he'd left? It troubled Steve that he may have just told Elena a lie. He hoped he'd make good on the promise he'd just made, but like Alan, whether he did or didn't come back wasn't up to him. Still, he maintained his faith—his belief—that he would.

# 16



*Shannon, Ireland, May 24, 2009*

Roland and Steve flew from Cherry Point, North Carolina, aboard a charter commercial aircraft ferrying Army National Guard soldiers from a motorized transportation unit based in Montana. They were green, unsure, and it struck Steve as odd that those people, up until the time they were deploying, had normal jobs in the civilian sector. Roland and he were military professionals and Roland, perhaps unfairly, derisively referred to the guardsmen as spares.

Steve sat next to their executive officer during the flight to Ireland where they would have a six-hour layover.

He'd discovered the XO was an investment banker and had left a lucrative job, as well as his family, for a one-year rotation in Afghanistan. Being a transportation unit, they would drive cumbersome vehicles along roads subject to roadside bombs and ambushes. It was decidedly dangerous and inglorious work. It was also vital, since it kept American units resupplied with any manner of items from ammunition to morale-boosting mail.

Spares or not, Steve admired they were doing their part in a war that many people in the United States didn't understand any longer. As much as he liked Roland, Steve disagreed with his contemptuous outlook of the Army soldiers. Steve didn't view the XO or his unit as being any less valuable or patriotic.

During the layover, Roland and Steve went to the small bar in the Shannon airport. Roland ordered them two pints of Guinness. "Irish Guinness is better. You'll see."

Steve took his first sip and whistled. "Damn. You're right!" It was creamy smooth and tasted different from the imported Guinness available in America because it was so fresh.

Roland touched his glass to Steve's. "I fell in love with this stuff on my deployment in the infantry. God, it was good. Plus, this is the last booze we'll have before we get into country. No drinking in theater due to General Order Number One." He referred to the American directive to military personnel that forbade the consumption of alcohol in combat zones.

Significantly, American service members were the only forces denied alcohol. All the other NATO allies could and did consume it. Shannon, Ireland, was decidedly not a combat zone, but the Army soldiers had already been ordered to obey GO-1 ahead of arriving in Afghanistan.

"Guess we'd better enjoy it while we can, sir!" Steve said, sipping again. He gestured toward the XO and a small group of his officers. They were enjoying a meal in the pub but not drinking because of said orders.

"Sucks to be them. Spares."

"You know, sir, I sat with their XO and got some perspective on their situation. I think they're in a worse spot than us." Steve recounted his discussion with the Army officer. "They got called up for this war. You and I do it for a living. I think some acknowledgement is warranted, you know?"

Roland glanced at the XO, happily eating a burger, then looked back at Steve. "Damn. You're right. That was narrow of me."

"Not trying to make you feel bad, sir. Just what I learned from the conversation on our way over."

"No, not at all. You're right. And I have to say, what I love about our relationship is that you and I can communicate honestly." Roland flashed a humble smile.

"Thank you. I feel the same way, sir." Steve sipped his beer again.

"You can call me Roland, Steve. If you want?"

"Aye, sir." He winked at Roland, who burst into laughter and put his arm around Steve's shoulder. "This is gonna be a great deployment!" He signaled the bartender for two more beers.

# 17

*Southern Afghanistan, May 26, 2009*

The Army MH-47 helicopter flew through the night sky, its twin rotors moving what was essentially an armored Greyhound bus. In the dimly lit interior, Steve and Roland rode in the back, wearing combat uniforms and night vision goggles. It landed in a cloud of dust at the forward operating base—FOB Prince, named after Staff Sergeant Mark Prince, a US Army Special Forces soldier killed earlier in the war.

After three days of traveling from the states to Afghanistan, they arrived to meet their counterparts with whom Roland's Special Operations Company would conduct a relief in place with the current one, MSOC Echo, commanded by Major Felix Osman, in twelve short weeks. The results of the trip would inform Roland's MSOC's final training ahead of their deployment.

The helicopter's rear ramp lowered, and they walked down it, met in the dark by Osman.

He embraced Roland and shouted over the noise of the helicopter. "Good to see you, Roland!"

"You, too, my friend!" Roland shouted back.

Osman guided him. "Let's get away from this thing!" Steve fell in behind and the three of them walked to a building behind the landing zone and went inside. The MH-47 remained at the FOB another five minutes to pick up a few passengers and pallets of outgoing items and lifted into the night sky, dust and quiet settling after its departure.

Steve and Roland followed Osman into the HQ, where they would be briefed on the current situation on the ground, one they would inherit. They removed their combat equipment and leaned their rifles against the wall, but they all retained pistols. A terrain model of an Afghan compound sat on one of the tables. The detail was impressive.

Roland introduced them. "Steve, this is Major Felix Osman. We came up as infantry platoon commanders, then served together at First Force before MARSOC was established." He turned to Osman. "And this is Steve Keller, my direct-action platoon commander."

Osman, a large African American built like the football player Bo Jackson, smiled a wide grin, and shook Steve's hand again. "Good to meet you, Steve!" Through an adjacent door, another Marine dressed in a green T-shirt and camouflage trousers sauntered in. "Ah, Jim! Gents, this is Captain Jim Eggerton. He's your counterpart, Steve." Osman gestured toward Eggerton, who leaned forward to shake Roland's hand, but stopped before doing so with Steve.

Jim Eggerton was the kind of guy who was easy to hate. Fit beyond measure, he was what America expected of their Marine officers and what Marines, in turn, wanted to embody their leaders. Eggerton sneered. "Keller. I didn't think you'd pass selection, let alone make it out here. You can't even land a parachute!"

"You two know each other, I take it?" Osman asked.

"Yes, sir," Eggerton continued, his tone patronizing. "Ol' Steve here is always one step behind me, aren't you buddy? First Infantry Officer Course, then MARSOC." He smirked at Steve. Steve locked eyes with Eggerton. The air grew thick with tension.

Steve's nostrils flared as he raised his middle finger at Eggerton. "You better smile when you talk shit to me, Jimmy!"

They both laughed, and Eggerton grabbed Steve in a bear hug. "Damn, Steve! It's good to see you! We can almost go home!" That took the pressure out of the room.

Steve was happy to see his old friend. "I'm glad to be here."

Osman laughed at their reunion. "All right, old home week is over. Let's get to business." He walked to a large map of their AO hanging on the wall. Next to it was a printout of a PowerPoint presentation. They all stood next to tables strewn with maps and photographs. Roland and Steve listened attentively. Osman motioned to a photo pinned on the wall. "This is Muammar Agha, also known as Objective Tenkara. He's a Taliban field commander responsible for several bombings and the deaths of his own countrymen. He controls a large number of fighters and he's worked his way up the Taliban command hierarchy as illustrated on this spider diagram."

He motioned to another printout next to Agha's photo. Starting at the top, Osman pointed to each corresponding photo, describing their roles and locations from the top commander down to subordinates. "As you see, Tenkara is a top-tier commander. He has five subordinates who are all his lieutenants, the most prominent being his son and heir apparent, Muktah Kalib."

Osman finished the diagram. Roland and Steve turned to Eggerton when he spoke. "Tenkara's also the number three man out here; the shadow governor and assistant governor are above him, so he's poised to become a shadow governor. He's the biggest objective in our AO, gents.

"That's right. And, lucky for you, tomorrow night, we're going to try and roll him up, so you guys don't have to deal with him when you RIP with us in a few months." Osman used the acronym for Relieve-In-Place.

Roland studied the diagram on the wall. To the left of it were a dozen photos with a red X over them. He crossed his arms and pointed with his left index finger. "Who're these guys?"

"Former members of the network, junior commanders mostly. We've eliminated them over the past four months." Osman sounded proud.

"That's a lot of leadership. If we suffered those kinds of casualties, we'd be combat ineffective."

"They're a resilient lot, and there's no shortage of players."

"Hmm," Roland said, skeptical, eyeing Agha's photo. Agha didn't look like much of a threat with his dumpy round face and salty black beard. "Why don't you drop a bomb on him? Less risk to force."

Osman sucked over his back molar. "Too risky. And besides, considering collateral damage, he's worth more alive. The intelligence value he would provide us would be fantastic."

Osman smiled more broadly, excited. "So, you guys interested in a little extra-curricular combat?"

A familiar adrenaline dumped through Steve as Roland looked at him, and Steve looked back to him. "Great live-fire training environment! Whaddaya say, Steve?"

"Fuck yeah! As if I have a choice, sir!"

Osman slapped Roland's shoulder with enthusiasm. "It'll be a good time!"

The following night, after resting up and learning a little more about their AO, Steve and Roland recalibrated their laser aiming devices ahead of the mission. The laser provided a decided advantage while fighting at night. Mounted on the rifle and operated by a pressure pad, it wasn't visible to the naked eye, but with the assistance of Night Observation Devices (NODs), all someone had to do was look at the infrared dot that emitted as a beam from the end of the laser.

Place the dot of the laser, adjusted to hit where the rifle was aimed on the target, and pull the trigger. Shooting someone would be like playing a video game.

After completing that, they listened to the mission brief to capture Tenkara.

Utilizing the terrain model from earlier, Major Osman pointed out various locations while describing the scheme of maneuver to his assault force, covering all facets of the operation. "We've confirmed Tenkara is at his bed-down location. It has two compounds—designated A and B—that are two hundred yards apart, but we don't know which one he's in." He pointed on the terrain model. "We'll fly in two MH-47 helicopters to an insertion point six klicks away from the objective and make our approach on foot. Since it's a big objective, we're going to split it in two. Once both elements are set, we'll execute; timing will be key, so we'll hit both compounds simultaneously." Osman paused for a moment, looking around the room at the members of his MSOC.

No one spoke. They looked back at him quiet, attentive.

"Captain Eggerton," Osman continued, "with Captain Keller accompanying him, will be the main effort and assault Compound A. My element, along with Major Joyce, will be the supporting effort and assault Compound B. I'll have command and control and overall air support approval authority. When we're finished, we'll move to extract and fly back here to the FOB. We should be mission complete by tomorrow morning."

Osman finished the briefing, and from there, they assembled their equipment and moved to the FOB's landing zone to load the two MH-47 helicopters and conduct the raid. Steve was eager, adrenaline already rushing through his veins. Danger aside, a raid was an adventure with the highest stakes. Steve wouldn't have missed it for the world.

# 18

Southern Afghanistan, Desert Insertion Point, May 28, 2009

The flight to their starting point took a half-hour. Through his NODs, Steve examined his part of the assault force seated in the black interior of the helicopter. Some guys were sleeping. Flying to conduct a raid was what he'd joined MARSOC to do, and he couldn't believe the opportunity had presented itself. He tried suppressing any nervousness, wishing to be more relaxed and confident. Then again, he was a combat tourist with no real responsibility on this mission. For him, it was the best of both worlds.

An electric, mellow excitement was palpable when the assaulters stood on the last thirty seconds of the approach. The helicopters made a final sweep of their landing zone to ensure it was cold—unoccupied—then settled down in a cloud of dust, their giant rotors creating green halos of static electricity around their arcs with dust sparking off the fine particulate when Steve viewed them through his goggles. Examining the rotors, the halo of Michael the Archangel, protector of warriors, came to Steve's mind.

The rear ramps lowered, and the assault force exited the giant machines, moving away from them to establish a security posture. Offloaded in less than one minute, their last form of armored protection lifted into the air, the door gunners manning seven-barreled miniguns and scanning for any approaching threats. They turned back toward the mountains to screen their movement, throttled up, and departed. Then it was silent except for the odd cough coupled with a few members taking a piss before they started their foot movement.

The assault force took stock of their location and their reconnaissance element moved out to lead them to Tenkara's compound. Roland nodded at Steve. "You ready?"

"Yeah, just a little edgy," Steve admitted.

Roland put his hand on Steve's shoulder. "Man, I get it, but tonight will be a quick mission. And it's better to get in a small action before you go to Hue City!" He smiled, referring to the January 1968 Marine assault against North Vietnamese forces during the Tet Offensive.

"Makes sense," Steve replied, more at ease.

They shook hands. "Good luck tonight, Steve!"

He looked at Roland and adjusted his NODs. "You too, sir. See you after we get this guy!"

Roland moved to join up with his part of the assault force. Roland's Velcro call-sign patch on his right sleeve, J06, reflected in the artificial light of his goggles.

***

After a six-kilometer walk, Osman's element broke away from Eggerton's at their release point. Osman got into position and told Eggerton's element to move toward Compound A. As they did, one of Eggerton's Marines carrying an assault ladder tripped, making a loud noise. Shots echoed from Compound A, and this alerted the enemy in Compound B, who also opened fire. Several bursts of small arms rounds impacted Osman's position.

Osman keyed the handset to his radio and called Eggerton. "Drifter One-Zero, this is Drifter-Six. Sitrep, over."

Eggerton's element engaged the compound moving via bounds. "Drifter Six, roger. We're one hundred meters to the west of the objective compound and taking fire but able to maneuver. We can press the fight."

"Roger. I can see your forward trace. Go! We're assaulting compound B now!"

Eggerton's element advanced. Viewed through NODs, lasers were seen on human targets followed by the dull snap of suppressed rounds and several enemy fighters went down. Eggerton called to Osman, "Drifter-Six, Drifter One-Zero. We're at the compound entrance and commencing breach."

"Roger. Continue," Osman replied.

From the main gate came the call, "Breaching! Breaching! Breaching!" followed by a large explosion that shattered the gate's double doors. Eggerton's assault team made entry and began clearing the compound. When they finished, they'd engaged and killed three fighters but found the compound otherwise empty.

Tenkara wasn't among the dead.

***

Osman radioed Eggerton. "Drifter One-Zero, we have two WIA. But the enemy's trapped in this compound. We'll gain fire superiority and continue."

"Roger, Drifter-Six. We're securing Compound A. Tenkara isn't here. Need us to consolidate at your position?" Eggerton replied.

"Negative. Remain in place until I call you up," Osman ordered.

"Copy. Standing by." Eggerton understood. He spoke into his radio on his platoon channel. "All stations, Drifter One-Zero. Hold your positions. Say again, hold your positions and continue SSE." This meant searching for anything of intelligence value like phones, weapons, or photographs, also called Sensitive Site Exploitation.

Steve, right next to Eggerton, asked, "What's going on?

"Osman said they've got casualties and told us to hold up coming to him." Eggerton pointed to the ongoing firefight in Compound B.

"Oh, shit," Steve said as they watched Marines exchange fire with enemy fighters, worried about what appeared to be violent combat and if Roland was in it.

***

Eggerton and Steve's objective compound was quiet. Too quiet. Until it wasn't anymore.

Over the company command net came a call. "Drifter-Six-actual, this is Alpha element. Over." The voice sounded concerned.

"This is Six-actual. Send your traffic. Over," Osman replied.

*"Drifter-Six, be advised, Juliet Zero-Six is down and KIA. Over."*

"What was that?!" Steve grabbed Eggerton's arm. "I thought I just heard on the radio, something about Juliet Zero-Six. That's Roland's call sign!"

Eggerton turned to Steve, his face grave. ". . . I'm sorry, but the word that was passed is that he's KIA."

"H-how?!" Steve's world began to swirl. He saw the starry sky, the Marines around him. His mouth tasted like dry copper, and he suppressed a wave of nausea. Eggerton asked something unintelligible, but Steve stumbled over to a wall to brace himself. His body grew chilled but in nonspecific ways. He fell to knees. The euphoric rush of being on the raid was replaced with frigid dread and shock. Steve's stomach knotted and he felt queasy again, though not sick; this was something he'd never experienced.

It was all very strange, how quickly the feeling of success was supplanted by a feeling Steve didn't expect: fear.

It seemed incongruous that Roland Joyce could be killed, but for Steve, the impossible had happened. Steve screamed, "ROLAND! NOOOO!"

***

The mission ended. The wounded Marines and Roland's body were flown to Kandahar, and the rest of the assault force returned to FOB Prince in a melancholy mood. Steve packed his and Roland's equipment and spent the day ruminating the events of the previous evening. It made for a long afternoon.

That evening, Osman approached Steve on the LZ before he flew to Kandahar to escort Roland's body back to the states. He would receive Roland's casket on the tarmac, the body prepared for the journey the day prior by mortuary affairs.

"I'm sorry, Steve."

"Me too, sir. I'm not sure how I'll share this with Roland's wife, Pam."

"I can tell you what I know: When we breached our compound, two Marines were hit, and the assault stalled. Roland saw what was happening and rushed to assist them. Before I knew it, he's inside the compound by himself, which isn't good in a CQB situation, as you know."

Steve nodded.

"I don't know what happened, exactly, but after we secured the compound, we found Roland with his carbine jammed and his pistol in his hand, so the carbine probably failed, and he transitioned to his secondary weapon. The enemy must have shot him when he did. There were no enemy dead in the room." Osman sighed. "I don't think he knew what hit him. He was dead before he hit the ground."

Steve winced.

"If Tenkara was there, we didn't find him; he certainly wasn't among the seven KIA we uncovered between the two compounds."

"It just seems so damn unfair for him to go out that way."

Osman looked into Steve's eyes. "He was a good friend of mine, Steve. I feel for you."

"Thanks, sir."

Osman clapped Steve on the shoulder. "Get him home, Steve. We'll see you in a few weeks."

"Will do, sir."

The sound of an approaching MH-47 ended the conversation.

# 19



*Wilmington, North Carolina, June 3, 2009*

Steve departed Afghanistan on what was called a Hero Flight. It meant he flew directly back to the States on a C-17 aircraft solely dedicated to the return of fallen service members. There were seven other coffins. He hardly slept, the weight of the raid where two of Osman's Marines were wounded, the helicopter ride after as he sat with Roland's body, of escorting Roland back to the United States at Dover Delaware, caused Steve bouts of breathless anxiety.

Roland's death was hardly the first or last in the Steve's life, but it was much more acute.

Five days after leaving Afghanistan, Steve arrived home on a rainy afternoon. Having called her ahead of time, Elena sent the kids to a friend's house to watch a movie. She met him at the front door. "I'm so sorry, Steve." Steve started to cry, and she pulled him hard against her, quivering with sobs of her own. He collapsed in her arms.

"Oh, baby! What—What happened?"

Steve attempted linking his thoughts together but sounded nonsensical. "The assault—came to help. Stalled. He went alone. Why alone? Funeral next week—gone. Why is he gone? Holy fucking shit. What am I gonna do?!" He broke down, absolutely shattered.

"Let's get inside. Get you settled. We can talk about it and just reset ahead of next week. OK?" Elena held his hand and helped Steve up, despite her own tears still wetting her cheeks. "Then we'll get the kids home and you can spend some time with them. They don't know about Roland, and you're being home will be a great surprise for them."

Steve laughed at the irony. "So, I'm just supposed to act like everything's OK?"

Elena shut the door behind them and moved to their bar to pour a few drinks. "In this case, yes. They only want you, baby, so we'll find a way to get through this together."

Steve wiped away a tear. "I love you, Elena." She was just doing her best to be there for him and their family. Even rattled, he needed to appreciate her for that.

"I love you, too. And I'm here for you." She hugged him again. "I'm glad you're home."

Steve returned her embrace. "Me too. Of that, I'm grateful. But it's a hell of a tradeoff."

"I know," Elena said. "But I'm relieved it wasn't you."

# 20



R oland had been dead two weeks.

Brian and Guido, both having known Roland from when they'd all served at First Force Recon years earlier, came over the night prior to the funeral, and Steve, Brian, and Guido coalesced in Steve's study to privately toast their lost buddy. It caused tension and resentment between him and Elena since she felt shut out from the grieving process and as though Steve chose his friends over the support his wife had to offer him. And maybe he had.

For all of Elena's desire to help Steve, and for all he felt for her, he pulled away in favor of the familiar territory of his teammates, of the men who understood the weight of the pain losing a man in combat caused.

***

Steve and Elena drove in uncomfortable silence until they arrived at the funeral home in Annapolis. Elena dropped him off and left to check into their hotel. She would meet him later to pay her own condolences before going to dinner together. Steve changed into his formal Marine Dress Blue uniform, and his medals shone. That uniform was reserved for the most formal occasions. Many of them happy, like celebrating the Marine Corps Birthday or a wedding, but in some cases, also sad.

Sliding the black Mourning Band onto his left arm, he greeted old friends and exchanged condolences with various attendees. However, compared to others in military uniform, he was somewhat embarrassed that he hadn't achieved what many considered the mark of the veteran: combat awards. He felt inadequate. Had Roland ever experienced that same situation? He doubted it since, well, who would do that to him?! Steve was plagued with self-consciousness and comparing himself to Roland, his hero.

Steve found Roland's wife, Pam. She was as stunning in person as in the photos he'd seen, though solemnly dressed in a black skirt and blazer due to the circumstances. He revealed the story of Roland's death to Pam. "Roland led from the front. He exposed himself to danger as a matter of course."

"I know. Being brave is what Roland did. It was all he Did." Pam said, somber but proud.

"Your husband went out on top, in other words. We all wonder if we're of the same caliber, made of the same material. But we know we aren't." He lowered his head.

"You're very kind, Steve. I know why he liked you so much. Did you know you're one of his pallbearers tomorrow?"

"No!" Steve replied, surprised.

She smiled. "Well, there you go. I appreciate your candor, Steve, and thank you for coming." She embraced him for a long moment of comfort, then moved on to other well-wishers.

Roland's life had affected an endless number of people who came to see his family, to console, to offer condolences. The governor awarded a posthumous Silver Star and Purple Heart to Pam and their young daughter, Kayla, whom Roland loved dearly. He was now a father she would never know.

Young children of deceased service members troubled Steve. He remembered the funeral for another Marine earlier in his career whose graveside ceremony in the freezing cold at Arlington Cemetery still caused him to shiver. It wasn't due to the weather, either. The Marine's little girl had walked among the tombstones in a pink jacket, stark against the gray sky and earth tones and military pomp of a final ceremony primarily for those who're left behind. Medals and apologies were hollow platitudes, and the family would trade everything for ten more minutes with their loved one.

Having lost another friend, Steve knew the feeling well.

Marines are unique in that when a fellow Marine dies, during the viewing at their funerals, they watch over fallen comrades in shifts. Steve arrived after the watch shifts had been assigned. Roland's friend, Major Jeff Mitcham, as the senior ranking man, took charge to establish the watch bill, and Steve was on it.

"When do I start, sir?"

"This afternoon, sixteen to eighteen hundred."

Steve looked at his watch; it was two-thirty. "OK. Any other times?"

"We need a midnight to zero-two watch," Jeff said.

"You got it, sir." Standing watch was a tragic labor of love, but one he was willing to put on his shoulders. Roland deserved that much.

"Thanks, Steve." Jeff looked weary. He and Roland were also very close. Steve squeezed him on his shoulder. Jeff had been Steve's company commander when he was a young infantry officer, and Jeff had served in Bosnia with Roland as Force Recon Platoon Commanders, but Jeff had continued his career as an Infantry Officer, deciding not to join MARSOC. Usually relaxed and jovial with soft blue eyes, Jeff seemed hollow, resigned yet not quite accepting the reality of Roland's passing.

At four in the afternoon, Steve stood his post over Roland. It was an open casket funeral, and Roland was being buried in his Dress Blues, complete with medals and his Sam Browne belt. His white-gloved hands were gently folded on his chest. His right eye closed in repose, the left side of his head was bandaged to cover his wounded left eye, concealing the bullet hole that had entered beneath the socket and emerged from the top of his skull, shattering the bone. The back of his head betrayed his fatal injury due to its mottled skin only visible if standing beside the casket like Steve did.

Roland appeared peaceful and dignified, despite the wounds incurred, as if he might wake up from deep slumber.

Jeff came in to ensure Steve was in place. "Oh, shit!" he exclaimed, looking at Roland.

"What?" Steve looked down at his own chest. Had he missed something when getting into his own uniform?

Jeff pointed to Roland's left pocket. "He's missing his jump wings and combatant diver insignia!" The funeral home embalmers overlooked a significant detail.

"Damn! That's a must. If anyone has the right to call himself a Recon Marine, it's him!"

Jeff tried to remove his own "dual cool" as it was colloquially called. "Help me with this."

Steve and Jeff dutifully—reverently—completed Roland's uniform, placing the insignia in the proper place on the left side of Roland's Dress Blue coat above his medals. It struck Steve that despite outward appearances, Roland's body was indeed a shell since the chest under that uniform was hollow and lifeless. At that moment, he accepted that Roland was gone, and Steve secretly, selfishly, wished for the opportunity to avenge him. For all his misgivings, Steve no longer doubted he would perform if called upon. He mentally repeated the mantra Roland had ingrained in him.

*You were born to do this job.*

"Thanks. You good?" Jeff asked of Steve, bringing him back to the task at hand.

"All good." Steve smiled at Jeff, then Jeff departed. From that point, people arrived in a steady procession, filing past the casket and out a door on the left side of the chapel to another area of the funeral home.

***

At five o'clock, the funeral home director, a rotund man with a thinning hair line, dressed in a charcoal three-piece suit and small glasses, entered the room. He announced in a soft, clear voice, "Everyone please depart the chapel so the family can spend private time with their loved one." He held out a pudgy hand, directing people toward the chapel's side door.

Visitors followed his instructions and the funeral director exited out of the chapel with the last well-wisher, closing the French doors behind him. The chapel was silent as Steve continued standing his watch over Roland, lying peacefully in his casket.

Roland's parents and brother entered from the rear of the chapel, leaving the door open. In front of Roland's casket, his father collapsed in an inconsolable heap. His wailing couldn't be stemmed nor absorbed, only released.

Steve marched swiftly to the funeral parlor's door to shut it out of respect for their privacy. No one else was permitted to enter. Steve would protect the vulnerable moment, of which he was only a part of due to the family's trust in him because of what Roland told them of him.

Roland's father's plaintive, anguished cries echoed through the room, embedding in Steve's memory for the rest of his life.

***

When Roland died, something changed in the way Steve related to Roland's friends. The signs started early but didn't become clear until later. In more ways than Steve realized, he was a periphery to Roland. Not that Roland didn't value him, but compared to the others in his circle, Steve was grudgingly accepted, probably because Roland deemed it, and no one questioned him. For Steve, Roland was the only person who thought he was worth his time.

After his watch, Steve and Elena went to dinner to decompress. A group of Roland's friends were in the restaurant. They ostensibly knew each other, but the group ignored Steve and Elena. Roland's friends weren't his, and he wouldn't be able to break into their ring for all his efforts. One of Roland's closest friends, another Marine major named Lars Ellison, who only appeared to tolerate Steve, cemented that in his treatment of him.

With Roland gone, Steve craved mentoring and assistance. Lars offered none of it, holding Steve at an arm's distance. Steve was unsure why. He found out a short time after the funeral when Lars rebuffed him for no other reason than Steve missed his friend, was sad, and wanted to talk to someone. Lars never took Steve's phone calls and inexplicably removed all ties with him. He and the others in Roland's circle enjoyed each other's company without them.

Steve and Elena ate alone, each the comfort for the other, while he wondered if seeking perfection in his own relationships was too much to ask.

Steve conducted his late-night watch and returned to his hotel for a little sleep. The funeral was at ten that morning. As one of the pallbearers, he would help carry Roland in and out of the US Naval Academy Chapel.

He and Elena arrived early. The chapel was packed to capacity. They found their designated seats, and Steve joined the other pallbearers outside. While he walked back to the front doors, he wondered if he knew that many people over the entirety of his own life, let alone those standing in that vast chamber. There was more than a century of history and tradition in one place, and Roland's funeral would add to its walls for permanent keeping.

Steve admired the fine woodwork, the celestial paintings, and the homage to past battles and heroes and exited into the warm sunshine.

A friend's death is strange. Their loss is immediate, but the impacts are harder to understand. Life continued uninterrupted, beautiful days passed in their course, and the misery that occurred on them didn't have bearing on anything at all. Steve learned valuable lessons during that process. Life is hard, unfair, and the difficulties encountered seem important to those who feel them, but, despite personal pain, the entire world continued to struggle to attain basic requirements.

First-world problems that a person might order a meal and get it for free if they're not satisfied and have successfully argued their point, that you can get gasoline when you want, or order a pizza online and change your mind to get something else after you've placed the order. Birds sung, a breeze came through the trees, and Arlington Cemetery would inter another tenant. The world continued turning when his friend died. Steve didn't know how else to categorize it.

Steve and seven other pallbearers engaged in small talk ahead of the hearse carrying Roland arriving. The heavy rear door swung open, and they extracted the coffin.

"We gotta be careful!" Jeff shouted.

"Fuck! It's heavy," came another. Roland's coffin contained his Marine Officer sword, his fraternal recon paddles, and a host of other mementos, adding several hundred pounds to the heavy oak casket.

"Jesus, who cares?! Just lift it!" Lars snapped.

"Once it's up, we won't be able to make any adjustments! That's not the way to move this!" another member argued.

Frayed nerves and emotions spilled out as each man grappled with the gravity and importance of the task.

"Gents, for God's sake!" Steve exclaimed. "It is Roland Joyce. Do we need any other reason?! There's only one opportunity to get this right, and that's now. Let's focus. Everyone breathe. We've got this!" They looked at Steve and must have recognized that he was right; the arguments stopped.

Roland was carried in with proper solemnity.

With the casket in place on the pulpit, Steve moved to sit beside Elena. Seated, he looked at his shoes. His socks poked through the open side seams. The weight of the casket had popped the stitching in his shoes at the balls of his feet.

Roland death was felt across the Marine Corps. His funeral was attended by more than a thousand people, and Lars gave a tremendously fitting eulogy. In it, he extolled Roland's virtues and impact on him and other people's lives. He concluded by telling a story from his own experience with Roland.

"In 2003, I lost several members of my command in combat and Roland attended the funeral for one of my Marines. After the ceremony, Roland shook the father's hand, looked him in the eye and said, 'Congratulations.' The father recoiled, incensed, and asked 'For what?!' Roland replied, 'For raising your son to be a man.'" Lars paused, folded his notes, and looked directly at Roland's parents and Pam sitting beside them.

"To you, Mr. and Mrs. Joyce, and Pam: Congratulations."

People openly wept.

# 21



*Smoky Mountains, Tennessee, October 2031*

Steve awoke with a start in his darkened study, the fire down to coals. Having fallen asleep in his chair, he was stiff and sore. He looked at his empty whiskey glass on the table, his neck aching. He rolled his head slowly to loosen the muscles, his mind back on Roland. Had he been a dream? More than an apparition? Roland had been dead for years, and that hadn't been the first time Steve had seen him, always appearing the same way: in his Dress Blues, wounded, haunting him. Still, Steve asked aloud, "Am I going crazy?"

Kelso raised his head.

Steve stood slowly, flexing his crooked left arm in and out. He stretched his shoulders, then his back and sighed, releasing the tension of moments and memory. He'd sleep better in his own bed, though it would probably be fitful, as usual.

"C'mon, old boy," Steve said to Kelso. He strolled down the hallway to the bedroom and slid under the covers.

He didn't sleep soundly.

***

Dawn arrived clean and clear, the sun working through the

trees to lend light to the cabin's interior. Steve awoke, and Kelso leaped from the bed to follow him to the kitchen. He let Kelso outside to explore and take in the morning while Steve prepared their breakfast.

Looking out the window, sunrays lightly illuminated the last of the rainfall hanging from the leaves in small prisms. While the coffee brewed, Steve refreshed Kelso's water and food bowls, then set to making an omelet, which again appealed to his sense of exactness. There were a few potatoes remaining from last night's dinner, and he cooked them to complement his meal. He turned on music from an era he liked and was sure no one else did to keep him company while he worked.

Breakfast was a ritual. His entire life had been one of predictable routines, and he strove to maintain that, though he preferred to own the pace of the task, not have it dictated to him. Steve cooked the fillings for the omelet quickly and set them to the side. He finished whisking the eggs, the pan now hot enough to quickly cook them without scorching. The eggs cascaded into the pan, and the room filled with the wonderful smell.

All items finished and assembled; he left the pan to cool as he ate. He placed the dirty dishes in the sink as Kelso came back inside, and after the dog's own breakfast, Kelso expectantly looked at Steve, as if to ask what the plan for the day entailed.

"Fishing," said Steve. He went back to his room and stopped by the linen closet to check the Glock pistol he kept there was loaded and safe. Of course it was. Who else would move it? Still, his brain needed the reassurance.

The day looked cool, but it would warm up enough to only require a light jacket and wear jeans inside of his waders. Steve retrieved his fly-fishing equipment and his waders from their place in the garage and put all the items in a day pack. He grabbed a snack and water to complete the load, deciding he would be home for lunch.

Returning to the pile in the sink, Steve tackled the dishes so they wouldn't attract bugs throughout the morning. He scrubbed each item, utensil, and the pan and put them on a red dish towel he set to the right of the sink, balancing all items to dry. Then he opened the freezer and removed a premade frozen dough ball from its wrapping, placed it in a bowl, and covered it with another kitchen towel to rise for dinner later that evening.

Satisfied with the kitchen, he dried his hands before putting on his coat and reliable Asolo hiking boots and grabbing his equipment and walking stick. His trusty M1911A1 .45 caliber pistol settled into his belt holster with ease.

Steve stepped out of the door and onto the path in the shade of the trees. Kelso ran ahead a bit. They set off on the hour-long hike at an easy pace, traveling down the field and into the tree line where Steve would cut through the copse and into another field to reach the stream and handrail it to his spot.

It was a glorious morning.

# 22



*Smoky Mountains, Tennessee, October 2031*

Yesterday's rain ushered a gusty day against a wide blue sky visible through the break in the trees, a perfect backdrop to the fall colors of the oak, maple, and dogwood trees that created the forest through which the wide creek ran. After working the line to set the fly into the water, a light breeze caused Steve to adjust his cast to counter it. Increasing the pace of his back cast, he realized he hadn't seen Kelso for a few minutes. Where had the dog vanished to? He wouldn't ever go far, so Steve was more curious than concerned.

The water swirled at his legs as he let the line out in front of him, laying the fly perfectly into a still pool behind a moss-covered rock outside of the flow of the stream. He hoped to entice a trout below the surface since the fish were generally stubborn to catch and even more difficult to set a hook into. The fly sunk to the bottom, and he began to slowly draw it back through the water, one small pull at a time, feeling the line for tension.

The wind increased and a piece of deadfall snapped behind him. His head turned and he dropped the fly rod into the water. Drawing the semiautomatic pistol on his hip, Steve turned with the pistol in a firm, two-handed grip, his reaction a programmed fingerprint in his mind from years of practice. He was still fluid and smooth, the pistol up to his eyes and pushed out in front of him. He stared ahead to acquire the target, adjusting his footing in the water to deliberately turn and orient on the source of the sound.

A light draft passed through the trees and the water broke against his legs as he stared into the face of his old friend Roland, killed on that starry night in Afghanistan more than twenty years earlier. Steve breathed deep, controlling his adrenaline, unsure what was transpiring.

Easing his finger tension from the trigger, he relaxed a bit. Shooting him wouldn't have done anything anyway. Roland's ghost stood in his Dress Blues and shoes, full medals with Reconnaissance Marine insignia above them, wearing the Sam Browne belt and white gloves, his head bandage on the left side, covering his eye.

Steve lowered the pistol to his side and stood, his gaze fixed on the apparition. "Hello, Roland," Steve delivered, unsettled.

"Do you know why I'm here?"

"No."

"Because you feel guilty and ashamed."

"Yes. Yes, I do," Steve agreed.

"You have a lot to release yourself from, Steve. And a lot of which to be proud." Steve stepped forward to greet the specter of an old and trusted friend taken too soon, but Roland turned toward the tree line. "We'll talk tonight." He strolled into the forest and vanished in a blink.

The brush moved, and Kelso emerged, splashing through the water toward him, shaking Steve into the present. Had what occurred been real? The sense of being followed yesterday, then seeing Roland in the rainy field? Last night by the fire? He wasn't asleep; he wouldn't be able to feel water in a dream.

His fishing rod had washed downstream when he dropped it. It was ensnared in a tangle of deadfall and brush on one side of the stream, a knot of extended line and rod. *Damn.* Steve holstered his pistol and moved to disengage the rig from the abatis of nature's course and flow to which he was merely a visitor.

# 23



*Smoky Mountains, Tennessee, October 2031.*

The fishing resulted in three decent trout for dinner. Steve exited the water and lay his waders out in the afternoon sun to dry. While he'd thought he would be home for lunch, he instead would spend most of the day on the water, but his snack would tide him over until he got home. It wasn't the first time in his life he'd been hungry, so that didn't bother him, either.

He reached into his pack and withdrew his pipe, tobacco, and matches from one of the pockets. "Perfect day for a smoke," he mumbled, looking at the fall leaves and listening to the stream move timelessly by him. The sunlight glanced off endless ripples of water.

He carefully packed the bowl and lit it, drawing sharply to pull the fire on the match down and into the leaf. The scent pleased him. Satisfied the pipe was lit and required no more coaxing, he pulled a flask of whiskey from his fishing vest and took a small sip.

The birds sang, the stream coursed on its ancient route, and the wind moved the trees in a steady breeze. Small white nimbus clouds filled the sky but didn't indicate poor weather. He smelled the moistness of rain in the air, though, and the dropping barometric pressure as a cold spot under his skin due to the titanium rod in his left arm, a lifelong souvenir from the jump accident.

He enjoyed the pipe and whiskey. These were the kind of days he was told would be worthwhile in his advanced years. They were indeed nice, but it was tough to go it alone. How had he got to that point? All the twists and turns of life that led him to sit on the bank of that stream on a beautiful fall day. He thought of Sammie as a five-year-old, a spring in her step, beautiful brown curls bouncing on her little shoulders, carefree and walking down a path between the apple trees of an orchard munching on an apple. That had been when he thought he'd always get another year to manage the things life ran past him.

There'd been times when he hadn't adapted, and there were days over the years where he'd wondered if he'd ever relax. He didn't think he suffered from post-traumatic stress disorder, or not the accepted version perpetuated and peddled to the public that somehow all combat vets came home with tons of baggage and drama. Even with constant inputs and reminders of things and events triggered by outwardly benign stimuli, he mentally felt pretty well considering all he'd seen and been through.

In Steve's early training as a Second Lieutenant at the Infantry Officer's Course, at Quantico, Virginia, his officer instructors had tried to prepare him for what combat was "like" and how a leader "should act"—their words. The teachers, for the most part, had no real wisdom to impart since they hadn't been there themselves. It was all a sham. But the propaganda worked on the ignorant, young officers. They all believed they were indestructible and would make all the right decisions, that the leadership above them was competent, and that there were no evil people in their own ranks who would betray them. Reflecting on it in the present, it shocked Steve at how naive he'd been.

Steve raised his flask a final time with a sip of whiskey, to the river, to Roland, and those who couldn't raise a drink again. He disassembled his fly rod, zipped his pack, and repacked his pipe to smoke on his return to the cabin. Using his walking stick to help him stand, he shouldered the load to hike back in the late-day sun. Kelso bounded out of the reeds after him and dutifully sidled into his position to his front on the right.

With his pipe relit, his head wreathed in aromatic smoke, Steve traversed the fields, admiring the grass still wet from yesterday's rain, and decided that for the time being, all was good in the world. At least outside of himself.

# 24



*Smoky Mountains, Tennessee, October 2031*

Another breeze passed through the trees, leaving a stillness in the early afternoon sunlight. "Let's go back, buddy." Steve gave Kelso's ears a good rub and swept forward on the dog's head to scratch under his graying snout. "You've still got a few great years in you."

He thought back to that part of his life when Roland had been alive and smiled; Steve had lived long enough to appreciate it. He wasn't sure that had always been the case, taking Elena and the kids for granted on more than one occasion. Unlike physical injuries, that painful thought made him wince.

Reflecting on that, he traced his way along the creek to the break in the trees that would send them northward to the cabin. He wondered just how much time he'd spent in the woods over the course of his life. Steve loved being in the outdoors. As a kid, getting out in the woods had been a treat. It started in the Boy Scouts. He'd lived for the monthly trips into various parts of the Montana wilderness his Scout troop had traveled to for hiking, camping, and adventure. He'd enjoyed the woods and those formatively important years in the Scouts where he'd earned his Eagle Scout rank. His first real accomplishment.

Steve walked with purpose, scanning for signs of threats, and didn't so much walk as patrol with a constant sense of awareness. Learned as a Recon trainee, it required supreme discipline to maintain focus. Because losing it could land one dead. He thought of the rainy, cold night he'd spent up above Case Springs, California, where he'd learned that during a training exercise. The entire team had fallen asleep, and their instructor woke them up with acrid CS gas, a potent riot-control agent that caused respiratory distress and the eyes to water. Lesson learned.

Ironically, the instructor had later been killed in Iraq because he'd let down his guard. Steve had received the news while training in England with the British Special Air Service. Another goddamn impersonal blow, meted out in life's punishments if for no other reason than it was "your turn."

Steve entered the field that would lead to the next tree line—the one in which he'd seen Roland yesterday—across another field, and to the cabin. Not much farther, and in the scheme of things, it really didn't matter how long it took. Much like sighting in a rifle. If you have ten rounds and ten minutes, that's how long it takes. It goes up exponentially from there with the ammunition and time available.

In the middle of the field, he sighed, recalling an attack across open ground with Brian Geraghty, fully convinced he would either step on a landmine or be shot in a firefight. Neither materialized, but later, one of his Marines got crushed when a rocket strike caused a wall to collapse on him and bombs fell within meters of their position.

Steve arrived at the cabin in the late afternoon. He showered and went to the kitchen to make some fresh bread from the bowl of dough he'd left to rise that morning before he and Kelso departed on their fishing expedition.

He spilled flour on the granite countertop. Steve fell into a rhythm of kneading. Roll, fold, punch. Repeat. He enjoyed the feeling of the dough, the consistency in his hands, so worn and scarred, covered in flour and specks of dough—the same hands that had held and taken lives.

Steve cleaned and ate the trout for dinner with the fresh bread, and afterward, settled in by the fire for the evening. Roland sat across from him dressed as he was at his funeral, but tonight his presence felt warm, familiar. The fire cast their faces in a reddish glow.

"Pour me a drink, Steve?"

Steve smiled as he got up and moved to the bar. "Bourbon, no ice."

Roland looked up at him with his uncovered right eye. "Good memory!" He studied the copy of *The Raider Patch* with Marko's photo on the cover. "Marko's getting a Silver Star?"

"Looks that way," Steve said, fixing their drinks.

"Are you going to the reunion?"

"No. I don't attend them." Steve turned toward Roland.

"You disagree with the medal?"

Steve's shoulders slumped. "Marko didn't deserve *any* award, let alone a Bronze Star to upgrade to a Silver Star. It's ridiculous." He returned to his chair, sitting to face Roland. He placed Roland's glass on the table between them. Steve raised his own in respect for his deceased friend. "Cheers. I miss you."

Roland picked up his glass. "Cheers, indeed. And I you." He sipped his drink.

Steve looked down at his own lap. "You were the man I wanted to become. I had the unenviable distinction of being a pallbearer at your funeral."

"No one appreciated that more than Pam." Roland smiled. Steve peered back at Roland sympathetically. Roland became serious. "Do you remember the last time we saw each other?"

The fire crackled, light dancing across their faces. "Of course," Steve murmured. "I'll never forget!"

"Tell me about Marko. Start at the beginning," Roland said.

# 25



After returning from Roland's funeral, Elena and Steve lay together in bed before going to sleep.

"That was rough, babe," Elena said, her voice weary. "Like with my brother."

"Yeah, it was," Steve agreed. Her older brother, Carlos, died by suicide in 2003 after serving in Iraq with a Marine Infantry unit. There'd been no warning signs, he just did it. "I thought about Carlos this week, too."

Elena sighed and rested her head on his shoulder. "What's on your mind, baby?" She sensed his pensiveness.

"I'm hoping they give me command of the company. I need to get the bastard who did this." Steve's voice was grim.

"Giving you command would be the right thing to do, but the way you're headed isn't healthy. I know you're angry, but you can't let it eat you up." Her voice reflected both support and concern.

"It's not eating me up, it's fueling a fire. I can't wait to get back out there."

She raised up on an elbow to look at him. "Babe, that scares me."

"Why? This is who I am." Steve frowned.

Elena countered. "No, it's what you're becoming. Since you've been home, all you've focused on is returning to Afghanistan."

"I have unfinished business there." He looked at her.

"Maybe so. But what really worries me is that you're more excited about getting command and going back than you are to be home with your family." Elena smiled delicately and placed her head back on his shoulder. "I know you see deployments as a reward for hard training, but I view them as a sentence to a solitary, fretful existence. Especially after Roland."

Steve bit the inside of his lower lip. "That's true. I admit."

"Some days, I wonder if I'll run out of prayers," she stated softly.

Steve sat up a little. "How do you mean, babe?"

She rolled onto her side, looking at him, "Because each day I negotiate with God for your safety."

Steve stared at her, then wrapped her in his arms, holding her close. Fearful of her husband's growing obsession, Elena closed her eyes and drifted off to a restless sleep. As her breathing eased, Steve observed the ceiling fan, its rotating blades reminding him of his helicopter ride to the hospital with Roland in Arizona.

# 26



The death of any unit's commanding officer is a staggering blow to that organization.

Over the next few weeks, Steve struggled at times to comprehend the loss of his mentor and friend. The MSOC's deployment was only one month away, and they still had work to do. Per Roland's direction, Steve assumed temporary command of the MSOC and continued their rigorous training in an attempt to blunt the acute wound Roland's passing created. Steve was pleased with the unit's progress and how they developed as a team.

Roland wasn't easily replaced, so finding another company commander on short notice proved difficult. Being a junior captain, Steve couldn't be frocked or administratively promoted ahead of the actual rank to take command of the MSOC. The officer who did was Major Everett Charles Ballentine. Ballentine was prior-enlisted and secured an appointment to the Naval Academy. He prided himself on being a "Mustang" officer, though he had been a reservist in a Navy transportation unit and only served there for a year before attending Annapolis. Roland had graduated a year ahead of his arrival.

He was a short man with a perpetual scowl, clipped dark brown hair, parted on the side, and piercing blue eyes. What he didn't tell people was that he had no social standing save his name, being from literally the wrong side of the tracks in Cincinnati, Ohio.

Ballentine was an infantry officer and a veteran of the Iraq invasion in 2003. He came to MARSOC from a reserve Marine training command in New Orleans. Though competent, he was cautious, calculating, and arrogant. He wasn't a reconnaissance man, was assigned out of exigency and refused to go to Selection. He only commanded the MSOC due to his personal connections within the Corps and was more interested in what being assigned to Special Operations could do for his career than being an effective leader. His reputation proceeded him ahead of Steve meeting him the day he assumed command.

When Ballentine arrived, Steve was out training with the MSOC. He came out of the field wearing a unique uniform, Marine digital pattern combat suits made by Crye Precision and Asolo civilian hiking boots. The uniform's innovative design stood in stark contrast to what the rest of the Corps wore to fight, the top being essentially a lightweight athletic T-shirt with utility sleeves attached to it, and the trousers having strategically placed pockets and knee pads built into them to protect the wearer. Almost every part of the combat suit was well-considered. MARSOC units were the first to receive the revolutionary clothing, a version of which later became standard issue within the entire Corps. No Marine fought in anything other than issue boots, so Steve's choice of footwear was nonregulation.

The rest of the Marines were cleaning weapons and equipment after being in the field that week, and Steve didn't change uniforms when he left to meet his new boss. He pulled up to the company headquarters and noticed the scarlet company guidon with the yellow Eagle, Globe, and Anchor insignia and the letters 'MSOC P' sewn on it was in its carrier out front, indicating the commander was in garrison. Roland had eschewed that formality, keeping the guidon hanging on the wall of his office. It made Steve uneasy.

Steve walked into the building and toward Roland's—now Ballentine's—office. The door was open, and he lightly knocked on the doorframe. "Hey, sir!"

"Enter," Ballentine replied. He sat behind an orderly and organized desk, wearing crisp camouflage fatigues, his forehead furrowed, and his dour mouth turned to a pronounced downward frown.

"Welcome aboard, sir! Steve Keller; great to meet you!" Steve ambled forward, extending his hand.

Ballentine looked at him icily before standing to shake it. His hands were small and weathered with long thumbs. "Perhaps you mistook our relationship, Captain Keller?"

Steve, sensing tension, replied, "Sir?"

"Meaning, I didn't tell you to be informal with me."

"Yes, sir." Steve moved to a modified parade rest. He looked to the side of Ballentine's desk at a box containing some of Roland's paperwork and other office items. Aside from the phones and computer on the desk, it was otherwise clean except for a small, leather-bound cigar humidor placed an angle on the front right corner.

Ballentine wore a wedding band, but there were no photos of his wife or family. "Where were you today?"

"Training with my Marines, sir. We've been out all week."

"*My* Marines, you mean. You knew I was coming?" Ballentine asked with a raised eyebrow.

"Absolutely, sir."

"Then why weren't you here when I arrived? Where was the company?" Ballentine scolded.

"As I said, sir, we were out training. I figured the training plan should be adhered to considering our upcoming departure in a few weeks." Steve didn't like the line of interrogation.

"Hmm. I'll get to know the company later, and you and I will go over the pre-deployment training plan this week." Ballentine talked glibly to Steve, like he was a newly joined Second Lieutenant. "Anyway, I'm sorry to be taking over the company under these circumstances. Major Joyce was a good man."

"I agree, sir," Steve said, his guard still up.

"He brought you here as one of his platoon commanders?"

Steve cleared his throat. "He did, sir. We were close."

"My condolences for his loss. But, while his death is unfortunate, it's important to move on in these situations." Ballentine sounded insincere, his platitudes a formality.

Steve looked at the floor, a dark brown, coffee-stained carpet. "OK, sir."

Ballentine leaned slightly forward to regain eye contact with Steve. "You don't understand: You're the next senior man in the company, to include being so to my XO, Nathan. I know you were running things before I arrived. What that means to you is that there's no transition period." He paused.

Steve grew uncomfortable. "Sir?"

"I'm in charge here, Captain." Ballentine glared from under his wide eyebrows.

Steve squinted. "Of course, sir."

Ballentine looked him up and down. "The next time we meet, you'll be in a proper uniform. Is that also clear?"

"Very, sir," Steve replied.

"I wouldn't want us getting off on the wrong foot." He winked at Steve, which was a bit unsettling considering the turn the conversation had taken.

"Understood, sir."

Ballentine absently waved his hand toward the door. "Good. You're dismissed."

Steve popped to attention. "Dismissed! Aye, aye, sir!" He shouted, so anyone in the hallway outside heard him. Ballentine startled. Steve performed a perfect about face and strode out of the office.

# 27



The following week, Ballentine observed Steve's platoon conducting marksmanship training. He stood behind the firing line, a cigar clamped in his mouth, trying to appear officious. Considering his short stature, he looked like a caricature of himself with his arms crossed over newly issued body armor, a service pistol on his hip.

Steve waved him over. "Hey, sir. Wanna join us?"

"Sure." Ballentine walked toward the Marines on the firing line.

Brian watched him from his position as the safety officer for the evolution. "No smoking on the firing line, sir." Ballentine looked at him, then placed his cigar on one of the loading tables behind him. He looked chastised, and several Marines chuckled. "You can take a position next to Captain Keller, sir," Brian directed.

"Yeah, come on over, sir." Steve motioned. Ballentine did, though Steve sensed his unease.

"OK, gents. We're gonna be shooting pistols for time, so don't get all amped up by the box!" Brian said, holding up a shot timer. When pressed, it would start and end with a 'beep' indicating the allocated time to draw their pistol and fire a round. Any shots after the second tone were disqualified. No one wanted to have late shots, accuracy being paramount. The object was to fire quickly and accurately. "Shooters READY?!" Brian yelled.

He pressed the shot timer, and an audible tone began the unknown countdown. Each Marine drew their pistol smoothly and began shooting at their targets, Ballentine included. He hit the target close to the center, but Steve wasn't sure if that was luck or if Ballentine possessed any shooting acumen.

"Good job, sir!" Steve complimented. He fired his own pistol into the middle of his target. The second beep sounded, and each Marine returned their pistols to their holsters. Ballentine looked at his target, then at Steve's, with a neat hole in the center of it and very few outlying shots.

The drill continued, and Ballentine's shot group grew erratic as he tried to keep pace with the Marines. Earlier in his career, Ballentine had shot on the Marine Pistol Team, but that was under controlled conditions, not like the combat shooting they were conducting. Ballentine was not only sweating, but his long thumbs were wrapped around the pistol grip like grotesque miniature horns, his hands shaking. He was nervous.

Brian switched the drill to slow fire. That meant shooting at a more sustained and relaxed pace. Doing so took the tension out of shooting with the timer. Ballentine seemed more relaxed and demonstrated that he could, in fact, shoot well.

"Drill's over, boys. Take a break!" Brian directed. The Marines returned to the covered awnings and sat on benches. Off the firing line, some smoked or got a drink of water.

Ballentine picked up his cigar and relit it, observing some of the Marines. He took a drag, then motioned to Steve to walk with him.

"You know, Steve, I'm impressed. Your boys sure can shoot," he commented as they moved a short distance away to stand under a tree.

"Yes, sir. We practice a lot but wait until this afternoon when we're shooting carbines. Some of these guys are amazing!"

"I won't be here. Got to get back to Battalion HQ for a meeting ahead of our deployment," Ballentine excused himself, likely saving face. "But I'm glad you created a good unit for me to take over."

"Sir, if anyone gets credit for that, it's Major Joyce."

"Er, right," Ballentine fumbled.

"Sir, were you excited to come here?"

"Of course. I like being in command. I don't care what it is, either," Ballentine said, smug.

Steve studied him. "Guess you got what you wanted, then, sir."

Ballentine took a long pull on his cigar and exhaled the smoke upwards. "Steve, I'm heading back to my car. I appreciate you having me out this morning."

"You bet, sir. The boys are always happy to see their boss." Ballentine eyed Steve with a particular stare. Was he unsure of whether he was talking about himself or Ballentine? It was a double-edged compliment that Ballentine perhaps didn't think Steve had the intellectual capacity to deliver.

"Good man, Steve." Ballentine said, slapping Steve on the shoulder.

As he turned to walk away, Steve called after him, "Sir, you can't leave the range with live ammo."

"Oh. Sorry." Ballentine looked embarrassed at his second admonishment. He walked back to the range to deposit his loose pistol rounds in an ammo can. With that completed, Ballentine turned without a word and walked down the path to the parking area.

# 28



Upon concluding their training program, the MSOC was granted two weeks of pre-deployment leave. Steve took his family back to Montana. Time on the family ranch, fishing and swimming in glacial streams, horseback riding, and campfires. But it was a tense interlude.

As most couples do, Steve and Elena found a rhythm leading up to the sad day of departure. Paradoxically, tensions grew so high, some people had to be away from each other at a time when they most expected to spend time together. Thankfully, that wasn't something Elena and Steve experienced.

One evening, Steve and Elena sat on the porch of his parent's house, sipping bourbon. Elena reached for his hand, "I love you, Steve."

"I love you too, babe," Steve replied, looking at her. "What's up?" Her voice had quavered.

She closed her eyes, seemingly holding back tears. "Something's changing, Steve. I feel a disconnection I haven't before." She sniffed.

"How do you mean?" Steve asked. He set down his drink and turned to her to hold her hand with both of his.

"I don't want you to die! I keep thinking about Carlos, what he must have gone through." She broke down, sobbing. "I wonder i-if it would have been b-better if he'd died in combat, r-rather than burdening my family b-by committing suicide. If it's gonna h-happen, maybe quickly is better!"

"Oh, honey, don't. Carlos wrestled with a lot, I know, but don't worry about me. I'm gonna make it home, and I'll be fine!" Steve moved his head to look under her own bowed one.

"God, Steve, I wish I h-hadn't said that!" she cried. "It's not like I w-wanted him dead. And of course, I don't w-want that to happen to you! It's more t-that I see your descent toward the d-deployment, and it means you're d-distancing yourself from us."

"No, baby, it's not like that! I know deploying is tough, but I try to compartmentalize. To make sure I stay focused, and unfortunately that means I have to start ahead of leaving, you know?"

Elena collected herself with a shaky breath. "I know. And I've adopted it too, but I . . . wish I didn't have to. I can't lose you like I did Carlos—you must come home, Steve. Swear to me!"

Steve dropped to his knees in front of her, gripping both of her hands. "I swear."

She leaned in and kissed him.

# 29

*Camp Lejeune, North Carolina, August 15, 2009*

No matter how many times they did it, leaving on deployment wasn't easy, and after returning to Camp Lejeune, the inevitable day arrived. The entire MSOC went to their Battalion HQ for a final farewell with their families and well-wishers. Three tour buses waited while they loaded their deployment bags in the luggage holds.

Elena watched Steve with their kids, each dressed in neat clothing to mitigate the heat of a North Carolina summer in contrast to his Marine desert digital camouflage utilities. Steve squatted in front of the three of them, holding their hands in a close circle.

"Daddy. How long will you be gone?" Sammie asked.

"About six months, but maybe longer, baby girl." Steve looked into her soft brown eyes.

"But why do you have to be gone so long?" Marta, already sad, sniffed. Although the youngest, she was the most intuitive.

Steve reached for and smoothed her hair. "As I said, sweetie, it's because there are kids like you who don't have a daddy to defend them. I'm going to help make their lives better in a place that's very different from here."

"You're fighting the bad men!" Michael exclaimed, his father the epitome of a swashbuckler in his young mind.

"Yes, buddy, I sure am!" Steve returned, upbeat at his son's realization. It was a simple summarization of what he and the MSOC would be doing, but going after bad people in the middle of the night was dangerous work. Steve didn't express that to his children, though a brief wave of apprehension came over him and he forced it away.

"At least we get to have our kiss every day!" Sammie exclaimed.

Steve tousled her hair. "That's right, and make sure that you do!" Sammie referenced what the kids called a "Kiss Jar," a large glass container full of Hershey's Kisses; one for each of the children for each day Steve was gone.

"Do we get one today?" Marta asked expectantly. It wasn't quite real to her that Steve was departing and wouldn't be back for a while.

"Yep! That's one day down!" Steve smiled at her, then looked at his children. "Now, let's get together for a family hug!"

The kids all leaned into him as he dropped to his knees. Elena joined them, holding his hand tightly. They hugged for a long time. Steve thought about them. His relationship with them that he wanted to have later in life, ones that he felt would be the reward for doing this work so that they could have him later. It made him sad, but he again suppressed it.

Steve stood. "OK, kiddos, daddy's got to go!" He smiled and gave each of them a kiss and a high five before turning to Elena. She was dressed in a floral print sundress and sandals. Her beautiful hair hung down in waves. Jackie O sunglasses hid teary eyes. Steve took a deep breath and tried to commit her to memory, praying it wouldn't be his last remembrance of her. "I love you."

"I love you, baby. Come home safely." Elena's tears welled up, and she looked down.

Steve tipped her chin up to him and kissed her. "Always, my pretty girl." He smiled at her, and she wiped her cheeks with her thumbs. They hugged and kissed again, and Steve turned and boarded a waiting bus with the rest of his platoon. He didn't look back. Doing so would only burden them with another memory of his own sad eyes.

The bus drove out of their Battalion compound, leaving the families behind, each Marine and sailor alone in their thoughts.

As much as Steve tried, he couldn't stop thinking of his wife and kids during the hour-long ride to board a massive Air Force C-17 Globemaster transport aircraft that would take them to war. He then thought solely of Elena and their awkward intimacy the night before, strained by his departure. It had felt difficult and unromantic, even though they'd tried to be loving with each other.

Pulling onto the tarmac of Cherry Point, North Carolina, in the busses, his compartmentalization took over, and Steve hardened his mind for what lay ahead.

# 30



Ahead of deploying to Afghanistan, the MSOC pre-staged in Djibouti, Africa. The company spent another week conducting close-quarter battle maneuvers with long training days in the hot sun and short nights under endless starry skies, completing the remainder of their pre-deployment training.

Ballentine demonstrated that he was increasingly uncomfortable with the autonomy the MSOC, and Steve's platoon in particular, displayed. Being an infantry officer with little patience for independent thinkers, he ensured he administered a rigid discipline at which the members of the MSOC braced, including Hackett's infantry Marines, who found being in the MSOC a refreshing change of pace. This widened the division between Ballentine as the commanding officer and his men.

One of Steve's Marines, a staff sergeant named Eric Rodriguez, though everyone called him "Rod," came to him, fear on his face, scared for what was coming. Steve calmly reassured him, even if Steve didn't feel it himself after what transpired with Roland. It didn't matter how brave one thought they were; the entire world evened up in combat, and the most tested vet could freeze up while the novice might rise to great heights of bravery.

Rod poured his heart out, but something strange happened. His voice faded out as though it were coming through a speaker and someone had turned down the volume. It seemed Steve was metaphysically detached from things outside of his body, though he was present in the moment. Everything seemed clearer due to an intense, surreal focus.

He felt for Rod. Tough, and quiet. He had a young wife and a new son. He had as much to lose as anyone, or more to the point, they all had a lot to lose. Their families had entrusted Steve with their most cherished item, and Steve didn't take his leadership duties for granted.

Ballentine potentially did, however. The guy was a callous, self-serving prick, and Steve didn't like him. None of his men did. Still, Steve recognized the chain of command, and he respected Ballentine's rank, even if he didn't personally care for him. But the feeling seemed to be mutual.

While Rod continued his confessional, Steve embraced him and let him sob on his shoulder.

Each night, the company trained and retired to their unit bar, called "The Bitter End." Drinking ensued, Steve and a few others played guitars together, though Steve admitted he wasn't very good. Alex, however, was particularly good, being a talented, professional grade guitar player who could have easily been in bands and made a decent living. He sang his lungs out while he played the most popular tunes he could conjure. He was indeed a magician. Guido sang along with them in his off-key New York accent, and he and Alex went at it constantly, since Alex was from New Jersey. Their good-natured rivalry was legendary. Everyone enjoyed the music, and the most carousing a unit can do was accomplished. They'd go to bed in the early morning and sleep off the night's activities.

Later in the afternoon each day, ahead of training, Fergus and Alex woke Steve to go sweat out a hangover in the African heat by getting in shape with a five-mile run in body armor along the airfield's perimeter fence while French Mirage jets took off to prosecute targets on the interior of the continent. *That's one way to sober up*, Steve thought.

One evening after training, while the unit was at the bar, Rod, with alcohol-fueled courage, got into an honest discussion with Ballentine. Steve's platoon was tightly knit and scorned outsiders, including Major Ballentine. He'd lost the respect of the company before the deployment even began when he told people that he wouldn't have taken the assignment to MARSOC if it required his taking Selection. It was clear he felt he was too good for it.

Ballentine sneered at Rod, "You know what you guys' problem is?!"

"No, what?" Rod said.

"You think because you're recon guys that you're better than everyone else."

"So? We are."

"Bullshit! I've got more combat time than you!" Ballentine slurred, poking Rod in the chest.

Rod poked him back, "No, you don't. And you're not a recon man. You don't belong here."

"Fuck you, you prima donna! I was at Nasiriyah! You aren't better than the infantry!" Ballentine burned, defending his own combat experience in Iraq in 2003.

The infantry Marines from Hackett's platoon looked at him.

"Didn't say I was. I'm just better than *you*. Certainly tougher, that's for sure." The two were now standing close to each other, Ballentine glaring at Rod, who wasn't showing deference to a commissioned officer. Rod wasn't backing down, to the major's chagrin.

"To hell with you! To hell with your *fucking* platoon!" Ballentine's envy of the Direct-Action Platoon was in the open. Alex and Steve stopped playing. The room filled with quiet tension.

Rod stepped closer, poking Ballentine in his chest, this time harder. "Go fuck yourself, sir. I see you. In your fucking collared shirt. Your asshole attitude. You came here by accident. You're no Roland Joyce! You might be the boss, but you'll never belong!"

Ballentine's face went beet red, his fists balled at his side. "You cowboys can't handle any discipline!"

"You didn't take selection. You're a fake-ass punk." Rod smirked.

"I made the cut at the Naval Academy! I don't need to take selection. I've got nothing to prove to you or anyone."

"Exactly my point." Rod spat.

Steve handed his guitar to Alex and intervened before the confrontation spiraled out of control. "That's enough. Both of you. Rod, get out of here. Now."

"Yes, sir."

Steve looked at everyone as Rod backed down. "Bar's closed, gents. Go to bed."

Alex packed up their guitars in their hard cases, and everyone vacated the bar.

Ballentine broiled with anger. "I want to see him tomorrow morning! You understand me, Keller?!" He jabbed his finger at Steve, then turned on his heel and stumbled out into the desert.

***

The next morning, Steve, hungover and tired, stood in front of Ballentine, fresh from the barber with close-cropped hair. He sat behind a desk in the tent that was the company's makeshift office. It made him look even shorter than he was. "What the fuck's wrong with your man, Steve?!" Ballentine sneered. "He's a disrespectful shit and should be court-martialed!

Sweat rolled freely down Steve's back and he felt light-headed, the heat inside the tent not helping matters. "Sir, we were all drinking. I also need to remind you that it was you who engaged Rod in conversation, you started it when you poked him. A court-martial isn't gonna happen."

"This kind of shit wouldn't happen in the infantry!"

"Sir, most of us came from the infantry. Hackett and his guys make it possible for us to do our jobs. We've got nothing but respect for them. No one doubts their combat mettle—or yours, for that matter—but my guys are prideful, and drinking doesn't help in a heated shouting match." Steve sighed. He was nauseous and sweat beaded on his upper lip.

"I still want to talk to him. Get him in here!"

"Aye, aye, sir." Steve sent for Rod.

Rod arrived bleary-eyed and disheveled. He may still have been drunk; he wasn't in any capacity to continue the previous evening's argument. Rod stood at a wobbly attention. Ballentine sat scowling, clearly unimpressed. The proceedings were predictable.

After a suitable dressing down, Ballentine dismissed Rod, followed by everyone else in the tent. Steve went outside in the dry desert air, cooler by contrast to being inside the tent, and put his hands on his knees, fighting the urge to vomit.

Ballentine probably felt vindicated at the outcome since he'd gotten the last word. But Steve's defense of Rod to Ballentine cemented his reputation. To the men in the Direct-Action Platoon, Steve could do no wrong, and there was nothing they wouldn't do for him. Loyalty. Total and utter hard-earned loyalty.

The following day, the MSOC boarded another C-17 for the final leg of their journey. Steve felt it was part of his destiny. Fate. The same fate that nearly killed him in the

Arizona desert only a few short years earlier. The fate Roland had tragically fulfilled. It was inexorable and bringing Steve along in another chapter in life. One he'd chosen, and one created for him by the alignment of sequenced events outside of his control.

# 31



The flight was long. The sheer magnitude and expense of getting their unit deployed with all their equipment and vehicles was probably the same amount as some small countries' deficit to the World Bank. Steve didn't sleep well on planes or any moving conveyances, and that trip was no different. He paced nervously at times and tried to sleep at others, envying those who could just put their heads down and rest.

Finally, the plane set down with a jarring jolt that woke all but the soundest sleepers. It taxied and came to a halt, the enormous clamshell door opening, filling the interior of the aircraft with warm dust that floated in the air, illuminated by the plane's red interior lights. MSOC "Papa" was in Afghanistan.

Their advanced logistics and quartering party, led by Brian, had departed Djibouti five days ahead of the company's main body, and he met them at the aircraft's rear ramp. Large and imposing, Brain was disarmingly intelligent and funny.

"Welcome to Kandahar!" Brian grinned, his face bathed in red light as he extended his hand like a sideshow carnival host, ushering them off the plane to waiting buses. From there, they spent a long night unloading and accounting for their equipment in a blur of activity and getting settled. Steve was shown his living quarters, which he shared with Nathan and Hackett, and immediately fell asleep.

Waking up to the noise of a dusty operating base, the MSOC got to work preparing for combat operations. Sleepy, Steve emerged into the sunlight dressed in PT gear. He put on sunglasses against the glare. Kandahar airfield was an old Russian fighter base during the Soviet-Afghan war. Parts of the base were cratered in areas or scarred by the shrapnel effects of indirect fire. It was built to last.

The concrete walls of structures displayed evidence of long-past attacks, pock marked with bullet holes and impacts from larger weapons like mortars or rockets shells. Their testimony stood in stark contrast to remnants of the Gulf War of destroyed buildings knocked from their foundations by Iraqi artillery fire Steve had witnessed while serving in the infantry on the Iraq-Kuwait border in 2000.

Clapboard and plywood structures with tar-cloth and tin roofs, called B-Huts, were neatly arranged along a roadway in front of the older, solid structures dating to the Soviet-Afghan war. The B-Huts had bunk beds to house sixteen occupants, and the Marines moved in with various equipment and personal items stacked on or around the beds.

Fifteen military trucks called Ground Mobility Vehicles, (GMVs) were parked in a small lot across from the huts. Custom-designed on a HUMVEE chassis, they were rugged and utilitarian. Another member of MARSOC went to the Letterkenny arsenal in Pennsylvania and designed them from the ground up. It may have been his greatest contribution to Special Operations in general since Special Operations Command adopted his version of the vehicle.

The four-wheel-drive GMVs were set up for communications and command and control, by having custom radio brackets. Weapons mounts and turrets allowed for the positioning of a variety of firepower like heavy machine guns. Armored and with bullet-resistant glass windows, one felt fairly protected inside of them. It included a rear troop compartment, which carried up to four people, though being open, it didn't offer the same protection to those inside the vehicle.

Several Marines, shirtless and sweating in the hot, dry air, cleaned weapons and inventoried ammunition and equipment to load into their respective vehicles. They bantered with relaxed confidence, the combat vets feeling familiar, those without combat experience excited by the prospects. The common denominator was everyone was eager to do their job.

Ballentine had Steve assemble his team leaders, Fergus, Alex, Guido, Marko, and Brian inside one of the B-Huts to explain their next mission. A map was spread out on a table at the back. The Marines sipped coffee or dipped tobacco and looked intently as Ballentine briefed them.

"We're relieving MSOC Echo, who'll take our key leadership on a three-day turnover patrol alongside theirs." Steve shuddered at the memory of being with his counterpart, Captain Jim Eggerton, the night Roland was killed. *This turnover will be different*, he told himself.

"We'll board helicopters this afternoon to get out to FOB Prince. I'll orient us." Ballentine pointed on the map with a pencil. "We'll get the lay of the land and an appreciation for our area of operations."

Brian asked, "Sir, how big an area are we talking?"

"It's the size of the state of Rhode Island." Ballentine sounded confident, like he knew something they didn't and was glad to reveal it.

Alex chimed in, "I played a few gigs in Rhode Island!"

Fergus shot back, "No one fucking cares!"

"Shut up, you Mick!" Alex quipped.

"All right, knock it off," Ballentine snapped. "This is important! When we finish this patrol, we'll get everyone else in the unit out to FOB Prince and take over the mission. Then MSOC Echo is going home."

Marko smiled. "Lucky bastards!"

"Make sure you stick close with your counterparts and learn all you can about what it's like out here. A few of us have been to Iraq, but this isn't Iraq." Ballentine looked at Marko, who stared blankly at the map.

Marko shrugged his shoulders. "Combat's combat, but right on."

"Anything special we need to carry?" Brian asked.

"Just our basic load out. MSOC Echo will bring all the heavy stuff. Be ready to fight," Ballentine said.

Brian nodded. "Cool."

"You never know." Ballentine ended the brief. No one had to tell Steve the accuracy of that statement.

# 32

---



MSOC "Papa's" key leadership boarded CH-47 transport helicopters and flew over the ancient landscape, passing over hamlets and the ruins of fortifications, some dating to the time of Alexander the Great. The flight to FOB Prince was uneventful. They arrived and moved to temporary living quarters. Each group of Marines went to find their counterparts to begin the turnover process.

Eggerton strolled up to Steve and warmly embraced him. "Man, now I'm *really* glad to see you!" He beamed.

"Yeah?"

"Yep! Now I can go home!" Eggerton laughed louder.

"Nice to see you, too, Jim!" Steve's sarcasm matched Eggerton's.

"The patrol starts tomorrow morning, predawn. We'll take you on a tour. Stir up shit and see what we can get into." Eggerton gave a wry smile. "And, hey, we were all destroyed when Joyce got killed. I'm sorry, brother. Truly."

Steve nodded. "I appreciate it, Jim." He tried to let the moment pass, to avoid it becoming awkward.

"And I've got something for you. After we interrogated the wounded fighters we took off site with us and confirmed through radio intercepts, we found out Major Joyce was killed by Muammar Agha—Objective Tenkara—himself. He was at those compounds after all but escaped through some tunnels we later discovered," Eggerton delivered.

Steve raised his brows, "Wow. Hopefully we'll get another crack at the son of a bitch."

Another group of Marines walked by. Steve had served with members of Jim's unit earlier in his career and recognized a few of them. In fact, the recon community being small, their being on the FOB had the feeling of a reunion gathering. They were going on a combat mission, and there they were bantering and carrying on.

"Let's show you to where you'll be staying," Eggerton said.

After dropping his bags, Eggerton gave Steve another tour of the base, stopping at the convoy of ten vehicles already in place for the operation. They typically rode in groups of five or six to a gun truck which would become home, and the crew of that truck would be the family of each individual. They relied on each other implicitly. It was required for any chance of surviving. There would be three in Eggerton's GMV. The driver, a fit, stoic Sergeant named Wilkins, in the front left, Eggerton the front right, and Steve behind Eggerton. The empty passenger seat next to Steve held two cases of bottled water. Steve was happy he'd ride in a different vehicle than Ballentine and Nathan.

"Hey, Taylor!" Eggerton waved to one of his Marines.

The Marine waved back. "Hey, Sir!"

"Who's that?" Steve asked.

"Corporal Taylor Ketcham. He's only nineteen, but he's energetic, tough." Eggerton nodded toward Ketcham. "Everyone likes him. He'll be in the trail vehicle tonight."

Steve watched his preparation, admiring the young NCO methodically going over his vehicle, checking its readiness. He clearly took his job seriously.

They walked on, and Eggerton continued, serious. "This movement outside of the wire tonight might be considered administrative, if not routine. Except that nothing here is routine. Nothing. You don't get to choose when the enemy attacks." He looked at Steve, who took in his friend's warning. "So, progress will be deliberate with overwatch positions covering each area we visit. And the overwatch positions will rotate so no one gets complacent. It allows for everyone to share the duties."

"Makes sense."

They tested and zeroed their weapons in the afternoon and took a nap after dinner. Ahead of step-off, they checked their night vision and laser targeting systems. Still in darkness, they mounted their vehicles and drove into the night.

In the GMV's dim interior, their night vision goggles cast a green glow around their eyes. Eggerton said over his shoulder, "Lemme tell you 'bout this place. It's the Wild West. When you leave the FOB, you're surrounded by the enemy. When we aren't conducting helo raids, our patrols are long treks through the desert. The vastness of it all is impressive. We're here to find the enemy and engage them. And, boy, do we ever."

*How many missions do you need to be considered a veteran with enough experience that people respect and take you seriously?* Steve wondered, filled with doubt and misgivings, aware he still had a lot to learn.

***

They drove for a few hours through sunrise. The day grew hot and dusty, and the vehicle convoy rumbled and bounced along, testing the shock absorbers on the trucks, often past capacity, the interiors of the GMV coated in ever-present dust. Passing through villages and areas that had been there since Byzantium, sad faces of weary Afghan people looked back at the column. Steve marveled at it all.

The column traveled across the landscape like an unwieldy, heavily armed snake. Though it packed a lot of firepower, it was hardly agile. "We need half of this," Eggerton lamented when they stopped on the outskirts of a town known for a lot of enemy activity. Some Marines dismounted to establish security on higher ground. Ballentine went off with Nathan and Major Osman to examine the terrain. Steve stuck with Eggerton.

"Look down there," Eggerton said, pointing to a village behind a line of dense green trees. "Most people live in villages by water sources, in this case rivers. The lush green trees provide shade during the dusty, hot days, and offer fertile ground for the primary source of income, poppy. These villages all link together in a connected sprawl that allow the enemy to move through drainage and irrigation ditches covered by the trees, which gives these areas the nickname, The Green Zone. The ditches also create excellent trenches for fighting. These lend the enemy a big advantage of cover and concealment." He swept his hand across the expanse to their front. "That's where the enemy lives, and they're very creative in fighting from buildings and preestablished firing positions for mortars and rocket launchers."

Steve looked at the typical rural Afghan village comprised of mud-brick dwellings. In the hazy heat, unhurried villagers went about their daily business, the odd moped or motorcycle moving through foot traffic, donkeys, and cows.

"Things seem benign enough."

"Seems that way, but we got our asses handed to us here about two months ago," Eggerton proclaimed with a slight chuckle. "We conceded the battlefield, that's for sure." He pointed to the whitening hulk of a destroyed GMV on a hill in front of a line of trees. It stood as a silent sentinel to the activity that caused it to rest there with all four of its doors removed in a forlorn heap. "Hit a Russian mine," he said. "I still gotta account for the truck on my hand receipt, if you can believe that!"

Steve shook his head that administrative idiocy described this wreck as an actual vehicle.

Eggerton continued to chuckle, acting out an exchange between him and an accounting officer. "'And where is truck such-and-such?' Some clown would ask. 'Well, you see, after it blew up underneath me, and I got in a firefight trying to extricate myself from it, without tires, I found it couldn't be driven any longer and bequeathed it to the enemy since I had no further need for it.' Shit. What would people think of next?" He laughed. Eggerton was an Iraq combat veteran, and after serving in Afghanistan for six months, it made him a little brash.

A few small arms rounds fired from the village snapped in the air.

"Yep, they see us. And they're warning us to stay away. IDF will be next," he said, using the acronym for indirect fire, which might encompass anything from rocket launchers to mortars.

One of Eggerton's Marines named Staff Sergeant Adams pulled his sniper rifle from the truck, withdrew it from its case, and set up across the hood. He sighted in on the suspected point of origin and called out, "I see them! Armed males moving to the Green Zone. Looks like a PKM." He grinned and winked, then went back to looking through his scope.

Eggerton said, "If you've got PID, take the shot."

The rifle boomed.

"Got one!" Adams crowed while making a small adjustment on his rifle scope.

More rounds cracked through the air in their vicinity.

Eggerton moved quickly to Adams. "I don't think the boss needs to call in a TIC since this is exploratory. Don't wanna get people worked up."

Adams remained focused through his sniper scope "No, sir, I don't think so. We're good right now."

"TIC?" Steve asked.

"Yeah, Troops In Contact. When the fight is on, you call into higher and open a TIC. That way they know you're in the shit and may need assistance. You need to manage your TIC, or they'll manage it for you, and you don't want that. Before you key that handset, take a deep breath and be cool and calm to immediately establish confidence. Then, you close it out when you're finished."

"What do you mean when you say, 'calling it in'?" Steve pressed.

"On the radio. Don't want to call in a TIC without a reason. Remember that everyone is listening, and you don't want a reputation for calling in little things you can handle on your own. Think of it as the boy-who-cried-wolf effect. A TIC builds its own inertia. You'll know when it's time."

"Did we do this on the mission where Major Joyce was killed?"

"Yeah, but Osman was running the show that night, and you didn't hear it on the external net. Now if you're out on missions it could be up to you."

"Ah. Makes sense." Steve nodded.

"So, no TIC. We'll see how this thing shapes up." Eggerton looked back at the village.

Adams kept up a steady rate of fire. Everyone else watched, many looking bored since they weren't directly involved in the action. Some munched on MRE crackers and others tried to stay in the shade of the GMVs. What was another bit of gunfire out here anyway? Steve took it all in carefully. There would only be this time to learn it. Then he would manage it all himself. He hoped his confidence would mirror Eggerton's.

Steve looked at his friend. Tall, good looking, confident, funny, and utterly unflappable, Jim Eggerton was the poster child for all good things, and his men adored him. *I should be so lucky*, Steve thought, watching Eggerton move easily among his men while Osman talked with Ballentine. Nathan stayed back and away from it all, seemingly not wanting to get his hands dirty as if combat were a distasteful chore to be endured.

Adams's rifle thundered again. "Holy fuck! I got another one! Damn, I'm HOT TO THE TOUCH!" he exclaimed, high-fiving Fergus now standing next to him. Other people laughed.

"Mount up, before it gets too busy out here!" shouted Osman. They did so quickly, leaving the village and the enemy behind them.

"I never really got a chance to know about your boss the last time I was out here, Jim. What's he like?" Steve asked of Osman after they remounted the trucks.

"Old First Force guy. He's got a couple combat deployments under his belt and is a good commander who really cares for the boys."

"He seems like a good man."

"He is. He has a rare gift to transfer his enthusiasm to his entire unit."

"I see that. Your Marines and sailors have a vibe about them. It's because of Osman's ability to make them feel like everything was going to work out in their favor." Steve leaned his head on the seat rest behind him.

"I'd say that's true."

"Wish I could say the same of mine." The adrenaline of that earlier small combat episode had worn off, and Steve dozed.

***

Twenty minutes later, the column passed through another village in such a way that the lead was outside of it and clear of the buildings and streets and the middle and tail were still inside the built-up areas. Steve awoke to excited shouts.

"We're taking IDF, but it's no big deal!" Eggerton said.

"No big deal?! For whom?" Steve said. Shit hitting the fan and there being no preparation was indeed a pretty big deal. It was another existential experience.

Four mortar rounds landed in rapid succession on the lead of the column, but no casualties were reported. More IDF erupted, and the explosive concussions reverberated through the village, canalized down the roads through the high walls of compounds. All the Marines dismounted to gain advantageous positions to determine the fire's point of origin and get away from the trucks. Ironically, the truck's armor-plated steel ostensibly should provide protection, except that the trucks were great targets. The earlier visit to the first village and seeing Eggerton's old truck in its final resting place was testament to that.

A mortar round exploded five hundred yards from them in a cloud of dust and invisible metal fragments flying in all directions. *Shit! This sucks!* Steve inwardly cursed and exited the GMV to find cover. The explosion was far enough away that the concussion was heard rather than felt, but he looked directly at its signature as it struck the earth.

It was up to Osman to call in the TIC. All of them were reliant on him to make the right decisions.

"There's got to be a spotter close by," Eggerton said as another salvo landed near the lead of the column. Miraculously, there were again no casualties. Small arms fire was heard up and down the column as the enemy engaged the US forces.

The satellite radio crackled, and Osman opened the TIC.

During a pause in the firing, Eggerton's driver, Sergeant Wilkins, yelled out, "For Christ's sake, has anyone seen anything?!" His outburst relieved the tension, and everyone laughed, even as the enemy fire resumed.

Adams grabbed his sniper rifle and was up in the bed of the truck, using the roof as a stable platform. "Sir," he called to Eggerton, "I think I found the observer. Fergus, spot for me."

"Will do," Fergus replied, looking through binoculars.

"OK, on you." Eggerton gave Adams tacit approval to shoot.

Fergus walked him on. "I see him, old man, white turban, dark brown robe. Icom to his ear."

"Yep, that's him. I'm dialing him in." Adams applied fine adjustments on his rifle scope.

Steve raised his own binoculars and looked in the direction Adams was aiming.

The target—the old man—was four hundred yards away. There were children surrounding him. He wasn't directly using the children as shields but trying to use them for proximity protection. A few more rounds of IDF landed, and there was no doubt that the old man was spotting for the enemy. The fire was increasing and becoming more accurate, even with the trucks more spread out and less an obtrusive target.

"I have him at four hundred and twenty yards," Adams stated.

"Concur," replied Fergus. "What setting are you using on the rifle?" Adams told him so Fergus could make corrections should Adams miss, though it was highly unlikely. Adams already demonstrated he was an excellent sniper and knew his weapon inside and out. There was no way he would miscalculate. But he didn't leave anything to chance, and he trusted Fergus and relied upon him for insurance.

The calculations complete, the rifle prepared, Adams took a deep breath. "I'm ready," Adams said in a low tone.

Steve watched the old man. His binoculars were very good, and he discerned facial lines, a beard, and the texture of the materials of his clothing.

The sharp report of the rifle surprised and startled Steve. Adams maintained focus on the target. A small spot of blood oozed into the old man's robes before he pitched backward, the children running in all directions. After another moment, Adams worked the bolt of his rifle, catching the expended brass casing in his hands, and calmly dismounted from the truck. He returned the rifle to its carrying case, and he and Fergus shook hands. They both lit a cigarette.

Steve wondered if the old man threatened the kids to stay outside to act as cover and they were being held against their will, terrified of what might happen to them or their families. The old man lay motionless, obscured by the children until they scattered out of the field of view. Steve looked again through his binoculars at the body and saw the outline of the tread of his sandals. Adams had been correct. With Fergus's assistance, they'd killed the spotter and the indirect fire stopped.

It wasn't a mistake to shoot the old man, Steve knew, but it unsettled him how easily Adams and Fergus facilitated his death. No one made any witty retort or comment considering a difficult situation wherein the enemy blended with the populace, and he was discovered among them, but it was the first human being Steve had personally seen die at close enough range to haunt him. He wasn't sure if it was the fact that the target had been old, that there were children present to witness his death—or perhaps, like Adams, he'd professionally disengaged from the entire event. Adams and Fergus ended a human life together simply because it was their job.

Nathan threw up.

Steve looked at him, laughing, "Having a good time, Nathan?"

He spat and wiped his mouth with his sleeve. "Oh, yeah, sure!" He took off his glasses and cleaned them on his shirttail.

"Bullshit! Ha!" Steve couldn't blame him, though.

Nathan got back into his truck, and Steve walked with Eggerton to their vehicle. Eggerton gestured toward Nathan with his thumb. "What's his issue?"

"He doesn't want to be here." Steve chuckled.

"Do any of us?"

"I do! So do your guys, by the look of it!" Adams said to Steve, sweeping his hand toward some of his men.

Marko approached, grinning. He'd found some packaged sunflower seeds and had a cheek full of them. "What's up, boss?" His smile shone on his rugged, dusty face. His teeth cracked the shells of the seeds, and he spit them out of the side of his mouth.

"Nothing. You?" Steve looked at Marko.

"Meh, got in a little scrape. Nothing too heavy. Fun, ya know?" Marko said, working another seed from his cheek.

Steve nodded. "Yeah."

"Gonna head back to the boys. Catch ya later, boss!" Marko spat another shell and walked away nonchalantly. Steve watched him with a furrowed brow.

"Who's that?" Eggerton asked.

"One of my team leaders, Marko Pech."

"He seems pretty at ease in all of this."

"False bravado," Steve delivered.

"Wouldn't know it looking at him."

Steve turned to Eggerton. "I think he's pretending to enjoy it out here, but inwardly, none of this excites him."

"What's his background?"

Steve took a sip of water from a plastic bottle. "Came in the Corps out of high school. Old Second Force guy. Exceptional at shooting, and he's tough as shit." Steve grew serious. "This is his first combat deployment as a TL, though. He'll be fine, I think, but I still wonder how he'll perform when we're out here alone."

Eggerton offered, "A leader needs to keep up appearances."

Steve squinted. "The men see the difference. Anyway, I'll need to keep my eye on him."

"Let's get moving!" Osman gave the command.

With the excitement over, they remounted the trucks to move to a RON, or remain-overnight site, where they would set into a defensive position, clean weapons, eat an MRE, and maybe get some rest. It was getting dark, and they put on their night vision goggles in the lowering light, green discs emanating on their eyes and the world was a mono-chromatic view of black and green. "Make sure your night vision goggles are well adjusted." Eggerton instructed. They each focused the lenses to see clearly. Doing this prevented a raging headache from straining to see through the twin, narrow tubes.

Eggerton turned to Steve. "It's also worth wearing a magazine on the back of your helmet to counterbalance these, which helps keep your neck from hurting while wearing them all night. Plus, you can retrieve it if you're in the prone. See?" He patted the magazine pouch mounted on the rear of his helmet.

"You're full of great tips, Jim. How long are we moving tonight?"

"That depends, but we'll find an area that's good for defense and get our heads down. Besides, we need to show you a few more things tomorrow, but it's easier to approach it at night since we would be too exposed during the day."

"Take the terrain at night you want to occupy in daylight. Got it."

"You're catching on, Steve." Eggerton chuckled.

# 33



The American column bounced along, the night turning black since they preferred to operate in the darkest periods possible for protection. A low rumble followed by a flash illuminated the horizon behind them. It reflected in the glass of the GMV, and radios crackled through an external speaker mounted inside the vehicle. Everyone was alert.

"What the fuck was that, sir?" Sergeant Wilkins asked, looking out the driver's side window. "IDF?" Although young, Wilkins was combat-seasoned. He was attuned to surroundings, displaying a sense of cynicism disproportionate to his years.

Eggerton replied confidently, "I doubt it. It's dark and we're moving. No way they could see us." The column began to stop. People fanned out in security positions. Radios continued to crackle. Vehicle strike. Mine? IED? Did it matter? No one knew exactly what happened.

A harried voice came over the radio. *"We have multiple casualties and a gun truck on fire. We need HELP!"*

It was from the last vehicle in the column. Ketcham's. Steve's stomach dropped.

"Stop the truck!" Eggerton said. Wilkins slammed on the brakes. Eggerton, Steve, and Wilkins exited and looked toward the burning wreck, a half mile behind them.

The radio crackled again. *"Ketcham's wounded, urgent surgical. We need help NOW!"*

Another voice, more relaxed, keyed in reply, *"Stay calm, we're on the way! We need to take it slow in case there are more explosive devices. We'll get to you!"*

Eggerton listened closely. "Holy shit."

"Yeah, you said it. Fuck. Should we go to them?" Steve asked, wanting to do something.

Wilkins and Eggerton both shook their heads, "No," Eggerton said, "they have it under control."

The fire grew larger. As they watched, another vehicle arrived at the site of the stricken truck and began extricating the wounded, at great danger to the responders. The second, calmer voice reported. *"The truck's totaled. The ammo and rockets'll cook off in this fire. We've gotta get outta here. Standby."*

*"Roger, we're organizing the medevac now,"* came the reply from Osman, using the acronym for a Medical Evacuation platform.

Outside of the scan of their night vision goggles, the glow of what was becoming a macabre pyre, laden with ammunition and gasoline, burned brighter. The view was medieval, and they looked in rapt fascination at the horror. There were men in there, and they were dying.

"Oh, fuck!" Eggerton said, turning to Wilkins. "Who was in that truck?"

Wilkins replied, not looking at Eggerton, focused on the conflagration. "If it's Ketcham, it was Halloran's truck. The four guys in there could be pretty fucked up."

"Damn," Eggerton muttered.

The extraction vehicle loaded with wounded moved away from the burning wreck. Shortly afterward, it exploded in a huge fireball of fuel and ammunition, shooting streaks of tracer and other explosives in all directions, the flames an offering to Hades and the Gods of War. They took their share. Always.

The explosion illuminated the faces of those watching, and Eggerton raised his goggles on their mount to look with his naked eye. "Oh my God! I hope they all got out. Jesus." He sounded helpless.

The calm voice came again on the radio, strangely balanced against the unfolding chaos. *"We need that medevac. We have four wounded, two urgent surgical, one expectant, but we have to try."*

Osman replied, *"Roger. We're working it."*

They all listened to the tense exchange. "Expectant" meant someone was going to die.

"This sucks," Wilkins stated.

The vehicle fire cooked off in one more violent explosion and began burning itself out. Eggerton sighed. "We're stopping here. We'll punch out security on the high ground and get some sleep."

"OK. But I doubt I'll be sleeping," Steve said. His adrenaline was coming down again and spikes were causing him to feel a range of fatigue; awake and alert at one moment, then tired and unable to keep his eyes open at another.

Wilkins replied indifferently, "You'll get used it. I did."

Steve frowned. "I'm not sure about that." Blood pulsed in his temples as his heart rate came down.

Wilkins, pulling his sleeping pad and bag out and sliding out of his body armor and helmet, sighed, "I wasn't, either."

As they settled down, Steve watched activity near the site of the burning truck. Two other vehicles established a helicopter extract landing zone. Within twenty minutes, a CH-47 helicopter buzzed over the landscape. It swung in and landed to pick up the casualties in a cloud of dust. Viewed through the night vision goggles, its twin rotors cast familiar ghostly halos, now akin to those of Angels of Mercy. The casualties were loaded, and the helicopter took off into the night sky. After it departed, silence descended.

Steve said, "God, it's quiet. The stars, the sky; it's so big. Who can imagine what we're doing out here? It's unreal." This stood in stark opposition to the violence they'd just witnessed.

Eggerton spoke up from his sleeping bag, somewhat annoyed. "Philosophizing, Steve? Shit. This is how it is out here. Violence one minute, peaceful the next. This place will never get its shit together."

"This wasn't how I envisioned earning my Combat Action Ribbon. Not losing Roland. And not like this," Steve lamented.

"What'd you expect? I wanted a CAR like nothing else, too. Once I got it, I didn't wish for it again," Eggerton offered.

"Well, either way, you earned it tonight," Wilkins observed.

Another vehicle approached Eggerton's and squeaked to a halt. Two men got out, silhouetted in the darkness. One was Eggerton's Platoon Sergeant, Gunnery Sergeant Valken. The other was Steve's, Brian Geraghty.

"Boss, you awake?"

Steve recognized Valken's voice as the calm one during the earlier radio exchange.

Eggerton sat up. "Yeah. What happened?"

"Halloran's vehicle drove over something, but we aren't sure what it was because we're in the middle of nowhere and weren't on a road. We'll know more in daylight."

"Got it. Casualties?" Eggerton asked warily.

"Yeah, all four of them. The gunner, Biggs, was thrown clear during the explosion but got frag in his legs. The three inside the vehicle got fucked up, but Ketcham was the worst. He was riding in the back right, on top of the fuel tank. He was burned all over his body, and he didn't make it. He was a mess. The docs tried, including Luke Milam, but goddamn, what can you do out here—hell, anywhere—to fix that?!"

"Luke helped?" Steve asked.

"Yep. And even the Special Operations Medic of The Year couldn't save Ketcham," Brian replied.

Valken went on to explain that the medics slaved to save Ketcham, begging him not to die, the procedure further complicated since they worked wearing night vision goggles. The medics, being Special Forces–trained, took great pride in their work, and rightfully so. A breathing tube had been inserted through his nose, and they'd made lateral and vertical lacerations to reduce the swelling on Ketcham's scorched body. Tourniquets were applied to the stumps of limbs that no longer existed. They'd used all of their collective knowledge to give Ketcham, broken and mangled, a fighting chance. It was for naught. By the time the medevac bird had arrived, Ketcham was already dead and packaged to be sent home. The rest of the wounded were treated and put aboard the aircraft.

Valken turned to Eggerton, "I'm gonna go check the lines and keep the rumors down. I'll see you in the morning."

"Thanks. Yep," Eggerton said. He shook Valken's hand.

Valken and Brian walked away. Brian nodded toward Steve before leaving, who smiled back at him.

"He's one cool operator," Steve said.

"Valken? He's the best. I'd be lost out here without him."

"I feel the same way about Brian. We both got lucky."

Eggerton perked up. "Yeah. By the way, I knew Luke was the Operator of the Year last year, but I didn't know he was also the SOF Medic of The Year!"

"Yep, and he's the only person in MARSOC to ever hold them simultaneously."

"That's awesome!" Eggerton was impressed.

"It is." Steve grew somber. "Something dawned on me, Jim."

"What's that?" He sat back down in his bedroll and loosened his boots.

"I've been riding in the same spot that Ketcham was. If we'd hit what they rolled over, that would've been me." Another adrenal spike coursed through his body. Fear which had to be overcome. Steve tried not to think about it.

Hearing them, Wilkins called from his bedroll, "But it wasn't. Now, both of you go to sleep, please."

"Yeah. It wasn't," Steve finished, resigned. Though he didn't smoke, a day like this might drive him to do so. Laying down, he conducted some breathing exercises to calm his nerves. He didn't remember falling asleep.

***

In the morning, the loss of Ketcham and the wounded Marines was acute. A grave pall hung over them when the mission, the last of MSOC Echo's rotation, concluded the following evening. Back at FOB Prince, they cleaned personal weapons while listening to music. They drank cold Krombacher near-beer, smoked, joked, and groused. A quick shower, and all sewer-smelling clothing washed and hung to dry outside, then it was time to eat.

Marko, Brian, Fergus, and Steve sat around a table eating dinner, generally served from pre-prepared tray rations that could be quickly heated.

Brian, in between mouthfuls of macaroni and cheese, said, "Ketcham's vehicle ran over a Russian anti-tank mine. Probably buried to get rid of it without the thought that another human would find it."

"Eggerton told me the Afghans get blown up all the time by old Russian ordnance. Shit of it is, Jim's vehicle drove right over it and, inexplicably, it didn't explode," Steve said, picking at some green beans on his tray. "Ketcham wasn't so lucky."

"The fact that anyone survived is testament to people doing what they're trained to immediately when they recognize they need to act." Brian finished his near-beer and stood up. "Time for bed. Night gents."

"Night, Brian. Good work out there," Steve said.

Fergus finished his meal too and stood with his tray. He looked at Steve with a cynical smile. "Hell of a way to go. No way I am going out like that, eh?! Make me a promise, Skipper." He was one of the few who called Steve that. "If it comes down to it, you'll slot me." Fergus used a British euphemism. "Slot" meant kill by execution.

"Only if you agree to do me in the same circumstances," Steve replied.

"Done." With a nod Fergus strolled away. Steve knew Fergus could be relied upon to make good on his word.

Marko watched him leave and turned Steve. "Don't be so glum, boss."

"I'm not." Steve tilted his head.

"Yeah? I know you better than that. You're thinking about Ketcham." Marko pointed at him and finished the last bite of his meal.

"Yep." He nodded. How could he think about anything else when Ketcham's fate kept Steve from being the one killed?

Marko stood and dropped his tray in the trash. Before he left, he said, "I don't blame you," and touched him on the shoulder. The door to their dining facility shut heavily when he exited.

Alone at the table, Steve thought about the past few months. Though he was technically a combat veteran, and his first engagements had been eventful, those weren't exactly what he expected. He wanted something more akin to the firefights, the true combat, that he'd read about as a young infantry officer. He feared this was all there was, and he felt slighted.

Steve stood up and walked to his quarters as the sun fully set. He went to bed exhausted.

The next afternoon, Steve, Ballentine, and the other company key leadership said farewell to their hosts, boarded CH-47 helicopters, and flew back to their waiting unit.

# 34

The members of the company who'd remained behind greeted their leadership on their return. Since they'd been out on a mission and taken some fire, they enjoyed a bit of celebrity, but that made Steve uncomfortable. Though inwardly, he admitted the edge had been taken off by being on another combat mission, and at least he felt that he was starting to fit in a little bit.

Showered and clean, Steve walked around the buildings on their part of the base, looking at reminders that war was woven into the fabric of Afghanistan. He occasionally ran his fingers over the weathered battle marks of bullets and shells faded white in the sun, wondering who'd made them and if the result had been worth it to either side. He smiled lightly that he might become a true battlefield philosopher, per Eggerton's admonition.

Steve and his platoon were waiting on a few other members of the company who were late arrivals in theatre, and Marines occupied their time working out and shopping at the base exchange. They stocked up on sunflower seeds, chewing tobacco and cigarettes, which could be used as a barter currency with each other, and other snacks like beef jerky and Starburst candy. Upon leaving a developed base like Kandahar, the options to obtain such sundries were limited, and the MSOC relied upon care packages from home to augment an austere diet.

After another day of rest, they would drive their GMVs to FOB Prince, a five-hour journey from Kandahar at night. They'd depart in waves, traveling in smaller columns to reduce signature and to allow for all the units' equipment to be transported over the course of a few nights. Of course, Ballentine and Nathan flew to the FOB, avoiding that unpleasantry.

Steve and his platoon leadership developed their movement plan, and they readied the vehicles for the drive. Three US Army Special Forces soldiers from the ODA, or Operational Detachment-Alpha, with whom they were partnered at FOB Prince would hitch a ride with them.

They approached Steve to discuss the drive later that night. "What you need to do, sir, is drive fast with your lights on, and people will move out of your way," instructed a Sergeant First Class named Schilling. He was squat with a bushy beard and reminded Steve of a dwarf from a mystical fantasy world. The two other SF soldiers who'd ride with them concurred.

"That doesn't sound smart to me," Steve replied warily. "But I'll take it under consideration." He went to find Brian to tell him what they'd suggested.

Brian balked. "Absolutely not. I recognize bullshit when I see it."

"C'mon. I called guys out in training all the time. You know that," Steve defended.

"We're in combat now, sir. The difference here is that even if someone gets away with something, the repercussions are far more grave." Brian squinted.

"I get it, and I don't exactly agree with their reasoning either," Steve said, "but it makes sense in some ways and these SF guys have been in country and fighting longer than us. Besides, we'll be driving through a lit-up city, so it won't make any difference."

"I still don't think it's a good idea." Brian shook his head slowly.

"After we get clear of the city, we'll go dark. Does that work for a compromise?" Steve seemed wedded to his decision.

"Whatever. We just need to get there. I'm going to conduct final inspections on the vehicles." Brian's irritation was evident.

The column of six vehicles formed, conducted radio checks, and exited the base on one of the few paved roads into the city of Kandahar. Many of the platoon members were nervous, particularly the inexperienced infantry Marines. Steve's vehicle was third in the column.

Riding along, something nagged at Steve. He tried to rationalize his feelings. It was their first real mission without Eggerton and his unit to guide them, and they were still cutting their teeth. Maybe they had a little room to make mistakes? But such erroneous thinking turned the troublesome feeling inside of Steve into full-on dread.

He saw the entire column working through the city, which also meant the rest of the world—and the enemy—saw it, too. On their left, they passed what looked like a parking garage but was an unfinished building, and the upper floors sparkled like fireflies as unseen gunmen opened fire on them.

"Go, push through!" Steve called over the radio since they didn't want to stop or become decisively engaged inside of urban terrain. Turret gunners strained to see from where the fire originated. They pinpointed it, but no one returned fire since the shots against the first vehicle were inaccurate, then died off. Spraying down each block with automatic fire was out of the question, and they moved quickly through the streets away from the engagement. The attack had been short-lived.

That was enough to convince Steve that he'd been wrong to listen to the SF soldiers, and Sergeant Schilling implicitly, while subjugating his own feeling, and Brian's protests that something wasn't correct. He didn't ignore his intuition again after that evening.

Steve called over the radio, "Turn out the lights and go IR!"

The order was duly followed, and a sense of relief came over the column.

They drove through the countryside the rest of the dark night without incident, only stopping to take a piss, and the entire five-hour ride Steve kicked himself for being so trusting.

It was his fault. He was the leader, and his own men had a ton of combat experience. He knew better and had gone against that, listening to Sergeant Schilling instead. *Fool.* He was lucky the entire column hadn't run into something more than they could handle because of presenting a fabulous target for the enemy and that the group of shooters that had engaged them in the city were rank amateurs.

The column arrived at FOB Prince an hour before dawn, towing a vehicle the last five hundred yards. Somehow, the driver engaged the GMV's four-wheel-drive while they were on pavement. The transmission burned out as he tried to keep up with the column. That night was a learning laboratory for a lot of people. Steve kept that in mind when Ballentine wanted to punish the driver. Mistakes happen. The vehicle was fixed the next day. Most things could be with a good night's sleep and daylight to examine them.

However, the enemy also learned American tactics and procedures. Steve turned in his patrol report detailing all that happened, to include the brief engagement. A few weeks later, the next group of Americans attacked by the enemy was a Special Forces ODA conducting another relief in place. That ODA, with Schilling now as their team sergeant, chose to ignore the report, and adhering to Schilling's directives, drove through the same area in the city with their lights on, and got ambushed. Of a twelve-man Special Forces-ODA, four were killed, and another four received wounds that medically retired them from the Army. The last four soldiers were sent to other ODA's as combat replacements. The unit hadn't been in theatre for a week, and it was tactically destroyed.

One of the dead was Sergeant First Class Schilling.

# 35



The company settled in on FOB Prince. It was not a large base but housed a few ISAF (International Security Assistance Force) units. Those were NATO nations, as well as other coalition forces, and FOB Prince had a Danish armored reconnaissance company on it that never left the confines of the base and a Czech commando unit that was gone so often the Marines rarely interacted with them. The Czechs had a reputation for being fierce in battle, and for questionable battlefield conduct bordering on war crimes. American forces universally looked upon ISAF troops with derision, saying the acronym stood for "I Suck at Fighting" or "I've Seen Americans Fight." This was disingenuous; ISAF units fought and suffered casualties too, particularly the British.

The base was divided into three sections for the respective residents to carve out their living areas with a large helicopter landing zone in the middle of it, the American's occupying the largest footprint. Most of the buildings were brick-and-mortar construction with solid roofs, left over from when the CIA first established the base earlier in the war. Most of the MSOC slept in those buildings, but some, particularly the junior Marines in Hackett's platoon, slept in expeditionary wall tents with cots. Those offered barrack style living with little privacy and provided no overhead cover from indirect fire. Everyone shared communal showers but considered themselves lucky to have hot water and flushing toilets. The water itself was non-potable and pallets of bottled water from some spring in Kuwait were stacked in various locations on the base so one could grab and drink it then throw it in the dirt. Try as the Marines might to keep a clean home, the bottles were everywhere.

Adjacent to the FOB was an Afghan National Army (ANA) camp which housed an ANA company that accompanied coalition forces on most missions, lending an Afghan presence to American operations, but those soldiers were largely disinterested, and no one trusted them. They smoked marijuana, and the pungent smoke carried across the base on the prevailing winds.

The MSOC settled in, and after a week began preparing for a large combat mission Ballentine planned for later in the month. They trained and made improvements to their equipment. One of these were the GMVs.

The GMVs did fine on paved roads. Off road in the harsh terrain, however, several shortfalls were realized, and the Marines further customized the vehicles by strengthening the suspensions and made improvements for storing a lot of ammunition, food, water, batteries, and other mission-essential items like readily accessible shoulder-fired rockets.

Fergus, having been a steelworker in his former life in Dublin, Ireland, further transformed the vehicles by welding on boxes for storage and making other pragmatic additions. Steve admired the Irish expatriate's welding skills, which explained his rough, calloused hands. The company mechanics made the engines more powerful and improved the speed by working the diesel systems to maximize output. It took a few days and long hours in the hot sun to get the GMVs ready. Steve was immensely proud of his men.

All of that was against orders to make any modifications, intelligent or otherwise, to the vehicles. Ballentine saw the handiwork and exclaimed, "How is this going to look? They modified government property; I didn't give permission to do it!"

Ballentine, ever the envious opportunist, worried how things, good and bad, would affect his career. The men saw right through it, but if Ballentine knew, he betrayed nothing. Conversely, Steve didn't care for regulations or stove-piping. The two of them were very opposite with few similar traits.

In the present, Steve had a job to do, even if he didn't exactly agree with the management or current situation within the unit.

# 36



*FOB Prince, Afghanistan, September 20, 2009*

Marines were still considered new to Special Operations. The inaugural deployment by a MARSOC unit ended ignominiously with that unit being drummed out of the country under investigation for war crimes. Later acquitted of all charges, the unit and its leader unfairly spent the rest of their lives trying to recover their good names and honor.

As a result, Steve's company partnered with a US Army Special Forces team led by a man named Captain Williams, who were presumably assigned to help the Marines learn the ropes and how to fight in Afghanistan. It held credence if the SF units' combat experience in the country established credibility, but many of the Marines felt the ODA was keeping tabs on them.

As they'd found with Sergeant First Class Schilling, the other SF units partnered with them often knew less than they did but tried to swagger appropriately. It was unnecessary posturing. However, Captain Williams and his ODA were battle-tested and very good at fighting.

"When you get into contact, get out of the trucks, dismount and fight on foot. The enemy hates that," Williams's team sergeant instructed.

Brian shared some knowledge of his own with their SF partners of how to maximize the use of the Claymore antipersonnel mine by cutting it in half and attaching a time-fuse to an initiator to allow for them to be emplaced inside tight urban spaces to deter pursuit. The first time it was employed, the effects were devastating since the alley in which it erupted funneled the steel ball-bearings down the mud-wall canyon and made shredded beef of two enemy fighters. Otherwise, the company continued to prepare for combat, and much of the month passed uneventfully except for a few small patrols that resulted in sporadic gunfire but no serious contacts.

***

One sunny, hot afternoon, an explosion erupted in the town adjacent to the base. It rumbled deep and foreboding, a black cloud of dust and suffering rising into the air, visible for miles. It was a massive detonation, and the shockwave was felt across the expanse that separated the base from the town.

People grabbed weapons and moved to defensive positions, most in casual clothes with body armor over top of it. A few changed into boots or running shoes. Some, like Alex, went in flip-flops. Scanning for threats, they assessed that the blast was localized to the town and that a follow-on attack wouldn't materialize.

"Shit, dude, that was huge." Alex stared at the enormous smoke cloud rising in the distance. "I'll bet that was an IED." He used the familiar acronym for an improvised explosive device.

"You think?" Steve asked, looking at the growing inky black plume.

"Yeah. Car bomb or something."

People began to stand down from being on alert, including Steve's medic, Luke Milam, a Navy Special

Operations Amphibious Reconnaissance Corpsman. He was tall, good looking, calm and soft-spoken. He started walking away from the defensive positions. "Luke!" Steve called.

"Hey, sir! We'd better head to the clinic. Civilian casualties will start arriving soon." He said, his blond hair reflecting the sun.

"OK. I'll get Abdullah and Grimace." Steve referred to their Afghan interpreter and the MSOC's counter-intelligence Warrant Officer.

"Good call, sir. See you there." Luke jogged to the clinic.

The heat was stifling, and the medics moved to the aid station to prepare it to receive the inevitable casualties that would arrive within forty-five minutes. The base was their only source of treatment, and, in this case, sanctuary. MARSOC ensured its members received plenty of live-tissue medical training to treat battlefield wounds. In a mass casualty situation, anyone with that training would be an extra hand to medics like Luke.

The Marines and Sailors, along with a few Army SF medics sat in the shade and waited, ready to assist the wounded. Most wanted to be a part of it since treating seriously injured people was the right thing to do, but also helped keep battlefield trauma skills fresh. Sunglasses on and smoking cigarettes, most wore PT gear consisting of a T-shirt and shorts. Some removed their shirts to tan scarred and tattooed bodies, bullshitting about what was coming.

"All the live-tissue training you can get, right?!" Someone callously commented, sounding base, cruel, and insensitive.

Afghans were seen as second-rate humanoids by some, though Steve didn't embrace that. They were humans, fated to live in a poor, dusty country short on hope. Whose fault was that? Shouldn't they receive care if it could be provided?

"Shut up," Steve snapped, despite knowing it was all just a coping mechanism for what was to come. The commentary stopped.

The biggest issue was, while US forces on FOB Prince offered treatment and packaging for further care if required, they weren't an actual hospital. Afghans who received medical assistance didn't have access to follow on care. But American medical supplies were first-world compared to anything the Afghans could obtain on their own.

Villagers came in a parade of ghoulish wounds. The first casualties arrived in cars, others followed in carts or even wheelbarrows, then the ambulatory, bloody and destroyed, limped in. There were thirty wounded with at least that many dead in the streets. They were in various states of agony due to shrapnel, blasts, getting crushed, and severing injuries. It was unforgivable. Triage began, and people got to work. Luke performed an amputation.

Abdullah and a massive redheaded man named Chief Warrant Officer 2 Corey Greeley, nicknamed Grimace, entered the treatment facility. His hair stuck out in an orange Afro, his beard making him look like a Viking. His right arm had a twisted scar from a bullet wound he'd sustained earlier in his career as an infantryman in Iraq. Grimace took notes in a small notebook, asking injured people for specifics about the incident while Abdullah translated. Steve was impressed by the stoicism of the Afghans, though they communicated through their eyes and faces, if somewhat impassively.

Steve saw a little boy, aged maybe twelve, but it was hard to tell since time didn't seem to apply in Afghanistan, burned across his body. His arms were the worst with third degree burns in places with charred flesh that slid off since the dead casing of skin couldn't cling to the live tissue underneath it. The boy was in shock. He arrived alone without any adult accompaniment, elders, parents or otherwise.

The boy implored in Pashtu. "He says he's thirsty," Abdullah translated. A cup of water was brought to him, but it didn't slake his thirst. The severity of the burns instantaneously dehydrated him.

Steve said, "Bring the boy in. I'll help Luke treat him." He felt compelled to do it out of a sense of duty, that if he didn't, he was no better than the monsters responsible for the boy's suffering. Good had to outdo evil. In his mind, Steve reinforced that that was why they were there, particularly after he told his youngest child, Marta, that he had to go away to help children that didn't have anyone to do what her daddy did for them. He was being lent to children to protect them from the bad men, as his son, Michael, characterized.

His children had accepted that as a noble pursuit, that if he was doing that for others, then their donation of their father to assist them was right and correct. His children didn't know that it might be a one-sided bargain. Their idea of what their father was doing didn't involve days like this one or high-end kinetic combat where death came without warning or reason.

The Afghan boy was put on the table. Luke worked with Steve in a good partnership; Luke ran IVs, Steve abrading the boy's wounded limbs, the necrotic flesh washing off his arms like molting skin, revealing new epidermal layers, raw and pink. It was hideous. Steve washed and cleaned and cared for the boy. He tried to be tender, but it was impossible, for the wounds required difficult attention. All the while, the boy was quiet, only continuing to ask for water, which he could no longer drink since it might induce shock due to the drugs. Water intravenously administered into his system was being sent to the wounded areas by the body to try and begin the healing process.

Steve's approach was systematic. He cleaned and sterilized the wounded limbs, then wrapped them in burn treatment gauze before applying an outer gauze to protect the wounded flesh. The burn gauze was soaked in a specific chemical such so it would treat the raw skin and charred areas but not stick to it the way dry gauze would.

The boy's pain increased, and he moaned slightly. Luke assessed, "I'm gonna increase his ketamine to take the edge off. It'll dull the pain but not eliminate it. But I can't give him an adult dose." Ketamine was potent stuff; Steve knew from his own experience with it during his hospital stay after the parachuting accident.

The medics worked as a well-trained machine, treating the people with swift, professional progress. Steve was impressed with his men's performance. Ballentine and Nathan didn't show up to this kind of work. Both were viewed as charlatans, especially Ballentine, whose compensatory, insecure measures made everyone uncomfortable. None of the Marines trusted their skills anyway.

The boy was stabilized for extraction from the base, along with others requiring follow-on and better care than could be provided with the limited support and supplies they possessed at FOB Prince. Steve pulled a black Sharpie from his pocket and marked the boy's forehead with a 'K' for ketamine and wrote the dosage and time of administering the medication so when he was passed off to the medevac, they would know what kinds of treatment the boy had already received and not make a mistake in giving him more.

Luke and Steve then tended to a grievously wounded woman. While doing so, Grimace and Abdullah spoke to her. Abdullah was an old hand at this job, having translated for American units for a few years. Grimace and Abdullah's working relationship was such that Abdullah could make the correct interpretation, not just parrot words.

Grimace spoke directly to the woman. "What happened in the village?"

She replied with each iteration of question and translation.

"She says a bomb went off in the market."

"Damn." Grimace swore with a slight shake of his head, his blue eyes focusing on her, "Who would have done this?"

"She says definitely the Taliban," Abdullah translated.

"Do you know who the leaders are of this organization?"

"She thinks she does." Abdullah nodded.

The exchange continued as Luke treated her wounds. He spoke to the woman, too. "You are very brave. I'm going to sew your wounds shut. It may hurt a little."

Abdullah translated the statement, and her reply. "She says thank you. And that she knows she is badly hurt. She doesn't mind."

"I never want to hurt a patient," he gently said to the woman. "The worst is nearly over. Please forgive me that it continues to cause you pain."

"She says she understands. She thanks you for your self-lessness. Your bravery."

Luke threaded a suture kit and began to sew the woman's arm wound shut. Grimace and Steve watched him. The woman said nothing.

Steve turned to Grimace. "What do ya got?"

Grimace examined his notes. "A vehicle-borne IED was placed in the market to go off during the busiest part of the day. It worked."

"Those fuckers." Steve winced.

Grimace gestured toward the woman. "She says the Taliban are responsible. She gave me a name, and I'll check it against our objective database. I'll bet he's in there."

Steve pursed his lips, "OK. Anything else?"

"She's grateful. For being treated. For Luke," Abdullah commented, capturing the woman's sincerity.

Luke glanced up. He smiled demurely and continued working on her.

The wounded were treated, and some required higher echelons of care. A medevac was called. The Americans carried the injured out to the landing zone. Dressed in casual clothes, they looked extremely out of place in the military camp. Two massive CH-47 helicopters flown by

British aircrews arrived to retrieve their shattered cargo. Steve moved with Luke to load the boy feet-first on the helo, preventing his head from sliding into gear boxes or instruments. The boy remained quietly detached from all of it due to the ketamine having fully taken effect.

Steve gave the turnover brief to the British nurse, a pretty woman under her helmet and equipment, conspicuous against the dust and the pain that the wind carried with it. "He's very badly burned. I cleaned and dressed his wounds. We gave him ketamine. I noted the details on his forehead." He squeezed the boy's hand.

"We've got him, sir," she said in a clipped accent. Steve nodded, barely able to hear much of anything over the powerful engines. Steve stepped back, and the ramp closed. The helicopter lifted off in a storm of wind and noise that was replaced with silence except for a light breeze and the odd cough or conversation.

Steve watched the helo until it flew out of sight, immense sadness sweeping in. The boy had arrived by himself, or at least unaccompanied. There wasn't any way to notify the boy's family, if they were even alive, about what had happened to him.

He never learned what became of the boy since the wounds he'd sustained required probably years of care that wasn't attainable in Afghanistan.

Steve shook his head.

A vehicle-borne IED, packed with explosives, detonated at a crowded market, killing and maiming indiscriminately without explanation other than it was everyone's bad luck that day. People who tried to chalk it up to some type of enemy protest or strike in retaliation for something missed the point. Bomb goes off, people die, and the cause for which it was detonated doesn't matter to the victims since all of them were innocent. War waged at the population level wins over no one. Even the Russians grasped that, if they didn't ever embrace it.

George Santayana was right.

# 37



Ballentine assembled the company to brief his plan to conduct a deep-penetration operation in enemy territory. Their patrols to date encountered little enemy contact. It was the first big mission they'd execute as a unit and all of them were excited to go on the mission.

While the members of the MSOC already earned their coveted Combat Action Ribbon, Steve still felt cheated somehow. He wanted a legitimate firefight and to prove himself, to be tested, and found that he "rated," to use a synonym for measuring up to standards.

That evening, the company and their SF counterparts gathered in an open courtyard outside of their berthing around a large four-sided terrain model illuminated by four floodlights. The Marines and soldiers stood on three sides, Ballentine on the fourth, pointing out key terrain and maneuvers with a long stick.

"Gents, we're going to conduct a five-day clearance operation in the Valley of The Jackal to our North!" He smiled satirically, but it seemed forced, plastic.

Someone called from the back, "Seventy-five of us in that valley?! Shouldn't a larger unit do that? It seems a gross misuse of Special Operations Forces!" With direct action being their primary mission, it wasn't exactly what Steve and his platoon had trained to do.

Ballentine scowled while looking for the unidentified speaker. "We just need to do what we're told. We can fight as infantry."

Fergus, rolling his eyes, muttered to Alex, "Go with what you know."

"Yeah, hyper-conventional forces," another Marine quipped.

Ballentine became annoyed. "That's enough—now listen up! We'll advance northwards in three elements up the valley. I'll be in the center with one part of the company and Lieutenant Hackett, Captain Keller and his platoon will go to the east, and Captain Williams and his team to the west." He gestured to each area on the terrain model, explaining various features while describing the plan. "If we get into contact, we'll attempt to support the others, but the enemy gets a vote. We step off tonight at 0330 hours. Good luck."

The briefing over, the unit broke into smaller groups to discuss the coming operation. Captain Williams, an African-American officer, approached Steve. "How ya' doin'? My name's Kelvin." Williams extended his hand. He had an easygoing demeanor.

"Nice to meet you!" Steve said, shaking William's palm.

"Gotta ask: What's up with your boss?" He sounded concerned.

"Huh?"

"This operation is something we would've done when I was in the Eighty-Second Airborne, not in SF."

"He wants to establish our reputation out here on a wide scale."

"Sure. But we'll be three units that are pretty lightly armed. If the enemy isolates any one of us, they'll cut 'em to pieces."

Steve nodded. "You've been out here a while."

"Yup. It's different from what I was taught at West Point, that's for sure. We can chat more, but I'll also tell you this: Your man seems like he's here for his own résumé. If all he wants is for this to be successful, so it makes him look good, that's a shitty reason to be leading troops," Williams saw right through Ballentine.

"Don't I know it." Steve was almost embarrassed, like he'd been called out on withholding information.

# 38

*FOB Prince, Afghanistan, September 24, 2009*

Ballentine called to Steve while he was talking with Williams. "Captain Keller? A word, please."

Overhearing this, Brian looked at him and smirked, and Fergus smiled like Steve was in trouble with the teacher. Williams departed. "Catch you later!"

Steve waved to him, then turned to Ballentine. "Of course, sir." He stepped outside the lit courtyard and into the night. It was still warm under starry skies, and though clear above them, the air was stale with dust.

Ballentine tried to sound paternal. "Steve. This is our first big foray together. I'm thinking you have the wrong perception of me."

"How do you mean, sir?"

"I know the majority of the unit has been together for some time, most of you coming from Force Recon, as Rod—ahem—duly pointed out to me in Africa. Not being a recon man myself, I wanted to allay any concerns you may have." Ballentine spoke slow and measured.

"OK, sir—"

"I have plenty of combat time. More than most people in this unit. Certainly, more than you. Losing Major Joyce was terrible, but make no mistake, I *will* lead it in battle. I know combat, and I know what I'm doing. I fought a Nasiriya in '03 and Fallujah in '05."

"We know your capabilities, sir." Steve hated Ballentine's condescension.

"That's just it," Ballentine said. "I don't think you do. Don't think being recon is all there is to being in Special Operations. It's a mindset."

Steve was glad it was dark save a small light over the door to a building behind them. It masked the look of distaste on his face. Ballentine was a hypocrite.

Ballentine reached into his pocket and produced two cigars, offering one to Steve. "I know you want to avenge Major Joyce. I want to help you do that, but my way."

Steve accepted the cigar after Ballentine cut the end. He allowed Ballentine to light it and spoke between each draw with the cigar clamped between his teeth. "What—way—is—that?" Each pull caused the flame from the lighter Ballentine held to grow larger, illuminating both of their faces. Ballentine looked like an evil counselor.

"This is a long war, Steve." He lit his own cigar. "I don't want to hate policymakers or those who seek conflict resolution by other, more peaceful means, but sometimes, goddamn it, war *is* the answer." He looked at the red ember on the end of his cigar, ensuring it was even. "The French understood this in Algeria and Indochina, but a national lack of political will to see things as they are instead of how their politicians wished them to be interfered. The United States is no different." He held his cigar in a light pinch between his thumb and two fingers.

Steve pulled on his own, thinking of something to say.

Ballentine cleared his throat. "The enemy requires multigenerational engagement. They're the worst of the horrendous and can't be reasoned with, negotiated with, or otherwise rationally engaged due to their apocalyptic views of world-wide destruction. They need to be eradicated—put to the sword to the last man, woman, and child. There's no other way."

Steve listened closer.

Ballentine's tone was one of conviction. "The war must be waged ruthlessly and without quarter until the desire of the enemy to reconstitute or put-up further resistance is so unpalatable, they wouldn't think of doing it for fear of what might happen to them. And that is what we're going to do tomorrow." He sounded monstrous, though a small part of Steve agreed with him. He didn't want to admire Ballentine, but the guy did have a point. Could Steve himself be both vengeful and measured in his own approach to fighting, too?

"Sir, again, we're a small raiding force—"

"Which means we'll be an adroit opponent." Ballentine cut him off again, much to Steve's aggravation. He looked at Steve as if to ensure he was understood.

Steve took a long drag on his cigar. "You're right sir. No better men to do it, either. A small force, completely sure of each other will fight to the death, to paraphrase Alexis De Toqueville." He exhaled smoke. Ballentine's taste in cigars was quite good.

"Good man! I'm glad we talked, though I admit I didn't take you for an intellectual." Ballentine laughed, patronizing, but now more at ease. Steve wasn't sure if he sounded that way because he convinced Steve of his point of view or if he'd just confessed something to make himself feel better.

"I'm full of surprises," Steve said sardonically.

# 39



The MSOC and Special Forces soldiers spent the rest of the evening readying for the long mission ahead, loading the GMVs, bristling with firepower, ammunition, and rockets. However, the toughest weapon in the vehicles were the men themselves.

Steve's was driven by a Sailor medic from Hackett's platoon named HM3 Chris Hoyle. Steve would ride shotgun beside him with 'Fruit Bat,' his newly-arrived Air Officer and JTAC, or Joint Terminal Air Controller, behind him. Fruit Bat was a Harrier Pilot named Captain Tyrone Cashiers, but no one called him that. He was responsible for controlling air support and employing aerial-delivered munitions in support of ground forces. Being approved to do so meant a lot of training and maintenance of his skills and his duties came with great responsibility. When he arrived in the country, his call sign was entered in a central database for being given permissions to drop ordnance.

Their vehicle's turret gunner was an infantry sergeant named John McConnell. Like Hoyle, he was a member of Hackett's platoon but assigned to Steve's vehicle. He loved being Steve's gunner. He was a smaller, round man, built like a squat football guard with a grease-monkey eye for working on the truck. Riding in the troop compartment would be Grimace and Abdullah. Steve liked his crew.

After a bit more preparation and a final scan of equipment, Steve and his mates went to bed in their small room. Hackett slept on the far bunk, Fruit Bat beside him. Along with Nathan, Steve was crammed in there, too, somehow. Each wrestled with their own apprehensions and hoped for some rest.

***

Steve was shaken awake from a sound sleep to see Roland's ghost sitting on the edge of his bed, dressed as he was in his casket in his Dress Blue Uniform with a bandaged head. "Wake up, Steve."

Steve rubbed his face, groggily trying to process the apparition which possessed physical qualities. "What? How? Holy shit, Roland! You're dead; how's this possible?!"

Roland looked earnestly at Steve and slowly shook his head. "You must listen to me carefully."

"What?! No way you're here!" He was still incredulous.

"Stop. I am, and this is very real. Listen to me." Roland applied an iron grip on Steve's arm, and Steve reacted to the all too real touch of what he assumed was a ghost. "You're going on a bloody, difficult journey."

Steve came to and leaned up on his elbows. It was no dream. It was real, though unbelievable.

Roland continued, "It's going to test you like nothing else in your life. But you're ready. You were born to do this job. Say it with me."

"I was born to do this job." Steve blinked.

"And it's gonna be OK. Do what you trained to do, and don't doubt yourself. Ever. Understand?" Roland peered into Steve's eyes with his own good one.

"I do . . . but . . . how?" Steve said, awake but still unsure of what was transpiring.

Roland again shook his head. "Don't worry about 'how,' Steve. I'm here. I'm with you. Trust that and trust yourself. Your men's lives depend on it. I'll be with you through all of it." He stood and left the room.

Steve fully sat up in bed and threw back the covers. "Roland! Wait!"

He ran out the open door to his room and down the hallway, looking for Roland, chasing a ghost. Steve emerged into the cool of the early light of dawn, taking the stairs to the rooftop fighting position, which at night doubled as a great place to smoke a cigar and contemplate life.

Arriving at the top, he conducted a panoramic scan. Sunrise. It was clear. The usual slight haze on the horizon that obscured everything wasn't present, and mountains he hadn't seen on the other side of the distant wadis lined the horizon.

Where was Roland? Steve conducted another circular scan. He needed answers. Who would die? What would be the cost? Could he ensure those things didn't happen? Would he make the right decisions? Would he be brave? Tears streamed down his cheeks. Steve sat on the bench seat and put his head in his hands and wept. He missed his friend, but he was also unsure of the prophecy he'd been presented. The outcome was pre-destined somehow and out of his control. He felt helpless.

The sun rose, heating the air like a giant convection oven. Steve collected himself and started descending the stairs leading from the roof. A door shut down below him. He peered over the deck railing to see Luke emerging from the showers. "Hey," he called.

"Morning, sir," Luke said in his even tone. He wasn't the kind of person to get excited or emotional.

*He's totally confident; everything we all want to be.* Steve's admiration for Luke was boundless. He stared out to the horizon one more time, then looked back at Luke. "Morning. Did you see anyone out here?"

"No. Why?" Luke tilted his head.

Could no one else "see" Roland? "A man was in my room, but I don't know who, and when I came out here, I couldn't see them."

Luke shrugged and chuckled lightly. "That's weird, but we've all got strange sleeping patterns. Mefloquine will do that to you! You sure he was there, and you weren't imagining it?" Mefloquine was an antimalarial antibiotic with psychosomatic properties for some users. They all took it weekly while deployed.

Steve leaned forward, growing serious. "I get what you're saying, but there's one issue."

"What's that, sir?" Luke shielded his eyes from the rising sun to look up at Steve.

"My door only opens from the inside. We close it each night. When I got up, the door was open. My three other roommates are all asleep. It isn't possible."

Luke frowned a little. "Damn. Well, I didn't see anyone."

"At this point, I'm not sure I did either." Steve sighed and turned to view the horizon again.

Luke started walking, then glanced at Steve again. "Today's the big day. Be careful out there, sir." He nodded and resumed walking away.

"It is. And you too, Luke," Steve replied, quizzically watching him disappear into his berthing.

# 40



*Smoky Mountains, Tennessee—2031*

Steve finished his drink. He stood up and stoked the fire. Kelso shifted and stretched, then lay still on his bed. Steve returned to the chairs and took his seat. He reached for the bottle on the table, looking at Roland. "The night before the big mission. When you woke me up. I couldn't believe it."

Roland finished his whiskey and offered his empty glass for a refill. "I wanted you to be ready. To be forewarned."

Steve opened the bottle. "I didn't know what to make of it at the time."

Roland nodded. "That was the point; to increase your awareness. It paid off."

"Yeah, but at a steep price." Steve topped off their drinks.

# PART II

After being in combat for a while, a service member passes through a second phase. They believe that if they're careful, and rely on their training, they'll stand a chance to get out alive, though they grudgingly accept that something *might* happen to them. Fussell explained the perspective: "It *can* happen to me, and I had better be more careful. I can avoid the danger by watching more prudently the way I take cover / dig in / expose my position by firing my weapon / keep extra alert at all times, etc. This conviction attenuates in turn to the perception that death and injury are matters more of luck and skill." *Wartime* (Oxford University Press, 1989), 282-283.

Steve reflected that after his first few missions, he felt he relied on his preparation, then later, after more protracted combat, a combination of training and luck. But he also feared he'd view killing the enemy as something he could rationalize. He worried he might not be able to influence that either, since, as World War II Marine Eugene Sledge wrote in *With the Old Breed on Peleliu and Okinawa*, men would just kill to kill. For Sledge, combat became so inhuman, so terrible, that after the war, he never went hunting again and became an entomologist, studying bugs. Steve didn't want to become that detached, so in Afghanistan, he attempted to influence the future through his own design. It provided him a sense of control. It was also complete nonsense.

# 1



At the appointed time in predawn darkness, the unit departed FOB Prince in a massive convoy that split into their three predesignated formations. They entered The Valley of the Jackal, and by late afternoon, all three elements were in engagements with the enemy. Steve found his own part of the war in a compound from where they took intense fire. Bullets popped through the air and gunfire came from all directions in utter chaos as Marines took cover behind vehicles and the compound's walls. Guido, Fergus, and Alex's teams assaulted the compound, pushing the enemy back and were finishing processing it for intelligence.

Steve's headquarters element parked by the compound when Ballentine's voice crackled through the radio speaker in Steve's GMV. *"Serpent Seven-One, this is Rogue Six. We're Troops In Contact, time now. Stand by for contact report. Over."*

*"Roger, Rogue Six. Send your traffic,"* came the reply.

"Ballentine just opened a TIC. Sounds like everyone is in contact," Steve said calmly. A mortar round landed three hundred yards away with a loud "crump."

Brian stood next to him. "Sir, we're taking pretty accurate small arms and IDF. We should displace."

"We need to process this compound before we can move." Steve keyed the radio handset, talking on the platoon net to reach Marko, whose team was providing security on their left flank. "Rogue One-Zero, this is Rogue Two-Zero. Status report. Over?" Another explosion erupted closer by, covering he and Brian in dust. Both remained standing, the speaker hissing without response.

Steve repeated his radio call, then heard firing from Marko's position. The radio silence continued. Steve was about to key his handset again when a voice came through the speaker in his truck.

*"Rogue Two-Zero, this is Rogue One-Zero. Roger. We're taking heavy small arms fire, and the enemy is attempting to flank us."* The voice was not Marko's.

"Roger. We're almost finished here. Keep them occupied and refuse our left flank, estimate five mikes until exfil call. Over?"

*"Roger, we'll work on it,"* the voice replied over the gunfire. The handset remained keyed, and the voice shouted, *"Luke, keep their heads down!"* followed by a long burst from a machinegun. Then it went quiet.

Hearing more gunfire from Marko's position, Steve scanned through his binoculars and saw Marines moving around but couldn't discern what was happening. The voice came over the speaker again. *"Rogue-Two Zero, this is Rogue One-Zero. Be advised, we have one WIA. Triaging now and will move to a medevac LZ. How copy?"*

"Solid Copy, One-Zero. Send WIA MIST report when able." Steve indicated the Mechanism of Injury and Treatment of the casualties.

*"Roger, Two-Zero. One-Zero. Out."*

The Marines at Steve's position completed their work in the compound. Brian yelled, "Sir, we're done! Let's go!"

Steve turned to answer Brian when a loud explosion came from Marko's position, obscuring it in smoke and dust.

The dust cleared and one of the GMVs was smoldering from what appeared to be a rocket strike.

"Damn!" Brian exclaimed.

"*Rogue Two-Zero, Rogue One-Zero. We have multiple wounded. Urgent Surgical medevac needed. Triaging now. Wait. Out.*"

Steve, seeing the resultant smoke from the explosion, replied into the radio, "Roger, standing by. Send SITREP when able." He turned to Brian. "Multiple casualties at Marko's position!"

"Who?"

Steve shook his head. "I don't know—"

The radio crackled. "*Two-Zero, we have four WIA; one expectant. Callsigns as follows.*" The voice read off the list of the injured. Steve copied them down, stone faced. He knew Ballentine was also listening, but he wouldn't cut in while important information was being exchanged. "*We're moving to a medevac LZ to the east of our position. Request you provide security to the north and maintain that position until casualties are extracted, and we can move to the RV. How copy, over?*"

"Roger, One-Zero. Copy all and will execute." Steve set the handset down and stared at his notepad with the call-signs of the casualties. "Brian, we have four wounded and one dead." He looked down.

"Shit," Brian said gravely.

Steve darkly read off the names. "An infantry corporal named Pelton. Gary McGuire. Kyle Miller. And Pech. Luke Milam is dead." He looked up at Brian. "This changes everything."

"Pech? Who was on the radio?"

"Don't know, but it wasn't Marko."

"It sounded like Iceman."

"Maybe so. Either way we need to establish that security position."

"Sir, let's hold off telling the boys until we get set."

"Good call. Give me a full accountability of men weapons and equipment. Let's move. The fire's getting heavier."

"Will do, sir."

Steve keyed the handset. "Exfil, exfil, exfil! All stations, Rogue Two-Zero is moving, time now!"

They both ran to their vehicles.

# 2



teve's part of the unit consolidated at a rendezvous point. The remainder of Marko's team remained in their position. A large moon rose in the faltering light. Steve looked toward Marko's position, night-vision binoculars glued to his face. Smoke and gunfire emanated from their stricken area, and the rest of the line opened up in a furious response to the loss of one of their own.

Staff Sergeant Kyle Miller was hit by machine gun fire in the initial salvo. He went down and shortly after he was stabilized, Marko's truck was hit by a rocket the circumference of a small telephone pole. It entered the lower left side of the rear troop compartment and exploded. The impact alone rocked the truck, and the ensuing fragmentation and blast did the rest. Luke was blown in half from his body armor down. Staff Sergeant Gary McGuire, manning a .50 caliber machine gun in the turret, was cut off at the knees with a stomach injury that would take years to heal. The driver, Corporal Pelton, was a mess due to a shrapnel wound to the left side of his jaw. Marko was knocked unconscious. A member of Marko's team, Sergeant Sean Covington, called "Iceman" for his resemblance to Val Kilmer from *Top Gun*, took charge.

Luke couldn't be saved, but the other medics did their best to provide the illusion of doing something for him, and Iceman had the wherewithal to grab both parts of Luke's body, the guts and entrails hanging out from two sides, and put them together to give the impression he was still whole. Psychologically, that was an amazing ploy. Steve later wondered if he would have possessed the same presence of mind to do that. Iceman created stability out of chaos. That was also why he was called that. Totally cool in the worst of situations.

Iceman and the remainder of their element established a secure landing zone for a British CH-47 medevac helicopter to extract the four wounded—including Marko, evacuated for concussive shock—and Luke's body. The medevac bird landed in a cloud of dust after swooping in and skimming the earth to reduce its signature. Iceman, assisted by fellow Marines, loaded the casualties into the rear of the helicopter. Luke's covered body was put on the helicopter last, Iceman saluting him. The entire process took four minutes, and the helicopter leaped into the sky in another cloud of dust, moving fast to one side, hugging the earth to fly to safety. Two RPGs were fired at the machine, crisscrossing in the air above it in an X. Steve marveled it wasn't hit.

After the CH-47 departed, the fighting had largely stopped, sporadic pops and shots being heard only in the distance, and a quiet settled over the valley.

He raised the night vision binoculars on their helmet mount.

"Brian, extract of our boys is complete. Get the platoon together. I'll break the news." Luke's death was still so fresh, out of place, it seemed impossible, despite having watched his remains get loaded into the helicopter.

"OK, sir. Most of them already heard it on the radio, though. This is tough but hearing it from you is the best way."

"This is the easy part, Brian," Steve said.

"Sir?"

"It's one thing to inform the troops, but I'm not sure what I am going to say to Luke's family. I guess one never knows." Steve felt completely unprepared for that impending eventuality.

Two GMVs approached over a small hill. It was Ballentine. He arrived at Steve's position and exited his truck. He didn't look dirty or disheveled like Steve and his unit. Steve wondered what he'd been doing all day. Steve and Ballentine stood outside of his vehicle. McConnell remained on security in the turret.

"Bumpy go of it today, eh, Keller!" Ballentine tried to sound cheery.

"Yes, sir. We're gathering up the platoon now to break the news to them in person. I was going to do it in about five minutes."

"Good man! I'll do it when they arrive." Ballentine probably saw the situation as a tremendous opportunity. It took a moment for Steve to realize his address was being hijacked.

"You got it, sir. They're your men." Steve glowered under his helmet at Ballentine, but he couldn't see Steve in the darkness. It was a caustic detail.

The Marines started gathering, and Steve turned to them. "Four brothers were wounded today, including Marko, and Luke Milam was killed. I know you were close with them."

"Men, strengthen your resolve, and be ready to continue out here," Ballentine interrupted. The Marines turned to him, their surprise thickening the air. They hadn't expected him to be there. "It sucks, but there's is a lot of this mission remaining. Stay focused and rely on each other. If any of you want to talk, I'm available." He sounded insincere, like the offer was a formality to save face, and a dark mood came over the unit.

Brian, sensing the melancholy, snapped them back. "All right, boys, get back to it!"

The Marines departed in groups and pairs, returning to their GMVs. Brian and Steve remained behind at his truck. Ballentine turned to them. "Hopefully, despite today's events, your trust in me as your commander is growing."

"This has hit everyone hard. Luke Milam was a stalwart member of the Direct-Action Platoon. Everyone loved him." Steve felt drained and weighted, the impact of what had happened catching up with him.

Ballentine shrugged. "It's tragic, I know. But for all of his experience and talents, he's dead, and the rest of the unit must carry on."

Steve clenched his jaw, then forcibly released the tightened facial muscles. "Easier said than done, sir."

"It's been a rough day, sir," Brian added, seemingly sensing Steve's growing anger.

Ballentine glanced at him, then back to Steve. "Yes. I've seen this before. Iraq and other places. I've lived other lives, you know? You needn't worry."

"You have, sir?" Steve raised his eyebrows.

"Sure. There are times, actually, when I feel I've served in other wars and time periods, as if some of my perspectives are not my own. And this will allow us to outmaneuver the enemy." Ballentine paused for effect. "Have you ever felt that way, Steve?"

"No, sir," Steve half laughed.

"Well, I do," Ballentine snapped, his tone superior. "And I believe I transcend the decisions that would trouble others. Today was no different."

"You sure, sir? I'm not convinced you know where we are on the map," Brian said. He was half kidding, but the situation was getting strange.

Ballentine became flustered. He blurted, "I served in Tarsus as a Roman soldier, and I understand where we are because I marched across Afghanistan in a former life as a British officer. The ground looks familiar; this is how I knew where to position our forces to get the drop on the enemy and absolutely destroy them!"

"If you say so, sir." Brian glanced over at Steve. If Brian could have seen Steve's face, it would have been one of stunned confusion. Steve couldn't believe Ballentine had just said what he had, and even more so that he believed it.

"It was a pretty even fight, but I'm not sure we got the drop on them, sir. Luke's dead and we've got four people in the hospital," Steve remanded. His frustration with Ballentine's breezy approach to today's events manifested as a burning behind his ears.

Brushing it off, Ballentine looked at both Brian and Steve through his NODs. "Nonsense. We have the enemy right where we want them, and we'll relentlessly pursue them, starting this evening. We have air support en route." Ballentine motioned to Steve to walk with him back to his truck.

"Keep your men alert and ready, Steve. There's still a lot of fight ahead of us." His countenance was grave, and he gripped Steve's forearm in an awkward attempt to shake his hand.

"No worries, sir. We've got it." Steve found Ballentine's hand and shook it. Even through gloves, he felt cold.

"Good man!" Ballentine climbed into his truck and drove away.

Steve watched for a moment before returning to his own position. "Brian?"

"Sir?"

"Walk with me over here a minute." Steve moved away from their vehicles. Brian followed him. "Iceman did a hell of a job today. I still can't believe Luke is dead." His loss was incongruous to Steve.

"He did. So did Luke, apparently." Brian glanced at the ground, then back to Steve.

"Marko was the Team Leader at that position."

"Yes, he was," Brian agreed.

"Why did a sergeant run this action?" Steve frowned.

"Iceman's a combat veteran of Iraq. Besides, Marko was in the vehicle when it got hit. He had a bad concussion."

Steve nodded. "That was after the fact. Marko never came up on the radio. Iceman did it all."

"I'll talk to Iceman when we get back to the FOB. See what I can find, sir."

"Be careful here, Brian. We don't know all the facts." Steve put his hand on Brian's shoulder.

"Understood, sir. I'll figure it out."

"Thanks." Steve released his shoulder, and they walked back to Steve's vehicle.

When they arrived, Brian started to chuckle.

"What're you laughing at?!" With Ballentine's demeanor still fresh in Steve's mind, he was overly sensitive.

Brian's body shook with amusement. "I was thinking, if Ballentine believes in reincarnation, with my luck, I'll come back reincarnated as me again!" He howled with laughter.

Steve joined him. "Better you than me!" He pointed at Brian, eliciting more laugher.

From the turret, McConnell chuckled too while he continued scanning for the enemy.

# 3

---



An AC-130 gunship arrived overhead later that night. Steve listened to radio traffic as he witnessed Fruit Bat, via the AC-130, deliver the most terrifying firepower. Through Icom traffic intercepts, Abdullah relayed that the enemy suffered so many casualties that they were out of vehicles to carry them away for any sort of treatment. No one would drive into the kill zone since the circling "Angel of Death," emitting a piece of metal for every square yard on the ground in its arc, pummeled the ground and its occupants.

"Yeah, fucking pound 'em," Steve swore and watched through his NODs.

Fruit Bat remarked, "The pilot's a chick. She sounds hot." Others listening commented on that fact, too. "I'm considering asking her out."

"You're a rake. And on a tactical radio in combat, too." Steve rolled his eyes as he listened to Fruit Bat.

"It could happen. I should ask what she's wearing," Fruit Bat said after calling in another salvo.

"Slob." Steve walked away, secretly wondering if, indeed, she was hot. *Pig,* he admonished himself.

Steve felt an overwhelming sadness. He needed some alone time. The late summer heat lingered even though the moon had fully risen. He shivered, the adrenaline of the day's events surrendering to fatigue. His joints ached and blood thumped in his temples. He slumped against the wheel of his truck and removed his helmet. The emotions of the day overwhelmed him, and his dirty, grimy, sweat-stained face streaked with tears as he cried softly into his hands. When he stopped, Steve wiped his eyes and lit a cigarette. He'd enjoyed an occasional cigar, but he'd never being a regular smoker, so he coughed a little when he took his first drag.

McConnell, breaking the tension, asked from the turret, "Do you really think Ballentine's lived other lives, sir?"

"No. But I think he believes he did—or is just imitating Patton, which would be just like him," Steve ridiculed. He licked his dry lips.

"I mean, maybe he did?" McConnell continued, intrigued.

"OK. Let's give him the benefit of the doubt, Mac. Why do you think that?" Steve was interested in McConnell's perspective, caring less about Ballentine's act. The AC-130 continued to drone overhead.

"He said he was a crusader of sorts, from the old days. He talked about walking as a legionnaire across Tarsus, like he'd been here, too." McConnell glanced down at Steve. "Where's Tarsus, anyway?"

"It's in Turkey, or at least I'm pretty sure it is. But go on."

"All I'm sayin' is that he *might've* done all that stuff. He's got a sense about him, like you. Know what I mean, sir?"

"Uhhh, not exactly." Steve propped himself up. "But I appreciate it."

McConnell maintained his scan on the horizon, while Steve considered their commanding officer. Did Ballentine have a hero's complex, a feeling of righteousness in his cause? Yes. And that made Ballentine self-centered to believe that he alone should be the judge of the people the MSOC hunted, Agha notwithstanding.

Leaning against the truck tire, Steve had an epiphany. His trainers also did nothing to prepare a leader for dealing with the death, the acute loss of someone in his unit. Roland's was always in Steve's mind, but nothing had prepared him for losing Luke—one of his own. And how would one even teach about it? The coal of fury welled in his chest, growing into a flame. *This isn't healthy*, he thought, but it was insuppressible.

If people read his mind, they might have thought of him as being existential.

# 4


*Southern Afghanistan, September 29, 2009*

The American offensive in the valley continued. They pursued the enemy for a few more days in a rolling fight. Steve's men tenaciously found the enemy, allowing them no sanctuary or rest. It was taxing on the Marines too, but they fed on the energy only vengeance from losing a teammate like Luke can provide. Each engagement became more violent and protracted. The enemy didn't stand a chance.

Late in the day, Ballentine made an assessment to gain a foothold in enemy territory by seizing and fortifying a compound situated on a small hill. He ordered Steve and his platoon forward to secure it. Evening approached, and Steve looked at the hill five hundred yards away. He understood his orders and briefed Brian, Alex, Guido, Fergus, and Fruit Bat.

Bullets snapped sharply through the air. The enemy was close. Radios crackled with Hackett reporting more enemy movement to their front. The assault brief completed, Steve and his platoon mounted their five vehicles and drove down a small road, essentially a causeway, leading to a field with a five-foot drop on its back side. Less than ideal, but the compound was the objective, and they could fight from it.

Rounding the first bend in the road, the lead vehicle approached the compound with Steve's being third in the column of five. Fire erupted from the tree line and on two sides of them, and the second vehicle exploded in front of him.

"Oh shit!" Steve exclaimed.

"What the fuck?!" Fruit Bat yelled.

"I think they hit a mine or IED," McConnell yelled down from his turret.

However, the lead GMVs kept rolling. "I think it was an RPG. It must have exploded underneath or in front of it since the vehicle isn't damaged," Hoyle said.

The world accelerated around them as a tremendous bump shook the truck to one side. Another RPG warhead bounced off the hood of the vehicle and skewed to their left and into the drop-off, exploding with a deafening concussion. Shrapnel and rocks marred the side of the truck.

"Holy Fuck! RPG! But we're OK!" Fruit Bat yelled, the understatement of the day.

The two lead vehicles stopped and were heavily engaged by the enemy. Steve grabbed the radio handset to notify Ballentine. He steadied himself, drawing a deep breath despite the chaos. "Rogue-Six. We're Troops In Contact, receiving fire on three sides by small arms and rocket-propelled grenades. Wait. Out."

An initial report would feed Ballentine's voracious appetite for information, and it was necessary with all five vehicles stopped and engaging. He remembered what the Special Forces soldiers told them about dismounting from the trucks to fight.

"Out of the truck!" Steve commanded. He looked out the window; his men were already obeying, some throwing hand grenades. Rod fired a belt-fed squad automatic weapon from his shoulder, laying down a withering suppressive fire with his light machine gun at six hundred 5.56 mm rounds per minute.

"I'm out," Steve said to Hoyle who nodded back.

Steve opened the door and met with a maelstrom of bullets which impacted all around him. The roar of his own men returning fire added to the din. It didn't seem real. Earlier in his career, his instructors told him training would take over, but no training could replicate a firefight of this ferocity. He turned to move and find cover on the other side of the truck since he was exposed to the enemy, and they were clearly trying to hit him.

Hoyle yelled, "Sir, please shut the door!"

*Idiot.* He ran back to shut his door to protect Hoyle. How that must have looked to the outsider or adversary . . .

Steve sprinted the length of the truck, firing his M4 carbine as he went. Grimace delivered long bursts with the bed-mounted M240-G machine gun, and McConnell blasted away with his .50 caliber. His firing shook the entire GMV, its expended brass and links falling into a pile at his feet. Fruit Bat exited the vehicle on the opposite side and was down the precipice preparing a 9-line for an airstrike. Abdullah lay in the back of the truck, holding his AK over the edge and indiscriminately shooting. It would have been comical except that he hadn't been in a lot of firefights and was scared shitless.

Steve viewed it all through a narrow, clear lens, his sensory perception more acute. While it didn't seem they had gained any sort of upper hand, they were causing the enemy to pause and figure out who those crazy guys were who weren't taking getting a licking sitting down. Steve feared his men would conduct a close-in assault by bounds, where one group supported another in a leap-frog fashion across fifty yards of open terrain to close with the enemy, further increasing the likelihood of casualties.

It was time to withdraw.

The fire intensified. Steve needed to be back in the truck and on the radio, but that meant he had to return the way he came. He checked his weapon to ensure it wasn't jammed and replaced his magazine with a full one. He was getting ready to run back to his side of the truck and expose himself to more enemy fire when he remembered something that a former Green Beret told him when they were training in the United States:

"If you're barricaded, don't go running right past the cover. You don't know what's on the other side of it or what's waiting for you. Take your time, and pie-off the angles to engage from cover, then move forward, firing to gain advantage."

Steve positioned himself such that the truck and its giant tire shielded his body and leaned out slightly to look through his rifle sights. He saw three enemy with a PKM machine gun over their shoulders with ammunition running in the trees. He placed the red dot of his combat sight on the middle man with the gun and pressed the trigger twice, sweeping to the front, then back to the rear man, calmly and deliberately firing two rounds into each one. Then he fired one more into the middle man. All three fell out of view and didn't reappear. They were dead, and they were the first men he'd ever personally killed.

It took less than three seconds.

Satisfied he'd eliminated the threat to his front, Steve broke from cover, firing as he moved to his left. Time slowed, like when he was talking to Rod in Djibouti that night before they'd deployed. Each pull of the trigger was acute, and he felt the spring reset. The hot spent casings flew through the air, and he read the writing of the bullet's manufacturer stamped on the base. All while maintaining focus on the enemy, whose bodies littered the tree line. He reached the truck's door and opened it.

How he didn't get hit, he wasn't sure. Bullets whizzed pass by him, hot and angry. It was as if he were being outlined in a cartoonish manner with the bullets creating his silhouette on the truck as he moved. The rounds smacked into the truck's armor plating like a handful of metal washers being thrown against a wall. He fired a few more times and climbed in the truck.

"What the fuck?!" He laughed at Hoyle. Hoyle, smiling, shook his head.

Steve got on the radio. "Rogue Six. The position was untenable; we're withdrawing."

"*Roger,*" replied Ballentine. "*You're cleared to proceed.*"

Steve said nothing except "Roger" in return, but thought, *Well, fuck what you think. We're out of here!* He called on his platoon tactical channel, "Fall back! All assaulters mount their vehicles!"

People began to move, and Fruit Bat climbed in the truck. "I've got an airstrike coming. A-10s." The Flying Retard they called it. Awfully insensitive nickname, but it was apt. The main 30 mm seven-barreled Gatling gun emanated a low noise resembling a vocally disabled, deaf person when it fired.

"How long?" Steve asked.

"Not sure. He was at lunch when I called him." Fruit bat shrugged.

"Shiiiitt. You're funny, Fruit Bat!" More bullets impacted. The enemy was recovering from their shock. "Time to go," Steve said to Hoyle.

The column reversed direction one vehicle at a time, and the others continued to fire on the enemy. Gunner's gunned; driver's drove. Each truck crew knew their jobs and did them well. The rear two GMVs were in the lead and began to drive out of the kill zone. More RPGs exploded near the small column.

"Fuck this," Steve said. "Gas it, Hoyle!"

Hoyle obeyed, and they turned around. Fruit Bat lowered his window. He pushed his rifle out and fired at the enemy. His rifle had a short, close-quarter battle barrel, handy inside of a vehicle, though the muzzle didn't extend past the opening of the window and exploded inside of the truck when he fired, the concussion deafening the occupants. Hot brass flew out and onto Hoyle's neck, burning him.

"Fruit Bat," he asked calmly, "would you please put your rifle a little further out the window?"

"What the FUCK, Fruit Bat?!" Steve yelled, temporarily semi-deafened from the ringing in his left ear.

"Strange thing to be mad about when bullets are flying!" Fruit Bat squinted and continued firing.

They were gaining speed, and Steve began to believe they might make it out of the nightmare.

The radio crackled. It was Guido. *"My truck's stuck! Fuck! We need a tow."*

The vehicle to do that was Steve's, but they were ahead of Guido's and would need to back up. "Stop the truck, Hoyle."

"W-What?!" he stammered. Hoyle looked at Steve as if he'd told him that he was the sole inventor of cheese or the uncredited creator of the Oxford comma.

"We gotta back up to get Guido unstuck."

The trail vehicle's driver had the presence of mind to move forward around Guido's truck to position itself to tow them out. Guido's rear right wheel dangled over the precipice and the weight of the truck potentially tipped it into the ditch, making it inextricable.

What happened next was unclear to anyone who was present. Perhaps the hand of God reached down and lifted Guido's truck, weighing nearly seven tons, out of the ditch and back onto the road, for he elatedly yelled into the radio, *"We're out! We're OUT! GO! GOOO!"*

And they did. All five vehicles weaving back to the relative safety of their start point.

# 5



Behind the cover of a hill, Steve exited his truck and was met by Ballentine, who looked at him dumfounded as to how, exactly, they survived that, and all without casualties.

"Holy. Shit." Ballentine smiled and clapped him on the shoulder.

"Yeah," Steve replied, breathing heavily. He moved away from Ballentine to check on his men.

It was almost dark. The fight was dissipating, but they were still being engaged. Steve put on his NODs and moved to join two other Marines on the top of a hill to fire down on the distant enemy. He was in between them when the position was raked with fire. The man on his left was hit in the head and the one to his right in the chest. Both went down. Steve remained unscathed.

The one hit in the head narrowly escaped death. The bullet had entered his helmet, circled the inside rim, and flew out the other side. It gave him a rather close haircut which bled a lot, but he was alive. The one shot in the chest lay gasping, having been saved by his bulletproof ceramic plates. He later sported a "dead spot" on his chest that was bone-white with a massive bruise all over him.

Picking themselves up, Steve couldn't believe how stupid they were to reexpose themselves. *File that one away in the harsh-lessons folder.*

He returned to the truck and retrieved a break-open, single-shot M79 grenade launcher. He grabbed a bandolier of 40 mm fragmentation grenades and fired two high-explosive rounds in rapid succession at muzzle flashes in the tree line from which the fire was received. An enemy fighter was backlit by the explosion as he dropped. Steve fired two more rounds, but it was time to load up and fall back.

The A-10s Fruit Bat called arrived and pulverized the enemy positions with 30mm cannon fire and bombs with impressive destruction. Abduallah monitored enemy communications intercepts which came in loud peals from Afghan commanders wailing about their fate.

Now safely disengaged, Steve sat against the wheel of his truck. It was becoming his custom. Full night had fallen, and a large moon was up over the valley. It seemed quiet, save the odd shot here and there.

Fruit Bat wandered over to him. "Cigarette?"

Steve gladly took it, his second one in as many days. He lit it from Fruit Bat's to reduce the signature. The cherry of the igniting embers lit their faces, glowing red in their eyes as he smiled at Fruit Bat in gratitude. He inhaled deeply, letting the smoke and attendant nicotine coat and fill his lungs. *It feels so good,* he begrudgingly admitted. A few more drags led to him to wonder how he came to be sitting there, not ventilated by bullets without any serious casualties. It defied logic.

Later, they were told they'd been ambushed from the base of a large U-shaped enemy fighting position at the bottom of which was the compound they were trying to occupy. They'd driven right into the heart of the enemy and essentially attacked them face-to-face, though completely by accident. That they got out of the trucks on foot further shocked the enemy. They were unsure of what to do, and the suddenness and violence of the Marine attack broke their will.

MARSOC acquitted themselves in the first actions of what would come to define them as being legendary in battle. Steve's unit alone was credited with destroying an enemy Platoon-sized element by fire and close combat, just like any Marine infantryman.

Fruit Bat presciently pulled the pin and threw a purple smoke grenade in the ditch as they pulled off to mark the position for the A-10s.

"Head's up play," McConnell said.

That night was full of nervous laughter and congratulations.

The enemy was also smart. Hackett and his element established supporting positions on high ground to cover Steven's advance, and when Steve's element had driven into the base of the ambush, the enemy put mortar fire on those supporting positions, forcing them to withdraw. Steve and his team had been isolated while their support repositioned. After learning about that, Steve mentally tipped his hat to the enemy commander for a masterful use of combined arms.

The lesson was clear: those guys may be armed with light weaponry and fight in simple clothes and sandals, but they were tough and cunning. The Marines could not underestimate them.

Steve looked at the deep stars in the impressive Afghan sky. *Lord, if you get me through this, I'll live the best life I can, be the best man possible.* He'd also made a similar deal with God in the hospital delivery room with each of his children, especially when Marta was born with the umbilical cord around her neck, choking her as she fought for life with an energy that would define her.

*Dear God, if you only give me this, I will do that . . .* But Steve would compromise on those agreements by doing something to nullify the bargain and the negotiations would start over again. He continued, *If I ever get out of this, I'll never go to war again.*

That was a lie, both to God and himself. He was born to do this job, after all. It was what he was good at, excelled at doing it, but he didn't want to admit that to himself or anyone else.

Smoking that cigarette, Steve realized he was enormously hungry. He tried standing to get an MRE, but his legs wouldn't move. He was utterly exhausted. Overcome with fatigue, he passed out holding the cigarette. It burned down, and he awoke to it searing his fingers. Had that not happened, he might have slept all night.

# 6



That ended the company's first big mission. Luke was gone, and the four who'd been wounded, including Marko, were recovering in a hospital in Kandahar. The MSOC took a few days to refit and absorb what they'd experienced.

Steve examined the remains of Marko's truck, which they miraculously drove back to the FOB. The entire back troop compartment was deeply stained with blood that wouldn't come out of the paint. The company mechanic said he'd rebuild the vehicle, but no one wanted to ride in that. It was too disturbing.

He called Luke's parents to express empathetic offerings from him that he was sorry for their son's death and that it was he who was responsible. It was incredibly tough.

*"How did he die?"* they asked.

"Bravely," he replied. That seemed to satisfy their curiosity, at least for the moment. What was he to say? Steve hadn't lied; Luke remounted a truck that was already targeted, manning a machine gun to lay down suppressive fire. He gave his life protecting the wounded. He never knew what hit him, at least that's what Steve liked to believe.

"Boss?" Brian asked as he approached Steve, who was examining a jagged hole on the left side from where the rocket entered the back of Marko's wrecked GMV.

"What's up?" He ran his hands over chipped paint from bullet impacts on the plate-steel armor.

"I spoke to members of Marko's team regarding his performance during the operation." Brian studied the blood in the back of the truck and frowned.

"What'd you find out?"

"No one's quite sure what happened. From the outset, Marko didn't get in the fight. He sat in the vehicle."

"Was he scared?" Steve pressed.

"People say he froze up as soon as the bullets started flying. We all get scared, though."

Steve nodded. "True. Man, we're lucky Iceman stepped up. Without his leadership, I don't know what else would've happened. The day was pretty bad as it was."

"Yep." Brian sighed.

"I'll go talk to Ballentine," Steve said, still surveying the back of the truck, imagining Luke's last moments.

Brian raised a brow. "About what?"

Steve exhaled. "Relieving Marko."

# 7



Steve knocked on Ballentine's office door.

"Enter," Ballentine said and glanced up from some paperwork as Steve stepped inside. He sat behind a chintzy desk, an Afghan rug on the floor with two chairs in front of it. The office was dusty and hot, despite an air conditioner gently humming on the opposite wall.

Steve closed the door behind him and moved to one of the chairs in the sparsely adorned, windowless office lit by a ceiling-mounted fluorescent light. "Sir, you got a minute?" Ballentine looked at him somewhat annoyed, as if he hadn't given permission for Steve to sit. Steve got right to the point. "Sir, I think we need to relieve Marko for his conduct during the op."

"I make that decision. It's not a 'we.'" He added air quotes with his fingers for emphasis.

"Yes, sir."

"Though, now I'm curious. Why do you say that?" Ballentine leaned back in his squeaky chair.

"He froze up during the fight and didn't lead his team. Even before Luke was killed, he never got out of the vehicle. He isn't up to the job."

"It's hard out here for everyone. Maybe he was in shock by everything," Ballentine acknowledged, a slight jut to his lower lip.

"Marko didn't provide me any radio communications. He was nonexistent as a leader. Iceman took over."

"Iceman? Who's that?"

"Sean Covington, sir. He's a sergeant. Marko's a Gunny."

"I see. Well, Iceman's commendatory actions will be recognized, but I'm not relieving Gunnery Sergeant Pech." Ballentine lightly waved his hands.

"What?" A small rush of adrenaline trickled through him. "Sir—"

"Forget it. People need a break sometimes, and he'll get it while in the hospital in Kandahar. When Marko returns, the best thing to do is get him on a mission and back in the saddle."

"I disagree, he—"

Steve argued his position, further irritating Ballentine who ended the conversation with another wave of his hand. "That's all, Captain. Besides, think how this would look for us. For Marko. Don't be selfish."

Steve's eyes widened. "Selfish, sir?" He controlled his shaking hands, but anger with Ballentine coursed through his veins. People's lives were at stake, and Ballentine didn't care about the repercussions of retaining Marko. Which meant Marko and his conduct were no longer the focus of the conversation.

Ballentine was a master manipulator. Steve's stomach twisted.

"I said, that is all." Ballentine looked back to the paper on his desk.

Steve stood. "That is all, aye, sir!" He turned smartly and left the office before he could be tempted to say or do anything stupid.

**8**

---



On missions, the MSOC operated as a large formation, split into two platoons, with Steve commanding one and Hackett commanding the other. Ballentine ran the show with a smaller HQ element along with a complement of Afghan National Army soldiers. The MSOC fought that way for more than a month. The tether to SF units was released once the company demonstrated competency and Captain Williams endorsed their being able to serve independent of Special Forces oversight.

Williams and his team continued with their own missions. Marko recovered from his concussion and returned from Kandahar. Corporal Pelton, Staff Sergeants Miller and McGuire, the other three Marines wounded alongside Marko during the fight were on their way to the United States due to the severity of their injuries.

One day, Ballentine called Steve into the intelligence center and gave his direction for his next mission. "You're going out on your own to run an operation. In fact, you'll run all of your own operations from this point forward." By contrast, Hackett got the opportunity to do that periodically, but not like Steve was being granted since Hackett always had Afghan troops with him, who were generally considered poor quality. It was a level of trust Steve didn't think Ballentine would grant him.

"Thanks, sir. Awesome." He didn't betray how elated he was with this news.

"Steve, we researched the bomber in the market and who the Taliban field commander was the day Luke was killed. Enemy signals intercepts revealed they were the same person. It was Agha; Objective Tenkara. But there's more."

Steve listened attentively.

"We've also confirmed he personally killed Major Joyce."

This news stoked the fire for revenge in Steve's psyche. His expression tightened

"Don't let this cloud your judgment, Steve. You've got what it takes to go far in the Corps."

"Got it, sir," he demurred, quelling his own sense of fury.

Ballentine nodded. "Nathan and his intel crew think they've found Tenkara's compound. I want you to take your guys on a capture-kill mission and go get him. Any questions?"

"No, sir. I'll brief you when I'm finished talking to my guys."

"Good man." Ballentine nodded again, and Steve left to assemble his team.

# 9

While Brian and the team leaders prepared for the mission, Steve went to the company offices to examine the intelligence assembled on Agha.

He rested against the edge of the table facing the wall on which the spider diagram was tacked and studied each picture, trying to understand his adversaries.

"What're you looking at, Steve."

Steve turned to see Nathan Caldwell behind him. "Just who we're up against. Got any updated news, Nathan?"

Nathan sat down beside him. "About Agha? Well, let's see. He's 48, which makes him old by Afghan standards. He regards any Afghan government reps or forces as puppets of American imperialists. To his mind, only the traditional, complicated Afghan tribal structures can govern the country, and they should be left to do that. He's also fiercely religious, and the Taliban allow him to further his own means under their non-secular directives. In another era, he would've been a warlord, but the Taliban offered him an avenue for legitimacy. As a result, he's vehemently anti-American, whom he views as invaders."

"I have to respect him for his sense of patriotism and tenacity for their cause. In his own way, he's a Nationalist, even if he doesn't support the Government of the Islamic Republic of Afghanistan."

Steve focused on Agha's photo. "You're sure he killed Roland?"

"That's what the radio intercepts confirm. He was heard talking about it being Allah's will that he wasn't killed by the American he shot. He'd learned that he'd bested a great warrior. This has only increased his standing with his people. To Agha's men, their leader's a deity."

"Think we'll get him tonight?"

"I hope so. All the indicators are that he is there."

"Good." Steve switched topics. "How's it going working with Ballentine?"

Nathan removed his glasses and cleaned them on his shirttail. "Your boy is a pain in the ass."

Steve laughed. "He's not *my* boy!"

"I'm kidding!"

"It has to be tough dealing with him every day."

"Oh, it is! But I found out some things about him that explains his self-consciousness."

"Like what?"

Nathan finished with his glasses, held them up to check their cleanliness, and put them back on his head. "My brother was two years ahead of him the Naval Academy, and they rowed together. One night, the team had an initiation of sorts for new members, drinking and stuff, you know. Anyway, Ballentine gets drunk, and the senior members of the team start to grill him about his background, and he breaks down. Turns out, he grew up poor on the margins of a small town outside Cincinnati, literally on the wrong side of the tracks. His father left his mother and him along with his younger brother when they were young. She was always on the dole. His brother died of a methamphetamine overdose in high school. Becoming a Marine Corps officer was a way out of abject poverty for Ballentine, but the shame of who he really is has never left him. He tells people he's from Ohio, and that's it."

"Wow. No wonder he's so uptight. That almost makes me feel sorry him."

Nathan gave Steve a side glance. "Almost."

Steve smiled at Nathan. He hadn't considered Nathan's daily interactions with Ballentine and what he experienced as the guy's XO. Steve developed a newfound respect for him. Steve punched him playfully in the arm. "God bless you, Nathan."

"Good luck, Steve." Nathan smiled in return.

# 10



*FOB Prince, Afghanistan—October 7, 2009.*

Steve gathered his Platoon around a briefing table at the company headquarters to inform the twenty-man assault force of their mission. "Gents, tonight we're going in after the Taliban commander and weapons facilitator, Muammar Agha, also known as Objective Tenkara."

Fergus blurted, "I know he's the guy our predecessors were after, but isn't he just another dirt farmer of little consequence?"

Steve crossed his arms. "In most cases, I'd agree with you."

"But?" Marko asked.

Steve nodded to Agha's photo on the wall, his arms still crossed. "Tenkara is evil, even by Afghan standards." He pointed at the picture with an outstretched hand for emphasis. "He dressed up like a border patrol policeman and got assigned to a checkpoint. He poisoned fourteen people with a sedative he put in their evening meal and killed them in their sleep. Then he cut off their genitals and stuffed their cocks in their mouths."

People murmured in outrage and disgust. Marko raised a brow, and Brian recoiled. "Damn! What an animal!"

"That's not all." Steve continued, calming everyone. "Last week, Agha and his goons ambushed a convoy of Afghan soldiers. They took twenty prisoners, forced them to take off their body armor, and executed all of them."

"I stand corrected," Fergus acquiesced.

Steve looked at him, then back to his men. "We've also confirmed he was the triggerman who personally killed Major Joyce, that he planted the bomb in the village last month, and that he was also the field commander fighting against us when Luke died."

Marko frowned and said "Jesus. Fuck this guy!"

"Gents, Agha's got to go, and tomorrow night, we're gonna help him make an informed decision."

"Visit us before we visit you! Right, skipper?!" Fergus quipped.

Steve nodded. "We'll get some sleep this afternoon, then depart at night and move under cover of darkness to make the best progress through enemy territory. When the bad guys wake up, we'll be in their backyards. Got it? Good. Now, get to it."

The men turned to assemble their equipment and loaded it into vehicles to conduct the raid.

They woke at midnight, but Steve got hardly any restful sleep. He'd waited months for another opportunity to get Agha. Excitement thrummed through his veins.

Hackett walked with him to their staging area. "Going out on your own, away from Ballentine?! You lucky bastard!" He shook Steve's hand, smiling in a warm but serious way.

"See you in a few days!" Steve smiled back.

"Bring Tenkara back, dead or alive!" Hackett yelled over the noise of the GMVs diesel engines starting up.

Steve gave him a thumbs up and moved down the line to shake hands with each of member of the assault force. He did so with each of Hackett's men, too, who supported them as gunners and drivers so the DASR could operate as a cohesive unit. He always shook their hands and tried to say good things to them.

Other members of the MSOC joined them as well, including Ballentine, who stood to one side.

Shaking hands with your mates was a sign of fraternity, the warrior bond. One never knew what might happen to their friends, if that was the last time they might see someone. And they didn't know the same of you. No one wanted to die alone. Everyone hoped someone would give a shit about them afterward.

At the appointed time, Steve wordlessly looked at Ballentine, gave the order to the platoon, and their small column drove into the blackness.

After sunrise, they drove for most of the morning and established a secure site in the desert to wait out the afternoon. They needed to be patient. Agha's bed-down location was in a small compound on the outskirts of a village, but still deep in the Green Zone. They didn't have a lot of men, but they had the right ones.

"Success on the battlefield does not depend on the number of men you bring to the fight, but upon who they are." Roland had told him that.

Steve divided his force into two parts. The security team under Brian with Alex and Guido would maintain the cordon. And the assault team, commanded by Marko with Fergus in support, would attack the compound. Steve set aside his misgivings and, second-guessing himself, he considered his conversation with Ballentine and designated Marko's element as the main effort. His headquarters section would manage the assault from a hill overlooking the objective.

When it was fully dark, they mounted up and drove to a drop-off location three klicks from the compound. When all maneuver units were in place, Steve would drive and establish command and control; quiet and secrecy wouldn't need to be maintained after the raid began.

Under cover of darkness, Alex, Guido, and Brian set the security cordon to isolate the area. Marko and Fergus's teams crept forward toward the compound, and after what seemed an eternity, Marko's team reached the door of the compound; Fergus established his team just outside of it.

Marko reported in a soft tone on the radio, *"Rogue-Two-Zero, Rogue-One-Zero. We're at the compound entrance and setting breach."*

Steve gave the order to commence. "Roger. Execute."

# 12



Marko called, *"BREACHING! BREACHING! BREACHING!"* Followed by a large explosion.

Steve's vehicle drove as fast as possible to the overwatch position. From his vantage point, through his NODs Steve saw the main gate buckle under the pressure of the explosive charge. A burst of gunfire from within it ripped through the open doorway and hit the lead breacher. He went down.

Marko and his team attempted making entry into the compound and the enemy delivered a withering volume of fire. Through NODs, lasers and suppressed rounds flew, and Steve witnessed another Marine go down. Someone ran to the stricken casualties, returned fire, and dragged them to safety.

Marko's voice rose to a higher pitch as he yelled into the radio, *"We've got two casualties! WE'RE GETTING THE SHIT SHOT OUT OF US! We need to extract and reduce the compound with an airstrike!"*

***

Steve shouted, "I'm calling in a TIC! Fruit Bat, get our CAS in the overhead for a run in. We may need a bomb on that compound."

"Roger that. I'll get us some close air support."

Steve finished calling in the TIC and keyed the handset to call Marko. "Rogue-Two-Zero, this is Rogue-One-Zero. Sitrep, over!"

"*Bro; Iceman and Murtaugh, WIA! Taking fire.*" Marko sounded panicked.

"Calm down! I need a sitrep. Now!"

Marko stammered, almost hyperventilating. "*W-we gotta pull back! Holy shit!*"

"Rogue Two-Zero, get it together! I need you to lead!"

The radio went silent. Steve scanned the night landscape. The staccato of gunfire carried in the night. The low concussion of a grenade was seen, then heard, the flash coming from inside the compound. Things were getting worse.

Marko came back on the radio. His voice rattled between breaths. "*W-we got everyone back out of there, but we're pinned down. Request any kind of close air support. Danger-close!*" Danger-close meant that the probability of friendlies being hit or affected by the bomb was as high as that of the enemy. It was an incredible risk, and one that Steve, as the Ground Force Commander, would assume entirely.

Steve took a breath, then keyed the handset. "Confirm you've accounted for all friendly personnel, to include two WIA. Confirm no civilians. Over."

"*Goddamn it! Dude, yes! We have them! And no civilians. We need to get the fuck out of here!*"

Brian now radioed, "*Rogue One-Zero, this compound isn't worth more casualties.*"

"Concur." Steve replied, then unkeyed his handset. He turned to Fruit Bat. "How're we looking on that CAS?"

"They're inbound. They're scanning to confirm location of friendlies."

"I'll have Marko keep the enemy contained. I haven't seen any civilians, have you?" Steve asked.

"No, but I haven't been looking. The shit's hit the fan, ya know?! I'll have the aircraft conduct a scan." Fruit Bat had a downlink from the aircraft's cameras to his computer he could access in real time.

Steve picked up a pair of infrared binoculars from inside his truck and watched his teams withdraw under covering fire from Brian's supporting positions. He said to Fruit Bat, "Good. Let's not add CIVCAS into the mix," using the acronym for civilian casualties.

"OK." Fruit Bat keyed the handset. "Hornet Seven-Two, Rogue One-Zero. Request collateral scan ahead of nine-line. Advise when ready to copy."

The pilot, twenty-five thousand feet above the chaos replied, *"Roger. Commencing scan. Ready to copy."*

Fruit Bat passed the information to conduct the strike. "Good copy, Hornet Seven-Two?"

The pilot responded with a double click of his radio.

Fruit Bat smiled. "Pretty cool!"

"What?"

Fruit Bat laughed. "He acknowledged me with double click! This guy's switched the fuck *on!*"

"Awesome . . ." Steve said sarcastically. He returned to speaking with Marko over the radio. "Rogue Two-Zero, what's your status? Over."

*"We're in a defensive position approximately two hundred and fifty meters west of the compound in defilade terrain with all personnel accounted for. Over."* Marko still sounded anxious. From Steve's elevated position, it appeared they were still under fire but had consolidated in the cover of a makeshift trench line.

Steve watched the spirited fight down below. His men moved and positioned their teams. Alex and Guido's group dispersed and shot down two fighters who exited the compound. Fergus and his team chased three fighters down an adjacent trench line.

"What the fuck?" Steve said out loud. "This is getting ridiculous."

Fruit Bat continued talking to the air support, who were running low on fuel.

Fergus radioed, *"We pushed them out of the trench line! The enemy's on the run toward the Green Zone!"*

"Hold up!" Steve cautioned. "Don't need to get wrapped up in there. We'll take care of them with an airstrike."

*"Roger,"* Fergus replied, but Steve knew from the tone of his voice that Fergus was in the trench line and begging forgiveness for something he was already doing.

***

From Marko's makeshift command post, he radioed Steve, panting heavily. *"We're engaging the enemy right now. But where's that bomb?! We need to drop that compound. NOW!"* Steve watched several members of Marko's team return fire at the enemy shooting at them from the compound.

"How're we coming on the strike, Fruit Bat?" Steve asked, insistent.

"Three minutes out."

"OK. Confirm still no civilians," Steve told him.

"Roger." Fruit Bat called on the radio, "Hornet, Rogue. Confirm no civilians in collateral scan."

The pilot returned, *"No civilians identified. Only combatants firing from the compound. Two minutes out; time on target, one zero."*

"Roger. Thanks. Copy two minutes. TOT one zero." He turned to Steve. "Two minutes out, boss. Time on target, ten after."

"Roger." Steve keyed the handset to talk to Marko. "Rogue Two-Zero. Rogue One-Zero. TOT is one zero. Collateral scan complete. Confirm you're still Troops In Contact and have not seen civilians. Mark your position with an IR strobe. Over."

"*Still in contact. Copy, one zero TOT. No civilians. Mark is out. Over.*" He still sounded unsteady.

"Roger. Still in contact." Steve turned to Fruit Bat. "Marko put out an IR strobe. How're we looking?"

"Yeah, I passed the mark to the pilots. If we don't drop, it'll be at least a five-minute turn around, if they don't run out of gas first."

"OK." Steve scanned through his NODs at the compound. Despite Brian's support, enemy fighters continued firing at Marko and Fergus's positions.

"On final. Thirty seconds." Fruit Bat informed Steve.

He closed his eyes for moment. "Clear 'em hot."

Fruit Bat keyed his handset. "Hornet. Cleared hot—cleared hot—cleared hot."

Steve muttered, "Here we fucking go." He looked intently through the IR binoculars, and his eyes widened. A small group of people, which appeared to be two women and three children, were exiting the back of the compound. One of the women also appeared to be carrying another small child in her arms. "Jesus!" Steve shouted.

"Two away, twenty seconds."

"Oh my God! ABORT! ABORT!" But that wouldn't be possible. The bombs were in the air. There was no way to stop them.

"What?! It's too late!" Fruit Bat shouted. He looked at the feed from the aircraft. "What the fuck, Steve?!"

"We can't change it!" He keyed the handset and spoke to Marko. "Rogue Two-Zero. Rogue One-Zero. Get your heads down; two away and twenty seconds. Danger close! Over."

"*Roger!*"

***

At Steve's position on the hill, he and Fruit Bat observed the impacts. Two five hundred-pound bombs delivered a tremendous explosion followed immediately by another one that lit up the night, vaporizing the compound. The explosions whited out their NODs and illuminated the entire area. Steve turned his NODs back on and tried to scan through the resultant dust and smoke, then switched to the IR binoculars. "Oh, man. That was unreal."

Fruit Bat asked, "Want me to clear dash two?"

"No. Not yet. Tell them to get us a battle damage assessment."

"Roger." Fruit Bat keyed the handset. "Hornet two. Abort, abort, abort. Return to the overhead, conduct BDA scan, and await further tasking. You may be making a run in on same attack geometry. How copy?" The radio clicked twice to indicate the pilot understood.

Steve keyed his handset to contact Marko. "Rogue-Two-Zero. Sitrep, over."

Marko replied. *"W-we're good. That was fuckin' amazing!"*

"Are you still in contact?"

*"No. No fire coming from the compound."* Marko was calmer.

"Roger. Need you to go forward to confirm BDA."

*"Wait, what?! No way! We aren't going back in there!"*

"Rogue Two-Zero, I need an EKIA count, any SSE, and to confirm if objective Tenkara is among the dead. The mission isn't over!"

*"You do it, then!"*

Steve shouted into his radio, "What the *fuck* did you say?! Get in there! I'll join you shortly." He unkeyed the handset, exasperated.

***

Five minutes later, Steve and Fruit Bat examined the scene. The compound was completely leveled. Brian's team remained on security while Marko's and Fergus's teams moved cautiously through the rubble conducting sensitive site exploitation. In the wreckage, they found five dead enemy fighters. Along with the other five in the trench line, that put the count at ten enemy killed in action, but none were Agha.

Steve and Fruit Bat moved to where the civilians were last seen. Marko joined them, turning on a headlamp mounted on his helmet. Stark against the smoke and debris, scarred and scorched in a drab pile of dirt walls lay the shattered bodies of six civilians, including a baby. Two were women. One was a male but was also not Agha. The male was dressed in drab or black and juxtaposed against the backdrop were the colorful robes and shoes of three little children.

Marko clucked his tongue. "Dude. I didn't know." He sounded wooden.

"What?!" Steve snapped. He suspected Marko was lying, or at very least, hadn't done a well enough check to have been able to properly confirm no civilians had been in the area. "How?! You were in here!"

"There's no way I could see them. They must've been in one of the buildings inside the compound."

"I can't believe I killed civilians!" Fruit Bat exclaimed.

"It isn't your fault." Steve clasped his shoulder. "I approved it."

Fruit Bat, tearing up at the site of the three little bodies in the rubble, became more distraught. "Yeah, but I asked what the pilots saw. We should've known about this!" He shrugged off Steve's hand.

"I saw them at the last minute, but the bombs were already in the air. It was too late to call off the strike. Besides, the fighters that opened fire on Iceman and his assault team used them as shields. We did what we could."

Fruit Bat snapped back, "Holy fuck, Steve!" He walked away in disgust, shaking his head. "I'm getting a CASEVAC going for our wounded."

Marko shrugged his shoulders while taking a sip from his Camelback, then wiping his mouth. He spoke nonchalantly. "Bro, shit happens." He was too calm about the situation, which increased Steve's suspicions.

"Marko, it isn't enough to say that 'shit happens.' I'm the ground force commander. I have overall responsibility for this mission and the airstrike, even if there was no way to get those bombs back on the rails. And Agha wasn't fucking here. But I'll have to report it. This is all on me."

Iceman and Murtaugh were put aboard a CASEVAC helicopter after Brian's element secured a landing zone outside of the village. Steve consolidated the rest of the unit, and they drove back in a dark mood to FOB Prince.

Arriving just after sunrise, Steve dreaded his confrontation with Ballentine.

# 13



During their post-mission debrief, they dissected what happened on the mission. As Marko's team placed the explosive breaching charge on the door of the main gate to the compound, one of the fighters heard the commotion and fired a burst from his AK-47 out a window from within the house. The bullets went through the sheet-metal door that the lead breacher, Iceman, had been in front of when he and his secondary, a staff sergeant named Murtaugh, placed the charge. Iceman had gone down as Murtaugh detonated it.

Abdullah was with Marko's team to conduct interpreter work after the compound was secure. He moved forward and lay down fire against the enemy behind the door and maneuvered to assist Iceman, dragging him to safety behind the cover of a wall where a team medic began treating him. With Murtagh also wounded, Fergus moved forward to return fire, covering Abdullah as Murtagh crawled to safety.

After the fight, Murtaugh was flown to Kandahar, then onward to the United States to recover at Walter Reed Medical Center in Washington, D.C. Iceman, however, got it the worst.

Iceman had a young wife and baby at home. He was enthusiastic and enjoyed being an operator. Luke having been a good friend of his, it came as no surprise that he'd been first at the compound to apply the door charge since Agha had supposedly been in that house.

He'd been lying in the compound's entrance while the rest of the team waited outside, themselves pinned down since the first burst, followed by more fire from other fighters primarily directed at them. Murtaugh had tried to push inside the door into the interior of the compound when he was hit, but Murtaugh had been able to crawl back out and get behind cover. Iceman also tried to fight back, but his wounds had been too egregious, and if not for Abdullah, he would have died.

Steve reminisced as a child when he used to play war with his friends and they'd would pretend to be wounded, how they would say that they were fine because they'd only been hit in the arm or leg. What did they know of such things? None of it was real.

Actual wounds were devastating, requiring multiple surgeries, months or years of recovery, and the mental anguish remained long after the physical pain faded. Bones were shattered, along with lives, and some people never really recovered the full use of the limb, as was the case with Iceman, who would later be unable to shake hands due to the massive trauma a single round inflicted on him, the bullet entering his right hand, traveling up his forearm and exiting his elbow. Steve looked at Iceman's arm before he was evacuated and knew the hard part had only begun for the young man.

After his first surgery, Iceman was moved to higher echelons of care until he eventually returned to the United States to Brooks Army Medical Center in San Antonio, Texas. Steve called Iceman's wife and Murtaugh's parents separately to convey his condolences, express his support, and conduct the pantomime he'd developed. He learned that with Luke's parents, even if he was sincere. It never got easier, either.

Nathan and his intel crew later confirmed Agha wasn't at the compound, instead sleeping in another house deeper in the Green Zone. Steve's platoon assaulted what was determined to be an enemy barracks of sorts. Coupled with the CIVCAS and US casualties, the raid didn't achieve its objective and was an intelligence failure.

Fruit Bat had a hard time reconciling what had happened. A similar issue had arisen with a Special Forces Team in another area of the country. The Team Leader and his JTAC were relieved and expelled from theatre as a result. The circumstances were a bit different in that they knew civilians had been there, dropped anyway, and lied about it, but CIVCAS made headlines, and headlines were bad press in a war without clean lines.

Steve complimented his men's performance but acknowledged the enemy might be learning something from them and that their growing losses might become a point to be exploited. But enemy commanders knew who they were up against and reluctantly respected Steve and his men as fellow warriors because of an unwritten code that both sides inherently knew. Still, that didn't mean they didn't want to destroy the Americans.

The debrief finished and Steve's team left to clean their weapons and equipment. Steve grabbed Fergus and indicated he wanted him to remain behind. Just the two of them occupied the briefing room.

Steve crossed his arms. "Tell me what happened after you all pulled back from the compound."

"Marko got us set into a defensive position. Medics stabilized the wounded."

"And how was he?"

"Marko remained seated under cover, his rifle in his lap. He was out of it, kept repeating, 'Fuck. Fuck. Fuck!'"

"So, he wasn't in control?"

Fergus shook his head. "Like I said, he stayed on his ass while we returned fire on a determined enemy. Fuckers nearly kept us pinned down. Marko at least yelled to us to take cover before the bombs fell. We all hit the dirt, me and my team lay flat in the trench line when that shockwave swept over us."

"Then what?

"I heard Marko crying and found him all balled up with his arms around his knees."

"But that was later. You had pursued the enemy in the trench line. Right?"

"Yeah. It was so easy. Like we were on a training range." He acted out the scene. "I shot down three of 'em in rapid succession after another Marine kept their heads down with enfilading fire. One enemy fighter was still alive when my team arrived to process the bodies. I placed the suppressor of my rifle to the fighter's head and pressed the trigger. The wounded guy's brains flew out like cherry pie filling." Fergus chuckled.

Steve studied Fergus. One of the best close-quarter-battle marksmen in the entire unit, he displayed no emotion or remorse and was proud, amused, even. Describing what occurred reflected Fergus's near-robotic and systematic approach to everything he did. Even jumping, his heartrate seemed to stay at a steady forty beats-per-minute.

Fergus finished telling Steve what he'd done to the wounded enemy fighter with a small grin. "No prisoners, eh, skipper?"

Steve looked at him, serious. "Don't tell people about Marko. And never repeat what you did in that trench line ever again to anyone."

"OK, skipper," Fergus replied, a scolded child berated by his father.

# 14



After the platoon debrief, Steve went to Ballentine's office to explain the civilian casualties. Ballentine sat behind his desk. Steve stood.

"CIVCAS?!" Ballentine frowned.

"Yes, sir." Steve's voice was tired.

"How?! Did you know they were there?" Ballentine's tone was accusatory, as if this initial round was perfunctory.

"Only after the bombs were in the air." Steve drew his lips together tightly.

"Shit. This'll look really bad." Ballentine winced.

"For whom, sir?" He didn't have to wonder. He knew what would come out of Ballentine's mouth. But he asked anyway.

"You, mostly. Maybe me, not sure. There'll be an investigation."

"Sir, I made the call based upon the information I had."

"Who was leading the assault?"

"Marko, sir." Steve looked at Ballentine. Would he finally accept the problem with allowing Marko to return to service?

Ballentine raised an eyebrow. "Really? I thought you didn't think he had what it took."

"I don't, but he was the senior Staff NCO I had to do this mission. And, per your admonition, he was still a team leader. I guess I was looking at giving him another chance."

"Hmm. Where was Brian?"

"He was running the security cordon." Steve focused on Ballentine. "Sir, Marko isn't up to the task. We need to relieve him. First for his lack of performance during the firefight when Luke was killed. And now this."

"This is war, Steve," he spoke condescendingly. "Unfortunate things happen. He hasn't done anything wrong. He's learning the ropes as a TL, and no one knows how people will perform in combat. Besides, he's not the one they're going to investigate. Even if it is cursory."

Steve jabbed Ballentine's desktop with his index finger. "Sir! His conduct cost Luke Milam his life, plus several civilians!"

"Seems a bit shortsighted to have Marko take the fall for last night when, perhaps, he hadn't really processed the outcome of the fight in the valley! Maybe you shouldn't have had him out on the mission!"

Steve, shocked, yelled, "I put him out there at *your* direction, and against my better judgment!" He sighed and straightened up. "With Gary Maguire, Miller, Iceman, Murtagh, and that infantry corporal, Pelton, going home to the States, and Marko just back from the hospital, that makes six wounded and two dead incurred by this MSOC, including Major Joyce!"

Ballentine sniffed and sneered, "That's nothing next to what my infantry unit suffered in Fallujah in '03."

"That's the problem, sir," Steve snapped. "You think this is a big competition between SOF and the grunts! We're a raid force, and your 'clearance operation' up the Valley of the Jackal amounted to shit! It got people hurt and killed, and I stand by my request to relieve Marko before it gets worse!"

Ballentine put up his hand, ending the conversation. "Relieving someone for happenstance things is bad for morale. We can't have that. We'll give Marko a rest. Take him off missions for a while. He stays. That is all on this subject, Captain."

Steve's head and neck burned. "Understood, sir." His face tightened when he ground down on his back teeth, seething and tense, but determined to not reveal it to Ballentine.

"Good man. Get all the people who were there to organize their statements." Ballentine wagged his index finger, "We don't want to appear to be hiding anything."

"Will do, sir." Steve snapped to attention.

Ballentine looked down at his desk and away from Steve, then back to him. "You know, your passion for your men is impressive. I'll say it again: if you'd let me mentor you, there's no telling how far you could go." He flashed a droll smile.

"The fuck, sir?" Steve pinched his forehead and bit the inside of his lower lip. The smile, coupled with Ballentine's beguiling approach, struck him as Machiavellian.

Ballentine closed his eyes and rubbed his temples. "Now go prepare your after-action report." He exhaled before looking at Steve again. "Sorry to hear about Iceman and Murtaugh. And good job out there."

Steve turned to leave. "Aye, sir." He left the office in a dejected mood. Ballentine's compliment was an empty cliché.

# 15



*FOB Prince, Afghanistan, October 11, 2009*

A US Army officer named Colonel Malcolm Hutchinson, a bookish, slight man, arrived at the FOB to conduct interviews about the CIVCAS incident. The investigation was indeed sensitive. His not being a Marine or in the direct chain of command would prevent a conflict of interest.

Hutchinson and Steve sat across from each other in folding chairs in the shade outside of the company command post. Steve wore PT gear and running shoes juxtaposed against Hutchinson's tri-color desert camouflage utilities and boots that might have one time been starched.

Hutchinson leaned back in his chair. "My condolences on your casualties, Captain Keller."

"I appreciate it, sir. It's tough. The boys have taken it hard." Steve sat with his forearms on his thighs, his hands clasped in front of him.

Hutchinson nodded. "War is a rough business."

Steve eyed the colonel's Army Special Operations combat patch on his right shoulder, indicating his experience. "Agreed." He nodded twice.

Hutchinson sat forward, placing his elbows on his knees. "So, what happened with the CIVCAS?"

"Sir?" Steve knew what he'd been asked, but he wanted to hear it spoke out loud.

"The civilian casualties resulting from the bomb you dropped. These investigations are a matter of routine, but there are repercussions." Hutchinson waved his hand for emphasis.

"Yes, sir," Steve assented.

Hutchinson pressed, "So, what of it?"

"There was a lot happening, and by the time the bombs hit, I was more focused on saving my own guys than who was in the compound."

"You didn't know those civilians were in there?" Hutchinson sounded skeptical.

"No, sir. Marko would've told me."

"Marko?" Hutchinson raised his chin.

"My assault team leader, Gunnery Sergeant Marko Pech, sir."

"I see. I just mean, it wasn't one or two people. There was a baby."

"I saw, I was there, sir."

Hutchinson sighed. "Captain, cut the bullshit. I'm not asking you to tell me something I want to hear. I'm also not telling you to tell me something you don't believe. I want the truth."

In a flashback, Steve saw himself at his MARSOC board answering Roland's question about his integrity. He exhaled before answering. "The truth is, we went onto an objective at night to capture a high-value target, got into a hot fire-fight where two of my men were wounded, and to extract from that situation, I cleared bombs hot from the aircraft. That there were civilians in that compound wasn't known at the time, and there was no way we could've known under those circumstances."

"And Gunnery Sergeant Pech, the assault element leader, didn't know?" Hutchinson pressed.

"No, sir. He didn't." Steve looked to the side. He felt nervous and guilty. He'd just compromised his integrity. He didn't like lying, even if it was for one of his men. But he couldn't take it back.

Hutchinson wasn't convinced. "You're sure?"

"Sir, I know it looks bad, but it was all we could do." Steve accepted defending his position, even if he knew the truth. Still, he'd just betrayed his own code. The guilt nagged at him, but he suppressed those feelings.

"OK, I see." Hutchinson eased his interrogation and made notes in his notebook.

Steve stood to leave. "Anything else, sir?"

"No, that's fine, Captain." He resumed writing in his notebook.

"Thanks, sir." Steve came to attention, turned, and left smartly.

# 16



Thinking of the interview and awaiting the outcome of Hutchinson's investigation, Steve was uneasy. He sat in the chow hall sipping on a cup of coffee. It wasn't a very good blend, but it was readily available. He wrote in his journal, trying to capture the emotions of the past few weeks, and set down his pen to ruminate more on Roland's death and the mounting losses his platoon sustained. He broke from his pensive analysis when the screened chow hall door slammed shut under its spring-loaded weight.

Steve looked up to see Marko.

"Hey, boss," he said, pouring his own cup of coffee from the brown plastic tureen.

"Marko." Steve returned. "Hutchinson get with you yet?"

"Yeah. I just got done talking to him." He tightened his lips.

"And?"

Marko kept his back to Steve as he opened a package of creamer. "And nothing. I told him what went down."

"OK. I guess we'll just see what happens."

"Well, we sure fucked those guys up, yeah?" Marko said, self-satisfied.

Steve held his tongue; Marko had hardly been active during the fight. Steve thought of Marko's team, who maintained a good front to act as if he was a good decision maker, that he was in charge. They did it straight-faced and performed well despite him. The frustrating thing was Marko's team had very good people on it. Including Iceman, and unlike Marko, was trustworthy. But Iceman was in the hospital.

Considering everything to date, Steve was weary and hesitated to argue with Marko about his performance, his skills as an operator aside, the civilian casualties being another issue altogether. Marko also didn't know what was happening between Steve and Ballentine, but Steve's sense of objectivity made him feel guilty for not telling Marko about his reservations. His own moral cowardice made him cringe.

He'd screwed up the courage to say something when Marko turned to him. "Sir, I have a question."

Steve raised an eyebrow. Marko rarely called him that.

Marko mixed his coffee with a small wooden stirrer and tossed it into the trash. "Do the Taliban lawyers come and investigate them for CIVCAS or any of the shit they do or get into?" Marko sounded caustic.

"Funny," Steve said evenly.

"I'm half serious. For all the shit we go through, I've never seen a Taliban lawyer in any town we've been in, ya know?" Marko exhibited a confidence Steve hadn't seen before. It was disarming.

He looked away from Marko for a moment, then straight at him again. "We have to play by the rules."

Marko sipped his coffee, looking at Steve over the brim, then left the chow hall.

# 17



The CIVCAS incident meant the entire company didn't conduct operations for two weeks. Steve sat on a bench loading 5.56 mm cartridges into rifle magazines. It was a tedious but easy chore, and he enjoyed the early evening. A nonalcoholic beer rested next to him, rivulets of warm condensation sliding down the can and forming a wet circle on the wooden bench. An ammunition can full of loose rounds sat on the ground at Steve's feet.

Reaching into the can for more cartridges, Steve paused. He thought of the bodies of the Afghan civilians in the rubble after the airstrike, of the dead children. How could he ever explain what happened to his own children? He couldn't characterize what he'd done—accidental or not—in any way to develop an acceptable vindication.

Ballentine approached, smoking a cigar. "Got some good news for you," he said.

"Oh?" Steve looked up at him, shaken from his internal deliberation.

"CIVCAS investigation is complete. Hutchinson said that you, Fruit Bat, and Marko were not found culpable. You guys are exonerated." Ballentine sounded excited but more like he was relieved things wouldn't affect him.

"Wow." Steve paused loading the magazines to sip from his near beer.

Ballentine snorted, "That's it? 'Wow'? Thought you'd be more excited than that."

"That investigation shut us down, sir. We haven't been out in two weeks." Steve finished loading the last of his rounds into a 30-round mag.

"You guys needed the rest."

"Sure. And there are still six dead civilians, regardless." Steve exhaled. He stacked six full magazines to the side before reaching down and closing the ammunition can, latching it shut.

"We'll get you back out there." Ballentine dragged on his cigar and exhaled upwards. He opened a small case and withdrew one, cut the end, and offered it to Steve. Steve examined it for a moment, marveling Ballentine made no mention of the dead Afghans. Still, he accepted it, lit it with Ballentine's lighter, and said nothing.

Puffing on their cigars, they looked out onto the dusty landscape. Steve took a sip from his beer, but it was hot and bitter. He spit the residual of the lukewarm liquid into the dust.

# 18



*Southern Afghanistan, November 4, 2009*

The company regained approval to go out on missions. Steve gathered his platoon to brief the patrol order for a three-day patrol deep into enemy territory. Satisfied with their preparation, the Marines went to bed for the rest of the day.

They departed at one-thirty in the morning and drove until sunrise where they took a security break. Then they spent the day ranging from that base of operations conducting reconnaissance. It was uneventful, but a fight could erupt at any time.

In the late afternoon, Brian's part of the column came under attack. First it was sporadic fire, then it increased. Steve, Marko, and Fergus established his command post on a high hill overlooking a valley. He directed Brian to take his part of the unit with Alex and Guido to locate the enemy at the edge of the Green Zone at a compound from which they were taking fire.

Steve opened a TIC and watched their progress. The shots from the compound were heavy for a moment, and Brian's section immediately returned fire from their vehicles until they gained superiority and the enemy broke contact to the safety of the Green Zone.

Brian called over the radio, *"Rogue One-Zero, this is Rogue One-Two. We've gained entry the compound to our East. Request you come here when able. How copy?"*

"Solid Copy, One-Two. I can see you. Give us a minute, and we'll be there. Over." Steve replied, then closed the TIC.

*"OK. You gotta see this."* Brian replied.

Steve and his vehicle crew drove to Brian's location. He met Steve outside. "What's up, man?" Steve asked.

Brian ushered him inside. "Just wait." Walking with him, Brian took Steve to a part of the compound set up to receive wounded personnel. Steve assessed it; it was no ordinary treatment facility. It was supplied with gauze, blood clotting agents, IV bags, two operating tables that doubled as beds, and even had antibiotics and other drugs inside metal and glass medical cabinets. Whomever would treat someone in that compound for a battlefield wound or otherwise would have to know what they were doing. Steve was unaware of any Afghans living in rural areas with that kind of sophisticated medical training.

"Who uses this place?" Steve wondered, examining the inside of the clinic. It was more of a field hospital, though there wasn't any evidence of recent casualties having been treated there. The place had a sterility Steve also hadn't encountered, such as it was, since fine particulate dust still covered everything. Looking at the IV carriers by the beds he said, "I wouldn't want an IV in this place!"

"You wouldn't care if it was all you could get," Brian observed.

"That's true, but I'd prefer not to have hep C, at a minimum." Steve laughed. He continued examining the room, impressed with its inventory as he looked through various drawers and cabinets. It was well organized. "Who put this thing together?"

"No idea, but it's pretty slick for being out here, right? What shall we do with it? Call it in?"

"No." Steve thought of the Taliban, of the enemy the facility would support. He thought of his wounded men and the dead. He disconnected himself for a moment from the dark anger welling within him. "Burn it." It wasn't a suggestion.

"What?!" Brian's eyes widened. "Sir, we can't do that! This clinic might be for locals; it may be all they have!"

"Seriously, Brian?! You took fire from this compound. Look around you!" Steve swept his hand across the room. "It's not like they treat their own people here. They came to us after the market was bombed, remember?! This is an enemy medical aid station. It provides them the ability to keep fighters in the fight!"

"Doing this is against the Geneva Convention. We can't destroy a medical treatment facility any more than they could do it to us!"

"Are you fucking serious?! The enemy doesn't follow the Geneva Convention! They kill their own people; they've killed our people, to include Major Joyce and Luke. Fuck them!" Steve nearly screamed.

"WHAT?!" Brian came back, incredulous. "We're supposed to be held to a higher standard! You even said it!"

"Brian," Steve grew calmer, "would they let us keep this place if the roles were reversed?"

Brian stared at him. "Probably not. They'd loot it for what they could use . . ." He didn't disguise his frustration. "But I think you're taking a turn on this you shouldn't, and I don't want any part of it if you do. We're US Marines, not the Waffen SS!"

Steve studied him, then surveyed the room once more. Brian was right. "Get your guys loaded up. We'll head to the RV, and I'll call it in." He scuffed his boot on the floor and swore as he left the clinic. "Goddamn it."

# 19



*Southern Afghanistan, November 5, 2009*

The platoon mounted their GMVs and departed to set into a patrol base for the evening. The enemy fired a few more shots at them that likely wouldn't hit, but no one wanted to test the theory of what a lucky bullet would do to any of them. Twenty minutes later, they arrived at the rendezvous point.

Brian exited his vehicle and confronted Steve. "What the fuck was that, sir?"

Steve removed his helmet. "If you want to talk, Master Sergeant Geraghty, we can go out in the desert away from here." The entire platoon were looking at them.

"Roger, that, SIR!" Brian replied disrespectfully.

The two of them walked a good distance away from the rest of the unit, all of whom watched their leadership in a heated exchange.

Brian spoke first. "Really? You pulling *rank* on me out here?!"

Steve recoiled. "Watch what you say and when you say it."

"Fuck!" Brian swore.

"Just remember who we are, regardless of familiarity. I know you're pissed." Steve kept his voice even.

"Do you?! I can't believe you were gonna do that!" Brian pointed at him with an open hand.

"You saw the situation, the bind it put me in, and—"

"You're justifying behavior out of revenge, Steve!"

"That's . . . true." Steve admitted. "But only due to the circumstances. Put yourself in my shoes."

Brian rolled his eyes. "Like hell! I can't believe it. What if you'd done it? Then, what if the boys were to follow your example? Where would it end? It would only have gotten worse. What would you have done then, sir?"

"Let's not get too hypothetical. It was the right call to pull away from that compound," Steve said, admonished.

Brian stared at him. "Only *after* I talked you out of it. So, yeah, you did make a good choice, just like you did with Marko."

"WHAT?! This is totally different!"

Brian stepped forward, getting close to Steve's face. "Bullshit! If I hadn't been here, you would've done it in direct violation of the Laws of Armed Conflict! That kind of shit isn't something I want to explain to my own girls. Do you REALLY want to have that on your conscience?!"

Steve leaned toward him in return. "Fuck you! You have NO idea who they treat in that compound!"

Brain took a step back. "I know you're upset, but letting the heat of battle and internal aggression take over is no substitute for clear thinking and solid leadership. I think you're slipping, sir. Don't lose your edge! Don't lose sight of what we're doing here. We're the *fucking good* guys!"

Steve put his hands out to his sides. "It's not that way—"

"Whatever!" Brian turned and stormed off, helmet in hand. Mid-stride, he turned back to Steve and blurted, "When we get back, I'm transferring to Ballentine's element!"

# 20



*FOB Prince, Afghanistan, November 7, 2009*

They returned from the patrol in the evening.

Changed in clean jeans, a T-shirt, and a hooded sweatshirt, Steve sat on a bench in front of their quarters playing his guitar. He was mentally distracted, however, ruminating over his confrontation with Brian. He *was* slipping out there, that much he acknowledged, but was he really losing his edge? Was that the perception people had of him? He didn't want that to be true, and he also wanted to be honest with himself.

He considered the weight of leadership, along with the ramifications of decisions. Was that what Roland meant when he told Steve he'd been "born to do this job"?

Ten minutes later, now clean and dressed in PT gear and flip flops, Brian found Steve strumming "Peaceful Easy Feeling" by the Eagles. "Hey, sir. Got a minute?"

Steve stopped playing. "Hey. Sure. What's up?" He put the guitar down next to him.

Brian looked to the side, then back to him. "I don't want that transfer."

"No?" Steve perked up, relieved.

"No. I thought over things and, regarding our losses and the enemy, I see where you were coming from." That was a big admission for Brian; he could be prideful.

Steve breathed a little easier. "That still doesn't give us permission to do things like that. I'm glad you talked me out of it, Brian. You and I are a good check and balance to the other. Thank you for being a voice of reason." It was Steve's best attempt at an apology.

"No thanks needed. You're a good officer and a good platoon commander. You're worth your salt." Brian extended his hand.

Steve stood and shook it while looking Brian in the eye. When Brian walked away, Steve resumed his seat, slightly stunned.

Brian would know if he was worth his salt.

Steve reflected on ancient origin of that statement. On the island of Malta, there are small pools cut into the granite coastlines to collect sea water on the high tides of the Mediterranean. The water pools in those collecting basins and evaporates, leaving behind salt that is fresh, flaky, and of the best taste anywhere. During the Roman occupation of Malta, that salt had to be collected and was used to feed Legionnaires their daily salt rations. It was said that if you were a good soldier, you were worth your salt; you'd earned it. The highest of praise, not easily provided and only delivered as deserved. And that coming from Brian, one of the most reserved of people . . .

Steve compared it with when Elena told him before he'd left for deployment that he was too distant and didn't value her as much as his job. Both sunk in deep.

Brian's compliment was one he wasn't sure he deserved, and of Elena's comment, he wasn't convinced he didn't deserve it. *Why is it all so intertwined?* He wagered he might be the only person that thought that way, and he hoped so, since it was such a tortuous mindset.

# 21

*Southern Afghanistan, November 15, 2009*

Steve and his assault platoon embarked on another independent patrol, traveling for three days through the Afghan desert. The enemy engaged them on two occasions, but a TIC wasn't necessary in either case. When the Marines stopped for any protracted period, they circled their six vehicles in a desert laager site to rest and refit in an isolated location with extended visibility and good fields of fire in case they had to defend themselves. After a long movement, they rested for a day. Most of the platoon tended to tasks such as weapons cleaning or basic vehicle maintenance. All were dusty and dirty from campaigning. They and their vehicles looked like shit.

McConnell sat in the turret resting his arm on his M2 .50 Caliber machine gun, a pair of binoculars close to hand. He scanned the horizon for enemy activity idly munching on MRE crackers. A radio handset connected to the vehicle was clipped on a strap so he could respond to any traffic. Steve, Grimace, Abdullah, Fruit Bat, and Hoyle all rested on the ground in the shade of the truck.

"Hey, Fruit Bat?" McConnell called down from his perch in the turret.

"Hmm, what?" Fruit Bat said drowsily.

"Where're you from?" McConnell scanned a moment with the binoculars, then set them down.

"You woke me up for that?"

"Just askin'." McConnell shrugged.

"Miami. My mom's Cuban and my dad's from Trinidad. How about you?" Fruit Bat kept his eyes closed.

"I'm from the Bronx, New York City," McConnell said proudly.

Fruit Bat muttered, "I knew you were from New York."

"No, I'm from *the city!*"

"Fine. Now let me go back to bed."

"Why'd they call you 'Fruit Bat'?"

He sighed. "Jesus. The questions. I was flying Harriers with the Spanish a few years ago, and they asked what my call sign was. All of them had ones like 'Tiger' or 'Lion Heart' or 'Shark.' So, I told them I was a ferocious animal, a 'Fruit Bat.' They didn't know what it was. My guys thought it was funny. It stuck."

"DUDE! That's hilarious!" McConnell laughed.

The radio crackled next to McConnell. *Rogue One-zero, this is Rogue-Six. Over?"*

He reached for the handset as Ballentine's voice emitted from it. McConnell answered in his thick New York accent. "Rogue Six, this is Rogue One-Zero, Roger."

*"Roger, Rogue One-Zero. Put Rogue One-Zero actual on the net. Over."*

McConnel replied, "Roger." He unkeyed the handset and called down to Steve, "Sir? You need to get on the net. Rogue Six is callin'."

Steve sat up on his poncho liner, groggy. "OK, OK. I'm up." He climbed into the vehicle. McConnell passed down the handset. Steve pulled out a notebook and pen before keying the handset. A brief exchange ensued; the details unclear. Finished, Steve handed the handset back to McConnell and exited the vehicle. He shook his crew awake.

Grimace stretched. "What's up?"

Steve winked. "Get Brian and the team leaders over here now."

# 22



Steve spread a map out on the hood of his truck and assembled Guido, Fergus, Alex, Marko, and Brian around the map. All were in various stages of undress, most in utility trousers and T-shirts with a pistol or rifle. The rest of Steve's vehicle crew listened in on the brief, McConnell in the turret, Fruit Bat and Grimace sitting on the roof with Hoyle in the driver's seat with his door open.

"What do ya got, sir?" Brian asked.

Steve smiled. "Just received word from Ballentine that Tenkara is in a village six klicks from here."

"No shit?" Fergus asked.

"No shit," Steve confirmed.

Alex asked excitedly, "We gonna go get him?!"

Steve nodded. "We've been tasked with capturing him, if able."

Guido smirked. "That's 'if able.'"

Steve looked at him. "If anyone wants him dead, it's me. But you know we don't do that. It'd be good to get him alive."

"I know, I know." Guido held his hands out in resignation.

"So, what we're going to do is this: Brian, you, Alex, and Marko are going to take your three vehicles to the south, down and around this village and set up a blocking position here." He indicated the location on the map with the tip of his knife. "While me, Fergus, and Guido wait here for a half hour, then move on to the village to isolate his building and capture Tenkara."

"Won't he be alerted by our movement?" Marko asked, his tone not hiding his frustration at being assigned to the security element, probably viewing it as a demotion.

Fergus added, "Yeah, and how many guys are on the objective?"

Steve looked at Marko. "There are a lot of vehicles moving around out here, so they may not be paying too much attention if we don't get too close, too fast. Timing will be key." He turned to Fergus. "And I don't know. I'm not that comfortable with going after Tenkara in daylight, but we know he's here now, and he may not be later. We have to try."

Fergus half winked. "Just like the other time?! Fuck, skipper, this sounds risky. And fun!"

"You're crazy, you dumb Mick." Alex quipped. "Do you know that?"

Fergus shrugged. "Yep."

"Where's he located in the village?" Brian cut in, refocusing the brief.

Steve again indicated to the map with his knife. "That's what makes this doable. The building is on the outskirts of the village, not in dense compounds, so we have a pretty good shot at him."

"OK."

"I want you to go back and brief your teams, then come back to me in half an hour for a final synch and radio checks. Then, Brian, you'll step off. Questions?" He looked at his leaders faces. There were none. He nodded and said, "Let's go."

All departed for their respective vehicles.

Brian stayed back to talk with Steve. "You're sending Marko with me?"

"I need someone I trust to keep an eye on him."

"That aside, do you think this is wise? Us going into the village after Tenkara?"

"I wanna get this bastard," Steve said.

"Everyone does, sir."

Steve drew his lips into a tight line. "Just go get in your truck, OK?"

Brian stared at Steve for a long moment. "Yes, sir." He nodded and strolled to his vehicle.

Steve finalized the plan, and he the key leaders met a final time. He briefed Ballentine over the radio, and he approved Steve's proposal. Radio checks were conducted, and Steve shook Brian, Alex, and Marko's hands, then they mounted up for the drive south.

They departed, and Steve looked into the clear blue sky. An enormous bird of prey, an Afghan Golden Eagle with a giant wingspan, circled above them. He pointed it out to McConnell. "You see that, Mac?"

He looked up, shielding his eyes with one hand. "Yes, sir. Where'd it come from? It's huge!"

"It is! And I dunno. The bigger question is what does it eat?"

McConnell rubbed his chin and frowned. "Small animals. Kids. Who fuckin' knows?"

They chuckled as they looked at the circling bird while Brian and his three vehicles melded into the dust.

# 23



Steve's section of three vehicles moved through the desert toward Tenkara's location.

The radio crackled. It was Brian. *"We're set. Very little activity in the village. Over."*

Steve passed the message to the occupants of his vehicle over the noise of the engine. All rode in silence otherwise.

On the outskirts of the village, Steve's vehicle stopped on the high ground above Tenkara's potential location, from which snaked a spur that led deeper into the village and Green Zone. The objective was a single dwelling inside of an eight-foot compound wall constructed of Afghan mud. The compound had a sheet metal door, but the building looked unfinished. It didn't have glass windows or other solid doors, only holes open to the elements. A road led from the compound below, down and toward the spur, around a curve, and disappeared between two hills.

Steve called to Brian on the radio. "We're in position. Going to begin movement in two minutes." They began to dismount when small arms fire came from the compound. Steve keyed the radio to Brian. "We're taking fire!" Then he yelled to Fergus and Guido, "GO! Get in that compound!"

Fergus and Guido drove their vehicles to the edge of the walls and deployed their teams to make entry. The door was unlocked, and Guido's team entered while Fergus covered them. Steve's vehicle followed to just outside the compound. Hoyle, Fruit Bat, and McConnell remained in the vehicle. Steve, Grimace, and Abdullah jumped from it and moved to the outer wall. Small groups of women and children began leaving the village.

Steve yelled to Guido, "Let me know when we can come in." He turned to Grimace, "You see all those people leaving?"

Grimace nodded. "Yep. Sure sign we're gonna get in the shit."

Behind the wall was a small house. Like the building in the compound, there was no door or windows, but its empty holes were covered by colorful cloths hung on the inside. They swayed with a slight desert breeze. Noises came from inside the house, and Steve motioned to Grimace and Abdullah to follow him.

Grimace moved to the edge of the doorway, covering it with his rifle. Steve stepped behind him and withdrew a grenade from a pouch on his vest. He removed the safety tape and wire from the spoon and held it in his right hand. He squeezed Grimace's arm to let him know the grenade was ready and then gripped the ring on the pin with his left index finger, the last stage of safety before arming it. If he employed it, it would explode in less than five seconds.

"Abdullah, tell whoever's in there to come out!" Steve's voice was even, though he was sweating. Grimace remained focused on the doorway. Abdullah repeated the order several times when the voice of a young boy called back to him. Steve breathed a little easier, though he knew anyone could be inside the building.

"He says he's afraid," Abdullah translated.

"Ask him if there are any other people inside; any weapons?"

Abdullah conversed with the young man. "He says he's the only one. There are no weapons. He's scared and will not come out." From inside came the cry of a baby.

"Tell 'em to get the fuck out here!" Grimace snarled, not taking his eyes off the doorway.

Abdullah spoke more firmly and a young boy, about thirteen, emerged from the hut, followed by two girls about eight-years-old and three women in burkas. One of the women held a baby.

Steve eased the tension on the grenade, firmly reseating the pin and replacing the safety wire with a spare he kept in a small pocket on his trousers. Checking it, he returned it to its pouch. "Tell them to leave and follow the rest." Abdullah relayed this, and they departed.

"Whew . . . that was close." Steve exhaled.

"No shit," Grimace agreed.

Brian came over the radio. *"A large number of women and kids are leaving the village. It's like the book of Exodus."*

"Roger. We sent a few more out of the village," Steve replied, then turned to Grimace, "God, I hope Tenkara's here. I don't want to get stuck in a fight."

Guido shouted from inside the compound, "Come on in, sir!"

Steve, Grimace, and Abdullah entered and jogged into a single building. Its interior was dark save streams of fading sunlight coming through the open windows, flecks of dust hanging in the air, turning the light into dirty shards. An AK-47 assault rifle leaned against a wall. On the dirt floor were four expended copper shell casings. Separated from it and standing in a corner while being covered by one of Guido's Marines, sat a skinny fifteen-year-old kid, trying to look stoic and tough but got nervous when Steve and Grimace entered the room. Steve's eyes swept the space.

He spoke to Guido. "Find anyone else?"

"Nope." Guido gestured to the kid. "Just him."

Steve glanced at the boy. "Grimace, you and Abdullah chat with him." He turned to Guido, pointing at the AK. "Come with me. And disable that weapon." Guido grabbed the AK-47 from the wall as he and Steve exited. He deftly unloaded it, removing the bolt and spring. He threw them over the wall into the dirt, rendering the rifle unusable. "Good call, boss."

"Can't have them using it against us. What else did you find? Anything?"

Guido slightly shook his head. "Nah. Nothing else is in the building. We got here, and the kid was just standing there. It was weird."

"He was left behind to distract us. There were a bunch of women and children leaving as we arrived. Tenkara might've been with them. Either way, he ain't here." Steve looked at the inside of the compound walls.

"Damn."

Loud voices emitted from the building, Abdullah yelling at the Afghan kid. Steve went inside to see Grimace glaring at the kid as he held him off the ground by his shoulders. His massive hands engulfed the boy's slender frame.

"What's up, Grimace?" Steve asked.

"He says he doesn't know anything." Grimace scowled.

"Yeah, he does. Abdullah?"

"Yes, sir?" He stood ready to relay.

"You tell him this: the guy holding you is entirely loyal to me. Do you know why?"

Abdullah translated, and the boy answered in hurried Pashtu. "He says he does not." He looked at the kid. The kid looked at Abdullah, to Steve, then to Grimace, who grinned evilly.

Steve stepped closer to the kid, then spoke matter-of-factly while glaring at him. "Because to work for me, he had to kill a member of his own family. If he did that, what do you think will happen to you when I leave this room?"

The youth's eyes widened to tea-cup size as Abdullah translated.

Desultory gunfire was heard outside of the compound, then more to the south near Brian's position. Steve yelled at the kid, "TELL US WHAT WE WANT TO KNOW!" With that, Steve left the room as the kid blathered in quick, panicked tones.

After a moment, the kid sprinted out of the compound and into the desert, following the path of the other women and children.

Grimace came out smiling. "Nice one, sir."

Steve shrugged. "Had to get creative. What do we know?"

"Like you said, the kid was a remain behind. Tenkara boogied five minutes ahead of us, but he's still in the area. This village is a Taliban hotbed. There are a lot of fighters here." Grimace gestured across the expanse of the village toward the Green Zone.

Steve raised an eyebrow when his radio crackled. It was Brian, *"One-Zero, we're in a fight. It's picking up."*

"Roger," Steve returned.

Guido came in from outside, breathless. "Fergus saw Tenkara! He's pursuing him, and his team's engaged up on the hill! I'm taking my team to help him!"

"Go!" Steve ordered.

Guido took his vehicle to join Fergus at the top of the hill. They dismounted their teams and moved forward toward where they were taking small arms fire. The closer they got, the more the enemy fire intensified, indicating a concentration of enemy fighters.

Steve, Grimace, and Abdullah arrived at their truck. Hoyle kept it running, and from the turret, McConnell actively scanned in front of him. Fruit Bat spoke on his own radio in anticipation of needing air support.

Opening the front passenger door, Steve grabbed his handset and knelt behind the door for cover, his rifle slung across his chest. "I'm calling in a TIC!" He keyed the handset—BOOM! BOOM! BOOM!

Grimace fired his M4 carbine right past him. Steve recoiled and dropped the handset, his eardrum ringing. He turned to Grimace with an annoyed scowl while remaining on a knee. "WHAT THE FUCK! I'm on the radio!"

Grimace yelled, "RPG!"

Steve's ears rung, and the world slowed to a crawl. Grimace pointed at an Afghan fighter one hundred yards away pointing an RPG at them. The fighter was dressed in a burgundy robe with a black turban, his angry, tanned face squinted as he aimed.

Steve rested his own M4 in the space between the door and the vehicle and, through the sight of his rifle, the red dot of it settled on the chest of the RPG gunner. He fired twice. The spent shell casings ejected in slow motion, the hint of cordite lingering in the air.

The Afghan fell backward, launching the RPG rocket into the air in a cloud of dust. The rocket arched into the sky, sailed over them, and exploded directly behind Steve's vehicle. Hot shrapnel ricocheted off the gun truck. Grimace slapped him on the back. McConnell opened fire with his .50 caliber machine gun, the recoil rocking the truck on its springs, brass and disintegrating link ejected from the gun and rolled off the truck into the dirt. Steve looked up into the sky, and through the haze of smoke and dust caused by the battle, circled the enormous Golden Eagle.

Steve keyed his radio handset. "Serpent Seven-One, this is Rogue Two-Zero, we're Troops In Contact, time now! Over!"

# 24



*Southern Afghanistan, November 15, 2009*

At his truck, Steve stood up, the door still open. He watched Fergus crest the top of the first hill. "Oh, shit!" he said, observing the hilltops in front of them.

Grimace, standing behind him, asked, "What's up?"

Steve pointed. "Check this out! The two hills ahead of them are actually a combined trench line!" Taliban fighters moved through them as McConnell fired from the turret at the enemy. To the left, gunfire was heard as Guido and Fergus's teams fought in the trenches. Grimace watched a team member throw a grenade. "Whoa, shit!" he shouted, awestruck.

Steve studied Guido and Fergus's teams leapfrog forward, engaging in close quarters fighting inside of the trenches. Taliban fighters were being killed, smoke filled the air, punctuated by the low, deep concussion of hand grenades.

Steve yelled to Grimace and Fruit Bat. "If we take the road below, we can cut off the back side of that hill! Let's go!" He pointed at the road leading away from the compound, the fighting in the trenches intensifying. Steve called into the radio, "All stations. Rogue One-Zero is dismounting to help Fergus and Guido's teams."

Leaving Hoyle and McConnell behind in the gun truck, Steve, Grimace, Abdullah, and Fruit Bat ran down the hill, onto the road. Ahead of them, Guido, and Fergus's teams gained ground, killing several more Taliban fighters. By the they time arrived at the next hill, Guido and Fergus's teams had driven the enemy out of the trenches.

Steve ascended the hill on which his men spread out across the top of to see them firing down the other side. Grimace and Fruit Bat moved to Steve's left as they advanced up the hill, following a swath of destruction wrought by the teams. Steve spotted a large bunker entrance at the base of a hill behind them. It went under the trench lines they'd just cleared. Bodies lay inside the trenches, and it was possible that other fighters escaped down and into the tunnels inside the hill.

He called to Grimace, "Has this been cleared?!"

Grimace shook his head. "Beats me?"

"Shit. We can't have this at our backs. We don't know who's inside." Steve looked at the doorway.

"Throw a grenade in it!" Fruit Bat suggested.

Steve moved to the bunker entrance. "Grimace, throw in a frag!"

Grimace prepared a fragmentation grenade. Steve, his weapon ready, slightly offset from the doorway, reducing his exposure. The door was framed by massive timbers. Grimace threw the grenade. It sailed through the air, moving in slow motion.

The spoon flew off. The detonator popped. The yellow stencil 'M67 Fragmentation' was clearly readable. It hit the top beam of the bunker entrance and dropped to the ground one foot away from Steve.

He gasped and dove toward the close hill, putting the bunker entrance between him and the grenade. It exploded in a deafening roar. The explosion lifted Steve off the ground, the concussion wave passed through him followed by a cloud of smoke, shrapnel, and dust. He picked himself up and looking back at Grimace with the same annoyed face from earlier.

"Goddamn it! *Fuck* the Taliban. YOU'RE gonna kill me today!" He pointed for emphasis. Grimace sheepishly looked at him, wordlessly shrugging his shoulders with his hands out as if to say "sorry, bro."

Steve prepared his own grenade and threw it into the bunker, yelling "FRAG OUT!" It exploded and dropped the roof of the entrance, effectively sealing it. Satisfied with the result, he glared at Grimace again.

"Ma'bad," Grimace muttered.

Steve shook his head.

# 25



*Southern Afghanistan, November 15, 2009*

Steve, Grimace, Abdullah, and Fruit Bat resumed their ascent. On the hill top above them, Guido and Fergus's Marines occupied the trench line and were furiously engaged with the enemy on the opposite side of the hill.

Abdullah's Icom radio sprang to life with excited chatter. He listened and translated to Steve. "Sir! They say they're getting ready to shoot!"

"Shoot what?"

"They call it 'the big weapon'!"

Steve drew a breath to reply when far to his left he saw the signature of a 107mm rocket launch followed by a WHOOSH! As it sailed toward Steve and his men on the hillside.

*"Allah Akbahar!"* came from the Icom.

The giant Golden Eagle soared overhead, looking down at the ensuing battle. It flapped its wings hard, and the wind picked up as a massive explosion knocked Steve's group to the ground.

The rocket's impact sent a shower of dust, debris, and fragmentation in all directions. Steve pitched violently to the ground as if he'd been hit from behind, his face pressed into the dirt, cheek wrinkling from a massive weight bearing down on him. He couldn't move and he mumbled, "Get off of me, Grimace!" A blast of wind swept over them.

The pressure on him lessened and Steve peeled himself up, yet no one was near him. Grimace, Abdullah, and Fruit Bat were lying prone twenty yards away. Could either of them gotten to him to keep him on the ground? He couldn't explain how he'd been knocked over and held down with such force otherwise.

They looked at each other as the wind cleared the smoke and dust from the impact of the rocket.

Wet, warm liquid trickled down Steve's back and legs. "Oh, shit." He frantically swept his hands, but they emerged clear. The shrapnel cut across his back body armor, lacerating his ear and neck, and causing him to bleed, but the adrenaline kept him from noticing. If he was hit elsewhere, he was unaware. He sipped from his Camelback, but it made a dry sucking sound. Shrapnel had shredded his water source. The wetness on his back was water, not blood. Steve tossed the tube in disgust.

Another rocket exploded between two Marines atop the hill. Steve flopped to the ground, dust and rocks sweeping over him. "Fuck. Now I gotta clean *those* guys up," he said out loud, then breathed a sigh of relief as the Marines emerged from the smoke grinning, miraculously unhurt.

"WHOA!" one laughed to the other. "That was CLOSE!" In the face of death, they high-fived each other and launched a shoulder-fired rocket of their own.

Steve's command group crested the hill. The Marines were in a fierce engagement, laying down a withering fire on an enemy staging area containing one hundred and twenty Taliban fighters who were preparing to assault them when the Marines surprised them from the high ground. They fired into the mass of fighters below, throwing grenades, creating a chaotic mess of dead and wounded bodies. To his left, Grimace and Fruit Bat joined the Turkey Shoot. Steve looked down in amazement at the carnage.

Guido yelled, "Sir! We need more ammo!"

But it was a near impossible request since in order to retrieve more of the coveted ammunition, Steve had to return to his truck at the bottom of the hill where Hoyle pulled forward as close as he could. He'd then grab three cans and run it back to the top of the hill. At the rate his men were consuming the ammunition, it would be deficit spending to do so. However, Hoyle's decision to put a mobile fire support platform in place covering their rear and supporting a withdrawal proved prescient.

One of Steve's men fired a grenade from his M203 under-barrel grenade launcher in a direct-fire mode, blowing the head off his target. The body kept running for five or six more steps, apparently unaware of its decapitation. So many of the enemies were running, it looked like the Marines had kicked an anthill. He was mesmerized. Steve didn't fire his weapon so much as flip the safety and depress the trigger. Everything else happened in the absolute clarity of combat.

Steve snapped back into focus; they would run out of precious ammunition and be stuck on that hill awaiting an enemy counterattack. Already being bracketed by rockets, it was a matter of time before one finally found a true mark, the first two being close enough.

He yelled to Guido, "I can't get you ammo fast enough! We gotta pull back! Fall back, fall back! Alternating bounds with Fergus! We're out of here!"

Guido looked back, his rifle still in his shoulder. "Roger, sir!" He fired a few more rounds. Steve, Grimace, Abdullah, and Fruit Bat, followed by Guido's team, and finally by Fergus's team, withdrew under pressure, clambering down the hill. The firing intensified. McConnell provided cover with his machine gun, rounds hitting Taliban fighters.

Brian radioed that Steve's group were being flanked. From their position, Alex was engaging with his .50 caliber sniper rifle, firing bullets the size of small ketchup bottles into the enemy who, tired of having the shit knocked out of them, maneuvered through an adjacent trench line to attain an advantageous position.

As they consolidated on Steve's truck, McConnell noted in his thick New York accent, "Sir, they're in the fuckin' trees," while continuing to engage the enemy in and around trees one hundred and fifty yards across an empty field to their left. The .50 caliber bullets destroyed them. Limbs flew off as the heavy, anti-armor rounds slammed into them.

More fire came from the tree line McConnell was engaging.

Fergus called, "Contact Left!" and his team executed a perfect peel as fully automatic fire raked the enemy, and the Marines bounded past each other.

Steve looked through his sight. The magnifier had fallen off somehow. It was lying in the dirt along with a smoke grenade fifteen yards behind him. *I can get them.* He took a step toward the items but halted when a strip of bullets kicked up dust in front of him. "Fuck it." He returned fire. "They can have 'em!"

Amazingly, Hoyle managed to drive the truck in reverse while McConnell hammered away with his machinegun. "Last mag!" Steve yelled. Fergus handed him one of his own so Steve would have a spare. Fergus was selfless with no thought of needing that magazine otherwise. That stood out to Steve amid the chaos. Hoyle got the vehicle moving forward again. Steve opened the door to retrieve spare magazines, but Hoyle had already loaded all of his old ones. They were neatly stacked on his seat.

"How the hell'd you do that, Hoyle?"

"Just what I do, sir." Hoyle was completely unexcited.

Steve, grabbing freshly loaded magazines and getting his rifle ready, handed one in return to Fergus. He turned to see Fergus firing on full auto, waves of heat rippling off the shroud of his suppressor.

Fruit Bat retrieved an AT4 rocket from their truck and ran up to the edge of a ridge to fire down into the enemy trapped in the trench across the field.

"You're a brave, stupid fucker," Guido yelled.

Fruit Bat primed the rocket. "BACK-BLAST AREA SECURE! ROCKET!" He engaged the trigger, and everyone stopped, awaiting a satisfying 'Whoosh-BANG' that would emerge from the missile system.

Nothing. Misfire.

"Shit!" Fruit Bat yelled. He recocked the weapon, got to a high-knee, and aimed in again. Nothing.

Fergus looked up at Fruit Bat, and from his angle, saw straight through the rocket. Fruit Bat had grabbed an expended tube that was thrown in the back of the truck by accident. When Fergus pointed that out, laughter erupted and the smack talk began, all while people were shooting.

"Try it again, sir. It's gotta work THIS time!" Guido yelled. It just wasn't real to be laughing so hard when they could be killed at any minute, but perhaps that's precisely why humor had bubbled up.

They broke contact and made it all the way back to their vehicles, mounted up and started driving away from the smoking ruin of the trench line and enemy staging area.

Once they were moving, Steve called Brian on the radio. "You need to withdraw to our rendezvous point."

*"Roger. En route."*

Above all of it, the massive Golden Eagle continued circling above them, watching.

# 26



It was early evening when Steve's part of their force linked up with Brian, then they all moved back and away from the enemy position, setting up on a ridge to get more powerful weapons like rockets, mortars, and heavy machine-guns into play and engage the enemy from farther distances. An hour later, they drove further into the desert and away from the village.

Steve called over his shoulder to Fruit Bat, "What's the status of that air support?"

"I got an AC-130 gunship on the way."

"Good."

A few breaths later, the gunship arrived to deliver more death on the enemy.

Fruit Bat looked at the expended AT4 tube again. He was dejected, sad, even, about his foray with the rocket. "I won't get an opportunity like that again," he groused.

Grimace snorted a laugh.

At dusk, the unit halted in another desert laager site. It was confirmed they'd sustained no casualties. None. It didn't seem possible.

Steve was famished. He hadn't eaten since that morning, and they'd fought all day. He opened an MRE and bummed a cigarette from Fruit Bat. How would he ever describe what he'd been through to anyone? Who would understand? Who could know unless they'd been there with them?

The sun had almost set. Steve removed his body armor. As his vest swept over his head, his ear stung. It was tender and painful to touch. He looked at his shirt and trousers; they were covered in blood.

Hoyle noticed the blood, too. "Oh, shit, sir! I should take a look at you." He approached with trauma shears drawn, ready to cut off Steve's clothing should he be wounded elsewhere on the body. Steve was sure he hadn't been hit but didn't know why he had so much blood on him and couldn't ascertain where the resultant wound was located.

Hoyle looked him over. "Turn around, please."

"Not if you are going to cut off my clothes. I swear, you guys look for any excuse to use those damn shears. If you want to see me naked, just ask!" Steve was coming off an adrenaline high and felt punchy.

Hoyle smiled. "Don't flatter yourself, sir. Now, please turn around. Whoa . . ." Dried blood crusted on Steve's neck from where he'd been cut. Hoyle and Steve analyzed what happened.

When the rocket impacted and knocked Steve to the ground, shrapnel went across his body and perforated his camelback. A piece of metal, very thin and sharp, pierced his left earlobe and cut across his neck, but his adrenaline had been pumping, and he'd been too focused on the action. Blood had run down the back of his body. Diluted by sweat and water, it had soaked into his combat shirt and trousers, making it appear more extensive.

Removing his shirt, Steve rinsed the dirty garment with bottled water to lay it out to dry. The trousers would have to wait until he got back. He shivered once. "Tough day," he commented.

"Yeah," said Hoyle, "but you're all right. I'll write you up for a Purple Heart when we get back, no worries."

"No way," Steve insisted. "Not when guys like Gary McGuire are on ventilators and others are on their way home with missing limbs. And not after Major Joyce, Ketcham, and Luke being killed. This is a scratch, and we'll just chalk it up to a good story." Steve popped an aspirin to dull the soreness.

Hoyle never again brought up the Purple Heart. Steve didn't ask after it, either.

# 27

---



It was dark with little moonlight; the air grew chilly. Relatively safe in their new patrol base, people loosened their combat equipment, the AC-130 droning in the overhead as Fruit Bat called in fire missions on enemy forces remaining in the village. Fruit Bat's air strikes seemed never-ending until the AC-130 departed after it ran low on fuel and expending most of its ammunition. Fruit Bat sent them on their way, and Steve closed the TIC with Serpent Seven-One. The fight had lasted ten hours.

Abdullah intently listened to his hand-held Icom radio as several Afghan voices spoke in stressed and harried tones.

McConnell, watching through his night vision goggles, called down from his turret. "I don't know what's more badass: The AC-130 or that giant bird that was with us all day. If that isn't true overwatch, I don't know what is."

Steve frowned. "Really? Shit, you're right."

"Yep. And I was thinking something, sir."

"What's that?" Steve said after a bite of his MRE.

"That bird mighta been Luke watching over us. I mean, Luke was like six four, and the bird was huge."

Steve considered that comment. "Hmm. Damn. For all we went through, we didn't have a single casualty. What a strange day." Could the bird also have been a manifestation of Roland? He was equally tall.

"Sir, since Iceman and Murtaugh, we don't have casualties. Ever. No one gets hit when we're out with you."

The Pashtu chatter on the hand-held radio intensified. Abdullah interrupted them, excited, "Sir, you should hear this!"

"Really? What're they saying?" Steve was curious.

Abdullah laughed. "It's the man we're after, Muammar Agha. They have very bad casualties. It's terrible for them."

"Tenkara?! Damnit!"

"Yes, sir!" Abdullah smiled. Grimace, Fruit Bat, Hoyle, and McConnell listened intently, too as he continued.

"He said, 'They are worse than the Russians'!"

Steve chuckled. "That may be the highest compliment I've ever been paid!" His chuckles turned into laughter, and the others laughed with him, their combined mirth echoing into the desert.

# 28



*Southern Afghanistan, November 16, 2009*

Though the enemy couldn't attack them over open terrain, Steve and his unit were essentially surrounded in hostile territory. The Marines sat in their laager site eating MREs and listening to Icom traffic. The reports from the enemy of their conduct to date continued to flatter them. Steve was proud of their work, but the enemy was determined that they shouldn't get across the wadi—a large, dried-out riverbed—on their way back home and tried to determine which crossing point to return to FOB Prince the Americans would utilize.

By design, Steve and his men never took the same way home as they went in. Still, the Marines didn't have many options since the large wadi between them and their FOB was cut into the earth by an ancient river. The shelves of each, ostensibly banks, could be one hundred feet high, so it was important to find the right access point and move quickly through it.

In daylight, they would observe the point for a few hours before approaching it, with constant and uninterrupted civilian traffic being a good sign. It was dark, however.

"Sir," said Abdullah, "they're saying they're going to set an ambush for us. They said to watch each crossing point and be prepared to attack us when we're spread out across the wadi."

Steve nodded and ate, chewing slowly, looking at the map under a red lens light with Alex, Guido, Fergus, Marko, Brian, and Fruit Bat. He curled his lips into a small smile and studied the map more closely. "They can't be everywhere at once." He narrowed his eyes.

His men looked at him, listening closely.

"We'll cross tonight. They'll track us while we look for a crossing point, but we'll have Fruit Bat get some air support up and observe those ahead of our crossing. We'll listen to Icom traffic and see where the enemy is setting in or giving directions.

"Once we determine a safe crossing point, we'll check it out ourselves to be sure, then enter the wadi, but instead of going straight west, we'll turn to the south. We'll drive down the middle of the wadi on IR lights as fast as we can go, skipping two crossing points and coming up and out of the wadi at the one next to this place, called Russian Hill. That'll allow us to set in behind it and, if required, be on dominating terrain when the sun comes up. If not, we'll drive back to Prince.

"It's faster to move in the wadi and the enemy won't expect it. Even if they can reposition or call ahead to stage another ambush, they won't know which cut we're going to use. By the time they figure it out, we'll be long-out of the wadi and have regained the initiative. What do you think?" Steve traced the route on the map with the edge of a cracker to illustrate his idea.

"Damn, sir, that's just awesome!" Alex exclaimed, smiling. "I mean, realistically, who's ever going to expect us to use their own roadway against them and work down the wadi on our terms?"

Fruit Bat added, "I'll have fixed wing stay high above us and track our movements. It'll be a good standoff observation platform."

Steve nodded. *How did I get so lucky to lead these men?* He smiled back. "OK? Let's go."

Everyone moved from the hood of Steve's truck to their own to get ready for the next movement. The air was electric with excitement. By the time the plan was disseminated, the unit was in high spirits. They liked the sneaky nature of the mission. They wanted to succeed, to snub and get over on the enemy and cheat death without firing a shot.

"Sir, you always make the right decision." McConnell looked at Steve like a son proud of his father.

Steve smiled. "Thanks, Mac, but we're not back yet." It was a high compliment, but to his decisions, he made them, and his men obeyed. They never questioned him out of admiration and respect. Steve's main misgiving was that he wasn't so sure, knowing he could in fact make a poor decision. Brian correcting him in the enemy medical facility was still in the back of his mind, his near-error haunting him.

"I'm gonna take care of my girl, sir." McConnell clambered up the truck to his turret to give his machine gun a good cleaning.

Steve took a bottle of water and walked off into the desert to rinse his face and clean the grime from his neck. Would the plan work? *It has to,* he thought, *and if it doesn't, we'll be used as an example of what not to do. If it does—well, we'll just be that much more confident in our own immortality.*

He finished his refreshing rinse, but the water just bounced off his hair, failing to penetrate through the accumulated sweat and dirt. He smiled at that, too, as he ambled back to the truck to slide into his damp shirt and prepare for the crossing later that night.

If all went well, he would get a nap at the base of Russian Hill, named due to the remnants of a bygone Russian fighting position consisting of a trench line and observation posts on a piece of dominating terrain overlooking the wadi.

# 29

*Southern Afghanistan, November 16, 2009*

Even at night, the land was inhospitable and desolate. A cool wind swept across the desert, swirling dust which later settled over everything like a blanket. Steve climbed onto the hood of their GMV and sat with his back against the windshield, thick bullet-resistant glass surrounded by armor plate. The materials had absorbed the heat of the day, and even at night, the warmth of the metal and glass at his back caused him to sweat a little.

He quietly laughed to himself. He was so lucky to be alive, to feel that wind, to smell the dust, to see the stars, all senses awake. He wondered how he ever took that which he could enjoy for granted, and for a moment, he thought of Elena and his children, then banished them to the back of his mind again. He couldn't lose his edge.

Steve knew he was changing, though the full impact of those changes wouldn't be felt for a while, some of them many years later. Delayed PTSD? Probably. Post-traumatic stress disorder issues manifested in different ways. It wasn't the killing, though taking a human life never was natural to him—and he was glad of that—but that he was comfortable with doing his job, even the violence. Like he was programmed to appropriately initiate action. He acted without any hesitation or fear. He shot the enemy without remorse. It bothered him that it was easy for him, and it further troubled him that he still didn't flinch under fire unless it was IDF. Then, anyone would take cover in a hurry.

Did any of the other men feel the same way? They all seemed to go about their business good-naturedly, with a high sense of humor, although that could be morbid.

Steve identified with them. It was due to their not wanting to appear fearful or lacking to their comrades and they put on a good front and kept it under control. Some, though, couldn't help themselves and their fear was palpable. The problem with uncontrolled fear was that it's contagious and could lead to panic in poorly led units, as well as people. In the MSOC, any person who exhibited an amount of fear that was seen as unhealthy, and that was admittedly subjective, was a leper of sorts and immediately ostracized, if not outcast.

To paraphrase William Manchester's *Goodbye, Darkness*, people like that were truly damned. No one ever spoke of them again.

*After all I've seen and done, I'm going to need some serious therapy.*

***

The moon rose over hills that masked their position. Steve studied the horizon. They were relatively safe in their spot, at least from direct fire; not like when in the Green Zone where the enemy enjoyed plentiful natural cover and concealment to move freely to obtain a flanking position like they had earlier that afternoon. The enemy was always tracking them.

Steve thought of the enemy, of how adaptable they were, yet so undeveloped. It didn't matter that they weren't a professional military. For an illiterate society, they were good at fighting in the manner they knew how, and that culture bested the Russians. He didn't understand that part, either. The Russians must not have appreciated these people or their tenacity. The Afghans fought for their country and livelihood. The Americans fought for the guys on their left and right, the strategic impact of the war they were fighting in Afghanistan having very little effect on their daily existence.

It boiled down to finding the enemy and killing him. Pretty simple.

Steve's platoon mounted up later that night and drove into the wadi. True to the plan, they turned south, and while the enemy radio traffic revealed they were bent on setting an ambush, Steve's feint worked. The enemy didn't understand when the column didn't come out of the wadi at the place they guessed. Unable to see them, they surmised the Americans hadn't crossed yet, though the enemy heard the vehicles turning in the wide cut of the riverbed. The platoon hit the gas and drove all-out on NODs and IR lights, deep in enemy territory, avoiding the odd civilian car and moving quickly past the two other exit points from the wadi, to the third, just at the base of Russian Hill.

The deception and foiling of the enemy's plans complete, they were safely out of the wadi.

"All stations, keep going to FOB Prince," Steve radioed his men.

He hung up the handset, satisfied, but also extremely tired. Steve leaned his helmeted head against the window and attempted to sleep. Before he nodded off, Hoyle talked in low tones to Fruit Bat.

"Ballsy, man. The guy's just ballsy. No way anyone else coulda come up with something like that."

Steve woke with the sun breaking the horizon. They were ten minutes from FOB Prince. He'd slept for three hours and felt great.

# 30



They recovered to the FOB, and after checking in with Ballentine, Steve took his first shower in five days, the water cascading over his grimy body. He sighed when the hot water hit his skin. He stood in the stream of the shower, fists balled in front of him, leaning on the wall, and took another deep breath, exhaling through his nose to release both the exhilaration and emotional stress of combat. Reaching to turn off the water, drops ran lightly down the drain. He wrapped himself in a towel and exited the shower. The cool air felt bracing, and he ran the water in a sink to shave.

Grimace entered the shower room. Steve studied him through the mirror. "Good work. That was a huge victory over a larger enemy force."

Grimace laughed. "I'm still amazed no one on our side got killed or hurt! Well, sorry about your ear. Oh, and the grenade!"

Steve turned up his cheek and removed a few whiskers. "We still didn't get Tenkara." He frowned. "And thanks, Grimace."

"For what, sir?"

"You saved my life yesterday." Steve finished shaving and splashed water on his face.

Grimace squinched his eyes, "What're you talking about?"

"C'mon. When that rocket hit, you slammed me down."

Grimace frowned even more, his eyes squinting further. "No way. I was laying down myself. Besides, I was like twenty yards away."

Steve blinked and reflected on that. But it lined up with what he too had witnessed. Who protected him, then? " . . . I guess that's true. That's so weird."

# 3l



Steve turned to Roland. "You kept me alive that day going up the hill—it was you who shoved me out of the way of that rocket, wasn't it?"

"Yeah." Roland smiled.

"But things like that didn't happen every time. Aside from that, I honestly don't know how I survived. Or why, for that matter."

"I intervened at that critical time because I told you I'd be there for you." Roland raised his glass. "And you did fine on your own."

"To a point. Then things changed." Steve touched his glass to Roland's.

"I know."

The fire's coals ignited on a dormant log. They both gazed into the flames.

"Ballentine . . ." Steve said.

# PART III

Four months into being at war, Steve felt he couldn't both be good at his job and simultaneously not revel in being at war. It was an odd juxtaposition. He enjoyed parts of combat. The adrenaline dump. The excitement of war fighting. But the further he got into his deployment; he became more indifferent to surviving.

For service members, Paul Fussell described this third and final phase as one of incredible, fatal cynicism. There is no way to influence if you'll live, and you'll either be hit or killed as a matter of course. This concluding part in a soldier's combat transformation is one of acceptance. "It is *going* to happen to me and only my not being there is going to prevent it." *Wartime* (Oxford University Press, 1989), 283.

In other words, resign yourself that you'll be destroyed, and you might be pleasantly surprised. Steve hoped this mindset wouldn't grip him entirely, for that meant he was giving up somehow. But really, nothing could be done to stop it.

# 1



Steve and his platoon had been back almost two weeks. While they were resting, Hackett went out and got into a good scrape, sustaining two wounded, one of whom was evacuated to the States. That brought the MSOC's total wounded sent home to ten. Things were as dangerous as ever.

Within the month, the rainy season began. It was cold, wet, and damp. Missions abated, though if the weather supported it, either Hackett or Steve's platoon would go out and conduct reconnaissance or interdiction missions. Most of the time, the biggest enemy was boredom. People killed time by working out in the gym, watching movies, shooting on the range, and sleeping.

Being on the FOB allowed people to catch up on mail and packages. Getting mail to the remote areas in Afghanistan in which the US service members served was its own chore. By the time a box of cookies arrived from a well-wisher, they could be stale, dust, or both. Still, everyone anticipated mail calls.

A small package arrived for Steve from Elena. It contained some chocolate chip cookies, an early Christmas card, and photos of the kids and her.

*My Dear Steve,*

*I hope this letter finds you well. We are preparing to see my family for Thanksgiving. The kids are excited, and Marta asked if you would be home in time. It's tough to explain to her that you will be gone for a while; she really doesn't yet have the concept of time.*

*Michael has taken up karate. It's so cute to see him in his little uniform. He loves it!*

*Sammie is growing faster than we want, I think, and more by her maturity (read: attitude!) than physically. She likes to test me. I wonder where she gets that? Ha!*

*Each night after dinner, we have our "Daddy Kisses" and each of the kids tell me what they are happy about. It helps that we all do it together, and I think it allows them to feel close to you.*

*Life continues for us as it does for you, though I admit, you feel far away from me, and not just because of distance. I know it isn't personal. I know you are out there with your tribe and community. But selfishly, I don't like sharing you with them; nevertheless, I understand. I know it's how you cope with deployments, so I await your return so we can get back to us, you and me.*

*I pray for your safety and that of everyone in the unit. The news of Luke was tough for people here, along with the numbers of wounded you all have sustained. I don't know how you do it, honestly, but then again, that detachment you exhibit is probably why you can.*

*Otherwise, there isn't much to report, so I'm going to wrap this up. It's a sunny day here, the kids are playing in the backyard. One day closer to your safe return.*

*We love and miss you. I'm proud of you. I love you so much.*

*Always yours,*

*Elena*

When he finished reading it, Steve reread it while munching on the cookies. He looked at the pictures and thought of his wife. How much he missed her, his family. The news of the children was nice to read, but he also acknowledged the primary message of the letter from her perspective, even if he didn't like it.

True, he hadn't really kept in touch except via emails and the occasional phone call, but out here, he had a job to do, and his mental acuity was paramount to his survival.

Like all her letters, he kept it to himself. A part of him that was exclusively his.

He'd address the issue of his detachment when he returned from deployment. The clarity he sought as a leader in combat couldn't be interrupted, and he subjugated their memory to another part of his mind.

Steve started feeling hopeless. He questioned what the war was about. The combat losses. His desire to avenge Roland by killing Agha was continually denied by circumstances. It wasn't as if Agha wouldn't be replaced, either. Enemy losses in Afghanistan were filled with the next promotable candidate. That type of advancement could be a bane or a boon, depending on one's ambitions. In Agha's case, his successor might not easily be found, but one would be appointed eventually. Hell, it might even be his son, Muktah, who would continue the fight, filled with *Badal*, the Afghan word for revenge.

Paradoxically, though he certainly identified with needing vengeance, the endless cycle seemed pointless to Steve. In the main, he fought in a poor country so people in America could feel safe again, but citizens in the United States had lost that perspective a long time ago. They'd forgotten how scared they were when, on a brilliant September day, a terrifying few hours thrust a shadow over the world.

That night, Ballentine assembled the MSOC's key leadership, including Steve, his team leaders, and Brian, in their company spaces. He said he had big news.

# 2



When Steve arrived at the meeting, Ballentine and Marko stood outside the side door of the operations center, talking. Their interaction concluded, and Marko laughed as they shook hands and entered the company spaces.

"What's all that, sir?" Steve asked Ballentine.

Ballentine turned toward him. "Ah, Steve! Good to see you! Just giving Gunny Pech a pep talk. He's been through a lot." He smiled condescendingly. "We all have."

Steve sensed something was amiss. "Anything I need to know about, sir?"

Ballentine jutted his lower lip. "No. And it's my prerogative to speak to any member of this unit. I'm still in charge."

"Of course, sir, I—" Steve held up his hands. Adrenaline coursed through his veins and his fists trembled. Even in the cold air, sweat broke out along his lower back.

"Good man. I'm glad you still agree. See you at the brief." Ballentine entered through the same door as Marko. Steve watched it close and took a deep breath to collect himself before following Ballentine inside.

# 3



*FOB Prince, Afghanistan, November 28, 2009*

Nathan stood to the left-hand side of a large wall upon which a PowerPoint presentation was projected. He wore camouflage utilities and sported horn-rimmed glasses. The rest of the MSOC dressed like vagabonds in a mix of camouflage trousers and Patagonia puffy coats and sat or stood around tables strewn with maps and photographs, listening attentively.

Nathan began in his crisp, even tone. "As you all know, this is Muammar Agha, also called Objective Tenkara." He motioned to the screen as Agha's photo appeared. "He's the Taliban field commander responsible for bombing the village we treated casualties from and was on the field directing fighters when Luke was killed."

"Don't forget that he killed Major Joyce," Steve added.

Nathan nodded, pushed his glasses up the bridge of his nose, and pointed at another photo to continue the brief. "Yes, the blood of many Americans is on his hands—"

"That's right," Ballentine spoke up, overriding Nathan. "And we've had two chances to get him through capture raids without success." Looking around, he appeared to castigate the men in the room, as if they'd somehow failed. "So, now we're going to try to apprehend him through a classic SOF tenant, the indirect approach." His smug smile supported his arrogance, like he'd developed a master stroke.

"How's that, sir?" Steve asked.

Ballentine motioned to the back of the room. "This is Marlon Geddes."

All turned to see a middle-aged man of average height and build with a scraggly, brown salt-and-pepper beard behind blue eyes. A Patagonia trucker hat on his head covered shoulder-length hair. Tattoos adorned his arms. Dressed in a Carhartt T-shirt and 5.11 pants, a pistol on his hip, he stood, arms crossed and nodded. "Sup, gents."

"Officer Geddes is a policeman from Nashville. He's been working with the Afghan National Police to professionalize their force as part of the Law Enforcement Professionals program. He currently is teamed with a US Army Military Police unit down to our South. He's located Tenkara."

Geddes corrected him in a low drawl, "Respectfully, it's Detective, sir." Geddes was confident but understated and imposing despite his average size.

"Er, right, sorry! You still have a lead on him?" Ballentine queried.

"Yep. All we gotta do is go roll him up." Geddes's blue eyes flashed.

Brian looked over at Steve as if to say, 'what's all this?' Steve acknowledged him with a thin smile. For having limited Special Operations experience, Ballentine sure presented having a good handle on mission sets he hadn't heard about—let alone executed—a scant five months ago.

Steve pressed, "It's that easy, eh?"

Geddes glanced at him and icily replied, "My way is." He stepped forward and to a map on the table, pulled a knife from his pocket, opened it with one hand, and pointed to a village on the map. "He's about fifteen klicks from my FOB in a village called Wadi Mali."

Geddes coughed and continued. "Down here, he's a long way from home, or where you guys have been operating, anyway. He probably left his own town to lay low for a while."

Ballentine's face brightened. "Detective Geddes, this is Gunnery Sergeant Marko Pech. I'm going to send him and Staff Sergeant Donald Reid with you to formulate a plan to get Tenkara. Hopefully, you guys can make an arrest."

Shock flowed through Steve's body. The adrenaline returned, causing his temples to thump with his heartbeat. How Geddes had arrived on the FOB remained a mystery, but Steve surmised what he missed was that Ballentine somehow planned it in isolation.

"Good to go, sir," Geddes said. He looked at Marko, who appeared bored at best. Reid, one of Marko's Assault Team leaders gave Geddes a quiet nod. He had dirty blond hair and brown eyes and an athletic, cross-country runner build.

Ballentine gestured toward Marko. "You and Reid leave with Detective Geddes tomorrow morning. The rest of the company will be on standby in case you need more support. Got it?" He seemed excited.

"Yes, sir," Marko said, slightly turning his head toward Reid.

The briefing broke up, and Steve stormed over to Ballentine.

He sighed. "What's up, Steve?"

"Sir, I—"

"Marko?" Ballentine cut him off. "I might've guessed." He seemed exasperated.

"Never mind that. Where'd Geddes come from?!"

"As I said, Geddes works in the LEP program designed by US lawmakers to work with US forces to turn the ANP into a robust police force. The ANP occasionally go on presence patrols to enforce Afghan laws inside of neighboring villages, and Geddes accompanies them to help with evidence collection that will lead to convictions of Afghan criminals.”

“I know about the program, sir, but how did he get in touch with *you*?”

“A roundabout way. When Agha showed up down South a couple of weeks ago, his reputation led Geddes to carefully track him. I was on a list of people looking for him, so when Geddes confirmed he was in Wadi Mali, he gave me a call. I flew him up to the FOB.”

“Sir, this mission is pretty sensitive—”

He shrugged, dismissive. “Don’t worry about it. He’s a great resource!”

Steve forcibly breathed through his nose. “Do you think it’s a good idea to send Marko out on this? And given his track record out here . . . I should do it.”

Ballentine nodded. “I understand your reservations, but this would be good for him—for us as a unit. It would help us close out Luke’s death. I can think of no better man to capture the guy who did this.”

Steve leaned forward. “‘Close out?!’ Sir, we aren’t getting past Luke or Major Joyce! And Marko’s the wrong guy!”

Ballentine held up his hand. “We’re all emotional out here, you most of all.”

Steve glared. “It should be *me* going after him!”

Ballentine brushed him off. “I think you’re letting your personal vendetta to avenge Major Joyce affect your outlook. If you just let your men do the work on this, you’ll come out looking great, Steve. One day, you’ll see it more simply, like I do.”

“No doubt because of the perspective gained from your past lives, right, sir?” Steve scoffed.

“Exactly! Now you’re getting it. It’s a matter of my experiences trumping yours!”

“Oh, God, sir . . .” Steve sighed, speechless.

Ballentine poked Steve's shoulder, perhaps finally cluing in that he'd meant it as a barb. "That's *enough*. Drop it! I'm going to Kandahar with Nathan for the week to coordinate our return home. Track Marko's progress and keep me informed."

"Roger, sir," Steve hissed between clenched teeth. He glared at Ballentine's back as he sauntered away. No matter his frustration, Ballentine commanded the unit. It was his ultimate ace card.

# 4

*Smoky Mountains, Tennessee, October 2031*

Roland lamented, "I wish I knew what transpired that night between Marko and Ballentine in front of the company offices."

Steve shook his head. "It's not your fault. My senses were up; it was just too convenient that Ballentine assigned Marko to go do that mission." The fire had burned to red coals. Steve tossed another two logs on the pile and emptied the last of the whiskey bottle into their tumblers. "It was meant to happen the way that it did, I suppose."

"That's true. But when they got to Geddes' FOB, they planned it out meticulously."

Steve sipped his whiskey. "Man . . ."

"It was tough to watch," Roland delivered. He exhaled. "You didn't deserve any of that, Steve."

"Maybe, but it doesn't change anything," Steve reflected.

# 5



Steve sat in his office in a white Ramones T-shirt and soft blue jeans, drinking a Krombacher near-beer, watching a football game on the Armed Forces Network playing on a flat-screen TV hung in the corner of the office. On his desk sat a computer and a bank of phones from which he could call various entities depending on classification. Elena's letter to him was open and he was crafting a response. He'd called her on a satellite phone, but the conversation was strained. They'd hung up without closure.

He thought about Marko and felt a twinge of guilt. Though he hadn't performed as expected, Marko had helped him on his own Selection journey, and Steve felt he owed him a little bit. Maybe that's why he'd lied for him to Hutchinson. Plus, Steve mentioned nothing of Fergus essentially murdering the wounded Afghan fighter in the same engagement Steve dropped the bomb on Marko's behalf. Dead civilians or dead fighters, at this point, what did it matter? *Best to let things lie.*

Still, Steve couldn't help thinking about Ballentine talking with Marko ahead of the meeting with Geddes. He felt uneasy but couldn't put his finger on it. Though after not having heard from Marko in a few days, he wondered if he should call down to Geddes' FOB and chat with him.

The SECRET phone on his desk rang, startling Steve. The red light on the handset pulsed in time with the phone's choppy cadence. The ringing continued. Steve frowned, the phone's ringing unabated. He reached for it and answered, "Keller, secure—"

It was Ballentine. *"Steve, there are allegations of a possible Law of Armed Conflict violation. NCIS is flying to FOB Prince to pick you up and take you to the site."* Ballentine's tone painted a vivid mental image of the man standing, face red with fury.

Steve rose from his chair. "NCIS?! LOAC?! Like what?"

*"Like a murder!"*

"WHAT?! Who?! Where?!"

*"Marko. In Wadi Mali. You guys are going to pull security for NCIS."*

"Wadi Mali? In daylight?! We'd need a fucking infantry battalion to secure that place!"

*"You ain't getting it. Get a team together. NCIS and their assault escort will be at FOB Prince in two hours. Questions?"*

Steve calmed himself with deep breaths. "Tons, sir. I'll call Marko first to get the story."

*"No way!"* Ballentine shouted. *"We don't want him tipped off!"*

Steve grit his teeth. "OK. I got it."

*"Good. Don't fuck this up."*

The phone clicked, dead.

Steve replaced the handset. He stared at the phone. What had he just heard? After taking another sip of his Krombacher, he left the office to find Brian, who was sitting outside reading a magazine and enjoying the sunshine. "Hey. I got a call from Ballentine."

"Oh?" he said from behind mirrored shades.

Steve nodded. "I need you to get Fergus and meet me in our CP in five minutes."

"You've got it, sir." Brian sat up and went to find Fergus without asking questions. Once again, the loyalty of his team struck Steve.

Fergus and Brian entered the CP. They sat in the conference room. "We need to go to Wadi Mali."

"What?!" replied Brian, checking that he'd heard accurately.

"Something bad may have happened in that village. We're supporting NCIS and their investigation," Steve said.

Fergus immediately protested, "In Wadi Mali?! We'll get shot to pieces!"

"Fuck what you think, Fergus. We're going, and I'm going with you."

"What if I refuse, skipper?" Fergus sternly asked, his eyes blazed.

Steve measured his response, but he said it anyway. "I'll relieve you on the spot."

Fergus stared. Brian said nothing.

Fergus knew not to call Steve's bluff, and Steve was glad Fergus didn't. Steve recanted, relieving the tension.

"Look, gents. It's all gonna be all right." Steve looked at Fergus, an incredible warrior. He liked serving with him. Short, fit, tough, and resolute, Fergus could carry his weight, fight, and do all things required of him without any assistance or hesitation. He was exceptionally adept and maintained an enthusiastic demeanor with boundless energy for any task. He inspired confidence and was the right man for this situation. "Brian, you'll stay here and manage things. I'll take Fergus and his team with me." Steve looked at them both. "And keep it quiet."

"Roger, sir," Brian said.

They set to planning how they would go to where Marko, Reid, and Geddes allegedly committed the atrocity. Steve didn't want to believe it to be true, and he prayed he was right.

# 6



Six years passed. In the interim, Steve was promoted to major and considered for a Marine Raider Company Command. He wasn't selected on his first look and was in his second Command Screening Board interview. A marine colonel named Adrian Montclair, the MARSOC chief of staff, presided over a board which reviewed prospective candidates' fitness for continued command assignments. Steve and the colonel had a long history with each other.

The panel consisted of five members, the colonel in the center, two other senior officers seated on either side of him. The board room's dark wooden paneling made it feel stuffy. Photos of various MARSOC personnel and unit crests hung on the walls. It was carpeted in a deep maroon with overhead florescent lights and sunlight coming through the floor-length curtained windows. The flecks of dust suspended in the light reminded Steve of Afghanistan so long ago. Other than the members seated at the long table perpendicular in front of him, there were no other furnishings besides the folding chair in which Steve sat.

Colonel Montclair was a large, powerfully built African-American man. In his late fifties with a close-cropped Marine haircut, his appearance was offset by grandfatherly spectacles. His gruff demeanor bordered on condescending. "Major Keller, why were you not given a company till now?"

"I'm not sure, sir. I have the right résumé, I think, but these command boards are competitive. The right men get chosen."

"Very diplomatic of you. Your record, while excellent on paper, has to have something in it that people don't like. I'm sure there's some reason." Montclair paged through Steve's file.

"I guess I spent too much time being operational and being good at it made people uncomfortable. Or maybe I didn't give enough to the Corps, in someone's estimation, anyway."

Montclair peered over his glasses. "Indeed. Why don't you tell me what happened in Wadi Mali? I'm sure that's got something to do with it, don't you?" He pointed for emphasis.

A jolt of electricity shot through Steve, like he'd been caught omitting something. He let out a slow breath, placed his open hands on his thighs, and leaned back. "It was a bad day, sir. I could hardly believe it myself when I learned what had happened."

# 7



Geddes told the Army MP's they'd accompany them on a presence patrol to Wadi Mali with the ANP. An eight-vehicle column departed Geddes' FOB in darkness. It was cold, and Marko, Geddes, and Reid rode together in an up-armored Toyota land cruiser, driven by an Army private named Vaughn, the heater on full blast, which made the interior smell of gasoline fumes and dust. The ANP drove five unarmored Toyota pick-up trucks to the approaches of the village and established the small cordon Geddes designated. Further outside of the cordon were two US GMV trucks driven by US Army soldiers. The containment set, the ANP announced they were there to arrest Muammar Agha.

On the edge of the village, a shadowy figure tried to flee from one house, but Geddes was prepositioned in his path. He shone a flashlight mounted on his rifle at the figure and yelled in Pashto, "STOP! Get down on your stomach and put your hands out in front of you!"

Agha stopped, hesitated slightly, and did as Geddes instructed. Despite the temperature, he was dressed only in a long Afghan *shalwar kameez* without a cold weather coat.

Marko closed on him, tracing Agha's body with his weapon-mounted laser. "Not tonight, motherfucker," he murmured in English. Reid joined them, and while Marko covered him, he swiftly bound Agha's hands behind his back with a pair of plastic flexicuffs.

All looked at Agha, then at each other, smiling under the green glow of their NODS.

***

Marko, Geddes, and Reid locked Agha in a small building on the outskirts of the village. They stood just outside of it, ensuring the building's door remained shut.

Hearing the commotion, the Afghan owner of the building approached them, asking what was happening. Geddes conversed with him in Pashto and said it was nothing to worry about. Then Geddes sent the owner away.

Marko was giddy. "This piece of shit's the guy who killed our CO and my man, Luke. He was also the guy we were after where two others were wounded trying to take down his compound. He's a coward who hides behind women and kids. I can't BELIEVE we have him in there!"

Geddes smiled. "Yep! A real, live criminal."

"Guilty as fuck!" exclaimed Reid

Geddes rolled his eyes. "Aren't they all?!"

Marko looked at Geddes. "So, what do you want to do with him?"

"The problem's that even if Agha is arrested and taken to trial for his crimes," Geddes responded dryly, "there's really no glaring evidence to get him convicted in an Afghan court. It's a lost cause to capture him because he'll be out within weeks and back to his old habits, know what I'm saying? So, what do *you* think we should do?"

Marko smiled, revealing his enthusiasm. "All right! I like how you think! We'll need the truck." He turned to Reid, "Reid, go get it."

"Roger," Reid replied. He departed to grab the Land Cruiser. Geddes turned to Marko and held his gaze. "I'm gonna need your help for the set up."

Marko nodded, grinning. "You got it!"

# 8



*Afghanistan. Village of Wadi Mali, December 1, 2009*

Vaughn drove the Land Cruiser. Reid, sitting in the passenger seat, reiterated, "No lights. Drive with your NODs on."

"Will do."

The vehicle was beat up, with dirt-streaked windows, making it hard to see in the darkness. Reid looked behind him and ensured the back seats were down, then turned to Vaughn. "You good with killing an Afghan?"

Vaughn shrugged. "Yeah, no issues. It's what we do out here."

Reid clapped Vaughn on the shoulder and chuckled. "That's my boy! OK, drive until I tell you to stop."

"OK. Where're we going?" Vaughn sounded apprehensive.

"Just drive."

Vaughn steered them to the nondescript Afghan building. Reid got out, motioning for Vaughn to remain in the vehicle, and talked with Geddes and Marko.

"What the fuck, Reid?! What's he doing here?!" Marko exclaimed. "I thought you'd get the truck *from* Vaughn, not have him drive it!"

"Relax, man, I talked to him. He's cool."

Marko wasn't so confident, but the three of them went inside the hut regardless.

What was said inside the hut wasn't recorded. Geddes shot Agha in the head with his M4 carbine, and Marko put two more rounds from a .308 rifle in his chest. The large bullets went clean through Agha, who pitched backward against the wall and flopped forward, bleeding onto the carpeted floor. Geddes pried two of the three bullets out of the mud wall and carved out the piece of carpet before they rolled him up in it.

***

They brought the rolled carpet out to the truck where Vaughn was waiting. When they opened the back of the Land Cruiser, Vaughn yelled, "I heard shots! What the fuck did you do?! What the hell?! Is that a body?!"

Reid snapped, "What do you think?! Help us load this fucker!"

Vaughn shook his head vigorously. "No way. I'm not helping with any of this."

"Yes, you are," Marko joined in. "You're in this with us!"

Vaughn remained in his seat. "This is absurd! You murdered a guy!"

"Those are strong words, kid!" Geddes protested. "You didn't see what happened in there. He moved on us, and we had to shoot him!"

Vaughn slapped his hands on the steering wheel. "Oh. My. God. I don't believe this." He remained seated while they loaded Agha's body into the vehicle. They then all climbed in and drove to a deep ditch where Marko and Geddes unloaded the body.

"Off you go!" Geddes said when they unceremoniously tossed it in. They stood there, looking down at the rolled carpet, then got back in the Land Cruiser to drive to the link up point.

An uncomfortable silence filled the vehicle as it bounced along through the village.

"You did good tonight," Reid said. "Good work."

Vaughn half-glanced at him. "Fuck this and fuck you."

Reid poked him. "Lose the attitude. You said you were good with killing an Afghan."

"Not in this way. Shit . . ."

Another long silence passed, punctuated by the creak of the vehicle's strained springs and dust swirling around them.

Marko spoke up from the back seat, "What's the difference in killing Agha, a known commander and murderer, and a named objective at that—a total Taliban—and those we kill in in a firefight?"

The growing light of dawn revealed Vaughn's weary, gray eyes looking at Marko in the dirty rear-view mirror. "They're combatants. Besides, do we really know who that guy was?"

"We do know who he is—er, was," Geddes reassured him. "And it depends on how you look at it. We take bad guys off the battlefield. And that's what we did."

"That viewpoint is totally wrong! Killing people in combat is one thing. But this is premeditated. This is morally corrupt."

Geddes pointed at Vaughn. "You know, if anything comes of this, you'll go down with us, right?!"

Vaughn nodded in nervous acknowledgement.

Marko looked at him. "Who cares? Fuck it. Let's go get breakfast."

Vaughn sighed, defeated, and kept driving.

They arrived at their staging area outside Wadi Mali, then all eight vehicles returned to base. Geddes, having been the only person to detain Agha, made no mention of it to the attendant Afghan police or the other Army soldiers, except saying Agha wasn't there. He acted like nothing had happened.

Vaughn got out of the Land Cruiser last and stared at the other three as they walked ahead of him, laughing.

That day, he requested to go to Kandahar on the next available flight he could get.

# 9



"Like I said, I was shocked when I found out about it." Steve repeated.

"How did you learn all this?" Montclair pressed. "And what did you do?"

Steve slowly dragged his lower teeth back across his upper lip. "Major Ballentine ordered me to go to the site to ascertain what happened. The owner of the house they'd kept Agha in spied on them after they'd sent him away. And Vaughn confirmed his own witness account."

"But it sounds like you went to Wadi Mali reluctantly?" a member of the board, a lieutenant colonel, asked.

"Sir, I went to prove that people were wrong about them."

Montclair looked over his glasses. "And because it directly reflected on your leadership, I'll wager?" He sounded patronizing.

"Sir?"

"A leader is responsible for everything his unit does or fails to do. You know this." Montclair glowered deeper over his specs.

Steve slid his hands along his trousers. "Yes, sir, but how was I to have known—"

"Everything, Major Keller."

Steve took another deep breath, then quietly exhaled before he spoke. "Yes, sir. The whole point of our training allowed for decentralized planning and execution at the lowest level with supreme trust and confidence."

"And apparently, that's what they did. And you *did* believe it."

Steve bit the inside corner of his mouth. "I suppose, yeah. Deep down, I knew it was true. But we went back into Wadi Mali to see."

*Village of Wadi Mali, Afghanistan, December 3, 2009*

The helicopter ride from FOB Prince to the village took an hour. In flight, it was cold at altitude. On the ground, the helicopters landed in a cloud of talcum powder-like dust on a pleasant, if hazy sunny day. Steve and a small group of Special Operations Marines and Afghan soldiers moved to Wadi Mali.

While the Marines and their partnered forces secured a small perimeter, Steve and Fergus stood under the overhang of a house close to the scene of the alleged crime. In contrast to Steve's concerns, the populace went about their business and the town seemed sleepy.

Fergus asked, "What're we waiting for out here again?"

"NCIS. They're flying the investigating team here in a Huey. They landed at our FOB, but had mechanical issues, as you know. I said we'd fly ahead of them and set security. We'll guide them in, then take them to the house they want to look at and let them do their work."

Fergus cleaned his sunglasses on his shirt and put them back on. "Sounds fine to me." He looked out into the haze with a slight smirk and withdrew a package of cigarettes and a Zippo lighter from his shoulder pocket. Lighting two cigarettes with flourish, he handed one to Steve.

"Thanks. I wish we weren't out here, Fergus."

"You and me both. I need a nap." He snorted. "We generally sleep during the day since we operate so much at night. This is fucking up the rhythm!"

Steve grew curious. "You know about this situation? Do the boys?" Aside from Fergus and Brian, no one in the platoon really knew why they were out here, but Steve didn't assume anything.

"People know something's up. Otherwise, we wouldn't be here in broad daylight. The lads aren't stupid, you know?" Fergus exhaled smoke through his nose.

"Yeah. I know. Of course they know something is up. And people talk. Fuck." He took a drag on the cigarette.

"How much do you think this investigation is costing at the moment?"

"What?" Steve said, exhaling smoke.

"Us, coming out here. Them being flown out here from Kandahar. Just to investigate some dead Afghan? Who cares?"

"Fergus, I need to remind you that none of this is confirmed. It's, as of yet, circumstantial. Our own boys deserve the benefit of the doubt."

The whirring of another helicopter was heard in the distance, growing louder. Radios crackled for guidance, and Fruit Bat answered telling them where to land.

"You're right. That was shitty of me to say. I'm sorry." Fergus took another drag.

"All good. We're all frustrated." Steve finished his cigarette and tossed the butt into the dust. He winked at Fergus.

"Just another day!" Fergus laughed and winked back, coughing a blast of smoke.

A Marine Huey helicopter flew low over the village, banked, and landed close by on a pre-set yellow smoke grenade Fruit Bat threw out as a marker. A cloud of yellow smoke and dust engulfed Fergus and Steve and the Huey engine dropped to idle and settled on its skids. From the dissipating cloud emerged a woman and two men carrying a large plastic Pelican case, followed by Private Vaughn. They were dressed as if they'd shopped at REI just before deploying. Their gear was new, and their helmets and vests didn't fit. But they carried themselves as professionals, and given the gravity of the situation, Steve took them seriously.

The Huey lifted off, circled over them one more time, then departed. Out of earshot, the air again was still. The day was clear, slightly warm given the time of year, and the agrarian smell of dung hung in the air, intermingled with dust and depression.

Fergus and Steve looked at them through their Oakley sunglasses. Steve moved to greet them. Fergus remained leaning against one of three upright poles that held up the porch of an Afghan home.

The female agent approached Steve with an extended gloved hand. "I'm Special Agent Juliet Blaise, NCIS," she said, introducing herself and displaying her NCIS badge and credentials. She was an athletic Hispanic woman with neck-length hair and spoke with a light, clipped Spanish accent sounding like Penelope Cruz or Salma Hayek.

"I'm Steve!" He removed his own glove to shake it, he was a gentleman, after all.

"Nice to meet you!" she returned.

He smiled. "Juliet?! How romantic!" He tried to ease things with a joke. She reminded him of Elena.

She wasn't amused. "The other two are Agents Laurel and Hardy." She directed a thumb at Laurel, a tall, thin white man, and Hardy, a larger African-American with a small, neat moustache. The two men struggled carrying the bulky Pelican case.

Fergus, already irritated they were there in the first place, grunted. "Fuck...Real comedy troupe, you fuckers are!" He crossed his arms.

"Who're you?" She sounded annoyed.

But Fergus remained steadfast. "Groucho Marx, or the guy making it possible for you to do your work. You could say 'Thank you!'" He stared at Juliet, whose eyebrow began to twitch under her ill-fitted helmet.

"Thank you!" she said with sarcasm.

Steve sensed the increasing tension and commanded, "Fergus, go check the perimeter and make sure people are paying attention. I'll take the NCIS agents to the house."

"Roger." Fergus shifted from the upright, not taking his eyes off Juliet until he turned the corner.

She regained her composure. "I know this is a pain in the ass, but we appreciate your being out here for this. I know it's tough. We can't do it without your support."

Steve nodded. *You have no idea about 'tough,'* he thought. *Two of my men are accused of violating the Laws of Armed Conflict via Capital crimes, abetted by a law-enforcement officer.*

Outside of the house, Abdullah called out to talk to the Afghan owner. He emerged from his home, closing the door behind him. After a brief conversation in Pashtu, the owner gestured toward the hut.

Abdullah turned to Juliet, translating, "He said this is where the Americans killed him."

Juliet said, "That's why we're here. Can we talk to you after we finish inside?" She didn't apologize for the crime. Juliet was careful.

Abdullah turned back to converse with the Afghan owner. "He says of course."

Juliet thanked him with the only Pashtu phrase she knew. *"Ah Shookran!"* Abdullah, and the owner walked to a shaded area to continue their conversation.

Steve looked after them, then turned to Juliet, "So, this is it."

She nodded and looked at the door, then at her teammates. "You guys ready?"

Laurel and Hardy nodded and put down their box. They opened it to reveal cameras, a selection of evidence collection items, tape measures, and other tools to investigate a murder scene. Off to one side, Juliet briefly conversed with Vaughn and motioned for him to stay outside.

"Shit..." Steve said under his breath as the NCIS agents opened the door.

# 12

Fergus came back, and he and Steve waited outside. Vaughn stood a short distance from them, pacing nervously as he packed chewing tobacco into his lip. Steve sniffed to get the dust out of his nose. Vaughn spit tobacco juice and opened a package of beef jerky. *Ugh, what a combination.*

Fergus looked at Vaughn, then asked Steve, "What actually happened, skipper?"

"Marko and Reid killed Tenkara," Steve replied, drained.

"Really?!"

"When you see them, you can slap 'em."

Fergus shrugged. "Eh. Reid's a good enough bloke. But Marko, he's always been kind of an asshole."

"That bad, huh?" Steve ran his tongue over his dry lips.

Fergus nodded emphatically. "I've known him since Second Force and our days as your instructors. That's what you get sometimes, though."

"I think Geddes is the main guy. He's the kind of person who can influence and take advantage of people. I can see it."

"What makes you think that?"

"I didn't trust Geddes the moment I saw him. I'll bet he got Marko and Reid to go along with the plan he concocted to mete out some kind of vigilante justice. Having SOF guys like them working with him gives the entire operation an air of legitimacy. Plus, it's easier than making an arrest and dealing with the Afghan justice system," Steve proposed glumly.

"Yeah, probably. This situation's like back in Ireland."

That piqued Steve's interest. "What do you mean?"

"Geddes likely figured they could just shoot this guy and be done with it. In the IRA, when they dealt with dissenters, they did so on their own. Looks pretty much the same. Street justice, Robin Hood, or some such shit." He spit out of the side of his mouth and fished into his sleeve pocket for another cigarette. He put two in his mouth and deftly lit them before handing one to Steve.

"Thanks. That's two I owe you." Steve took a drag and stared out into the hazy day, blowing smoke slowly out of his nose. They stood silently for a few more moments.

Steve made eye-contact with Vaughn and glanced at Fergus. "Stay put." He flicked his cigarette into the dirt and walked to Vaughn to talk to him out of earshot. "Hey, private?"

"Yes, sir?" Vaughn sounded scared.

Steve raised his open hands in front of him. "You aren't in any trouble with me. I just want you to tell me what happened here."

Vaughn spit tobacco juice again, nervous. "I was Geddes's driver. Geddes knew this guy was laying low here and came up with a plan to have us go arrest him." He then recounted the details of that night.

"What about the rest of the Americans with you?"

"The other US soldiers on the mission were on the outskirts of the village letting Afghans handle Afghans. This ensured the ANP didn't come to where he was," Vaughn explained. "When Geddes captured the dude, the three of them took him in that building and shot him. Then, they got me to pick them up in our truck and they loaded the body, rolled up in some carpet, in the back. They threw it in ditch outside the village like a piece of trash."

"After they detained Agha, did you know what they'd intended?" Steve was still letting what Vaughn relayed sink in.

"No! I didn't!"

Steve nodded. "How did Geddes cover it up?"

Vaughn spit again. "From there, it was pretty easy. Geddes told our Afghan counterparts that Agha eluded them again, and we returned to base. When we got back to the FOB, Geddes filed a false report with his own higher that the guy tried to run and was killed in a firefight."

Steve asked, "Did you feel your life was in danger?"

"Fuck yes, sir; Geddes told me that if I told anyone what happened, he'd come find me in the States. After what they did and how they acted, I couldn't sleep. Even if I was an accidental accomplice, there were three crazy people on a remote outpost who might kill me! I left the next day and reported it to my chain of command."

He put his hand on Vaughn's shoulder. "We'll get you home safe, don't worry."

Vaughn timidly nodded.

The door to the crime scene opened. Juliet stood in the doorway of the hut. She motioned to Steve. "You should come in here."

Steve walked to Juliet, leaving Vaughn standing alone. He looked inside. The carpeted floor had a section cut from it, and what appeared to be three bullet holes in the wall.

"Don't touch anything," she cautioned. The three agents wore nitrile surgical gloves. Laurel shut the door and turned on a black light. In the dark of the room, blood stains and splatter illuminated on the walls and floor. Steve's eyes widened and his mouth slowly opened, his face drooped in shock. It was impossible to believe that Vaughn's account was fabricated.

Juliet said, "Well, that ain't good."

Hardy agreed. "Shit happens. And it appears that shit happened out here."

Juliet turned to Hardy. "You getting this on tape?"

"You bet, boss," Hardy said, videoing the scene slowly with a small camera.

"Great." She wrote on a small note pad while Laurel and Hardy processed the room, took measurements, and searched for forensic evidence.

Laurel examined the bullet impacts in the wall. "Boss! Check this out: a bullet! Looks like a .308!" He dug it out with the tip of his knife.

She held open an evidence bag, and Laurel dropped it in. "Nice!" Juliet studied Steve. "With the bullet, the missing carpet, and the blacklight photos, all I'm missing is a body. This is getting interesting."

"I gotta go outside," Steve said. His stomach knotted with revulsion at the confirmation that his own men had betrayed him.

Juliet followed him, and they exited into the sunshine. They walked a short distance from the house, away from Fergus and Vaughn.

Juliet said, "I need to talk to the Afghan who owns this place."

"OK." Steve motioned to Abdullah to come to him. "Abdullah, please get the owner."

"Yes, sir." He darted off to do as asked.

Through Abdullah, Juliet conversed with him. "Do you know where they put the body?"

"He said he watched the entire thing from over there." Abdullah pointed to a collection of trees one-hundred yards away. "And that they threw it in a ditch." He gestured to the outskirts of town.

The owner held up a pair of plastic flexicuffs and conversed with Abdullah. "He said he had to remove these to properly prepare the body."

Juliet took the flexicuffs and put them in the cargo pocket of her trousers. She pointed to where the owner indicated they'd disposed of Agha. "Is it still there?"

Abdullah shook his head. "He says it is not; he buried it the next day."

"Afghans bury their dead within twenty-four hours," Steve interjected.

Juliet shrugged. "So, we'll just dig it up."

Steve shook his head. "It's not that easy. To exhume a body, you'll need a letter from the Afghan government. That could take a long time. Sorry."

"Shit. By the time we do that, the body will have decomposed!" Juliet turned back to the owner. "Thank you for all your help. We'll return if we need your assistance, *Ah Shookran!*"

Abdullah translated and turned with the Afghan owner, leaving Steve and Juliet.

"You seem to enjoy your work." Steve looked away from the village at the dust swirling off the land.

"I enjoy finding the truth of things." She smiled and returned to the building.

Steve rubbed his left eye with his index finger to remove some dust. Another wave of nausea followed by disgusted anger assaulted him. Not only had Marko and Reid betrayed him, they'd also taken the one thing he desired above all else: Agha. Steve had wanted to be the one to stare into Agha's soul before pulling the trigger. But that had been denied him.

In another flash, he selfishly confronted the thought that the situation would end his career.

"Man, fuck," Steve said flatly.

An hour later, the NCIS agents completed their investigation and arranged with Steve to be recovered by helicopters.

Fruit Bat called for extraction. "Twenty minutes out, boss."

Steve gave him a thumbs up.

Fergus positioned the ground force in a security position while Juliet talked with Steve. "Now what?" Steve asked. Helicopters buzzed in the distance.

"We arrest them," Juliet said, as if she knew he wanted confirmation to something he already knew.

Steve picked up a small rock. "Figured." He tossed it.

"Do they know we're coming?" Her tone turned cautious, almost suspicious, as if she didn't trust him.

"Not likely. I didn't tell them if that's what you mean."

"No, nothing meant," she backpedaled. "Good. I also like to deliver surprises."

The helicopters grew steadily louder. Two Apache gunships flew overhead, followed by a MH-47 helicopter and a Marine Huey which landed in a gigantic cloud of swirling dirt and exhaust. Fergus and the security element loaded onto the MH-47. The NCIS agents, Steve, and Vaughn loaded onto the Huey.

They lifted into the cobalt blue sky, turning toward Geddes's FOB.

# 13

*Geddes's FOB, Afghanistan, December 3, 2009*

eddes, Marko, and Reid emerged from Geddes's team room and looked up at the aircraft as they approached. Steve looked down from the open door of the Huey. Geddes shielded his eyes against the glare of the sunlight while they flew over.

Steve pointed down at the FOB. "That's them!" he told Juliet on the helicopter's internal intercom.

"Let's go get 'em!" she directed the pilots to land in front of them.

Steve and the NCIS agents moved toward Geddes, Marko, and Reid, who walked to meet them, trying to be casual. Marko approached Steve. "Great to see you, boss!"

Steve was amazed Marko could be so upbeat, like nothing had happened. "WHAT?! Holy shit, Marko. You *know* why we're here!" He pulled him to the side away from Juliet and her crew, the whir of the helos masking any conversations.

Marko put his hands out and yelled, "Why do you care?! You wanted him dead. Hell, you wanted to do it yourself!"

Steve's eyes widened. "There are rules! We were supposed to do this the right way!" He ran his hands through his hair, then drew them down over his cheeks. "You need to come clean with this, Marko!"

Marko smirked but said nothing.

The helicopter blades remained spinning as the NCIS agents arrested them and read them their rights. Steve looked at Marko while the NCIS agents loaded them onto the Huey. Steve departed back to FOB Prince on the MH-47.

Those on the Huey flew to Kandahar where Ballentine awaited their arrival.

# 14



*Southern Afghanistan, December 4, 2009*

From the time they were arrested in Afghanistan, Geddes, Marko, and Reid mounted a counter-information campaign. They told any and all who would listen that the charges were unfounded and assured everyone that the "truth" would reveal all in what was a big misunderstanding. It was the same obfuscation and malfeasance that all guilty people use.

To further deflect pressure from them, as the investigation unfolded, Marko and Geddes branded Vaughn a coward, a traitor, a troublemaker, and a weak-minded soldier who only wanted to go home and would do anything to get it.

They also accused Steve of selling them out, of not supporting them, and that Steve didn't care about their well-being and that they'd essentially been abandoned to the post with Geddes. It was a hell of a blow to Steve's morale.

A huge division formed in the MSOC while they were still deployed. Those on Marko's and Reid's side shored up their reasons for supporting them and set out to discredit any who thought otherwise. Those who didn't or had no opinion formed another camp, and between all of them, were men with whom Steve never regained their loyalty as far as trust and leadership were concerned.

Steve was caught in the middle, though he eventually got an audience, albeit by phone, with Marko.

The discussion was terse and difficult.

*"The NCIS chick said you told her that we did it?!"* Marko accused.

"I didn't say that. I said I didn't want to believe it to be true, and I still don't, despite the evidence pointing to the contrary. Juliet told you that I believed you did it to sow doubt, so you'd confess!"

*"We're smarter than that!"* Marko sneered.

"Yeah, I know, but that hasn't stopped the narrative that I don't support my own men. Now it's gotten back to the families. I have a real problem on my hands."

*"You're the one who betrayed and alienated us! What'd you expect?!"*

Steve almost crushed the phone's handset in his anger. "Really, Marko? You've offered nothing to counter the sequence of events. If you've done nothing wrong, what are you afraid of? Incriminating yourselves?!"

*"Whatever, bro!"*

With that they hung up the phone.

# 15



"Then what happened?" Montclair asked.

Steve surveyed the room, the other board members, then looked back at Montclair. "I read the NCIS report. It made a strong case, but without a dead body, the evidence was all circumstantial. And there was no way to take them to trial with foreign witnesses. The long and drawn-out investigation yielded nothing. The case remains open.

"They murdered a guy in cold blood and tried to cover it up. They were proud of it. It destroyed my men's trust in me as people chose sides."

Montclair's surprise seemed genuine. "Some *sided* with them?"

"Of course. Counter accusations were levied. Nothing had to be true, only credible. Marko was very experienced and popular among some members of the company. So, he took advantage of that to protect himself and Reid and was further assisted by Geddes, who had experience in these situations."

"Geddes sounded like a good asset," Montclair frowned.

"He was sir. He did what we couldn't by locating Agha. He could have written his own ticket, except for one flaw."

"Which was?" Montclair looked up from taking notes on a yellow legal pad.

"He spent most of his career as a vice cop and he specialized in drug and prostitution busts. One needs guile to survive in those environments, and Geddes had tons of it. All those years of deep-cover counter-narcotics work made him sly and exceptionally careful. He also had a history of shady dealings in his own past. In the States, primary suspects due to appear in court in cases where Geddes was involved would end up dead under mysterious circumstances. He undoubtedly encouraged them to go forward with the scheme and knew how to cover it up. It was the perfect crime."

# 16



*FOB Prince, Afghanistan, December 11, 2009*

A week later, Ballentine returned to the FOB in the early evening. To his frustration, Steve didn't meet him when he flew in on a resupply helicopter. He immediately sought Steve out, who was shooting his carbine on the base small arms range.

"CEASE FIRE!" Ballentine yelled.

Steve finished shooting another two rounds and turned to his boss. "Sir!"

"Don't play coy; the private was right!" Ballentine's face was red.

Steve checked his weapon was safe, then let his rifle hang on its sling. "Appears so, sir. What happened was confirmed by the Afghan owner in whose hut the crime occurred. He corroborated Private Vaughn's story nearly to the word and action."

Ballentine swore. "Damn . . . . Well, at least they'll be taken care of."

"How do you mean, sir?" Steve dreaded the response.

Ballentine, calmer now, spoke like he'd come up with another master stroke. "NCIS is filing the charges today. But for their own good, and the good of the unit, I've arranged to get the three of them out of country to avoid further scrutiny."

"WHAT?!"

"They deserve a fair shake."

"I agree a fair trial is warranted, but this is a travesty!"

Ballentine slammed his fist into his open palm. "Let me tell you something. I don't appreciate how you second-guess my decisions! You have and continue to do so. This is best for all of us. End of discussion."

Steve was aghast. "You're *protecting* them!"

Ballentine extended his open palms and leaned toward him. "One thing I do know is, regardless of the outcome, this is not going to go well for *you*."

Steve looked at his commander with wide eyes. "What?! HOW?! You ignored my request to relieve Marko—*twice*—then cut him over to Geddes! And look what it got you, sir!"

"Don't pin this on me!" Ballentine shouted. "You had your chance with me and refused it! And they were under your command at the time. I was in Kandahar, remember?!"

Steve was speechless and welled with fury, but he had to be careful. "They committed murder. I saw where it happened. Two people with the same account of the same event, in two different languages, who've never seen each other otherwise, isn't happenstance!" Steve shook his head vigorously, then pointed at Ballentine. "You should relieve Marko and Reid, refer them to be court-martialed, and press charges against Geddes."

"Let it go, Steve."

Steve's unleashed his anger. "What do you stand to gain from all of this? Are you jealous, sir? That I belong to this tribe and, as an outsider, you won't be accepted into it on your own, regardless of merits? Earning it can only be achieved by taking Selection, but I know you would never undergo that process yourself. So, was Agha your ticket?"

Ballentine ignored Steve's outburst and remained collected. "Your passion is one of your positive traits that I admire. You and I have a lot in common, believe it or not."

He smiled, smug. "If you stay quiet about this, we'll all come away with what we want."

Steve stared, and though his mouth didn't move, his mind raced at a mile-a-minute. "We're nothing alike, sir," he said, resentful that Ballentine wanted to include him in the cover-up.

Ballentine eyed Steve for a moment, then wordlessly walked off the range toward his quarters.

Steve resumed firing his carbine on full-automatic, the short bursts of reverberating through the camp.

# 17



After Wadi Mali, Brian and Steve walked along the perimeter of the FOB Prince helicopter landing zone on an overcast, chilly afternoon. Brian stopped and faced Steve. "We hate Ballentine. Everyone knows about the Marko situation. I know it's rough for you, but we're on your side."

"I appreciate that, Brian," Steve sighed. "In hindsight, this past April, prior to deployment, when you told me about Marko, you were right. A better course of action would have been to relieve Marko altogether. Not doing so obviously proved disastrous because Marko was corruptible, and Geddes took full advantage of that. But he also apparently has a staunch ally in Ballentine."

"You really think so, sir?"

"Yeah. No doubt in my mind. Ballentine's spineless. He didn't relieve Marko or Reid on the negative premise of things they may or may not have done. They've kept their rank and won't receive bad evaluations. Of course, I disagree with all of this, but it's not my decision to make since Ballentine took it out of my hands."

Brian nodded. "We know. Ballentine's single glaring shortcoming is his arrogance. Where it stems from, I don't know. Maybe it's all those lives he's lived." Brian shrugged and smiled at Steve. "We see how he acts. Ballentine is self-assured and thinks highly of his own intellect. He can't be told anything, always seems to have the solution, and smugly answers questions with fake and plastic, foolhardy confidence."

"It's awesome what you guys notice, too." Steve smiled.

"You can't fool the troops, sir," Brian returned.

# 18



One of the international counterparts the MSOC shared their base with was a group of Czech commandos. They deployed with a large shipping container full of fine Czech pilsner beer. While GO-1 meant alcohol was forbidden to US forces, no such restriction applied to foreign troops. The Czech's gladly sold two cases at black market prices to the ever-resourceful Fergus, who invited select MSOC members to a Christmas party. Ballentine wasn't on the guest list.

Sitting around a large firepit, they enjoyed cigars and a few chilled beers in the cold air of Christmas night below a bright tapestry of stars. After drinking near-beers for months, the real thing was a godsend.

Steve had grabbed a beer from one of their coolers and was returning to the fire when he stopped. His men thought he'd stepped away and were talking about him.

"Damndest thing I ever saw," Guido commented. "I don't know how the dude lived through a hail of gunfire and emerged unscathed."

"Yeah. I can't believe he wasn't shot or dead by now! I'll tell you; we got lucky. Keller's the best officer I've ever seen.

You go out with him, you'll definitely get in the shit, but damn, he's good," Brian complimented.

"Yeah, stay with the Captain. He'll get you through," Fergus added.

"Keller is the ultimate combat machine; nothing fucking stops that guy." Alex smiled. "The dude's a myth!" He blew smoke rings for emphasis.

"He's too much," McConnell recalled, "Fuck, I saw him fire a warning shot at a guy on a motorcycle. I thought the 'ghans were going to light them up, but that guy had it under control."

"Shit, I remember we were taking a break on a patrol, and he was taking a nap on a stretcher, and we started taking IDF. One burst close by, and Grimace dove on him to protect him and woke him up. He was more pissed off about that than getting shelled and not having on any body armor. What the fuck?" Hoyle laughed, and they all cracked up.

Steve smiled at the memory. Steve and his men—hell, the entire company—had been through a lot. Much more than he thought they ever would. Though ten Marines in their MSOC had been wounded, they hadn't lost a man since Luke had been killed. Regardless of the rift within the unit, his men saw Steve as a Talisman.

Listening to them, Steve thought of his wish earlier that year to see more protracted combat. To be in real firefights. To be measured. He shuddered; the wish had been granted, yet he would take it all back instead of making a Faustian bargain.

He popped open his beer, signaling his arrival. "Sounds like a hell of a guy!" Steve joined, coming to the fire.

They looked at him sheepishly.

"What can we say?" Rod piped up. "You're the man everyone wants to be around. In combat especially. You're lucky." He was buzzed, but Steve felt his sincerity and smiled regardless.

Everyone nodded and turned to other topics.

***

The party broke up. It was snowing. Steve stood alone in front of the firepit watching the dancing flames. He thought of the irony of Agha being murdered and how, selfishly, the satisfaction of his death had been snatched from him. The moral issues Steve wrestled with were compounded by the loyalty he thought his men had for him in the same manner he gave them. That loyalty—fraternity—put him at odds with his own wife and, as she'd written in the letter, her perception was that he valued them more than her.

She, too, had a point.

For Ballentine, it was about the win. Ballentine could always distance himself if things went bad on an objective. Marko killing Tenkara got a named objective off the battle-field and made Ballentine look great, but in this case, where there were complications surrounding how Tenkara was killed, Ballentine could absolve himself of any wrongdoing by blaming it on his subordinates.

Under Ballentine's command, Steve realized how jaded he'd become, how he'd lost focus on why he served anymore. It further bothered him that he was responsible for the deaths of so many people. When it came to punishing the enemy, he was filled with a rage and single focus for revenge that couldn't be abated until he completed the task to his own satisfaction. Whether he did it by his own hand or helped to facilitate it, he was inextricably intertwined with the outcome.

He'd done it all for Roland, for Luke, for his uncle, for the weak, for the nameless and the oppressed, and the people who were guilty of nothing more than having been born. The only problem is that, according to a Sicilian proverb, "Revenge is a season in hell."

His thoughts turned to Rod's earlier compliment of him being "lucky." Steve didn't like that assessment. It weighed heavily on him. Perhaps he'd developed skills that gave his men faith in him and that he was a good leader through steady application, but being lucky, while apt, wasn't something he wanted to accept. For a leader, being called lucky brought an enormous amount of pressure.

Steve admired all kinds of military leaders from over his years in the Corps and different periods of history. From World War II, General James Gavin, Lieutenant Colonel David Stirling, Colonel Evans Carlson, and Colonel "Red Mike" Edson. From Vietnam, Major Dick Meadows, Colonel Bull Simons, Colonel Charlie Beckwith, Major General Gary Harrell, Major General Eldon Bargewell, Colonel James Ripley, and Major James Capers. From Iraq in 2007, Major Doug Zembiec. And the founder of Special Forces, Major Robert Rogers, an Indian fighter for the British during the French and Indian War, rounded out the list of leaders Steve tried to emulate.

Rogers was a respected commander with an incredible military record, including some spectacular victories. He also suffered crushing, dazzling defeats, but his men followed him unto death. Ingloriously, he died a debtor, divorced from his wife, nearly penniless and forgotten by the Crown he'd served. Steve admired the "White Devil," as Rogers was known by the Abenaki Indians he fought, flaws and all, and also knew most of the heroes he held in high military esteem were deeply flawed, troubled people. They were humans, in other words, but their contemporaries didn't seem to see them that way, for whatever reason.

Two and a half centuries later, Rogers was still a legend in SOF. His *Fourteen Rules of Ranging* were adapted by all SOF and were still part of the operational guidelines for the Army's Ranger Regiment. "Ranging" was the name for the type of war Rogers conducted, operating out of "range" of his supply depots, living off the land, and taking the fight to the enemy on their own terms. He raised units for near-suicidal expeditions and missions by reputation alone.

Rogers' men believed *he'd* been lucky. They followed him because they trusted that luck would work in their favor. Rogers hated that assessment. He felt the pressure was too great for a leader to be seen as lucky, to remain so, since that became the expectation, and no leader could sustain that reputation. But Rogers's luck held.

Steve identified with the pressure Rogers spoke of and it became hard to focus and function as a leader due to the cyclical nature of the expectation of survivability. Rogers had also written about it, and Steve appreciated it since it was now he who was "lucky." And he, too, didn't want it.

His men felt safe with him, that they would make it, and he couldn't convince any of them that it was luck for all of them, not him exclusively, that was working in their favor since individual fates could pull someone else into your path despite their not wanting to be a part of it like Portnoy. Roland. Ketcham. Luke, and all of the rest. They didn't have a choice in the matter.

What made people think Steve would somehow change the course of things?

But then it dawned on him that, perhaps, Roland's ghost had been even more of an influence than just that day on the hill or the foreshadowing of Luke's death. Roland was protecting Steve, and his men benefitted from that protection. Even with Roland's unseen shield, Steve braced against the pressure he felt to bring them all home, to be the guiding hand, to serve as their savior and messiah. In his mind, there was no way he could ever do enough for them or live up to performing to their expectations, but with each mission his reputation grew along with their confidence in him. It was a terrible burden.

*Sometimes, you don't get what you want,* Steve thought with resigned acceptance. He was the shepherd, and they his flock, though he was no angel or protector. It was something he never grew used to or liked.

It was also irrelevant.

Steve stared into a fire. What was next on the other side of the deployment when they went home in a few weeks? Looking into the dancing flames, he thought back to finishing the long walk at Selection only a few short years ago. Where Fergus had taken his pack. Of the satisfaction he'd had for completing the march and his first meeting with Roland Joyce. Then standing at the warming fire waiting for other candidates like Guido and Alex to arrive, unaware of their future. Of Marko waking him. Steve pushed his hands deeper into the pockets of his Gore Tex jacket.

"Merry Christmas," he said out loud. The snow sizzled on hot logs.

# 19



By the time the company was being relieved to go home, as Steve did with Eggerton back in August—only six months earlier—he was more than ready. The incident at Wadi Mali was hard to keep quiet, and Steve didn't like having the reputation of a leader who didn't back his men. Being called a coward was one of the worst things he could think of, and he never wanted his name associated with any kind of craven activity or action. He detested it in others, and Hackett tried to have one of his own men court-martialed for refusing to go out on a mission. Steve supported that, felt it justified, but Ballentine didn't share his sentiment. The man stayed.

As a result of all he'd endured as a combat leader and being betrayed by his own men, coupled with a growing yearning to return to his family, Steve never openly admitted his depression. It was hard to express, and his body rebelled against the intense stress. Exacerbated by the antimalarial Mefloquine tablets, it led to gastrointestinal disorders and chronic pressure and pain in his stomach and bowels. Over time, it in turn enlarged his prostate and he urinated near-constantly. His sleep patterns were nonexistent, and he struggled to get any rest.

Steve was heading down a dangerous path for the remainder of the deployment. He was miserable and drained both physically and mentally due to the fatigue and pressure of being a leader in a high-stress environment where his decisions affected lives. He'd lost men, killed and wounded, and his wife felt detached from him. He struggled with the illness he'd developed. He wasn't getting better, and he was dealing with it daily, all the while having to perform at a peak level. There was no relief from his men's expectations of him either, and he felt he had to be always perfect.

When he went on operations, he sought the most dangerous missions so he would expose himself to the worst and toughest situations. Combat was not a tourist venture; he had to be an active contributor. That was where the danger manifested, and Steve no longer wanted to live.

Ironically, he'd established himself as a fighter and leader to be emulated, so that took care of the fear of being perceived as a coward, and it also allowed him the best opportunity to get killed, and in so doing, it would be honorable, for he felt he had no honor left and that his own good name was ruined. He would also be out of his private misery. After a while he stopped questioning whether he was sane, he just wanted things to end, but he wouldn't do so by his own hand. Fate would have to deal the final blow.

Steve stopped ducking rounds as they whistled by him, figuring it was too late if he could hear them, and if he did get hit, he wouldn't have a say in the matter. His reputation became cemented as a fearless, unflinching, and complete warrior.

But he was tired. That was a supreme understatement, and when he left on a mission, he knew it would also take a little more out of him. It was a perpetual, self-destructive cycle.

The shit of it was that he loved the operations and how he felt on them, his physical maladies aside, and wanted—sought—the adrenaline that came with combat. Paradoxically, he became convinced that he was invincible, and at the same time, because of his deteriorating physical condition, that he was being punished.

Each mission was dangerous enough without him seeking the most difficult parts of it, but he didn't know any other way. If it meant driving at night, scaling ladders, putting himself in harm's way, or attaching himself to the team or formation most likely to get into contact, he sought it. His reputation was such that people asked if he would come out with them, if only to be near his infectious energy. He didn't betray any nervousness to anyone, if he felt it, and through all the things he experienced, he didn't remember feeling any fear, either. Though it must have been present for there was nothing worse than not feeling scared.

Having no fear meant you were already dead inside.

So, no, he couldn't not be scared. He just knew how to harness the energy to better deal with difficult situations. In combat, it was easy for him, but in relationships, he feared being hurtful and cruel more than anything.

He hoped Elena knew that.

***

Captain Chris Macksey, Steve's counterpart in the MSOC that was relieving them, revealed his own reservations as a new leader in MARSOC. Steve assured Chris that he'd felt the same way when he'd swapped out with Eggerton.

During their turnover patrol Chris asked a lot of questions but gone was the jovial nature of Steve's orientation before Ketcham was killed. Before Luke died. Before Agha.

"What's it like here?" Chris asked from the back seat.

Steve glanced back over his shoulder. "Combat in Southern Afghanistan is hard due to the rugged high-desert, mountainous terrain. It can be brutally hot in the summer and bitter cold in the winter. A rainy season in late fall replenishes the ground water, but generally, it's arid."

Steve cleared his throat. "Most of the population live in villages by water sources, typically near rivers. The dense vegetation causes these areas to be known as The Green Zone. The enemy lives and fights from these villages which all link together in a sprawl that allows for movements through drainage and irrigation ditches covered by the vegetation. These also create excellent trenches for fighting and give the enemy a decided advantage of cover and concealment, though they're very creative in fighting from buildings and pre-established firing positions for mortars and rocket launchers as well." It was a near-verbatim repeat of Eggerton's orientation to Steve.

"Huh, wouldn't expect that from a bunch of rag heads," Chris mocked.

"Don't underestimate these guys," Steve snapped. "They excel at defense in depth and can mass troops quickly and effectively. They're certainly not invincible, as we found, but every operator in the company respects the enemy since they can kill you as easily as anyone whether they're well-dressed, possess the best equipment, or other gear. It doesn't matter if a child or a seasoned fighter shoots you with an AK-47. Dead is dead."

Chris didn't ask any further questions.

Steve mutely stared out the window at the rocky, barren terrain. Hoyle drove. McConnell manned the turret. Grimace and Fruit Bat rode in the back with their counterparts. Abdullah, hoping for a better future, would continue serving as a US interpreter for Macksey.

Afghanistan remained unchanged.

# 20

*MARSOC HQ, Camp Lejeune, NC, July 16, 2016*

Colonel Montclair took a sip from his water glass. He grew serious. "You know why we're screening you, don't you, Steve?" It was the first time Montclair had let any familiarity between them slip.

"Yes, sir, absolutely."

"Do you think you have what it takes to lead a Marine Special Operations Company?"

Steve's reply was equally straightforward. "Emphatically, sir."

"Even in light of what you've told us?" Montclair arched his eyebrows. The other members of the board looked at him, stone-faced, following his lead.

Steve felt like he was presenting closing arguments at a trial. "You asked me difficult questions, and I answered them. I learned a lot from that event. And besides, I risked my life to prove them wrong. One doesn't go back into the heart of Taliban-held country in broad daylight after a prominent member of their society was murdered by Americans!" He leaned forward in his chair. "Do you really think I didn't take all of that into account when I went in there?! Haven't I demonstrated tough leadership in combat?! Isn't that the definition of courage, sir?!"

Montclair looked over his glasses again, his mouth curled up to one side. "Undoubtedly. But I must say, it still doesn't reflect well on you. Your leadership and judgment will always be called into question because of this. You know that, right?"

"Sir, it already is. It always is."

Montclair formed a peak with his fingers, his elbows on the table. "Steve—Major Keller—I need you to step outside while I confer with the rest of the board."

Steve sprang from his chair to attention. "Aye, aye, sir." He turned smartly and left the room.

He waited in the hallway. Steve exhaled deeply and ran his hands through his hair. Birds chirped outside as he reflected on his relationship with Colonel Montclair and knew, despite the crime in Wadi Mali, that the die was cast before he'd ever walked in the room.

Montclair had made his decision years ago. The interview was a formality.

# 21



After leaving the MSOC in the Summer of 2010, Steve was reassigned to II Marine Expeditionary Force (II MEF), another Marine unit outside of MARSOC, to gain distance from the stigma of Wadi Mali.

In early 2012, Elena began experiencing heavy fatigue and abdominal pain. Diagnosed as ovarian cancer, she underwent periodic treatments and a partial hysterectomy. The cancer took a toll on her physically, including the loss of her hair. It eventually went into remission, but they were warned it could return someday. They learned to live with it, and if Steve wasn't being punished, someone would have to convince him otherwise.

His latest assignment was a training command within II MEF that worked with line Marine Corps units preparing them for deployment. Steve, being from Special Operations, was immediately at odds with the unit's Executive Officer, Lieutenant Colonel Loren Baxter, a career Infantry officer with little use for SOF. He disliked Steve from the beginning.

Baxter was from a rich family in Pittsburgh, Pennsylvania. A Naval Academy graduate who had wrestled and rowed crew, he was six foot four inches tall, bellicose, and exuded a stereotypical caricature, hallmarked by an aristocratic air full of supreme egotism and bombast. He considered all officers who didn't earn their commission via a service academy "pretenders."

If he didn't like them, he'd research his subordinate officers to find out as much as he could, then bring them into his office and subject them to two-hours of character assassination, playing on the psychology that he knew more about them than they thought. He viciously engaged his charges like prey in an attempt to keep them in check. Baxter couldn't be appeased, no matter what someone did well, and certainly not if they failed at something.

Baxter played the good and bad jailer of sorts, switching tactics at random, and promised if they played their cards right, he'd be an ally. Some took him up on the offer to stop his attacks on their reputation, but those who stood up to him found themselves in a nightmarish world without support, no defense, and no respite. His counseling sessions left people psychologically shaken and visibly upset. He was a cruel sadist.

Baxter's deep-rooted insecurity might have stemmed from a chemical imbalance in his brain, if he were not an outright sociopath, since he didn't display any kind of empathy. He only expressed regret if he were caught or chastised by a senior officer for doing something; Baxter wasn't equipped to reach that conclusion on his own.

Steve kept to himself, but that seemed to be enough for Baxter to find faults with him. Combative by nature, the fact that Baxter didn't scare Steve meant Baxter had nothing else to lord over him, and he resorted to personal attacks.

"I see here you have the Outstanding Volunteer Medal," Baxter said in a session where he'd pulled up Steve's service record. "That's a bullshit award, you know? You aren't even going to ask why, are you?"

Steve remained impassive, studying Baxter's every facial expression, quirk, and tic, including his clipped, precise diction. Baxter's assumptive nature meant he controlled people through fear and intimidation, it was all the worst of being in a prisoner of war situation. Steve didn't answer the questions.

"That's just like you," Baxter derided. "I'll tell you why. You have to submit yourself for it. Essentially, it's a self-promoting award, and the individual who does so is a badge-hunter, an aggrandizer, and selfish. That's what you are."

"Actually, sir," Steve replied, surprising his interrogator, "my old platoon sergeant submitted it for me."

"For what?" Baxter snorted.

"For the work I've done in the community teaching and coaching youth lacrosse. I've given countless hours of my time over the years promoting the sport."

"Well, I heard about *that* from another guy who doesn't like you," Baxter said, "and you aren't very good at it, so what does that make you?"

"I still got the medal for the work I did. Some people don't share my methods, and I admit I could be better in some areas—"

"See! There you go admitting your shortcomings, but these are things you don't see on your own. This is why you have so much to learn as an officer. I know more about you than you know. I know you struggled during MARSOC Selection. Didn't think I knew that did you?! Impressive that you passed, but still, you placed almost last among officers. Yeah, you still got into MARSOC, but now here you are, working for us. Must suck for you." Another dig into Steve's psyche, for he was indeed sensitive about the Selection issue and didn't bring it up in conversation with anyone. Baxter had reopened a wound.

*I don't remember seeing you there with me.* He held off saying it out loud. He'd learned to stay quiet during the sessions and not get into trouble by opening himself to an attack, which, as frequently happened, occurred even if imagined items were introduced. Steve didn't understand why he was targeted, but it didn't get better, even when he worked extra hard to avoid scrutiny.

***

On one occasion when he'd been summoned to Baxter's office, Steve had reported but Baxter wasn't there. He'd gone out riding his motorcycle for the afternoon. It had been a beautiful day, Steve recalled, so he couldn't blame Baxter for taking advantage of the weather. He'd left and returned to his duties.

The following day, he'd been told to report to Baxter.

"GET IN HERE!" he'd roared at Steve, rising to his full height. His beady blue eyes glinted with indignation. "I thought I told you come to my office yesterday!"

Steve had tried to explain the situation. To ease the tension in his mind, he'd pictured Baxter as a large bear on a small motorcycle with a party hat on his head. He'd stifled a laugh.

"Bullshit!" Baxter had spewed. "It's not any of your business what I do with my time, but you'd better damn sure respect what I told you to do. Why didn't you wait for me?"

"Sir?"

"You fucking heard me, Major. Why didn't you wait?!" Baxter fumed. "Are you smirking?!"

Steve had tried to sound reasonable. "I had work to do, sir, and figured waiting was inefficient. And no, sir, I'm not making faces!"

"You insolent prick. When I was coming up, and I was asked by a senior officer to meet them, I waited."

"I'm glad things have changed in that regard, sir."

"THIS IS WHY YOU AND I HAVE NO RELATIONSHIP! YOU ARE SO DISRESPECTFUL!" Saliva had flown from a corner of his mouth.

Steve stood at parade rest, his hands clasped behind his back, and endured the rest of the session.

# 22

---



Over the course of two years, Baxter sent Steve on every detailed assignment he could that took Steve out of the office, and, in turn, away from his family. He traveled a lot around the country as a result, which also took him away from his primary duties, but that didn't seem at odds with Baxter's requirements of him so long as Steve was being inconvenienced. Steve joked that he had so much time in the Las Vegas airport that he was having his mail forwarded there to read it in a timelier manner.

It wasn't that he minded being out with and training Marines. Far from it. It was that he was always on the manning documents for training events requiring an officer evaluator, and even then, it wasn't unusual for him to be put against another emerging requirement. Steve was frustrated, but there wasn't much he could do.

On the other side of the tasks, Steve was one of the most experienced people in the organization and the units he coached performed very well in training and excelled in combat. He gained a reputation as being a fair and good trainer, being knowledgeable and free from any bullshit. It was refreshing for a lot of Marines who just wanted to be treated equitably, fairly, and most importantly, well-trained for the missions they would undertake. With the soul of a teacher, Steve enjoyed being in the field with Marines, helping them hone their skills that they would later employ in the zero-defect environment of combat. He didn't take the responsibility lightly.

During one of the training evolutions to California, Steve was in his hotel room when his cell phone rang. The number was scrambled and not identifiable, but instinct told him to answer it regardless. And he was glad that he did.

Master Sergeant Scott Kelton, an old and good friend, was on the other end. They'd known each other for years. Kelton worked in various SOF units outside of the Marine Corps. He'd left the Corps, joined the Air Force as a Combat Controller, and later rejoined the Marine Corps because he missed the structure and camaraderie. Kelton was as tough as they came, and Steve admired him.

He had an enticing offer to serve as an Operations Officer with a unit considered the pinnacle of Special Operations assignments. Steve listened intently. It was excellent; he was being requested to do a coveted job, and he had to be able to leave inside of two weeks. He couldn't believe his luck. He would have to get through Baxter, first, however.

Steve accepted but cautioned that he would have to get back to him about the permissions.

"Don't worry," Kelton assured. "We'll take care of the requests from our end. We're just glad you can help, my friend."

Steve hung up the phone and smiled.

However, it wouldn't be as easy as it sounded, primarily because of Baxter, not only because he wouldn't want to give up the personnel, but moreover his entrenched hatred for Steve festered and expanded over time, and each interaction only deepened the rift.

By the time he returned from this particular trip, the request for Steve via II MEF from an outside entity had already reached Baxter. He was poised and ready to strike when he ordered Steve to his office, put him at parade rest, and berated him with renewed vigor.

"I received the request. We've already told them No, and you're not going anywhere." Steve stood in stoic silence but internally felt defeated. "Do you know, Major, that I would never play poker with you? Your face betrays nothing." Baxter offered. Steve reasoned that fact irritated the shit out of him. Baxter persisted with the same tactic. Steve stared out the window and pondered the universe, or at least the clouds and sky that he could see on this late fall day. Baxter was furious and downcast. "Get out."

Steve popped to attention and turned to leave the office. He curled his fingers into fists, his nails digging into the palms of his hands.

"Major Keller," Baxter said, "it doesn't have to be like this."

Steve stopped and turned slightly, his back still mostly facing him. He didn't want Baxter to see the anger on his face. "Like what, sir?"

"Our relationship. I want to be a fan of yours, but you aren't letting me." Baxter put the onus on him for their poor interpersonal exchanges. Steve likened this situation—and the one that every other officer found themselves with Baxter—as that of battered wife. Not the ones who try to dress better, cook the right foods, protect their children by taking the brunt of things to protect herself from her abuser. More that of the sort that after being beaten for the umpteenth time, that they couldn't take it anymore. The mistreatment followed by the olive branch to make amends was all a cold, calculated, manipulative ploy.

"Aye, aye, sir." And Steve continued out of the office.

# 23



Kelton's organization wasn't easily deterred. They submitted an official message to obtain support and requested Steve by name to fill the role. The request came through the commanding general of MARSOC, and it so happened that he and the commanding officer of Kelton's unit were old and very good friends. From there, the MARSOC Commanding General called the II MEF Commanding General in charge of Steve's current unit.

The deal was struck.

The order came down to Baxter that he was to source the assignment with Steve and only him due to his reputation as a combat leader within the SOF community, Wadi Mali aside. Baxter was infuriated, and the day of the notification—the order—he called Steve to his office.

"Let me tell you something, you disloyal fuck. If I find out you had *anything* to do with this, anything at all, or that you engineered this in any capacity, I am going to fuck you over. And I mean fuck you over hard, and make sure it sticks for a long time. Fuck you, Major, and if the Master Sergeant was responsible, that's one thing, but if you were the mastermind, I *will* destroy you!"

Steve's body trembled at the threat, but he kept up his guard. By referring to Kelton by his rank, it was again clear Baxter had done his research but couldn't find the smoking gun he was sure existed to link Steve to influencing the request. Baxter fumed indignantly, trying to get back at Steve for circumventing him, or at least that's how he perceived it. Steve was ready for a confrontation but was ultimately relieved it didn't happen when Baxter again threw him out of the office.

# 24



*Camp Lejeune, NC, November 2014*

On the eve of his deployment, Baxter summoned Steve to his office.

*Make it through this, and in forty-eight hours, you won't have to deal with him for nearly six months.*

His own immediate supervisor, Lieutenant Colonel Donald Mason, came with him. Mason was not a particularly strong officer, but he sensed something might happen and came along, if only to be an object to blunt Baxter's ire.

The three of them stood outside of Baxter's office in a small conference area. Steve and Mason stood on one side of a conference table, Baxter on the other. Baxter glared at Steve and sneered, "You think you're so smart. You think you got away with it, but I know. I know all about you, and more than you know about me."

Steve stared at him without betraying anything on his countenance to reveal the boiling anger building within him. *This entire situation has gone on long enough.*

"I know about your wife," Baxter stated. "That she lost all her hair. Whaddya think of that?!"

"It isn't something I hide, sir," Steve stated, his eyes narrowing and his ears beginning to burn. "Do you know why?"

Baxter snorted. "No!"

"She has cancer, sir."

"Well, that sucks. Does she have tits?! I mean, that would be fucked up if she didn't have tits."

That is all Steve remembered, and in all the years that passed, when he focused on trying to piece together what happened, all he recalled is the rage he'd somehow subjugated and repressed. Mason had put his arm on him to restrain him, but his memory failed after that.

Steve imagined jumping across the table and wrapping his legs around Baxter, bringing him to the ground to get on top of him and driving a pen through his eye sockets.

Baxter didn't know how close he'd came to being killed. The only thing that saved him was the table between them. Mason apparently walked him away from the situation and went back to talk to Baxter, but that did little good.

Later, in his office, alone, Steve simmered with undiminished rage, debating whether he should go back up the hall and finish the job. He didn't. He loved Elena. He regretted that he didn't defend her honor then and there instead of sacrificing it to go on deployment, to escape the mental hell in which he worked, and why, for all of the wrongs inflicted upon him and his friends, he didn't attack Baxter.

Steve felt he had no dignity, no integrity, and, because he didn't act, that he was also a coward, the thing he hated most. In his incensed state, he began to craft a statement. He determined that the following day he would tell his mentor and ally, Colonel Adrian Montclair, what transpired.

# 25

*Camp Lejeune, NC, November 2014*

Militaries work through discipline and adherence to orders. If Steve had assaulted Baxter, despite his own feeling of vindication, he would have gone to the brig. That is exactly what Baxter had hoped for, but Steve didn't take the bait. It was a brutal ploy.

There was no law against a senior officer being an asshole or toxic to a junior. It might lead to an investigation, but one couldn't have senior officers being assaulted for using colorful language and insulting their Marines, regardless of provocation or the sense of righteousness on the part of the assaulter.

It would have immediately ended Steve's career, yet doing the right thing was never more a bitter pill to swallow. Instead, the entire incident scared Steve. He was far from ready to forget it, and he never forgave Baxter for putting him in such a compromising position.

Unsure of where to turn, Steve sought a senior officer outside his chain of command. The next day, he asked to visit Colonel Montclair in his office at MARSOC. Montclair was one of Steve's mentors from his early recon days and had known him a long time. Though he had a bit of a murky past, Montclair was also a legend in the Corps within the recon community and SOF because of his assignments and avid pursuit of martial arts.

He spent an hour in Montclair's office, bordering on tears at the intense insults he'd endured, culminating with a personal attack in the workplace that had no place in the Corps. He recounted how his wife, while battling cancer that took her hair and weakened her physically, worked with wounded female service members whose entire lives were turned upside down due to their injuries, helping them to tie their shoes, put their hair up, put on a bra, apply makeup, and feel not only pretty but whole and human again. Steve bristled at the memory, a raw, fresh burn that wouldn't scab. Elena was the love of his life.

Steve asked Montclair, "How is such a man allowed to continue serving? How can this be allowed to happen? I should file an IG complaint!"

"I'm glad you brought this to my attention. *I'll* take care of this, don't you worry."

Steve trusted Montclair would be true to his word.

Unfortunately, he was unaware of Montclair and Baxter's long-standing relationship dating back nearly twenty years, to their time when Montclair had been an instructor at the Naval Academy and Baxter's wrestling coach. Steve's own relationship with Montclair didn't win against it, and Montclair only upheld part of the bargain.

Montclair was supposed to impartially refer an investigation to the Inspector General of II MEF, the unit to which Steve was assigned. The reason he told Steve he was glad that he'd brought the incident to his attention was because it allowed him to keep it compartmentalized and handle it the way he wanted. Montclair gave Baxter a stern counseling and some cautionary language (in a 'don't do this again; the stakes are too high with him' way), but nothing to really make an impact and absolutely nothing on the official record regarding the incident, that it was reported, or the action taken.

Another cover-up.

Montclair placated Steve and ensured his acolyte, Baxter, maintained his good reputation and name, such as it was.

Prior to deploying the following day, Baxter called Steve to his office and delivered a half-hearted apology. "I was clumsy in saying what I did . . ." Steve listened to his insincere drivel only to the point of extrication from the situation. He didn't care if Baxter was sorry, and he knew he wasn't. Baxter only was contrite because he was told to be, fearing that there might be repercussions due to his behavior. He didn't actually feel badly about his actions. That required empathy.

For many years after, he didn't tell Elena of the incident. How Baxter insulted her honor, her beauty, and her goodness assaulted by a pig of a man. Some days, Steve was so enraged at the incident, that he felt revenge, some vindication, was necessary. But he turned the energy into something more positive. Or he tried, at any rate.

What he truly felt was as he had immediately afterward: that he was a coward and lacked integrity for not taking action. He hated that he'd compromised his family's honor and his wife's character for his own selfish requirements to serve with Kelton and his crew.

On one level, it was worth it, he begrudgingly justified, since it was a once-in-a-career opportunity that he couldn't refuse. But on the other, he knew deep down that he'd betrayed Elena. And he added that to the list of items for which she wouldn't forgive him.

# 26



Steve returned from the deployment and was supposed to enjoy some leave known as "dwell time." Ostensibly, one was to get nearly twice as much dwell time at home as had been spent on deployment. With the total amount of time he'd been gone, he rated nearly ten-months-worth of dwell. It wasn't the same as time off, but it meant for him to be home for regular, scheduled amounts.

Yet, Baxter continued to ensure Steve had nearly zero time to recover and reset from a combat deployment and again put him on nearly every training detail. "This is your pay back for having a good time overseas and getting to do what you wanted. You are, after all, the Stability Operations Training Officer, remember?"

Of course, no one else in the organization was so "rewarded" for their hard work. Steve didn't understand how he was in the same predicament as when he'd departed. He had done very well on the deployment, too, being roundly praised by Kelton's unit commander.

Steve again found himself traveling all over the country, his dwell time be damned and his opinion irrelevant. Baxter immediately got Steve on a rotation supporting a training event in Louisiana. Then another to Nevada. On the heels of that came ones to California and Virginia. In the time Steve had been home, he spent nearly four months out of five on the road attending various events. Steve understood that it was all part of being an officer, but he was gone so much due to Baxter's vindictive nature. Steve accepted it as a matter of course and bore down on his duties, attempting to do the best he could.

If any admonishment from Montclair occurred, its effects were long-diminished, if not forgotten. Baxter had a long reach.

When it came time for selecting new company commanders in MARSOC, Steve wasn't on a friend of Baxter's, named Lieutenant Colonel E. C. Ballentine—Steve's old MSOC CO—list of potential candidates.

Ballentine had become the Marine Raider Regimental XO.

Steve met with Ballentine. They hadn't seen each other in close to four years. Steve remained focused. "Why am I not on the list for Company Commander consideration, sir?"

"Look, Steve, there are plenty of quality guys to choose from, you being one of them, but not everyone gets to serve as a Company Commander. You're on the list, but not at the top of it."

"Why? My résumé is outstanding, including combat awards and proven performance, all of which you can verify."

"Steve, I don't think you're command material. But if you want an opportunity to screen for command within MARSOC, I'll give you one day to put your screening package together." That was, of course, impossible. All of the items to be assembled in that short period of time would require close attention, such as letters of recommendation, that most people wouldn't drop everything to assist him with.

"Is that how much time they gave you when you replaced Major Joyce, sir?" Steve delivered.

Ballentine glowered at him. "Time sensitivities are your problem, Major Keller."

Steve started to leave Ballentine's office, then stopped. "What is it about me you don't like, sir? Was it my popularity within the unit, or is it how Major Joyce and I had been a good team, one that you and I hadn't and would not achieve? Help me understand."

"No. It's your presumptive arrogance I don't like, Steve."

Steve departed, frustrated that he wouldn't be able to compile all the necessary items to be fully considered.

The day ended and Baxter chortled at Steve. "I agree with Lieutenant Colonel Ballentine, and *I'm* certainly not recommending you for anything! Besides, other people don't say good things about you, nor would you get a recommendation from them. I've already talked to them, so don't bother to ask them, and if you do, I will think you're checking up on me. Don't you trust me, Steve?" Baxter never defined who the "other people" he'd talked to were, but it was all part of Baxter's cruel plan and calculations anyway. Steve never stood a chance.

Had Ballentine called Baxter? It sounded just like the kind of thing both of them would do. But Ballentine's plan to stymie Steve backfired since when he submitted his final list of candidates to the MARSOC commanding general, the general asked where Steve's package was and why he wasn't on the list. Ballentine didn't have an answer and reluctantly submitted what Steve had been able to assemble and briefed it as an incomplete package.

A few days later, Baxter gloated to Steve about the outcome of the preliminary board. "Lieutenant Colonel Ballentine told me the presentation of your screening package didn't go well. The MARSOC general hasn't decided, but you can bet you won't get picked due to your lack of attention to detail. Truly, the mark of a poor officer, of which you are one." He winked at Steve. "You don't have any friends, Steve, but I *could* be the only one you have." He called Steve by his first name in an almost paternal tone, except that it was condescending and vitriolic.

Ballentine and he apparently attended the same charm school.

Steve stared at Baxter, though he didn't engage him. He knew at that moment what he would do and took action the correct way.

# 27



Steve had been recording a narrative of events for a long time. He took the opportunity to improve upon it, crafting a letter he brought to the civilian II MEF Inspector General—not Montclair and not MARSOC—enumerating all the items Steve submitted were true. He included a list of people who'd experienced similar treatment who could be interviewed for corroboration during an ensuing investigation.

He levied that if something was not done about what had happened to him, he would go to newspapers and tell them exactly what the II MEF command climate was like and blow the door open on how unprofessional and poorly led it was, starting with Baxter.

It garnered immediate action. An investigation was launched, and all of Steve's grievances were found to be justified.

The II MEF commanding general ordered Baxter to his office. He held Steve's narrative up and gave Baxter one minute to refute the statements. Baxter admitted to his wrongdoing and was immediately fired and thrown out of the building.

The general saw Steve in the gym later that afternoon and told him he was proud of him, that what he had done took courage, but it was a Pyrrhic victory since, no matter what, Steve would be viewed as a conniving rat who cried when he didn't get his way. And that's how Baxter and Ballentine characterized Steve to Colonel Adrian Montclair.

Somehow, Baxter survived being relieved for cause with a bad fitness report, either getting it pulled from his record or having some other administrative action taken to soften the blow. Baxter attained full colonel, and until the day he retired, never missed an opportunity to continue to make Steve's life miserable. He mounted an effective and long-lasting campaign against him through Ballentine and other influential friends assigned to MARSOC. His network was impressive, and Baxter made good in fucking Steve over, just as promised.

On his first real evaluation in July 2015 to take command of an MSOC, Steve was placed on the alternate list.

What had Baxter told those men? Did he ever admit the real reason he'd been relieved? It didn't matter. Steve's successes went against Baxter's very fiber, and to the day he left the Corps, the petty asshole hated Steve, thinking he'd engineered the assignment that Kelton sought for him.

Baxter and his cohorts ensured their influence followed Steve for the rest of his career. This sealed his fate.

# 28



Outside the building, birds perched in the full green oak tree canopies chirped in the heavy, humid air. Steve stood in the hallway looking out the window at a red-tailed hawk. It landed in the tree across the street from the headquarters. He chuckled softly.

Reflecting on Wadi Mali, Steve recognized that Roland's death propagated his own cycle of revenge and death and suffering since, in the tradition of the Old Testament, once you were out of eyes to exchange, you went with teeth, and there were at least thirty of them.

It never seemed to end, but in a sick way, at that time, and before Marko took the satisfaction of revenge from him, Steve had hoped it wouldn't. It had given him purpose. That fact alone concerned him since he'd spent most of his adult life in some sort of combat zone or focused on a mission of ultimately delivering death on other humans, combatants or otherwise. Granted, it wasn't as much as some, nor had he seen all things that were bad or worse than others, but the experience was his alone. In the end, Steve inwardly wished he didn't relish certain aspects of it so much.

The enemy aside, the loss of his own men and friends seemed unfair, too. Afghanistan was a war like any other, yet also unlike anything people had seen. General William Tecumseh Sherman said during the American Civil War, "War is Hell." He'd been right; war is man's basest obscenity. How would anyone sleep knowing that, unless they believed in their cause and that the people they were fighting were bad? Somehow, that made civilian casualties tolerable. And they were caught in the middle, and that was no one's fault, wasn't it?

Awaiting the momentous decision that would determine his next command assignment, Steve wondered why he'd been allowed to live while others had died, to have quiet days where he second-guessed the choices that let him achieve that which he rued.

War was hardest on the survivors.

Pulling Steve back to the present, a sergeant popped her head out of the board room. "Sir, you can come back in now." She departed.

Steve returned to see only Montclair in the boardroom, standing against the conference table with his arms crossed. "Steve, you're a fine officer."

"But?"

"But . . . the blemish of the incident at Wadi Mali is something that can't be overlooked. While it was refreshing to hear it from you in such honest terms, it's a gap in your leadership we can't ignore." Montclair might have been happy he didn't have to make it as personal as Steve felt the decision was.

"What?!"

"It's my recommendation that you do not command a Special Operations Company now or at any time in the future. While this decision will not affect your overall future in the Corps or MARSOC, the reality is, I don't think you're equipped to deal with the ambiguity of increased command responsibilities."

Despite his initial outburst, Steve found himself surprisingly calm. "That's pretty clear, sir."

"Steve—"

"I tried to do the right things." His voice carried his disgust as he stared directly at the colonel. "Seems goddamn wrong. I don't get it."

"My decision is final. Good luck, Major Keller."

"'Good luck, Major Keller'?" he lashed out. "What the fuck is that, sir?! Ten years ago, I was flat on my back in the hospital. I came back *from the dead* to serve in this organization!"

Montclair's face tightened in an irritated knot. "Careful. I know you're upset but remember where you are and who I am." He pointed at Steve. When he did so, for an instant, Steve was transported to the evening confrontation with Brian after they'd found the Afghan medical facility.

" . . . Yes, sir."

Montclair looked away. If he second-guessed his decision, it was his only betrayal. "You're dismissed."

Steve snapped to attention. "Dismissed. Aye, aye, sir!" He left the room, Colonel Montclair's gaze making the back of his neck prickle.

Steve walked a little way down the hall, noticed a chair, and slumped in it, emotionally drained. He reflected on the entire afternoon and his past for a long while. He thought about Baxter and Ballentine's toxic leadership, that they'd lasted in the Corps, serving full careers.

Steve examined Montclair and his hypocrisy and ruminated the mistake he'd made years earlier as a junior officer in choosing Montclair as a mentor. How Montclair, on his second marriage—to the same woman after a subsequent divorce and another looming—didn't have any character. His mediocre leadership record in combat and how, as a captain, he was confirmed running from the enemy during a firefight. How he was removed from a combatant command for propositioning an enlisted female airman at a BBQ. About how, as a major, Montclair had fucked a female enlisted

Marine and survived that investigation when she refused to cooperate with the investigators to save her own career.

Whatever Steve had done in his life, he at least had integrity and a sense of decency. And Montclair was the guy making decisions on Steve's command suitability?! Disgusted, Steve spit through his teeth, stood and smoothed out his uniform, drying his sweaty palms, before heading to his car.

Entering the stairway, Steve heard laughter. He looked and saw Marko, now a master sergeant, ascending toward him with Ballentine, recently promoted to full colonel. They stopped laughing when Steve locked eyes with the two of them.

No one spoke. Marko's face was impassive compared to the vitriol on Steve's. Ballentine glanced away.

They all moved past each other, not looking back, and once again, faded from each other's lives.

# 29



Steve took another sip. "Ballentine rose within the ranks of MARSOC, even commanding the Raider Regiment. What kills me is how he constantly espoused the need for Selection processes, touting the merits of the right people being assigned to the unit. Ballentine never put himself in any situation he couldn't ensure the outcome, his unbridled arrogance a form of cowardice. He was a hypocrite of the first order. And now Ballentine's a goddamn general officer!" He gestured toward *The Raider Patch* magazine, "And, as you see, Marko retired as a Master Gunny after becoming Ballentine's Senior Enlisted Advisor. Ballentine was his retiring officer!" Steve exclaimed with an ironic laugh.

"What happened to the rest of them?" Roland asked.

Steve poked the fire. "They all got away with it scot-free. Geddes finished his career in law enforcement. It's a shame about Reid, though. He'd served in platoons within the Force Recon community ahead of MARSOC's formation. Reid was a tough, combat-hardened, street wise kid from Florida. While intelligent, Reid should have known better than to get involved in the scheme to murder Agha, but he was easily influenced since he didn't possess the same mental or moral stamina of many others and wasn't equipped to work well independently.

"After the subsequent fallout when they returned home, Reid succumbed to alcoholism and ruined his life. What a waste of talent. I somehow wished I could have saved him.

"Geddes, however, in the least didn't have a moral compass and was at worst sociopathic, it became clear. He possessed a murderous penchant and a sick sense of justice." Steve pursed his lips. "Marko fell into the complicity of it all."

Roland sipped his drink. "Damn. I see what you mean about Marko's award."

Steve nodded. "He'll get the Silver Star. But he knows the truth."

"Of course he does. And he has to live with it."

"So do I." Steve stretched his chin and neck upward, relieving tension in his upper shoulders. "In the face of so much perceived unfairness as we collectively experienced in Afghanistan, someone forgot to tell Marko and Reid that what they did wasn't what heroes do. I guess I underestimated the ethics of my men. I thought we all saw things the same way. Apparently not, and I wonder if anyone can actually teach right and wrong?"

"I don't know," Roland said softly.

Steve sighed. "What I walked away with is an appreciation for making hard decisions. Leaders will be challenged. If you aren't clear about what kind of leader you are and make your expectations known, circumstances will come along that test both you and the fabric of your organization."

"That's very sage," Roland agreed.

Steve turned directly to face Roland with his whole body. "You taught me that, for whatever I gained from the entire experience."

Roland nodded and sipping his drink again. "I'm sorry. For what happened, particularly with Baxter. That I couldn't have done more for you. And I'm sorry about Elena—I liked her very much, and I know you loved her."

"She gave me all she could, but there were things I didn't really appreciate that she experienced, too. You could call her another casualty from the war." Steve stood and put two more logs on the fire. "The cancer was just the last straw."

# 30



*Wilmington, North Carolina, August 3, 2012*

After the MSOC returned from deployment, the unit broke up; most people went their separate ways within Special Operations. Some, like Rod, Mac, and Hoyle got out of their respective services to embark on other careers or attend college. Others, like Brian, Alex, and Guido, stayed in MARSOC and continued the cycle of deployments in support of the Global War on Terror. Fergus was selected to go work a three-year assignment outside of the Corps with an unknown government entity. Tyrone "Fruit Bat" Cashiers completed another deployment as a JTAC and returned to flying, and he and Steve lost contact with each other.

Time continued its eternal march.

Steve and Elena reconnected, recognizing the strain of deployment created artificial environments that could be put into context. Away from the intense stress of combat, Steve's health improved, and while his own internal issues abated, it took the better part of two years. Then came Elena's cancer.

Fergus visited Steve and Elena one evening while in town for some training at Camp Lejeune ahead of returning to his job in the Washington, D.C. area. He brought a bottle of Irish whiskey and, after dinner, Steve, Elena, and Fergus sat on their screened-in porch enjoying an early summer evening. Fireflies danced, and the noise of the kids playing in the yard filled the air with youthful, innocent laughter.

"Damn, it's been a long time, mate!" Fergus said, pouring another two fingers of whiskey into their tumblers. Elena held out her glass, and he reached across Steve to fill it. She smiled.

"Agreed! Too long! How's D.C.?" Steve asked.

"Bureaucratic." Fergus winked, indicating there wouldn't be too many details.

"Got it. Do you like it?"

Fergus sipped his drink and tilted his head to the side. "It's OK. Not like with our old unit, though."

"It was a unique group, that's for sure," Steve smiled, closed lipped.

"I miss it. I miss them. I miss combat." Fergus looked out into the yard, the light of the overhead fan casting a shadow on his face.

"Funny, I was thinking the same thing," Steve admitted. Elena looked at both of them, an Afghan *pashmina* in teal with silver accents wrapping her bald head, her hair having fallen out months earlier.

"I mean, a firefight. The exhilaration. The feeling of being completely alive! That's what I miss!" Fergus looked at Steve, and they brought their glasses together.

"Me too! I'd go back out to get that rush. I miss it too!"

"Well, I don't miss it," Elena said in a soft tone. The porch came under a heavy silence, the gentle turning of the ceiling fan the only noise outside of the children running around in the waning light of dusk.

Steve's breath caught in his throat.

"I went through all of that, too. All of us at home did. Never knowing. Waiting for your calls. Lying awake at night, praying for your safety." She sipped her own drink.

"Babe, I—"

"You all saw this as some kind of adventure," she cut in, yet somehow, spoken in a kind and compassionate manner. "For me, it was a lesson in emotional patience." She looked out into the distance, a memory floating in her eyes.

"I remember once a black sedan driving down our road with the casualty call team searching the neighborhood for the address to deliver the news. The worst news." She paused, took a sip. Steve and Fergus sat still, listening. "I know because the sedan stopped in front of our home while the Marine officer and Navy chaplain adjusted their uniforms and prepared to go to the house, but I thought they were stopping at mine. I watched them from inside, looking through the curtains and out the dining room window, wondering if I should open the door to meet them in an attempt to control a situation in which I had none. But they moved on."

"Moments later, our neighbor, Cassie Fletcher, cried out in anguish as they told her the news that her husband, First Lieutenant Mike Fletcher, had been killed in Ramadi, Iraq. Her wails were heard down the street and, selfishly, while I felt for her, I was relieved it was not me who'd collapsed into the Marine officer's arms in a pile of grief in their driveway. Her kids were at school, thank God."

Steve swallowed hard. This was the first time he'd heard the opposite side of his deployment, not really considering it since it had been he who'd detached himself from his family in order to survive. His family held on tighter to him as a result.

Elena wiped a tear from her eye, and Steve sat beside her and wrapped her in his arms.

Fergus said, "I should leave."

"No." Elena sniffed. "Please stay. I'll go in and prepare a little dessert." She kissed Steve on the cheek and stood to walk into the house. Steve and Fergus stood with her, and she gently shut the door behind her, holding back her tears.

Fergus looked at Steve. "Really, I can go, mate."

"No, it's fine. It's good for her to be able to say that. She wouldn't if she didn't feel comfortable with you being here, and I'm glad you're here, too." Steve glanced at Elena through the window into the kitchen where she was cutting an ice cream pie onto plates and pulling out ice cream sandwiches for the kids. Considering the heaviness of the evening, it was an oddly domestic scene.

"You've got a hell of a woman there, skipper," Fergus admired.

"Yes. I do." Steve reached for the whiskey bottle and topped off their melting ice cubes. "A toast to the families and fallen."

"To the lads and the ones remaining." Fergus finished his drink in one pull.

# 31



Roland stood and walked over by the fire. The dance of a small flame shone off his medals. "Elena's another one that we can't get back. Again, I'm sorry."

"The cancer returned three years ago and didn't let go this time. It took her quickly and when she passed away, she had her family. And at least she and I got to enjoy this house together for a little while." Steve glanced around the room, tears welling along and spilling over his lashes. "She's waiting for me in Arlington Cemetery, so we'll be together again at some point."

Steve wiped his cheeks and looked at Roland. "I owe you so much. I had a decent career on my terms, even if it became mostly staff work. Though I didn't command troops again, and even if I didn't go as far as I might have, I got out as a lieutenant colonel. My post-Marine Corps consulting endeavors were lucrative. For all of it, my life has been rich. Thank you for that."

"Of course. As far as command, though, remember, in the end, the Corps and MARSOC protects its interests above everything else."

Steve curled his lower lip. "They did. And do." He exhaled and shook his head. "I've always wondered why you mentored me."

"What?" Roland said, the coals reflecting softly in his single, exposed brown eye.

"I wasn't like you. I wasn't like any of the people who you were friends with," Steve admitted. "I felt you guys were the best of the best, and I didn't belong. And you kept me alive when you pushed me down on that hill, never mind other times, I'm sure. Why?"

"You've always been modest, loyal—and too hard on yourself." Roland took his seat and reached over to Steve, clutching his hand. "You were meant for more, Steve. As a father and a husband, and as a leader and a man, and whether you wanted it or not, I passed the baton to you."

Steve wasn't convinced. "But I failed." His voice cracked. "I lied to my superiors. I lied for my men out of perceived loyalty, out of fear of repercussions. I sinned and didn't atone for it." He wept. The shame he carried; as much as he wanted to blame it on others, it was he who had planted the seed of his guilt early on, his detractors be damned.

Roland didn't admonish him. "Yes, you did. You came around from the dark edge in the face of it all, and when the shit hit the fan, you did the right thing and served with integrity and honor. I think that's the most anyone could do, yet most people don't do it."

Steve nodded. "You had the most faith in me out of anyone. I hope I lived up it."

Roland smiled. "Brother, you did. You made the kind of decisions that allow you to live with yourself. Don't feel guilty about any of this anymore. I'm proud of you. It's time to let go of the past." Roland reached across to toast Steve, the glasses refracting the glow of the hearth seen through them.

Steve took a sip of his whiskey and poked the coals with a fire poker, igniting a dormant flame that popped up across a small log. "I'm going to that reunion."

Roland looked at him, then smiled more broadly. "Good. You need to. People want to see you."

Steve swirled the whiskey. "And there's someone I need to see, too."

# 32



*San Diego, California, October 2031*

The reunion was held at the Hotel Del, a waterfront luxury hotel on Coronado Island, California. Steve flew in the day of the main formal dinner, skipping the golf tournament and an outing to a shooting range arranged by the Raider Association. He mingled around the reunion and caught up with many people. Most were glad to see him, and the engagements were generally genial, and to Steve's relief, devoid of tension.

Dressed in his Navy-blue suit with an enameled Raider patch lapel pin, Steve grabbed a drink from the bar and was turning to move to a seat when John McConnell approached him. He pulled Steve into a huge hug, nearly spilling Steve's drink.

"HOLY SHIT! I can't believe you're here, sir!" McConnell shouted, his booming New York accent filling the room.

Steve recovered and shook off some of the whiskey that had spilled on his hand. "Wow, Mac! So good to see you!" McConnell had put on twenty-five pounds, but his charcoal-gray suit fit him perfectly. "It's been twenty years, at least!"

McConnell took a step back from him. "Yep!" He was still grinning.

Steve smiled back. "How're things?"

"Great! I got out and went into investment banking. I flew here on my own jet!"

Steve whistled. "That's amazing, Mac. I'm so glad things worked out for you!"

McConnell sipped from his own bottle of beer. "Yeah, but I know guys who'd give up everything to do what we got to do."

"I'll bet. And I wouldn't sell it for anything. Damn, it's great to see you."

They shook hands and hugged again.

Steve looked across the crowd and saw Brian. "You'll be at the dinner tonight?"

"I don't miss meals!" McConnell patted his belly.

Steve laughed. "Good! I'll see you there. I just saw Brian Geraghty. I need to go talk to him."

McConnell slapped him on the back. "No worries, sir, and I'll see you a little later."

"Thanks, Mac." Steve nodded and wove through the crowd. "Brian! How are you?"

Brian looked at him and his eyes widened. "Oh my God! Good! Yeah, how are *you*? Your family?" he stumbled over his own words, like he was giving a cursory greeting and asking polite questions but wasn't sure what he wanted to say.

"Things are OK. The kids are grown. Sammie and Michael are married, but no grandkids, yet. I got out in 2021 and fully retired and sold my leadership consulting company in 2025. Elena passed away three years ago."

Brian nodded. "I heard. I'm sorry, man."

Steve looked past Brian for a second, then back to him. "I appreciate it. It was difficult, but long overdue. She suffered a lot, but it was peaceful for her at the end. How about you?"

Brian brightened, pleased to be past a difficult introduction after so many years. "Danni and I are still together."

"Still having kids?" Steve winced.

Brian laughed. "No way! Seven was enough!"

"Seven?! I remember when you had four!"

Brian sipped his beer. "Yeah! But that's what happens when you marry a Catholic! She wanted a big family. And who was I to say 'no'?! Besides, making them was the best part!"

"Nice," Steve said in mock sarcasm.

Brian frowned. "I'm surprised to see you here, Steve."

"Well, that makes two of us." He sipped his drink.

"Why'd you come? I mean, you never do."

Steve delivered evenly, "Marko."

"You're here for *him*?"

Steve shook his head. "No. The upgrade. I guess I'm here to satisfy a curiosity."

"Really? How?"

Steve pondered. "Think about it, about Marko. When he got out, he wanted people to believe he was the classically disgruntled Marine. But he also wanted people to know what he'd done while he was in, to like him. It's why Marko's here tonight. He wants adulation. Approval. Justification. He wants the celebrity."

Brian chuckled. "Well, I could have sent you a video, you know."

"Ha. No, I need to see this shitshow for myself." Steve looked more intently at Brian. He leaned in. "I need to ask you something." Steve looked directly at Brian, the noise of the reunion falling away.

"Go ahead, anything." Brian studied his old commander.

" . . . Was I good leader?"

"Dude, you were the best!"

Steve smiled. "Thanks for saying that. But *were* you and I friends?"

Brian smoothed his chin. "I'm not sure. We were close. It might have been the circumstances of being at war, however. We needed each other out there."

Steve let out a light sigh. "That's true. But I think in some cases, we mistake affinity for friendship. Like I did with Marko."

Brian's jaw twitched. "I see that."

Someone announced that the dinner would begin in ten minutes. People moved to take their seats.

"I know another reason you're a good leader," Brian qualified. He snapped his finger and pointed at Steve.

Steve, mid sip, looked over his glass, "Why?"

"Because I always know where I stand with you. Your approval matters. You made me want to be a good Marine."

Steve finished his sip and shook Brian's hand. "So did you."

***

Seated in a large ballroom of the hotel, Steve dined with Brian and his wife and Mac and his girlfriend. After dessert and a few more cocktails, the awards ceremony began, emceed by Raider Association president, Major Felix Osman, USMC, Retired, whom Steve hadn't seen since they relieved his MSOC in Afghanistan.

The room was full of chatter when Osman, sixty-three, fit with mostly salt-and-peppered hair and a goatee, dressed in a navy-blue windowpane, three-piece suit, took the podium. "Ladies, gentlemen—and I use the term extremely loosely for the latter—please take your seats."

The talking in the room quieted as Osman waited for people to move to their tables. For a moment, Steve heard Osman on the radio that night so long-ago, announcing Juliet Zero Six—Roland Joyce—was dead. Steve closed his eyes in reflection.

After a requisite opening statement, acknowledging several guests, and a toast to fallen comrades, Osman took a sip of water and got to the main event. "It's great to see so many fellow unit members here this evening. In fact, this may be one of the largest turnouts we've had!"

He began to applaud, and the attendees joined in.

"I would love that you all were here to see me, but I know that isn't the case. Being as it is our twenty-fifth anniversary; I'll briefly recount how we got here. In February 2006, the United States Marine Corps established Marine Special Operations Command forming its core from 1st and 2nd Force Reconnaissance Companies. Though an earlier experimental unit called Marine Detachment One stood up in 2003 and served with distinction, it transitioned to MARSOC by 2006, and the new organization grew nearly overnight. All of you seated here are a part of that legacy. And tonight, we honor one of our own."

The room was quiet. Steve scanned the room for Marko.

Osman was somber. "In our line of work, awards are hard-earned and seldom talked about. Everyone works hard, and I dare say, everyone is brave. But tonight, we salute the bravery of one man with remarkable expertise. He's a founding member of MARSOC and received the Bronze Star with Valor device for single-handedly taking a known enemy commander and named objective off the battlefield. ladies and gentlemen, please welcome to the stage, former Master Gunnery Sergeant, Marko Pech."

The audience applauded loudly as Marko politely waved and ambled to the stage and podium. Osman warmly shook his hand, then Marko stood to the side. Steve watched him. The ill-fitting charcoal gray suit Marko wore looked out of place on him, like he'd borrowed it for the occasion, and he was uncomfortable wearing it. Marko was fifty-seven, and though his dark hair was long, past his shoulders, he looked largely the same.

Osman put his arm around Marko. "I have to say, reading your award from your original actions was impressive, but tonight, it's going to another level."

Marko feigned humility. "I'm a little shocked."

Osman played it up. "Modest much?"

People laughed.

"I try to be," Marko said, and the audience again chuckled.

"I think it's a hallmark of ours, as a unit. Of course, no one did it as well as the guy who just left, and the guy who just got there thinks the guy who just left sucks! You know?!"

That elicited more laughter from the audience.

"Well, we relieved your company in combat. Things were fine when we had them. So, I'm not sure what went wrong!"

Osman laughed. "Ha! That's hilarious!"

Marko made a smug face. "Sorry. But not sorry!"

"Anyway, Marko showed that he had what it took. He was a strong battlefield leader and worked hard to improve his team. Unfortunately, on the deployment he's being honored for the work that he did, he sustained a man killed." He paused for effect with the crowd. "I also spoke with General Ballentine. He sends his regrets and included a letter to you." Osman handed it to Marko. "So, without further delay, let's get to it. Master Guns, please read the citation!"

Master Gunnery Sergeant Valken, now sixty and bald with a round face and body, entered the stage. He shook hands with Marko and Osman and stopped at his appointed area on the stage and put on his reading glasses. "Attention to orders!" he barked.

His voice brought Steve back to the awful night Ketcham died, when Valken's voice flooded the radio, organizing the chaos.

The audience stood, and Valken read the citation enumerating Marko's actions the day Luke was killed and further how and why Marko rated being upgraded to a Silver Star due to his actions in combat by removing Objective Tenkara. Osman pinned the medal to the lapel of Marko's tuxedo.

Steve's face tightened. The citation was a fabrication and didn't reflect what really occurred when Luke died or what happened in Wadi Mali, but it did make Marko sound impressive. Surely, it was all due to Ballentine, who, significantly, wasn't in attendance.

Valken finished the citation. "By the President." He turned to Marko. "Congratulations, Master Gunnery Sergeant!" He moved to shake Marko's hand, and the audience erupted in applause, which turned into a standing ovation. Steve stood too but didn't clap.

Osman indicated for Marko to take the podium, and the applause faded.

"I'm not sure what to say," Marko spoke softly.

A voice shouted from the crowd, "How about 'thanks', then sit down?!"

The crowd laughed.

Marko chuckled. "I know that voice, and there's a reason I forgot the name!" There was more laughter from the crowd. "In all seriousness, though, I'm happy—humbled—to receive this. The deed is what matters. I don't have anything else, really. Thank you, everyone." He waved and departed the stage to continuous applause.

When the crowd died down, Osman retook the podium. "Thank you, Master Gunnery Sergeant. That concludes the ceremony, ladies and gentlemen. Please, join me at the bar and enjoy your evening!"

Marko worked his way through the crowd as well-wishers slapped his back and shook his hand. Steve waited his turn to meet him, and when he did, he grabbed Marko's hand and pulled him close.

"Congratulations."

Marko was dumbfounded but recovered. "Well, bro, you know . . ."

"Yeah, I do," Steve whispered in a snarl.

Marko whispered back, "Why's it gotta be that way?"

Steve released his hand. "I need a word with you. Tonight."

"All right."

Steve smiled stiffly and melded into the crowd.

# 33

———

*San Diego, California, October 2031*

**M**arko and Steve found a quiet place in a room away from the chaos of drunken people reminiscing about old times. They sat at a table and looked uneasily at each other. Marko demurely smiled while sipping from a glass of bourbon. He set his glass on the table. "Thanks for the assist with the upgrade! Couldn't have done it without you!" He winked at Steve and glanced at the medal on his lapel.

"You've got to be fucking kidding. You didn't earn that, and you know it."

Marko leaned forward and slammed his fist on the table. "FUCK YOU!"

Steve took a deep breath. "Typical response. Makes one wonder why we haven't spoken in so long. I'll be honest, I didn't really want to come to this thing, and on some level, I'm kicking myself for doing so. But if we get to have it out, so much the better."

Steve jabbed his finger at Marko. "Tell me what Ballentine told you that night before you left with Geddes."

Marko paused. "OK."

# 34



Ahead of the meeting, Ballentine had Marko meet him in the courtyard outside the side door Company Offices, backlit by the light over the doorway.

"How are you tonight, Gunny?"

"Fine, sir." Marko replied, suspicious.

"Good. Good. Marko, I'll get to the point." Marko's eyebrows raised; Ballentine wasn't known for relaxing his stiffnesses.

"You know Captain Keller's recommended to me that you be relieved of duties?"

"What?! No way! Why?"

"He doesn't think you have what it takes anymore. Not as a leader, and not as an operator."

"That motherfucker! I helped make that guy!"

"You rightfully feel betrayed. I need you to understand that I get it. I understand the stress of combat. I know what it's like to second-guess yourself." Ballentine shifted, looking at Marko with all the sincerity he could muster.

"What's happened out here isn't your fault. It's how things go in battle. You can't blame yourself."

"Who said I'm blaming or second-guessing myself?!"

"Easy, Gunny, I'm not suggesting you haven't done what you needed to do or accepted the outcomes of unfortunate situations." Ballentine put his hand on Marko's shoulder and looked into his eyes.

"Marko, I've been watching you since I took command. I couldn't figure out from where I knew you. But then it came to me." Ballentine removed his hand and pointed lightly at him.

"You and I served together as Roman Legionnaires in a past life. It's been a long time since we've seen each other, yet, here we are, in the middle of Afghanistan. It's uncanny." Ballentine smiled modestly with closed lips.

"Uhhh, if you say so, sir. Not sure I'm down with that."

"I don't expect you to embrace what I'm saying, just to understand that I have a unique perspective on things. The point, given my experiences, is that I recognize you. I know what you're looking for."

"What? What am I looking for?" Marko relaxed a little.

"Redemption, Marko. You want to make it all right."

He nodded.

"I have an offer for you. How'd you like to get Agha? To avenge Major Joyce, Luke, all of them? To be the one who closes the door on this son of a bitch?"

"How, sir?"

"You'll see, but it's right up your alley! And what it will mean is that you'll have full discretion to handle the mission any way you see fit. You'll be the one who made it right. Fuck Captain Keller! Fuck what people think! I'm gonna present you with an opportunity, but you need to be nonchalant. I know you're good at that!"

"OK..." Marko said, though he again sounded distrustful.

"And after all is said and done, and if you trust me, you'll get all that you want! I'll have your back. From there, you and I can do anything! Will you work for me?"

Marko nodded once. "I'm in."

"Good man!" Ballentine clapped him on the shoulder, and they shook hands.

# 35



Steve listened to Marko describe the conversation. He took a sip of his drink. "So that's why Ballentine said it was none of my business. What a perfect arrangement: If Ballentine's plan for Agha worked, his MSOC came away looking good, but most especially himself. If not, he could blame me *or* you. Hell, even both of us together. Either way, that self-assured shit got the better of me. I mean, what an ideal way for Ballentine to become a part of an exclusive group that he wouldn't be able to enter otherwise, with a guy like you, Marko, whose outward respect was well-known, carrying him across the threshold?

"What the *fuck*?!" Marko's face dropped, taken off-guard.

"Changing topics, when did you make the decision to kill Agha?"

"It was Geddes. He planned it," Marko refuted.

"But you had the real motive, and it wasn't because of Roland Joyce, or Luke, or any of it. It was because Ballentine told you it would make you look good. You got to be the hero."

"Bullshit—"

"Bullshit, nothing! They found a bullet from your rifle!" Steve pulled in his lower lip under his top teeth.

Marko stared at him like he'd been unjustly accused and threw up his hands. "So what? Good that he's dead. That fucker deserved it."

Steve sipped his drink and looked at the ice melting in the bourbon. "*Good?!* Yeah, we were meant to kill the enemy, and we did by the carload, but not like that."

Marko rolled his eyes. "Who fucking cares, Steve? That was a long time ago."

He stood up and slammed both hands on the table, spilling part of their drinks. "I FUCKING CARE!" Steve glared at Marko and pointed his finger at himself. "I care because I lied, I covered for you, I was so loyal, and you guys gave it to me in ass for nothing. My reputation was ruined because of your actions and my own—I'll own what is mine. Yeah. I *wanted* to kill Agha. And you *knew it* and took what I wanted most. But GODDAMN IT, YOU GOT AWAY WITH MURDER, YOU MOTHERFUCKER!"

Marko leaned back, trying to get away from Steve. He seemed surprised but not shocked. "Whoaaa, 'motherfucker'?! You calling me names!?" He kept his temper. "All right, all right, let's calm down. We've been drinking a lot, and it's been a long night, emotional, you know?"

Steve took a few breaths to calm down, but he started pacing. "Don't downplay this, Marko. Not with me. Are you comfortable with what really happened? Your cowardice? How I dropped the bomb to save you while claiming we didn't know about civilians when you clearly did?"

Marko stood, too. "That's some random shit, calling me a coward."

Steve closed the distance between them. "For whatever you've done in your life and the laurels you've received, you know as well as I do who you were at that moment. And with Tenkara, what you were upgraded with tonight doesn't reflect the true story. If not for Vaughn, you might have gone to your grave with a horrible secret!"

Marko recoiled. "That's bullshit! That deployment was tough for all of us. Losing Luke, the wounded!" He removed the Silver Star from his lapel and shoved it across the table at Steve. "Here! You want it?! Will this make you happy?!"

Steve looked down at the medal and picked it up.

Marko dropped back into his chair and leaned back. "Never mind! I don't want to hear your selfish shit!"

"Selfish shit?! Are you serious? How the fuck am *I* selfish?! I violated the Law of Armed Conflict for you! I risked my life for you! My career, everything. And you reaped the benefits right up to the end. I lied for you, even though I could have dimed you out with a clear conscience! And for what?!" Steve sucked in a breath to again compose himself and sighed.

He turned the medal in his hand and then looked at Marko. "You've gotten everything you wanted on the back of my decisions. Directly or indirectly. You may not give a fuck, but deep down, you know it's true. For all of this, whatever I gained or lost, I tried to do it honestly. I know the truth about you. About who you really are. And you do, too."

"Is that a fact?" Marko said, standing with clenched fists.

"What you did to Agha was for your own gain just to recover your ruined character. If you had any integrity, you would've turned in your Raider Badge tonight!"

"Again, you keep bringing up Agha."

Steve raised his chin. "He was a *fucking* human being! And we were the good guys! Right?!"

Marko picked up his drink and shrugged. "He was the enemy. A Taliban. He warranted it and more."

Steve pointed at him again. "*You* betrayed me! Damn it, Marko. You sold yourself out to Ballentine and rode his coat tails to the end, paying interest on your debt by supporting that asshole for the rest of his career. You made a covenant with that son of a bitch and turned your back on your community!" Steve breathed deeply through his nose. "I hope it was worth it."

Marko sneered, "You think too much, Steve." He sat back down in his chair.

"I went back to that village, you know. I took Fergus with me. I went back to prove the accusations wrong. But you did do it. And you made me look like a chump."

"You were gonna fire me!" Marko seethed, leaning forward, and jabbing his finger on the table. "And you didn't even have the stones to say it to my face?!"

Steve laughed. "Yep, and that was a huge mistake on my part. I should have relieved you; Lord knows I tried. In a weird way, my not being able to convince Ballentine to let me relieve you actually gave you a second chance. You went through your entire life and career owing him, being in his pocket, but really, because of the lie I told to protect you, it was me you owed." Steve paused a moment. "Here I was chasing Agha and the entire time the real enemy was right in front of me. My God, I was such a fool."

"So, what do you want me to do about it!? Afghanistan's a war that no one cared about. All of it is over! Give it up. You sound pathetic!"

"Pathetic?! What's pathetic is your lack of courage, even now."

Marko looked about. "*Excuse* you?!"

"If courage is defined by the choices we make under difficult circumstances, in all the years I have known you, you have NEVER made the right choice!" Steve threw the Silver Star medal across the table at Marko where it landed face down.

Marko's eyes widened. His brows pulled up on his forehead.

"We didn't go to war for Afghanistan. Shit, no one asked the Afghans what they wanted out of the arrangement—August 2021 proved that. We went to war because our country asked us to keep the wolves at bay. We did it out of patriotism. Duty. For Family. We went to war for us—our tribe." He looked into his whiskey tumbler. "But I've thought about the war for a long time and concluded that wasn't what drove us." Steve paused. "All we wanted was to come home."

Marko shrugged his shoulders and sipped his drink for emphasis. "We did what we had to do." Despite everything, his eyes teared up.

"It wasn't right. You got a full career on a lie. Mine ended because of it. But it's too late now."

Marko's tears flowed freely. "Whatever you may believe, people turned their back on me. *You* turned me away. I was alone. Did you ever consider that *I* was scared?" He dabbed at his cheeks with his cocktail napkin.

"We were all scared, and our fears were our own. I conquered mine. You succumbed to yours. You owe me." Steve stood across from him. He wondered if Marko had ever confronted his own emotions and momentarily felt sorry for him.

Marko remained seated, overwhelmed by the stark truth. He eyed the twisted ribbon of the medal on the table. Looking up at Steve, he choked up as he yelled, "Fine, FINE! YOU'RE RIGHT—I OWE YOU! I OWE YOU FOR EVERYTHING!"

Steve stared into Marko's pleading, reddened eyes, and before turning to go, said, "There. Now we're even."

# 36



*Smoky Mountains, Tennessee, October 2031*

Steve was exhausted upon returning from the reunion. After retrieving Kelso from a boarding facility and settled at the cabin he went straight to bed. He slept soundly and slowly awoke, an easy reveille where he opened his eyes to a room fully illuminated by a rising sun. He lazily rolled his head on the pillow and looked to Elena's side of the bed, remembering the scent of her shampoo, and, sometimes, perfume. He pressed the heels of his hands onto his eye sockets and lightly rubbed his eyes.

In a flash of memory, he knew everything that had transpired with Roland was real. Where had the time had gone since the incident with Baxter and the attendant issues that transpired as a result? These were odd things to think of first thing in the morning.

He lay a little longer, then pushed the comforter and sheet back and swung his legs from the bed. Kelso slept on the end of the mattress, though he woke and jumped off as Steve went to the bathroom to use the toilet. He washed his hands in the sink and splashed cold water on his face while thinking of the lifelong morning routine he had adopted since joining the Corps.

Steve walked down the hall through the kitchen. He looked out the window, watching the leaves move in a crisp morning breeze. He loved fall most of all, and each year that he got to experience it, he enjoyed it as much as he ever had in his early years. Entering the den, he saw the ashes in the fireplace and another wave of memories overtook him. Of years earlier with Elena, in better and happier times.

When he thought of how he missed her, he was heartbroken. He looked at the photos on the mantle of the kids. Later in the evening, he'd call each of his children and check in with them. The three little ones, who were no longer small—her babies. Their contribution to the world.

In his assessment, he and Elena raised three of the most beautiful souls that ever walked the earth. He felt he didn't deserve them for all of the bad things he had done in his life. God either decided to ignore all his faults or just gave him them despite his shortcomings. Yet, he was convinced that regardless of his inadequacies, he'd helped the kids avoid all of his stupidity by guiding them along in ways he'd never received. He also felt Elena deserved better than him and always had. He cursed himself at the many times he hadn't been the man she'd wanted.

Michael was tall, handsome like Steve McQueen, and athletic. Friends said he was like his father, the same person but at an earlier stage of development. He felt that the boy was better than him and twice as gifted, intelligent, and figured things out faster than others. He was an old soul and held his father as the example of what a man, a gentleman, should be.

Though he didn't publicly admit it, the boy admired and absolutely respected and loved his father. Steve raised Michael as his son, and, when the boy came of age, treated him like his brother. They were similar and very different. Same temperament. Same interests and shared them together, sometimes being at odds with each other, but their bond was deep, rich, and complete. He knew his son, and the boy knew his father, or at least he thought because the boy only was allowed to see what his father wanted him to see, and all of Steve's own limitations, mistakes, fears, transgressions, badness, and insecurities were not revealed to him. The image had to be maintained.

It had been a lonely frontier, but Steve kept careful sentinel to ensure Michael didn't cross over into territory from which he might not recover or even want to know.

The girls, Samantha and Marta, were beautiful, spitting images of their mother. They loved him unconditionally. He was everyman to them and the definition of masculine energy, but only in the best ways. Devoted husband, father, friend, and confidant. He was also the good guy in the parenting role, for it was impossible for him to be heavy-handed with them. They didn't take advantage of this, and, in fact, respected it. He only sought their approval and did so through compromise, often in their favor.

They had no idea of his internal struggles and his feelings of inadequacy at the private war he fought nearly every day of his life as his public persona wrestled with his internal, true knowledge of who he really was. He wanted to be free of it and looked for the outlet that would meet their expectations of him to cleanse himself and achieve a balance he'd come to believe was unattainable.

The children knew their father had killed people, or at least that he'd facilitated their deaths, but they didn't know how much he struggled with the demons of war. Of the deaths of the innocents, of his own men. Steve believed they wouldn't have understood. They knew him for who they thought he was, and he felt genuine with them, but wondered if any father truly gave his kids the full story of who he was and how he was created, what made him, his influences, and what real hopes and dreams are, and how to move forward when they're irrevocably dashed by forces outside of your control.

He couldn't explain to them that their mother, a beautiful, caring soul in her own right, had struggled with her own part of her husband being at war, and the things she kept to herself to protect them. They didn't know that while he'd loved her, his own devotion to his men had meant she felt something was missing in their relationship.

Afghanistan took more than lives, and it was never held accountable. When she'd died, there was nothing else. Steve deserved his loneliness. That is why he could live alone and mourn all of them not being with him anymore.

# 37



Moving back into the kitchen, he creased his brow and leaned lightly on the sink. Steve regarded his life as a combination of luck and happenstance. Fate. To meet Roland at Selection and serve with him. That he got to live. In these advanced years, Steve nodded to his old physical therapist, Kyle Tierney, wherever he was, in silent admiration. Nothing that had happened to Steve in his life after the parachuting accident would have been possible without Kyle and Roland being guiding hands. Then he thought of Abdullah. He and his family had made it out of Afghanistan and settled in America and opened a pizzeria. He owed Abdullah a lot, too, and Steve hoped that somehow, in an astral message, he knew that.

Kelso drank from his bowl in the kitchen and whimpered at Steve to let him out into the yard. He opened the patio door, and the dog went out toward the woods. He watched Kelso's black body flit and meld with the shadows of the trees and followed with his eyes as he stood barefoot on the cool flagstone patio.

In the distance, mountains covered with the rich hues of fall foliage were wreathed in silvery mist rising from the hollows. The leaves glowed vibrantly in the sunlight. Steve inhaled deeply. Rich moisture filled his nose, and he smiled. Then, he and Kelso went back inside.

They walked down the hall to get ready for their morning hunt. On the way, Steve looked at a few of the photos on the wall. Of times long past. Of men he didn't know anymore but would never forget. He thought of all the people he knew who claimed they'd go into Recon or Special Operations. Only he and a few others from his Infantry Officer Course class had done it. Over a twenty-four-year career, he'd been surpassed by only two of them in rank and position, Jim Eggerton being one of them. The rest either talked a big game or didn't try at all. Steve was one of the lucky few who'd achieved it.

For all of his trials, his rejections, his anguish at trying to be the "right man," he finally found his path, though it didn't conclude as he envisioned. There were days he still longed for another chance to see if his life would have had a different outcome if he'd had done things differently, but it didn't matter. What had happened, happened. What was, was.

Wearing jeans and a sweater, Steve pulled on his boots. Did he suffer from post-traumatic stress? He'd certainly experienced trauma. It wasn't that he didn't worry. He just processed it more incrementally. That didn't mean he didn't feel things, either, but was able to subdue his feelings until an appropriate time. He was simply better equipped for dealing with it than others.

It hadn't always been that way, however, and he lost emotional control after Luke was killed. Brian helped him cope, and his men loved him for his sensitive expression when he cried unabashedly, but Brian had also informed him that displaying his humanity could have dire consequences on unit morale.

Steve had learned a valuable lesson the terrible day Luke died. He'd learned how to lead.

Those experiences also meant he'd also learned to internalize, though it could also be called deflection or downright denial, since he never came forward and divulged having any sort of issues. They were there, undoubtedly, but he didn't wallow in self-pity or depression. Survivor's guilt permeated periodically, and he wondered if he'd indeed lived well and decently. That often put him at odds with people's opinion of him, like his children, and who he knew himself to be on the inside. Could one ever really come to terms with—let alone distance themselves by running from—their past?

*It's loneliest at the point of decision,* Steve remembered, thinking of those dead Afghan civilians on that awful night.

Kelso was ready and sitting by the door as Steve finished dressing. Zipping his field coat, he slid his hands down the waxed material and into the lined pockets to ensure the shotgun shells and his pipe and tobacco were in their proper place. Of course, they were, but he always checked. That was an old habit that never left him. Too many years of proper placement and memorization of where things should be to find them in the dark ensured that.

He opened the door, and the dog sprang into the crisp morning air. He picked up his shotgun from beside the door, broke it open, and examined the buckshot shells. Then he reconsidered and closed it gently, applied the safety, gave it a long look, and put it back in its place. He grasped his walking stick and stepped outside, shutting the door behind him.

Steve felt good in a way he hadn't for a long time. No longer did he ponder the last time he felt that way; rather, that feeling was the only thing worth focusing on since he was in a good place. Because of all of his tribulations, and what life threw at him over a career such as his, it took all those days past for him to stand where he was.

As the philosopher Dan Millman wrote, there were no ordinary moments.

His shoulders were light. He felt released from the heavy baggage he'd been carrying for so long. Happy, he walked down the path toward the grassy, frost-covered fields and into the warmth of the sun, Kelso at his side.

At the edge of the field, Steve Keller stopped, leaned on his walking stick, and looked up at the orange, red, and yellow leaves. A light wind moved the trees, detaching a few of them to dance on the air. And against an azure sky, a red-tailed hawk circled above him.

# ABOUT THE AUTHOR

Lieutenant Colonel Ivan F. Ingraham (Retired) served most of his 24-year United States Marine Corps career in Marine Special Operations Command (MARSOC). Ivan is a writer, speaker, and storyteller who has written for multiple online publications and appeared on several podcasts discussing writing, leadership, and his service. He is the founder of IFI Solutions, LLC, a consulting company. This is his first novel.

# ABOUT THE PUBLISHER

The Sager Group was founded in 1984. In 2012 it was chartered as a multimedia content brand, with the intent of empowering those who create art—an umbrella beneath which makers can pursue, and profit from, their craft directly, without gatekeepers. TSG publishes books; ministers to artists and provides modest grants; and produces documentary, feature, and commercial films. By harnessing the means of production, The Sager Group helps artists help themselves. For more information, please see TheSagerGroup.net.

# MORE BOOKS FROM THE SAGER GROUP

*The Swamp: Deceit and Corruption in the CIA*
*An Elizabeth Petrov Thriller (Book 1)*
by Jeff Grant

*Chains of Nobility: Brotherhood of the Mamluks (Book 1-3)*
by Brad Graft

*The Deadliest Man Alive: Count Dante, The Mob and the War for*
*American Martial Arts*
by Benji Feldheim

*Death Came Swiftly: Novel About the Tay Bridge Disaster of 1879*
by Bill Abrams

*Vetville: True Stories of the U.S. Marines at War and at Home and at War*
by Mike Sager

*Three Days in Getttyburg*
by Brian Mockenhaupt

*Secrets of Ash: A Novel of War, Brotherhood, and Going Home Again*
by Josh Green

*The Living and the Dead: War, Friendship and the Battles That Never End*
by Brian Mockenhaupt

*Hunting Marlon Brando: A True Story*
by Mike Sager

*The Sing Sing Follies (A Maximum-Security Comedy): And Other True Stories*
by John H. Richardson

*Going Home to Die No More: A True Kentucky Story about a Train*
*Robbery and a Hanging after the Civil War*
by Russ Witcher

See our entire library at TheSagerGroup.net

THE SAGER GROUP
Artifex Te Adiuva